Praise for Nicholas Nicastro's novels

The Isle of Stone

"From its explosive first pages, *The Isle of Stone* draws you into the gritty reality of Sparta during the Peloponnesian War. Nicastro writes powerful prose, but this is no exercise in debunking. With drama, passion, and a sure touch for the facts, Nicastro reveals the heroism behind the humiliation of the shocking day when some of Sparta's unconquerable soldiers surrendered. His images of life and death under the Mediterranean sun hit you like the glare of a polished shield."
—Barry Strauss, author of *The Battle of Salamis: The Naval Encounter That Saved Greece—and Western Civilization*

Empire of Ashes

"Great historical fiction. Nicholas Nicastro paints an entirely believable portrait of the world of Alexander the Great, with the period detail and nuance that gives the reader a true feel for the time period. Even better, he resists simply regurgitating our common understanding of Alexander, and instead presents an unexpected and at times startling picture of a hero we thought we knew, but perhaps did not. *Empire of Ashes* is both fast-paced and scholarly, a difficult combination to achieve, but Nicastro succeeds beautifully."
—James L. Nelson, author of *The Only Life That Mattered* and *Reign of Iron*

"*Empire of Ashes* manages to be many things at the same time. The book is a grand historical epic combined with a court-room drama and political intrigue. Believable characters rise off the page in clear, evocative language. Nicastro has a tale[...] motivations of historical [...] tell us something abou[...] he result is a captivating [...]

"A great read. I loved the style and thought the framing device of the court case was fascinating and gripping. The sights, sounds, and social life of ancient Athens came to life for me in a way that few historical novels seem to manage. The characters were carefully and convincingly created and forced me to make various judgments about them, and then revise them, just as real people do. The action scenes were great too. Grim and gritty and vividly brought to life. All in all a great achievement."

—Simon Scarrow, author of
The Eagle and the Wolves and *The Eagle's Conquest*

and Nicholas Nicastro's other historical thrillers

"Nicastro takes you by the scruff of your neck and yanks you into the action of history."   —*Ithaca Times*

"An effective storyteller [with] a deft command of the language."   —*The BookPress*

"Nuanced, insightful, and thoroughly believable. . . . Nicastro does what the artist can do and the historian cannot; probe the inner mind of the historical [figure]. . . . Carefully researched, accurate in tone and detail."
   —James L. Nelson, author of the *Revolution at Sea Saga*

"This maritime historical novel fairly shimmers with furtive lustiness and wry humor. Embellishing John Paul Jones's early naval intrigues and sexual liaisons, Nicholas Nicastro preserves the true spirit of a mercurial and moody hero."

—Jill B. Gidmark,
University of Minnesota Professor of English

THE ISLE OF STONE

Nicholas Nicastro

A SIGNET BOOK

SIGNET
Published by New American Library, a division of
Penguin Group (USA) Inc., 375 Hudson Street,
New York, New York 10014, USA
Penguin Group (Canada), 90 Eglinton Avenue East, Suite 700, Toronto,
Ontario M4P 2Y3, Canada (a division of Pearson Penguin Canada Inc.)
Penguin Books Ltd., 80 Strand, London WC2R 0RL, England
Penguin Ireland, 25 St. Stephen's Green, Dublin 2,
Ireland (a division of Penguin Books Ltd.)
Penguin Group (Australia), 250 Camberwell Road, Camberwell, Victoria 3124,
Australia (a division of Pearson Australia Group Pty. Ltd.)
Penguin Books India Pvt. Ltd., 11 Community Centre, Panchsheel Park,
New Delhi - 110 017, India
Penguin Group (NZ), cnr Airborne and Rosedale Roads, Albany,
Auckland 1310, New Zealand (a division of Pearson New Zealand Ltd.)
Penguin Books (South Africa) (Pty.) Ltd., 24 Sturdee Avenue,
Rosebank, Johannesburg 2196, South Africa

Penguin Books Ltd., Registered Offices:
80 Strand, London WC2R 0RL, England

First published by Signet, an imprint of New American Library,
a division of Penguin Group (USA) Inc.

First Printing, December 2005
10 9 8 7 6 5 4 3 2 1

 REGISTERED TRADEMARK—MARCA REGISTRADA

Printed in the United States of America

PUBLISHER'S NOTE
This is a work of fiction. Names, characters, places, and incidents either are
the product of the author's imagination or are used fictitiously, and any
resemblance to actual persons, living or dead, business establishments,
events, or locales is entirely coincidental.

The publisher does not have any control over and does not assume any responsibility for author or third-party Web sites or their content.

To Dr. Fred Keating, teacher, for his patience, good taste, and timely encouragement

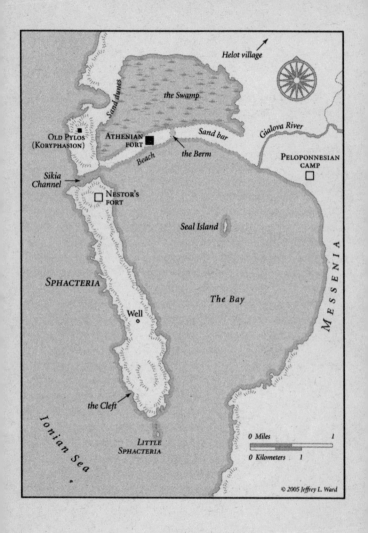

Helot village

the Swamp

Sand dunes

OLD PYLOS
(KORYPHASION)

ATHENIAN
FORT

Sand bar

Gialova River

the Berm

Beach

PELOPONNESIAN
CAMP

Sikia
Channel

NESTOR'S
FORT

Seal Island

SPHACTERIA

The Bay

M E S S E N I A

Well

Ionian Sea

the Cleft

LITTLE
SPHACTERIA

0 Miles   1

0 Kilometers   1

© 2005 Jeffrey L. Ward

Contents

Historical Note

The Peloponnesian War was the war to end all wars in antiquity: a conflict of unprecedented scope, length, and destructiveness, after which nothing was the same. Fought over a period of twenty-seven years, it pitted Athens and her sometimes-reluctant imperial subjects against a league of Peloponnesian states led by Sparta. This novel dramatizes one of the war's key campaigns—the entrapment and siege of hitherto undefeated Spartan soldiers on a narrow island in the west of Greece. The incident turned out to be a high point of the struggle for the Athenians, who still lost the war.

Readers unfamiliar with this subject may be confused by the varying ways the ancients referred to the Spartans and their allies ("Lacedaemonians," "Laconians," "Peloponnesians," "Spartiates," "Equals," et al). By way of clarification, "Lacedaemon" and "Laconia" are alternative names for the fertile valley region in the southern Peloponnese that encompassed the city of Sparta. Although all Lacedaemonians were Peloponnesians, the region of the Peloponnese included a number of other important city-states that were part of the Spartan bloc. Describing a force as "Peloponnesian" therefore emphasizes a preponderance of Spartan allies within (though at least some Spartans were usually part of such armies or fleets).

The term "Spartiate" is a more restrictive one than "Lacedaemonian." It refers to those adult males in the Spartan population who attained the status of full citizenship by completing the requisite course of education (the *agoge* or "Rearing"), being elected to a communal mess, and attaining the age of thirty. The number of full-blown Spartiates amounted to only a small minority in the city population and the army. This shortage of elite manpower obligated the state to accept into service noncitizen Lacedaemonians, including resident aliens called *perioikoi* ("circum-habitants," here designated as "Nigh-Dwellers"), ex-citizens stripped of their citizenship for conduct or financial reasons, and, in extreme circumstances, state slaves ("helots") who served in exchange for their freedom. Spartiates referred to one another as *homoioi*, which I follow certain authorities in translating as "Equals." Those who had graduated from the agoge, but were not yet thirty years old, belonged in an informal age-class called the *hebontes* (rendered here simply as "under-thirties").

The precise organization of the Spartan army has long been a subject of debate, including as it did a number of subdivisions that are unclear in nature and changed with time. For my purposes here I have remained agnostic on these questions. Since the names of the subdivisions are numerous and unfamiliar, I have opted to translate them into rough modern equivalents (e.g., "platoon" for the Spartan *enomotia* of thirty-six men, "battalion" for the *lochos* of one thousand, etc.). Similarly, the names of age-groups in the Rearing, which would have sounded archaic even to classical Greeks, have been changed here to the closest equivalents in American idiom: West Point class monikers ("Firsties," "Cows," etc.). My apologies to the purists.

A mixture of ancient and modern units of measure is used in the text. For the sake of convenience, modern units are used when they were more or less similar to their ancient counterparts (e.g., feet, hours, months). Verisimilitude has been served by including a number of antique units that are common in the relevant historical sources. Most prominent here is the "stade," a Greek unit of distance approximately equivalent to six hundred modern feet (and from which the word "stadium" is derived).

The common monetary unit is the Athenian "drachma," which is equivalent in value to six "obols." The superordinate units are the "mina," worth one hundred drachmas, and the "talent," equaling six thousand drachmas. We know that a decent house in a suburb of Athens in the late fifth century BC would set the buyer back five hundred to one thousand drachmas (or five to ten minas); a gallon of olive oil, more than three drachmas; a good pair of shoes, about ten drachmas; a healthy adult slave, three hundred to five hundred. Still, for various reasons, expressing the value of a drachma in today's currency is not as straightforward as finding modern equivalents for, say, distance. According to an oft-cited rule of thumb, the wage for the average laborer in classical Athens was one or two drachmas a day. A talent, therefore, works out to the equivalent of almost twenty years of work, or in modern terms something like a million dollars.

As for the calendar, the reader will notice there are no absolute dates given for the events depicted here. This is due to the simple fact that no universal system existed until recent times (and arguably, does not exist even today, given that the Chinese, Muslim, and Jewish calendars are still in use). Instead, years were designated either by counting the years since some important event, or on the basis of who held important magistracies at that time (in Athens, years were named for the so-called "eponymous" archons). For instance, the historian Thucydides dates the beginning of the Peloponnesian War to "the forty-eighth year of the priestess-ship of Chrysis at Argos, during the ephorate of Aenesias at Sparta and in the last month but two of the archonship of Pythodorus at Athens . . ." (2.2.1). This works out to the early summer of 431 BC by modern reckoning. The focal events of this book are the Great Earthquake in Laconia in 464 BC, and the battle at Pylos and subsequent siege of the island of Sphacteria, which took place over a seventy-two day period in the mid to late summer of 425 BC.

Finally, to help the reader navigate a plethora of similar-sounding Greek names, an index of characters is included at the back of the book.

The living are stretched bows, whose purpose is death.
—Heraclitus

I

A Hush in the Brazen House

1.

In the early morning of her wedding day, Damatria went out to the privy hole behind her father's house. She had just cut her hair in short, boyish style, in preparation for the traditional first-night visit from her betrothed. Squatting, she imagined the smell of Molobrus as he pressed down on her, reeking of the barracks, of swine blood and vinegar from the mess table. He would fumble down there, and she would need to guide him in the process of her deflowerment. How ignorant of women were the brave lads, who lived their youths naked on Taygetus but trembled, lost as lambs, in the foothills of the Mount of Venus! What responsibilities womanhood entailed, ruling these men of Sparta.

She was struck at once by a certain unsteadiness. After bracing herself against the ground, she realized it was the earth itself that was moving, not she. It was just a mild dislocation at first, as if she was perched on the wrist of a giant who was repeatedly clenching his fist. Then came a sick-making pulsation, wave upon wave, as if the earth became liquid. This went on for a few uncommonly vivid minutes, consuming her attention, until the waves ceased and she rose uncertainly to her feet, arms outstretched, as if expecting to plunge into the betrayed solidity below.

Her father's house lay at the outskirts of the village

of Mesoa. Where the structure had stood, there was now a cloud of plaster dust over a neat pile of debris. No houses stood intact anywhere she could see, though there were a number of other figures who were, like herself, standing unscathed. She met the gaze of the wife and mother who lived in the house next door; mute as a post, she was holding the handle of a broken water jug, her eyes reflecting a faint bemusement with the reordered landscape. The woman seemed not to register the interleaved walls of the house before her, where minutes before her infant had delighted in lifting his tiny head. Damatria looked to the skyline of Taygetus over the valley, ordinarily so comforting in its familiarity. This time, in a way she could not describe, even the mountain seemed changed.

She returned to her house and regarded its ruins. The roof appeared to have fallen in first, followed by three of the masonry walls in turn. Her father had been sleeping in the room at the front. He was on his couch, his lips smeared with the flesh of oversoft figs; she recalled how, before she went out, his chest heaved up and fell one time, as if making up for a history of shallow breaths. His walking stick was next to him, and it stood there still, resting against the house's last standing wall. Seeing the stick dispelled her reverie—the wreck instantly became a real place again, and the tangled mass beside the wall, a grave made by pitiless hands.

The timbers were long and half-buried, and the cobbles were heavy. She made painful progress at her excavation as the sun climbed above the peaks. Sparta was a quiet place on nonfestival days, and her people never wept or screamed at misfortune, but the quality of the silence after the earthquake was unnerving. The birds had stopped singing and never resumed; she could hear guttural exertions from next door, as intimate as the sounds of lovemaking, as her neighbor dug into the debris of her own house. Isolated, Damatria jumped when a voice suddenly spoke to her.

"Are you the only one?" asked the soldier. He was standing on the road, a sword at his side, a blazon of fresh blood trailing from beneath his helmet. Damatria thought he must be a fool, believing he could defend himself from the great Earthshaker with a sword.

"My father is here," she replied, indicating the wreckage.

The soldier stared at the pile. "By order of the ephors," he said, "the people shall show their dignity."

She made no response, as if such a reminder was beneath her notice.

The soldier moved on, then stopped, resting his hand on the grip of his weapon. "You should know . . . the disorder has encouraged some of the helots."

"If that is true, why are you standing here prattling with women? Go and be a man!"

The soldier hung his head and left. She bent to her digging again, scattering the stones around her as the afternoon waned, heedless of the cuts made in her hands by exposed nails. Suddenly—beneath a broken tile—a foot. Damatria paused, the sight affecting her more than she could immediately bear. She fell back on her haunches, regarding it, unsure whether to proceed.

This was to be her wedding night; by sunset, she was supposed to be seized by Molobrus' family and brought to her future home. Perhaps by now she would have been in the traditional belted chemise, awaiting the furtive attentions of the groom. She should not expect to be taken as a woman the first time, or even the first several times, the old wives advised. Shorn of her hair like a young recruit, the Spartan bride had to understand the mechanics of barracks love. Damatria had long imagined this and the other nights that followed, as she would initiate Molobrus, in subtle but due course, into the way between male and female. The end of the process would put him inside her in fruitful fashion at last. For it would only be at that time, perhaps months into a good Spartan marriage, that bride and husband were supposed to see each other's faces by daylight.

Did Molobrus' little house in Limnae still stand? Did her matrimonial bed contain only rubble? She must have stayed that way, thinking about such things, until she fell asleep. When she awoke, her head was in the dirt, with a glow from the west shining in her eyes. She realized, with some shame, that after all those hours she had exposed nothing more of her father but that single foot.

Resuming her work, she began to find objects from her quarters on the top floor. They were forlorn hints of her past life: a bronze mirror, bent askew; a handleless sickle; a clay lamp, now broken, from the souvenir booths near the Altis; a scroll of poetry by Alcman. By chance, she found the one illicit item in her possession—a sack of foreign staters. Possession of precious metal was still thought corrupting in Sparta, and was therefore illegal. That her Theban shields, Athenian owls, and Aeginetan sea turtles might see the light of day made her uneasy. She looked around for a place to hide them, until she was frozen by the figure of a man standing on the road, watching.

Thinking the soldier had returned, she asked, "Are

you back for your courage?" When he made no answer, she began to worry that he had seen the coins. She held the bag behind her back as the stranger stepped forward.

By the way he stood—by that slightly stoop-shouldered posture, and the way he twisted his neck as if to peer up at her—she knew he was a helot. His face was in shadow, but his hair was cut short in the manner best to distinguish servants from their long-locked superiors. His body, knotted with muscles telling of heavy, repetitive work, lacked the lean balance of a true fighting physique. At the end of one of those arms was a balled fist, and in that fist was a knife.

He was on her before she could get away. The attack felt at first to her much like a wrestling match in the gymnasium, the kind of test of strength she never lost against other girls. She felt a surge of confidence as she struck the first blow and spun nearly free. Indeed, in her contempt for this helot she had no inclination to scream, for to do so would have been to acknowledge some inferiority. In the next instant she lost her chance to escape: as he brought the butt of the knife down across her temple, Damatria, puzzled, felt her knees give way.

She woke up before she dared open her eyes. It was either hours or seconds later—she could not tell. She was on her back in the dirt with the helot on top. He kept on trying to bend her knees around his midriff, but even in her half stupor Damatria begrudged any opening, pressing her legs down flat on the ground. And so she waited, her jaw clenched so tightly shut with the pain that she cracked the crowns of her teeth. The physical ordeal, however, was not as bad as the sense of black despair, flowing like a liquid shadow into her every corner. It surprised her, so deep a well of loathing did she conjure in herself. Looking up, she saw a crow perched on a branch, cocking its head to regard her from one side. In that moment she despised that bird, so assured in its freedom, as much as she hated her own weakness.

After the helot spilled into her he seemed to linger there with piggish satisfaction. Still unafraid, she tried to wiggle free until he regarded her with mild curiosity. For the first time, she got a good look at his face: everything about it was heavy, from the lips like fattened grubs to the broken nose to the thick lids of his eyes. She was staring into those eyes, scorning them, when the shadow of his chiseled arm blotted the sky and he brought a fist down on her face. A thousand blossoms bloomed of every color she had ever seen; the force of the blow made her aware that her skull was composed of many parts that were designed, but straining, to remain together.

This time she did not pass out. Through slitted lids, she watched him take his feet, straighten his tattered work shirt over one shoulder, and step over her to continue on his way. After waiting a few minutes, she sat up. The first thing she noticed was that her half-spilled bag of silver coins was left untouched beside her. The second was that no matter which way she turned, one side of her world was dark. Reaching up, she felt the jagged ends of the small bones around what was once her left eye: the topography of the orbit above her cheekbone was alien to her, and something broken and soft was draining down to wet the corner of her mouth.

She pursued the helot into the fields without making any conscious decision to do so. She was suddenly full of the spirit of Artemis, able to read the lay of the twigs and disturbed soil, tracking her quarry like she did small animals in her girlhood. His path ran through the heart of the village of Mesoa, which she hardly recognized because it encompassed not a single intact building. Instead, it resembled a mine or a quarry. Some of the people were digging through the rubble, as she had; others stood by, detached, as if on an excursion to a dead city.

The helot skirted the southern slopes of the city acropolis on his way east, toward the river. Looking up, she saw that the Brazen House was still standing. The altar was below the crest of the hill, but she could see a curl of smoke rising above the temple gables as the Lacedaemonians gathered from every village to propitiate the gods. She would have been there too, if not on the present errand. Another black wave broke over her, making the light breeze seem to burn her skin. The handleless sickle from her father's house had somehow found its way into her right hand.

The helot disappeared from view as he descended to the banks of the Eurotas. She concealed herself in the rushes and crept forward to observe him. Removing his clothes, he waded in as deep as his waist, breathing hard as he entered the swift, cold water. He scrubbed his penis with a handful of dirt from the banks, then bent down to rinse the knob. The act filled Damatria with disgust for the squeamishness of men: in her haste, despite her degradation, she had not washed any part of herself, inside or out. She watched, feeling a kind of forlorn contempt for the helot's utter exposure, his damnable obliviousness. Cleansing himself of me! Her fingers gripped the rusty blade until they bled.

The helot floated on his back, as if savoring the taste of freedom for the first time. With a child's curiosity, he paused to inspect fragments of wood or wattle from shattered buildings as they floated by. When at last he pulled himself out of the water, he dressed and returned along the path by which he'd come. Damatria posted herself amid the plane trees, and knowing he would not be expecting her, hardly bothered to conceal herself.

He passed by without taking any notice of her.

She swung her sickle against the back of his head, lodging the broken end in the base of his skull. His body made sounds as it entered—a gasp of astonishment, a pop of dislocated bones, followed by a cluck of dismay. She wrenched his head around, watching him grimace and flutter his eyes in pain or stupefaction. She didn't know which; she didn't care.

2.

The earthquake destroyed all but a handful of buildings in Laconia. The death toll ran into the tens of thousands, but the ephors saw no profit in advertising the city's weakness and sanctioned no official count. What could not be hidden, though, were the large numbers of children killed of every age-class. Many boys were collected in the doomed gymnasia in the morning hours. Since every Spartiate adult was held to be protector and educator of every free-born child in the city, citizens gathered en masse to dig out the victims. Foreigners and helots, however, were kept away from such scenes. The sorrow of the Lacedaemonians was not for outsiders to witness.

When in doubt the Spartans mobilized for war. As aftershocks battered the city and unrecovered bodies stank in the streets, all five battalions of the infantry mustered in their appointed places. Mourning ceremonies halted for the families to comb their shattered storerooms for supplies to feed the troops. The soldiers practiced spearmanship, maneuvering to the pipes, and night fighting under columns of smoke from the fires of continuous funerals.

The thirty members of the city *Gerousia*, or executive council, convened in a goat pen and voted to declare war on the helots. Along with the usual immunity this conferred on any Spartiate who wished, for any reason, to kill a helot, the measure included the activation of the Hidden Service. Young men specially trained for these gangs were excused from their units and went into hiding. At night, they would sneak into the helot villages and murder any males they encountered; most often the victims were the most intelligent helots, or the most respected, or the strongest, or the finest artisans, or any that showed some distinction that might prove remotely threatening.

But these precautions failed to prevent an eventuality worse than the earthquake itself: the helots in Messenia, taking advantage of the misfortune of their masters, revolted. They were soon joined by several of the more restive Nigh-Dwellers and a few helots of Laconia proper. At a time when many of the granaries were already damaged, exposing the grain to rot, the helot farmers stood up and walked away from their fields. In a galling reversal, roving gangs of rebels made it impossible for decent citizens to travel at night. The army was forced to fight everywhere against the majority of the population of Laconia. The old men could not remember a less secure time in the life of the city.

All this seemed very far from Damatria. She was still haunting the ruins of her house when Molobrus'

father and two brothers came to see if she had survived. As they led her away, she was still not sure she
could reassure them. Certainly, there was a "Damatria" who lived—a figure in a play with the almond-
shaped eyes and straight teeth, the ingenue who still
ate, breathed, smiled, and looked with virginal tremu-
lousness on the mystery of her wedding night. According to this plot, she had stayed at her father's side
during the disaster, and her left eye was put out by a
falling brick. In this character she vested all the pro-
prieties to which she could never quite conform herself. Disfigured but dutiful, she seemed to her new
family a model of durable innocence; the match with
Molobrus was declared by all to be a more pleasing
prospect than ever.

The other Damatria was not a virgin at all. The violence of the rape had torn her inside and out. In the
streets, the sight of any face that even remotely resembled the helot caused her to be physically ill. At
night, when she most wished to escape her memories,
the dark half of her world did not remain so, but exploded with the same riot of phosphorescent colors
she saw when he first crushed her eye. The spectacle
forced her to relive the moment over and over, until
she grew to dread the attempt to sleep.

And so she went on simulating her former life, taking her place in Molobrus' Limnae house, pretending
to conspire in his schemes to steal hours away from
the barracks. The joy of these conjugal moments was
lost to her. The hot anonymity she once imagined was
repulsive, and Molobrus was too fascinated with her
crushed features to preserve the usual mystery. He
brought his round little face close to hers, whistling to
himself as he examined her wound. She, in turn,
looked back in smiling disappointment at his soft

cheeks, so obvious in their failure to produce a man's growth of beard. Everything turned out to be harder than she imagined, with only a single exception: she didn't have to fake a virgin's fear of penetration.

She became aware of her pregnancy a few weeks after the earthquake. For the sake of her sanity, she hoped that the child was Molobrus'. She subsisted on this hope for nine months, indulging her mother-in-law's compulsion to give advice:

"For the child's sake, you must not only bathe him in wine, but scrub his body with pinecones," Lampito advised her. "A baby's softness is better lost sooner than later."

"And if a girl comes?"

She frowned as if Damatria had done something akin to kissing her husband in public. "Sparta needs spears now," she said.

Of that, there was no doubt. After three months of fighting, the immediate environs of Sparta were mostly safe, with some of the compliant helots assigned to rebuilding. But the uprising was far from over in Messenia. Troops were dispatched west through the Taygetos passes on a daily basis; they returned almost as frequently, as the old saying went, "either carrying their shields or on them." It was rumored that the Messenians fought as if the intervening three centuries of their subjugation had never occurred. A startling proportion of Lacedaemonian deaths were from festered human bites.

Upon the birth of her son, before he could even be cleaned, Damatria demanded to see his face. Lampito laid his bloody form on his mother's belly, trusting that he would show enough Spartan vigor to claim the breast. The child inched up her body with clumsy but strong thrashing movements, like some swimming reptile. When he reached her breastbone he gazed up at his mother. There—unmistakable in the balled pucker of his rooting lips and thickly lidded eyes—she found herself confronted again with the face of her rapist.

For the next few days Damatria twisted in a vortex of disgust and guilt. In that time someone thought to give the child a name—Antalcidas—in honor of Molobrus' father, Alcidas. She allowed them to put the thing on her chest again, but she made no effort to help him nurse. As with many unwanted children, however, his hunger for life exactly matched his mother's longing for him to die. He taught himself to suckle, which transported Lampito into fits of admiration.

"What a fine boy!" she exclaimed. "And what a good Spartan mother, to compel the little warrior to find his own mess!"

"He will have nothing to fear from the tribe," agreed Molobrus.

Damatria perked up. Every Spartan infant was brought to the tribal elder when it was evident that he or she would survive the first days. The child would be examined, and if found to be in any way deficient, would be consigned to be thrown into Langadha Gorge. Most Spartan mothers respected the tradition, but dreaded the appraisal. To Damatria, it represented a ray of hope—a possibility that a lifetime ordeal would be cut mercifully short. She rose from her bed and took little Antalcidas in her arms.

"I will prepare him for the judgment," she swore.

Damatria's devotion to her son's improvement became legend in the village of Kynosoura. Molobrus returned to his regiment and was rarely seen since, but Lampito had ample opportunity to witness her daughter's commitment. Antalcidas was not only bathed in wine—his "bathwater" was pure, unmixed stuff. As the child screamed from the stinging in his eyes, Damatria ladled more over his head, until Lampito was quite sure she would drown him. When at last he began to convulse and vomit up his milk, she would relent, though she would never coddle him with swaddling clothes. Instead, she placed him outside her door to air dry. She did this even as winter came on and the temperatures plunged. His grandmother found him out there one evening, naked on the cold flagstone, his skin a color somewhere between wine-dark and hypothermic blue. Despite her pride in his Spartan toughness, Lampito feared for the boy's health. But when she brought him inside, she found Damatria impassively beaming.

"Don't worry, Mother," she told Lampito. "One day, when he is camped in the dead of winter on the Taygetos in nothing but his skin and a thin cloak, he will thank his mother for this training."

The day finally arrived for the judgment of children born to mothers of the Dymanes tribe. Seven women, stern faced and unaccompanied, gathered with their babies in front of the Shrine of Athena-of-the-City. This was called the Brazen House because the sturdy, four-square structure was decorated with bronze reliefs from the history of the Dorians. Between one plaque depicting Herakles' capture of the Hind of Ceryneia and another the defeat of the Messenians, the oldest surviving members of Damatria's tribe, Arcesilaus, son of Areus, Alcander, son of Pausanias, and Nicander, son of Cleomenes, had installed themselves on stools. Sadly, the earthquake had cost the city so many of her elders that these judges were not so old after all—Alcander was not yet sixty.

The order of presentation was determined by a pre-selection by the magistrates. The weakest candidates for survival were brought up first, so that the judgment could end with the state's happy endorsement of the stronger. Damatria was disappointed to learn that her son was picked third—too late in the round for her to be sure of the result.

The first child presented was a girl with a cleft palate. Arcesilaus glanced at her once, exchanged a few words with his colleagues, and nodded to the guards. A basket was presented to the mother; with a stricken look, she placed the infant inside and covered its face with a cloth. In exchange, they handed her a barley cake for Eileithyia so that she might assuage her grief with a dedication. A dutiful Spartan mother, she offered a proud, if threadbare, smile. The grimace vanished from her face when, as the basket was borne away to the gorge, the contents began to cry.

The second candidate was a boy. There seemed nothing outwardly wrong with the child until Arcesilaus tested his vision. Making him focus on a single finger moving laterally, Arcesilaus found the left eyeball at first tracked the target but then veered in the opposite direction. The boy's mother flushed with either fear or embarrassment: this was a defect she had not found. The elders murmured amongst themselves. Arcesilaus repeated the test, got the same result, and conferred again. To Damatria's surprise, the elders let the boy pass. The earthquake had changed more than the shape of Mount Taygetos.

Damatria presented Antalcidas, who was sleeping. She shook him awake. Arcesilaus regarded him, stroking his beard as the boy's head rolled on his tiny neck. They felt his grip, counted his digits, tested his reflexes.

"This one's eyes seem irritated," Alcander remarked. "Have you been bathing him in unmixed wine?"

"I have."

Arcesilaus shook his head. "Mothers should wash their boys in wine at half strength, not neat. Understand?"

She looked away, saying nothing. This was not going as she hoped: the elders were smiling at the boy, evidently pleased at his vigor despite the ignorance of his mother.

"Listen to his voice," she said. "His lungs are weaker than the other children."

Nicander scratched his freckled pate. "His cry sounds healthy to me."

"His movements are slow. And he nurses poorly."

"The nursing," thundered Àrcesilaus, "is something you must teach him!"

"I have tried."

"Try harder."

"Esteemed Equals," she sighed, "who knows this child better than I? Please . . ."

Arcesilaus' eyes widened. Anticipating what she meant to say, the other mothers regarded her with something close to horror. Damatria tried to continue, but couldn't.

"There is nothing wrong with this boy. Rejoice in your good fortune," Arcesilaus pronounced. With that, his gaze shifted to the next candidate. Antalcidas had been passed.

Damatria drifted a few steps away, her useless eye throbbing in its socket. Seeing the other women with their cherished babes made her dizzy with revulsion. The sound of Antalcidas' little breaths, his cloying smell, his very weight on her arm, filled her with unspeakable indignation. She whirled back at the elders.

"I see that wisdom is dead among you. Before the gods, then, hear me: one day, one way or another, this child will grow up to be the shame of this city! Remember that a Spartan mother told you this, when you lacked the courage to act!"

After this disaster she took the boy home and put him on the floor. She left him there a long time as she sat and thought. Might she have disposed of him earlier, she wondered, while sickness remained a plausible excuse? Could she still do so? Her mistake, she decided, was to leave her salvation in the hands of others. She resolved that she would not move until she knew what she might do to tolerate the prospect of her own future.

3.

Antalcidas was quiet at first, turning his head back and forth across the blur of the rafters above. At length he felt a discomfort in his stomach. He began to whimper, kicking off his blanket as he rooted for the nipple against his cheek. Feeling nothing, his fear rose, though he could not understand it as such, and he began to cry. His voice, scratchy and croaking, resounded through the soft tectonics of his skull, magnifying his dejection. He was alone.

He cried some more, grew tired, and stopped. In the silence he felt his need again, and went from quiet to full-on bawling in an instant. But then he stopped just as suddenly, and when the hunger ailed him again he produced only a murmur. What had been a bright blur above him was now an opaque gloom. Opening his mouth to root, he produced a yawn.

When he awoke he saw nothing but blackness. He had somehow lost his blanket, and felt a damp rigidity pressing against his back. His bladder had emptied as he slept, the fountain of his own water soaking him. In that instant his cold, his loneliness, and the discomfort in his stomach fused into a single knot of misery. He poured his heart into a long, arcing wail, and then a staccato of piercing sweeps. As he screamed, his face burned red and wet as his tiny fists punched the air. He cried with such violence that his breathing could not keep up. He choked, wept, choked. No one came.

Other voices came to him from beyond the walls. Across vastnesses he could not yet conceive, his brothers and sisters whispered to him from their stony cradles. They were collected at the bottom in their thousands, tender humeri scattered in the stream, toothless jaws rolled and polished by the water. Bits of scalp clung to some, covered with fine hair, residues of blood mingled across the boulders. Like Antalcidas, the bones lay in silence, but did not lack for attention from the rats and jackals that suckled their soft ends. As their mothers lived their days nearby, weaving their shrouds of forgetting, the children of Sparta lay gathered against that hard but eternally accepting bosom, calling to him.

Then something loomed at him from out of the dark. He felt it snatch him up, and through his tears he saw the gathering of a luminant mass, a moonscape of light and dark that resolved into his mother's face. What he could not recognize, though, was the peculiar shape of her mouth as she brought him close. For the first time, as she offered her breast, she was smiling.

4.

Damatria had realized a single, sustaining prospect—
to have a truly legitimate child. To that end, she attacked her husband in a procreational frenzy. Molobrus
kept up as best he could, but showed fear in his eyes
as she bared her legs for the third, fourth, fifth go in a
night. Even in his ignorance he could sense there was
no pleasure in the act for her, only the obstinate purpose of a commander marshaling his forces for some
greater end.

A son was born the following summer. Molobrus
took an afternoon to come home from the barracks,
looked down at young Epitadas, and pronounced
himself pleased. But to Damatria his arrival marked
the time of her own rebirth, of joys that were finally
unmixed. Her months of shame, of lies of omission,
were over.

She responded with a tenderness that surprised
Lampito. The infant's wine baths were diluted to one-
sixth strength and less. While Antalcidas lay without
cover in a basket across the room, Damatria took Epitadas to bed with her. His hunger and chills, his
teething, and the softness of his blankets, were constant matters for concern. One day, when Lampito
looked in on them, she was pleased to see that Antalcidas had begun to pull himself upright against
his mother's legs. Damatria, however, would barely
glance at him as she cooed at Epitadas.

"I would think you were a first-time mother, the
way you coddle him," Lampito said. "Remember I
told you that Sparta needs . . ."

"Sparta needs spears, yes," the other interrupted.
Breaking her gaze at Epitadas, she looked down at
Antalcidas with something more than her usual

severity. As she stroked his head, he became excited, trying to pull himself into her lap. She withdrew her hand.

It would be untrue to say Damatria never developed any feelings for Antalcidas. With the blessing of Epitadas' arrival, the well of her compassion overflowed enough for her to spare a few drops for his brother, who was really a fine, strong boy. When she thought about how cruel she had been to him, she was even inclined to regret—though for Epitadas' sake she did not take her self-recriminations too far. In time, she came to make peace with her secrets, and to the temporary weakness in her that had spawned her eldest. In place of useless resentment, she nurtured grandiose plans for achievement. Epitadas stood at the focus of her ambition, but his brother would have an important role to play. She pulled Antalcidas up and gave him the other breast; she fell asleep with both boys clinging to her, staring into each other's eyes across the chasm.

5.

The austerity of the Lacedaemonians was practiced in the richest landscape in Greece. Sheltered between the Parnon range in the east and Taygetus in the west, Laconia was secure, expansive, and fertile. The river Eurotas descended from the borderlands of Sciritis to water the estates of citizens in the valley. Figs, almonds, olives, grapes, pomegranates, pears, cherries, and apples fell from tree and vine; the climate was so congenial for barley that farmers reaped two harvests a year. The profusion of boar and stag in the foothills afforded ample hunting, while goats, sheep, and oxen flourished on grasses nurtured by pure snowmelt that persisted deep into the summer.

It was a common rite of passage for young Spartan males to climb into the lower reaches of Taygetus, to the very spur where, two thousand years later, the tonsured monks of Frankish Mistra would fly to escape secular corruption. The Spartan boys would flee nothing, but gaze in pride at the verdant tapestry below, comprehending better than ever the magnitude of their worldly good fortune. Even the helots seemed to go around in a permanent state of wonder at such stupendous plenty—the wealth that for some, in their secret hearts, was worth the sacrifice of their freedom.

In due course the damage from the earthquake was repaired. Houses were rebuilt larger and stronger, with luxuries such as windows. This drew the criticism of the elders, who wondered aloud if the Lacedaemonians were going soft. But in fact the indiscriminate destruction had pauperized, not spoiled, many of the citizens. Men who lost the produce of their farms by physical loss or the shortage of helots could no longer contribute to their dining clubs, costing them their citizenship. Families whose farms were spared could then afford to acquire more land. Some used the extra income to build bigger houses.

The loss of citizens-soldiers through penury aggravated Laconia's chronic shortage of manpower. Spartiates were enjoined to multiply, and spawn they did. But the fruits of this boom would not enter the army for another generation. Meanwhile, the revolt of the helots seemed interminable, costing the city more casualties, more ruined estates. At last, four years after it had begun, the toughest of the rebels were confined to fortified positions at the top of Mount Ithome, sixty miles northwest of Sparta. There they remained, resisting all attempts to dislodge them.

The Gerousia, envisioning operations against Ithome might drag on indefinitely, then did something unheard of in the history of Sparta: it asked for foreign help against a domestic foe. The Athenians, in particular, were known to be skilled in siege warfare. Why not let the allies of Sparta do the bleeding against the Messenians? At best, the Athenians would solve the problem; at worst, the rebels would hold the mountain, but Athens would lose men and prestige fighting them. Indeed, as the Athenians acquired alarming wealth and power after the Persian Wars, it was hard to say which result most benefited Sparta.

But the old men of the council had not anticipated the effect of four thousand Athenians let loose among the people. Damatria encountered them in the streets of Kynosoura: gangs of jabbering, overdressed, smooth-cheeked children. As respectable Athenian women rarely ventured out of doors, their men assumed every Spartan female they saw was a streetwalker. In her short peplos, her hair uncovered, Damatria got more than her share of attention.

"Look at that, will you! Give my pay for a go with her!"

"A real thigh-flasher, that one!"

"Hey girlie, look here!"

The Athenian parted his tunic to reveal what he carried there. As he stared at her unashamed, he commenced to yank back and forth on the foreskin. Furious, Damatria would have buried her fist in his face, but knew that would accomplish nothing. It was the third time that day she had been accosted.

Worse in the eyes of most Lacedaemonians was Athenian presumption. Gold and silver jewelry ap-

peared openly in Laconia for the first time in living
memory. The corrupting influence of these baubles
was the subject of much discussion around the mess
tables; the effect on Spartan women was feared the
most. The conceit of the Athenians went hand in hand
with their vanity: when one of them saw a desirable
helot, he invariably proffered either some high-
handed objection to Greeks enslaving other Greeks, or
else made an offer to purchase. Since helots were public resources, not private slaves, it was illegal to buy or
sell them. Yet few of the visitors seemed to respect this
or any other Spartan law.

In the end, the Athenian troops were as useless as
they were offensive. Cimon, their leader, took one
look at the ridge of Ithome, more than four stades tall,
and declared that the task required not siegecraft but
wings. This was the final straw: the Gerousia, with the
support of the kings Pleistarchus and Archidamus,
delivered an official disinvitation. The Athenians
were deeply insulted to be sent home. Some of them
(but not Cimon) went around claiming it was democracy, not Athenian arms, that Sparta feared most. With
their departure the treaty between Sparta and Athens
was finished. Insofar as Athens was a rising threat to
Spartan interests, the end of the alliance was not unwelcome in some quarters.

Soon after these events, Molobrus turned thirty.
According to tradition, this was the age when a married man was supposed to leave the barracks to go
live with his family. Damatria first thought she
would welcome this, but very soon realized how
wrong she had been. Her husband came home with
very odd ideas about running things in his own
household. The first days of his homecoming were
awkward, with Molobrus moping about, missing his

comrades. Soon he turned to making ignorant comments about the condition of the gardens, the olive grove, the hearth, the helots' work, and whatever else displeased him. The celebrated reticence of the Laconian male, she learned, was nothing more than a myth—or more precisely, a tale for ignorant outsiders. Spartiates chattered like sparrows when they didn't get their way.

Damatria soon tired of defending a way of life she had managed alone since the day of their marriage. Nor did Molobrus' actual presence do much for their physical intimacy. Spartan sex, predicated as it was on mystery and rarity, did nothing to prepare her for this stranger at her door.

Equally disturbing to her was the way he treated his sons. At first, he knew no other way of dealing with them than as barracks mates. In one instance, Damatria was upset to find an unsheathed sword in the hands of little Epitadas. She snatched it up, causing the boy to scream in protest.

"Are you a fool, giving a sword to a six-year-old boy?" she cried.

Molobrus shrugged. "He wanted to see it. Should a Spartan be kept from blades?"

"And how will he ever carry a weapon in the line if he loses a hand or some fingers?"

"I'm going to the barracks," he said, slamming the door. There was a cold winter rain falling, but he left in too much of a hurry to take his cloak.

In time, Molobrus acquired enough common sense for her to trust him with the boys. What soon became apparent to her, though, was that he was determined to treat Antalcidas and Epitadas with equal affection. She would stand in the shadows, watching him play war games with them. His ignorance sickened her.

True, she had never told him that Antalcidas was not his son. Yet some part of her could not help but wonder why he failed to perceive in him the bastard vigor, the doglike desire to please, the slave's devious cleverness. "Can't you see the truth?" she wanted to scream, making the wife's eternal complaint at her husband's failure to divine what she could not bear to say.

Fortunately, within the year Antalcidas was of age to begin the Rearing. The boy-herd, Endius, son of Melancidas, came for him one morning when Molobrus was away on the hunt. Damatria had not made the mistake of heaping warm clothes on her son's back, or packing him a last meal for the road, because she understood such things would be tossed in a ditch by his teachers. She had, in fact, not prepared him at all for his final departure from his parents' home.

The boy seemed to guess the nature of the stranger's business as he entered the yard. He ran to Damatria, wrapping his arms around her legs, and she looked down at him, frowning.

"Mother, who are they? Are they here for me?"

"What do you want from me, boy?" she cried, deeply embarassed in front of Endius. She yanked her skirt from Antalcidas' grip and lifted it to midthigh. "Do you want to crawl back up under here? Now off with you!"

The boy-herd pried him loose, and with the kind of curt nod given by someone collecting alms or taxes, carried Antalcidas away. But the boy bit down hard on his forearm. He ran back to his mother, this time locking his arms around her ankles. Damatria, not entirely willing to kick him, finally asked Endius to wait outside.

"This is very disappointing," she said as she got him to his feet at last. "Can't you see that everyone is watching you?"

"But . . . I . . . leaving . . . go . . . don't . . . wanna . . ." the boy uttered between sobs.

She gripped his arms tightly enough to make him yelp.

"Listen to me, you little shit. You will not unman this house. Don't you think your father did his duty? And his father before him?"

More tears. She brought his face close to hers, with almost their noses touching, and said, "Antalcidas, look here. I need you to be brave. You need to take care of Epitadas for me one day, when I can't be there. Do you understand?"

Lower lip aquiver, he nodded.

"To do this for me, you need to become strong. These men want to help you. Will you go with them?"

Uncertain, he showed a brave face as Endius returned and took him by the hand. The boy-herd had a poultice of mud and spit on his arm where Antalcidas had bitten him.

"No need for an apology!" declared Endius, though Damatria had not offered one. "We see all kinds of reactions . . . better tears now than in front of the other boys!"

He was gone. Damatria stood dreading the sound of him bolting back to the house, but she heard nothing more. Straightening the linen over her legs, she winced at the stains of Antalcidas' tears on the fabric. A torment to the very end! Yet with that, Damatria hoped the ordeal that had begun more than seven years before, beside the rubble of her father's house, was finally over. She looked to Epitadas, who had been watching through a doorway.

"By the gods, I don't expect such a fuss from you!"
she told him.

6.

Endius took him to a place in the fields where a wide
circle of grain had been trampled flat. Fifteen other
boys his age romped inside the circle. There were no
introductions and little talking—just the vegetal crack
of fifteen bodies jumping, wrestling, and flopping on
the stalks. Endius stripped off Antalcidas' cloak, leaving him with only a thin tunic. The boys halted to examine the new arrival. When Antalcidas looked up at
him with a questioning look, the boy-herd winked
and walked away through the rows of barley.

Antalcidas wondered if he was supposed to follow,
until he was shoved from behind. Turning, he was
confronted by an older boy, about twelve years old,
who bore a striking mole on his right cheek.

"Are you really just seven years old?" asked Birthmark.

"Yes."

"He's too tall," he said to the other boys. "Betcha
his mother kept him at home an extra year, maybe
even two!"

"Did not."

"Don't argue, Grub!" a redheaded boy ordered,
holding his little fist under Antalcidas' nose.

"Grub?"

"It's a kind of useless worm . . . Grub!"

"We call all the new ones grubs," said Birthmark.
"If you're lucky, you get a real name when you prove
yourself."

"Wake up! Scarecrow due east!" a third boy announced with hushed excitement.

All eyes looked to Birthmark, who Antalcidas realized must be the pack's leader. The boy crouched suddenly, and was joined in the huddle by everyone else. Redhead turned back to Antalcidas.

"What are you doing, Grub? Get in here!"

The others made a space for Antalcidas to join them. Birthmark was in the middle giving orders, jabbing a finger at each boy in turn.

"Frog, Ho-hum, Cricket, and Beast take flanking position. Redhead, Rehash, and Cheese guard against the countermarch, while the rest of you circle around with me to the front. . . ."

"Wait, what do I do again?" asked Rehash.

"I said, guard against the countermarch! New kid, you come with me too . . . on the double!"

As they scattered, each of the boys picked out a handful of stones from between the broken barley stalks. Antalcidas didn't understand what they were attacking—until they all crept through the grain and fixed their target.

The "scarecrow" was a solitary helot, walking along the verge with a hoe across his shoulders, a sun hat on his head.

Birthmark led his party through the barley a short distance ahead of the helot. He paused, synchronizing his approach with the flankers and the rear guard. The helot halted too, cocking his head as if he'd heard something, bringing the hoe down in blocking position across his body. There was a pause as hunters and quarry held still; Antalcidas had stalked hares on his own, in the grove behind his house, but had never before felt his heart beat with such anticipation. And then it began: the squad closed in on three sides with rocks on high, letting loose a collective squeal that seemed more rodentlike than dangerous. But there was no avoiding the ferocity of the attack as the stones pelted the helot from all sides. His hat fluttering off his head like a wounded bird, he collapsed to the dirt with his face covered. Birthmark and his more brazen foot soldiers came in close to hurl their missiles from inches away. The helot, who seemed to have some experience with these things, convulsed on the stubble to avoid the blows.

They tortured him with every rock they could find, and when they ran out of rocks they tried sticks, pebbles, and cow chips. Climbing to his feet, the helot uncovered his face to see where he might run. That was when Birthmark served up his last surprise—a shard of granite he had held back just for that moment. It struck the helot square in the mouth. An arc of blood, like a libation uncapped, poured out of him. He escaped into the woods adjoining the next field. Frog and Beast moved to go after him, but Birthmark called them back.

The boys gathered around the splash of helot blood and broken teeth on the ground, cheering. Birthmark broke into the middle of them.

"Quiet, all of you! What do you have to celebrate? Doing your duty?"

"That's one scarecrow who won't raise his head for a while!" declared Frog, a seemingly neckless, dimpled lad. He picked up the stump of a broken incisor and tried to fit in into the gap in his own mouth.

"Maybe. But there are always more slaves than men like us. Remember that."

"Look! New kid didn't throw!"

They all looked to Antalcidas—the only one of them who still had a sizable rock in his hand. As they all scrutinized him he burned red with embarrassment. The rock dropped from his fingers.

"Well, I'd say we'll be calling you Grub for quite a while yet," Birthmark said.

7.

For the next month, Antalcidas had no contact with the world of adults, but instead lived as freely as some wild thing sprung straight from the soil. No one came to feed the boys, but at the height of summer the trees and gardens and vineyards were heaped with food for the taking. After gorging themselves on fruit, they would go down to the swift Eurotas to drink, and then lie on the rocks as the rays of the summer sun filled them with warm indolence. Twilight was the time for deer and jackals to venture out, and so too for the squad to use the shadows to stalk helots. Soon enough Antalcidas was in the forefront of these attacks, coming at last to relish the look of terror on the faces of grown men as he came screaming upon them. The excitement plucked every string of muscle and tendon with the music of unabashed, consequence-free cruelty. With such power, he not only lost his fear of the dark, but came to take night and cold as his natural allies.

One by one, the amenities he had grown up with—a roof, hot food, clothes—became distant, even absurd to contemplate. The sound of human speech itself was stripped away, becoming in those days a rare thing to be indulged only for purposes of organizing war parties. In time they at last stopped calling him "Grub" and named him "Stone," after his deadeye accuracy with a thrown rock. But Antalcidas, having learned the essential unimportance of words, no longer cared what he was called.

He stopped missing his home. After two months of

sleeping under the stars, he could visualize the con-
stellations more easily than the features of his
mother's face. Looking up from his bed of rushes, he
imagined he had a new family all around him; the
lines of an old poem of Alcman, still sung by the older
boys, echoed in his mind:

The upland gorges are sleeping, laid among peak and crag
Hushed by rushing waters
As the nation of beasts enwombed in the black earth
Keep the silence . . .

His packmates all came to look alike, their faces
and knees caked with the same dirt, their feet hardened by the same calluses, their eyes burning with the
same appetites. Older men coveted them when they
glimpsed them in the forest, like prize game. Birthmark taught the younger lads to masturbate like men,
standing up as if to piss, legs together. In the end they
deposited their seed all together in a communal hole
in the ground. Antalcidas wrung what he could into
these viscous masses, imagining perhaps that the
mingling of masculine essences would give life to the
soil, like the warriors of Theban Cadmus sprung from
the earth out of dragon's teeth. Women who came
upon these wet spots puzzled over them; men who
had gone through the Rearing understood—and
smiled.

By the fall Birthmark—whose real name Antalcidas
never learned—passed into the lowest of the senior
age-groups. Beast took over as their leader, and boys
younger than Antalcidas entered the pack after him.
He bullied them in turn, calling them "Grub" just as
he had been. Helping his inferiors to struggle, adapt,
and finally to mature made him believe in his own

wisdom. Besides learning where the best berries grew, and which leaves to chew to settle an upset stomach, and where to obtain the sharpest cutting stones, he imagined he understood at last how a boy acquired manly virtue.

But he still had a lot to learn. Just as the chill of autumn mornings bit harder, the single cloak Endius had given him had become reduced to moldy, motheaten uselessness. It was no longer so easy to find fruit on the trees. The olives were not ready yet, and not many grapes were left on the vines after the harvest. Beast showed them how to stave off the pangs by chewing thyme leaves. He also showed them that, in a pinch, crickets and ants were edible (the former tasted like dry sticks, the latter like almond). But it was hard to eat his fill of these. The hunger gave him a constant headache; he found himself attracted again to settled places, where he thought he might steal some bread or cheese.

The boys were sometimes diverted from this torment by the intermittent presence of Thibron, son of Proclus. A smiling, handsome figure with preternaturally white teeth, Thibron was a Firstie—a member of the highest age-class, poised to leave the Rearing and embark on his career as a fighting member of the army. One of the duties of a Firstie was to school his juniors with advice and games. Thibron kept Beast's pack on the run with a steady stream of physical challenges, calling on each of them to exceed the exploits of the rest. "Which of you can climb this tree the fastest?" was a typical dare. Others were less innocent, such as "Who can take a punch in the chest from Beast and not flinch?" or "Who can stay facedown in the river the longest?" or, most ingeniously, "Who can bring me some hairs from the leg of Isidas the

Ephor?" Fulfilling these tasks broke up the monotony of long afternoons in the hills. It also gave Thibron an air of diabolical excitement—when he appeared, no one was sure what might happen.

But there were even greater dangers on the roam. The worse thing that could happen was to blunder into a gang of older boys, who would make them pay for their lack of discretion. This happened only once, during an afternoon when Beast led them down to the Eurotas to drink. Their favorite spot was occupied by a pack of fourteen- and fifteen-year-olds. During the chase Frog was caught from behind. Antalcidas heard him scream as the enemy gathered to kick him. Circling around, Antalcidas found a good round stone and, without thinking of the consequences, threw it at one of Frog's tormentors. The rock struck its target square in the back.

"Ow! What was that?"

"Somebody threw something."

"Where?"

They peered into the woods, but Antalcidas was well hidden among the laurel and holly oak. He had another stone in his hand, in case they came after him.

"I don't see anything."

"Somebody's in there—I can smell him."

"C'mon, let's go," said their leader, looking down on the supine Frog. "This little shit isn't worth it."

After each offered a parting kick, they left him on the ground. Antalcidas crept up, eyes and ears open in case their withdrawal was a trap.

"Are you all right?" he asked Frog. "Can you walk?"

The other boy moved his limbs, said something unintelligible, but otherwise made no response. Antalcidas turned him over to examine his chest and stomach. There were red marks there that would soon ripen into footprint-sized welts.

"Stone, what are you doing?" asked Beast, who was suddenly standing behind him.

"He's hurt."

"Got the wind knocked out of him. Hey, did you *throw rocks* at them?"

Beast had a look on his face as if he'd caught Antalcidas using a girl's spindle.

"I did . . . but only because there were so many."

"I didn't hear that."

"What was I supposed to do? There were five of them!"

"Listen, rocks are fine for punishing helots. But in battle, against real enemies, you don't demean yourself by couching behind a bush and throwing things. Don't you know anything?"

"I know you weren't there to help."

But Beast was already walking away, shaking his head.

After the new year they heard again from the boy-herd. The pack was summoned to the crest of the acropolis, where it was met by Endius and a man they did not know. Endius had the boys sit on the slope below them, obliging them to behold their teachers framed against the open sky. The boy-herd wore a simple tunic with one shoulder bared; the other man was dressed for war, with crimson cloak, short sword hanging from a leather baldric, and conical field cap made of felt on his head. His shield rested against his leg, its great lambda insignia—for "Lacedaemon"—facing out.

"Those who have lived thus far, congratulations," Endius said without welcome or preamble. "The first part of your education is over. Today you will begin to learn what you need beyond survival. You will learn what it means to be a citizen of Sparta. Listen."

He looked to the soldier, who leaned forward as if he was about to draw his sword. But instead he confronted them with a poem:

*I would not say anything for a man nor take account of
  him*
For any speed of his feet or wrestling skill he might have
*not if he had the size of a Cyclops and strength to go with
  it*
Not if he could outrun Boreas, the North Wind of Thrace
*not if he were more handsome and gracefully formed than
  Tithonos,*
or had more riches than Midas had, or Kinyras too,
not if he were more a king than Tantalid Pelops,
Or had the power of speech and persuasion Adrastos had,
not if he had all splendors except for a fighting spirit.
For no man ever proves himself a good man in war
unless he can endure to face the blood and the slaughter,
go close against the enemy and fight with his hands.
Here is courage, mankind's finest possession, here is
the noblest prize that a young man can endeavor to win,
*and it is a good thing his polis and all the people share with
  him*
*when a man plants his feet and stands in the foremost
  spears*
relentlessly, all thought of foul flight completely forgotten,
and has trained his heart to be steadfast and to endure,
*and with words encourages the man who is stationed
  beside him—*

"When I first heard these verses of Tyrtaeus," said Endius, "I was a child precisely as old as you are now, sitting in exactly the same place. The telling was done in just the same way, by a Spartiate as honored as Aeimnestus who stands here today, for the very same purpose. Savor this moment, boys, for it is given to none of us to hear Tyrtaeus for the first time twice. And like Aeimnestus, you will come to know every word of 'The Code of the Citizen' as well as you will know the fourth hour of a night watch, or what it feels like to take your place in the bronze-girt line. It has been this way since the sons of Herakles first conquered the kingdom of the Atreids, and so it will be thousands of years after we are all heaped on the pyre."

The boy-herd looked to the soldier, who picked up his shield and, with a comradely nod to the pack, departed. To hear that the reciter was Aeimnestus, the very man who had killed the Persian general Mardonius at Plataea, inspired each boy to look on him with new eyes. Those ropes under his skin were the very tendons that bound the muscles of heroism; those were the glossy locks that fell across the shoulders of legends. Looking down, Stone beheld the horn-nailed, callused feet of a veteran campaigner. In the proud, self-sufficient vacuity of Aeimnestus' eyes, he got his first look at a life dwarfed by its own renown— though it would be years before he understood this. For now, the moral of the man's mere presence, that such honor was within the grasp of anyone in the pack, was as compelling as anything written by poets.

Endius gave the boys their first official orders. They were to memorize and recite the first twenty lines of the "Code" by the next day. Omission or inaccuracy, he warned, would tell on the backs of those who failed. The same went for those who flouted the state's demand for them to learn their letters, and the dances of their fathers, and all the observances that sustained their city in the eyes of the gods. Then he asked the pack a question:

"For what purpose is the Spartan system?"

The abstractness of the question, and the sudden demand that they use their wits, at first kept the boys silent.

"My father said that his father told him that we suffer the Rearing to learn discipline," said Redhead. "So the answer is discipline, then."

"Too many words," replied Endius. "Never prattle. And you're wrong: discipline is never a goal, but only the means. Anyone else?"

"Victory?" Rehash ventured.

Endius kept looking, as if this answer wasn't worth a reply.

"Virtue?"

"Who said that?" asked Endius.

Stone raised his hand.

"I ask again, who said that?"

Antalcidas stood up. "I said it."

"That's better—never hide in the crowd, boy! If something's worth saying, it's worth standing on your feet and taking credit for it. Understand?"

"Yes!"

"You said virtue. That's closer to the truth, but still not right—virtue comes as naturally to the well-reared Spartan as fruit to the trees, but it is not itself the goal. Anyone else?"

No one spoke.

"There are two right answers. I'll tell you one of them: *freedom*. The Spartan citizen is as free as any mortal can be of enslaving passions. Most binding of all are the pleasures that men pursue. To teach you these truths, all children of citizens must suffer the Rearing, without regard to their families' honor or wealth. Remember this when you are hungry, or cold, or if you are lucky, facedown on the field of battle: you suffer because it makes you free.

"As for the other right answer—that is one you will have to learn on your own. It will not be told."

With that, Endius announced that he would answer precisely two questions. The youths looked at each other, as if unsure of what to ask or how to ask it. Beast shoved the nearest boy to him and snarled, "Come on now—any grub questions?"

Cheese straightened up and spoke, measuring out his words sparingly. "It is said that other Greeks live in proper cities. Why do our people still live in villages?"

"What you call 'proper cities' are the conceits of mortals," replied Endius. "The Lacedaemonians live in their five villages, and other Greeks in their cities. The Persians have the biggest settlements of all. Yet where do finer men dwell than here? Thebans and Corinthians assemble in vast meeting halls. Yet are the decisions of our elders any less wise for their meeting in the forest, where they are undistracted by roofs and statues and other vanities? The Babylonians have a city wall half a stade tall, and they have been conquered many times. We have no wall, yet we have never known an enemy soldier to plant his foot in our soil. Sparta's walls are the bodies of the men who defend her."

"How large is our territory?" asked Frog.

"You have seen the boundary yourself. It lies at the tip of Aeimnestus's spear. Wherever he carries it, that is the territory of Sparta."

The pack was dismissed. Their suffering, and therefore their freedom, was enhanced by a spell of cold weather that shrouded Taygetus and the folds of

their tunics with frost. They forgot their discomfort by
running through the woods, flying under the opposing limbs of the trees, lashing the trunks with fennel
stalks. As Stone charged, he struck a young laurel,
scattering the leaves behind him as he sang the words
Beast had taught him:

I would not say anything for a man nor take account of
   him
For any speed of his feet or wrestling skill he might have
not if he had the size of a Cyclops and strength to go with
   it . . .

8.

The raising of Epitadas consumed almost all Damatria's attention until it was time to let him go. In those
years she fed him, bathed him, swaddled him, and
taught him with the fierce possessiveness of a lover.
She rarely let Lampito hold the child; Damatria had
no patience at all with Molobrus' paternal fumbling.
Of his other kind of clumsiness, the one that afflicted
him in the bedroom, she no longer took notice. The act
interested her only insofar as it resulted in the salvation that was Epitadas.

In a most un-Spartan manner, she took pleasure in
her son's cooing helplessness. The freshness of his
smell possessed her, as in the night she tended to his
little cries, his spit-ups, his chubby arms held out to
her. Upon the spectacle of his first steps, she wept. For
four years she nursed him, seeking privacy so she
could gaze into his eyes. The power of his suck kindled a sensual glow that Molobrus' blunt pokings
could never match.

When the day came for him to take the Rearing, she

felt as if a piece of her heart was being cut out. She made Endius come three times, telling Epitadas to hide in the fields on the first two occasions. By the time his surrender could no longer be avoided, she left it for Molobrus to hand him over. Damatria watched him leave from a safe place, her hands grasping her milk-swollen breasts, too full of rage to let a sound escape the contorted mask of her grief.

She had to know where Endius took him. She followed them through the barley farms east of the villages, over the pelleted sheep tracks, to a hollow formed by two cypress-clad hills. An altar to mirthless Demeter lay in the center, its mass built up from centuries of solid ash tarred by dripping animal fat, scorched hair and bones and, on this occasion, the tears of a single Spartan mother as bereft as the goddess facing her daughter's exile to the underworld. From there she watched the boy-herd take the boy into the field to meet his fellows.

After a few days tracking the pack, Damatria learned its movements and could predict with fair accuracy where her son would be at any moment of the day. The paradox of it, that the movements of a group meant to be in a perfect state of freedom could be so easily forecast, was not lost on her. It was of use, though, in her efforts to keep the boy fed. Heedless of the scandal it would cause, she supplemented Epitadas' diet in secret, bringing him baskets of bread, apples, figs, almonds, olives, and cheese. The boy learned where to find his mother in the woods. They met without exchanging words—Damatria keeping watch for intruders, Epitadas stuffing the provisions into his mouth as fast as he could. On occasion, their eyes would meet. In her glance, there was the urgency of a need that transcended any prospect of shame; in his, Damatria saw neither thanks nor affection, but only the appetite of a starving animal.

From her vantage nearby, she could see the fruits of her crime. Where the other boys became undersized on their scanty diet, Epitadas came to tower over them all. In six months he outweighed boys three years his senior. With these advantages he dominated the competition, ruling his pack with intimidation backed by capricious outbursts of force. Damatria would watch him humiliate the other boys, strike them down, kick them, grind their faces into the dirt. She wished it didn't need to be so, and hoped that one day he would not take such joy in it, but mostly she was thankful it was Epitadas who gave the beatings and not the other way around. Then she set her mind to the pleasurable task of thinking in what other ways she could enhance his supremacy.

II
Redoubt

1.

Thirty years later, in the seventh year of the war between his city and Sparta, Demosthenes the Athenian invaded enemy territory with five ships and a thousand men. He did it midway through a trip around the Peloponnese, touching land in the extreme southwest of Sparta's dominion under cover of a storm.

The Athenians beached their vessels in a vast bay in the old kingdom of Messenia, beneath the capital of Homeric Nestor, just down the coast from the horseshoe strand where Prince Telemachus once sought news of his father, Odysseus. Millennia later, near modern Pylos, a combined British, French, and Russian naval force would help assure Greek independence by annihilating a Turkish fleet there. Centuries after that, the oily waters were plied by tankers whose size and ugliness would exceed the ancient imagination, but inspire no poetry. These gave way in their time to German and American holidaymakers escorted around Navarino Bay in motorboats, seeking camera-ready pathos among the drowned sarcophagi of six thousand Turkish sailors.

Unlike Telemachus or the tourists, Demosthenes came ashore with vengeance in mind. The region of Messenia had been the conquered territory of the Lacedaemonians for centuries, its population confirmed in its generational servitude. As the Athenians

walked lightly on the beach, imagining the very
ground might recoil from their weight, their eyes
sought out their general, seeming to ask him, "O
Demosthenes, do you know what trouble you invite
by bringing us here?"

To which the general answered, "Of course." He
understood that the passage around the Peloponnese,
with its storms and rocks, was exhausting enough in
peacetime. As his men waited for fair weather, they
might take their rest, cook a meal, or make repairs to
their ships. Demosthenes had no plan, except that
they should stay awhile and annoy the Lacedaemonians with their audacity. He would undertake no attack, he pledged, but conduct only those defensive
operations that would allow them to escape. "But for
now, let us do what the enemy has done to us for
seven years," he told them. "Let them know what it is
to have invaders on their territory! Let them wear
themselves out with worry for a change!"

With these declarations Demosthenes made them
forget their fears. The Athenians saw they had come
to a sandy beach on the northern limb of a crescent
bay some three miles in extent. An elongated island
sheltered the bay from the Ionian Sea, leaving only
two outlets: the narrow strait before them, and a
somewhat wider passage beyond the island's southern end. A cobbly promontory to their west protected
their flank; behind them stretched a marsh, half-salt,
that precluded attack from the mainland. The only
unimpeded approach was along the narrow bridge of
sand that formed the beach to the east. To even the
most tactically innocent of the Athenians, the spot
seemed a promising defensive position. The lack of
fresh water was the sole disadvantage.

"What is this place called?" someone asked.

"The beach and the hill the Lacedaemonians call Koryphasion. Before them, this was the Pylos of King Nestor, who went to Troy. And before him, it was the dwelling place of the cows stolen from Apollo by Hermes. They say the stockade is still here, in a cave under the rock."

"And the island?"

Demosthenes tossed his head.

Some Athenian soldiers took off their armor. After they had stood around for some time, distressing the pebbles with their toes, they resolved to prepare cooking fires, and at last to swim in the bay and play ball games. These diversions drew sneers from the ships' carpenters, who were obliged to tend to the inevitable cracked and chipped oars, popped strakes, loose oar tackle, and any of the thousand other things that went wrong with triremes at sea.

An alarm was sounded by Demothenes' lookouts on the promontory. Three figures were seen standing on the rock, looking down on the Athenians. The hoplites swam back to don their armor and loft their spears. They stayed that way, at attention, until it became clear that the intruders were just three young boys—probably Messenian helots from a nearby village. Even this knowledge did not reassure the Athenians, for the boys would no doubt return to their homes to report what they had seen, and it would not be long before the Spartans learned of their enemy's presence. Or so it seemed to everyone except Demosthenes.

"I would not count much on the Messenians' loyalty to the Lacedaemonians," he ventured. "In fact, I would say our secret is more safe here than if we had landed in Attica, at the estate of some aristocrat!"

Exactly as he predicted, the helot boys did not run

off to warn their parents. Instead, one of them—the smallest—clambered down the crags to have a look at the visitors. He was naked except for a sweat-soaked leather fillet around his head, and he seemed to weave and slip through the nettles with the ease of a snake. Closer, and the Athenians could see the scar on his arm of an iron brand—a mark of his helotry— standing pale against the flush of his exertions.

"Are you Athenians?" the boy asked.

Demosthenes presented himself with palms upturned.

"We are," he said, "and therefore come as allies of the Messenian people."

"Are you here to fight the Lacedaemonians, or are you going to run away like all the others?"

"We will do what is necessary to preserve our honor."

The boy reversed himself and started back up. At what seemed like a safe distance, he turned and shouted down to the beach:

"What took you so long?"

This question, though it had come from a mere boy, had an encouraging effect on the Athenians. The blessing of the local Messenians could only improve their position, for the invaders would need local supplies of food and fresh water if they decided to stay. What little was stored in the ships was needed for the trip to Corcyra, where the admiral, Eurymedon, expected Demosthenes' help in breaking the Peloponnesian siege on the capital.

Demosthenes did not so much order his men to fortify the Pylos beachhead as allow the idea to germinate in their own minds. His only command was a quiet one to his lieutenant, Leochares, to retrace the path the helots had used to approach them and keep watch on it. This was, after all, the sort of thing a responsible commander would order. He would then retire for the night to his hole in the sand, where he would fold his limbs carefully so as not to break them, as this responsible commander had for some time been convinced that his legs were as fragile as the clay stems of one of those high-pedestaled drinking cups. This was no metaphor: ever since his defeat in Aetolia the year before, he had become convinced that no pair of greaves could hide the fragility of those legs, which would shatter if he stepped on them too abruptly. Leochares and the rest of his men had noticed the tentative way that he had come to walk, placing his feet just so, and had supposed it had to do with some old battle wound. Little could they suspect that their general had in his mind an image of himself toppled, helpless among his own shards.

That night Demosthenes was visited by the same dream that had tormented him for months. In his sleep, he is back in those blasted hinterlands the day he lost his entire army. His men cry to him from the canyons. Rising up, a winged thing, he goes to them and finds only gnawed bones. His enemy that sad day, the Aetolians, did not fly, but knew the lay of the mountain paths. He awoke to his daytime command a ball of nerves and sweat.

His men constructed a barricade across the narrowest point of the strand. With their bare hands, they excavated a trench and used the sand to make a berm. Saplings from the edge of the marsh were cut, shorn, and fixed into the sand with sharpened sides out; the obstacle was topped with cobbles gathered from along the beach.

"Save the straightest poles and the biggest stones for later," Demothenes advised, somewhat cryptically.

The barricade, in addition to their command of the

heights of Koryphasion, and the marsh at their backs, made the Athenians more or less secure from the land. Demothenes was pondering their exposure from the bay when the helot boys returned, this time bearing three sacks. These contained a supply of milled barley, a jar of unmixed wine, and a skin of fresh water.

"There will be more," said the boy, "as long as you keep to this beach, and do not come into the village."

"I understand we must not endanger your people," Demosthenes assured him.

The boy took an appraising look around. "You still have some work to do, then."

The Athenians laughed at the child's presumption as he darted back up the rocks. When this died away Demosthenes shouted the last outstanding question in his mind:

"Can you tell us, boy, what that island is called?"

"Sphacteria!"

2.

The inevitable occurred on the third day, when Lacedaemonians were sighted some distance down the beach. There were three of them, shieldless, with their cloaks wrapped tightly around their lank forms. The Athenians could feel the eyes on them, appraising the strength of their defenses. And though his men so far outnumbered the enemy one thousand to three, a wave of disquiet rolled through their ranks, confronted as they were now by the certainty that a fight must come. With the exception on their glorious stand at Thermopylae, the Lacedaemonians had not lost a significant engagement in more than two hundred years.

"Tell us now, O Demosthenes, what we should do!" cried one hoplite.

"How can we fight these Lacedaemonians on their own territory?" asked another.

"Is there still time to escape, Demosthenes?" asked a third.

Demosthenes mounted on the bronze ram of a ship, climbing carefully so as not to damage his clay limbs. The Greeks, who were busy arguing with each other, did not notice him until he began to speak. The riot died down by stages, and every pair of eyes fell on him.

"Athenians, all of your questions have answers. But I ask you, are these the questions you want to ask? Are they worthy of you? Or should we all be facing our fates with different questions on our lips—ones that will redound to the glory of our city? Shall we not ask, instead, how our adversaries will take a prepared position when they are so loathe to risk the lives of their precious Spartiates? Instead of taking this place to be enemy territory, shall we not ask how we may make it Athens' own?

"No doubt you are thinking that our forces are few, while the Lacedaemonians will attack us by land and water with every able body they can muster. In such cases it is wise not to think about the odds against us, but to get on to the fight with as little reflection as possible. Did Militiades fret about Persian numbers at Marathon? Did your grandfathers count the enemy fleet at Salamis before charging their ships against it? You know the answers to these questions already.

"In any case, I will say two things about the size of the forces for and against us. First, numbers are irrelevant if an army cannot bring its advantage to bear against the opposition. With no way to reach us on land, the Lacedaemonians will no doubt come at us from the bay. But can you imagine those clodhoppers, who never glimpse a body of water bigger than a river, presuming to fight their way in from the sea? Do you imagine we will let them?"

Panic fading, the men laughed at the image of the waterlogged Spartans.

"Second, it is not we who are outnumbered, but the enemy. For never forget where we are—this is the kingdom of Messenia, a land of proud Greeks who have chafed in the Spartan yoke since before the days of Solon. This land is filled with our allies, men who would eat a Spartan raw if they had the chance. Our allies have but to be mobilized, and the first step will be the defense we put on here.

"And so for many reasons we have but one choice today: to govern our fears, to stand our ground here, and save ourselves. Does that answer your questions?"

The Athenians gave a thunderous cheer that reverberated off the heights of Koryphasion, and set to work.

The stretch of beach they needed to defend measured less than two stades. Using the heavy stones they had formerly put aside, they made submerged obstacles to block an enemy landing. In the places that were too deep for stones they anchored three of their ships broadside to the shore, and filled them with dry grass to help them burn in case the Peloponnesians tried to tow them away. The stones and the ships were disposed so as to funnel the enemy craft into just a few narrow approaches. These were the places where the outnumbered Athenians hoped, with luck, to defend themselves.

As most of the Athenians were sailors and not

hoplites, there was a shortage of weapons among them. Demosthenes sent his unarmed men into the marsh to gather green wood and willow fronds; with these they fashioned wicker shields. Straight branches served as pikes, and smaller stones as missiles. Demosthenes ordered the straighter, heavier piles to be positioned where he expected the Peloponnesians to force their way ashore. With these he intended his men to push the enemy ships away before they reached water shallow enough for their hoplites to disembark.

As they made these preparations, the Athenians kept watch on the horizon. Columns of smoke from enemy fires began to multiply by the third day; horsemen were seen riding back and forth on the shore, no doubt with dispatches coordinating the coming attack.

On the fourth day a fleet of sixty Peloponnesian ships sailed through the south passage into the bay. With their arrival Demosthenes' garrison was surrounded: it could not escape by land, and the ships could easily be used to block the bay's two entrances. To tighten their grip, the Lacedaemonians ferried a garrison onto Sphacteria, to prevent escape or relief via the island. The soldiers there would be in an excellent position to take any prizes or prisoners that might wash up.

But Demosthenes had never meant to make a secret of his little fort on Spartan territory. Before the Peloponnesians blocked the northern strait, he sent out two ships to find the Athenian fleet at Zacynthus. This was a calculated risk that reduced his force by three hundred rowers, but for Demosthenes the decision was foregone. Once the enemy disrupted his supply of food and water from the helot village, outside relief would be his only hope. Nor did he believe that Eurymedon could conceivably deny such aid.

When he at last came to rest, he was startled to dream of Aetolian mountaineers running along a ridgeline, trailing long ropes decorated with Athenian heads like beads on a string. In the way of certain visions, he could see both near and far at the same time; the living heads were breathing and blinking as they bounced along the goat paths.

He lay with the ground around him soaked with sweat when welcome news at last came down from Leochares. A force of forty Messenians from the local villages had come down to fight for him. They wore little more than breechcloths and the scars on their arms, and were armed with farming implements, but the expressions on their faces left no doubt of their zeal to kill Lacedaemonians. Hailing them, he found the Messenians even more laconic than the Laconians. Only later, when the three boys returned with more supplies, did he learn that these forty men were all parentless bachelors, with no family to suffer retribution for their acts. Demosthenes assigned them the task of reinforcing the archers defending the barricade.

The Athenians had arrived at Pylos dreading battle with the Lacedaemonians. Now that they had managed to make a fight inevitable, they wanted it to come as soon as possible. A hush of expectation came over the fort whenever a Peloponnesian ship set out across the bay; the place was abuzz when enemy troops showed themselves on the high ground of Sphacteria across the strait. But for another two days the enemy did nothing more than observe, probe, and blockade. Just two ships were enough to seal the northern channel; the southern one was far wider, but did not need to be physically blocked as much as guarded. The Peloponnesians stationed ten ships at a camp there, prepared to charge out and take broadside any Athenian vessels that attempted to enter.

During this time Demosthenes exhausted every trick to keep his men busy. He had the shoreline obstacles built higher and higher, until they protruded from the water in a kind of rustic stockade; he also had a ditch dug on the marsh side, in the unlikely event the enemy attempted to attack there. Any attempt on their position, he supposed, would be made in the morning, when the waters of the bay were most calm. The camp was therefore on a war footing hours before sun broke over the Aigaleon hills.

The wait ended on the fifth day.

3.

The Peloponnesian ships were of similar design to the Athenian: slim and sharp, more than one hundred feet long, with three banks of oars projecting from their hulls and outriggers. To Demosthenes, Athenian triremes resembled breaching dolphins, with painted eyes, metal rams for snouts, and upswept curl at their sterns for lobbing flukes. The enemy ships had eyes too, painted on their prows. Now forty of the wooden beasts turned their unblinking eyes on the Athenians' little outpost.

The enemy fleet approached in broad formation. The devices on their sails showed them to be a motley force—Corinthians, Aeginetans, Sicyonians, Anactorians, Megarians—each no doubt with a Lacedaemonian on board to command its contingent of hoplites. The Athenian camp was in an uproar as the men gathered their rude panoplies and took up their assigned positions. All of them could see that the Pelo-

ponnesians were rowing in hard, as if they meant to
ground their vessels on the rocks. This was a tactic
Demosthenes had not counted on.

*In his fear, would his body shatter just standing there,
like a flawed pot in the kiln?*

The ships halted just out of bow shot from the
shore. The Lacedaemonians, it turned out, were intent
on offering sacrifice at the last possible moment. On
the deck of the lead vessel, a Spartiate elder stood
forth with his crimson robe faded from salt spray and
dressed locks falling over his shoulders, brandishing
a knife over a braying goat. The Athenians could see
his unshaven upper lip move in unheard obeisances
to the patroness, Artemis Agrotera. The Corinthians
and Sicyonians stood by, fretting over the lost momentum of the attack. But their masters would not be
rushed as the entrails came out for proper examination.

Something was wrong. The Lacedaemonians huddled around the goat as they disputed among themselves. After some time they all began to wag their
ponderous heads, leaning back from the sacrifice as if
afraid to partake of some pollution. As the Athenians
and the Peloponnesian allies looked on in amazement, the Lacedaemonian commander gave an order
to the captain of the Corinthian flagship. The entire
enemy fleet then turned around and retired to the
other side of the bay.

In this way, thanks to Spartan attentiveness to the
portents of goats' livers, the garrison got a one-day reprieve. *Such an admirable reverence for the gods!* thought
Demosthenes, hoping that the delay would not invite
his men to think too much. As a precaution, he absorbed them in laying yet more obstacles and building
up the berm yet higher.

The next day dawned under a few clouds but no

wind. The ships came on and paused again for the sacrifice. This time the signs were favorable; libations of blood and wine were poured out in the proper order until, with the consecration of the bones, the Lacedaemonians at last pronounced the auspices satisfactory for the day's labor.

The Corinthians piped the signal to resume pulling for the beach. In good order, the ships sorted themselves into three columns, each aimed at an opening in the Athenian stockade. A stiff wind suddenly came onshore, bringing with it the bodily stench of seven thousand Peloponnesian oarsmen. To see one's enemies coming on was one thing, but to smell their very sweat made for an unnerving kind of intimacy.

"This is it, boys!" Demosthenes cried. "Let's let them know we're here!"

The Athenians roared in defiance of the enemy. They were outshouted, though, by the forty helots at the barricade. These produced a baleful snarl that, in its bottomless sadness, was just big enough to contain the thwarted hopes of untold Messenian lives. Projected down the slope of the berm at the approaching land attack, the cry seemed to wither the hearts of the Peloponnesian allies. But the Lacedaemonians were somehow quickened by it, charging faster, as if they were bred to the sound.

The Athenians let the Peloponnesian ships come as close as they dared before revealing their defense. Just as the first ram passed the outer line of boulders, the defenders rushed out with their straight timbers and braced them against the enemy bows. Demosthenes hoped that in this way just a handful of upright men, leaning hard in the shallow surf, could hold off laden triremes of 170 oars. At first, it worked: the Lacedaemonians hung over the rails, striking at the timbers,

but their spears were too light to dislodge them. Other
Spartan hoplites tried to reach shore by jumping in
the water, yet found themselves submerged too deep
to stand and too encumbered by their weapons to
swim.

The arrest of the first ship in each line caused all the
rest to jam up behind. The ensuing disruption traveled like a wave throughout the Peloponnesian fleet,
costing it all semblance of order. Demosthenes heard
voices with Dorian accents screaming at the captains
to break through the obstacles by smashing their hulls
on the rocks. But the Corinthians were too jealous of
their assets to make such a sacrifice.

The first serious challenge to Demosthenes' strategy came when two enemy ships collided with one of
the anchored Athenian vessels. The Lacedaemonian
hoplites swarmed all over it before his men could set
it alight. As the flames exploded through the shred-
ded sailcloth and pitch-soaked cordage, some of the
enemy managed to leap overboard into hip-deep
water. Demosthenes sent a squad of reserves against
them, half a dozen hoplites armed with spears and
wicker shields. Having lost their own spears in the
tumble off the deck, the Spartans struck at them with
short, daggerlike swords. The shallow water under
the Athenians gave them the decisive advantage: two
of the Lacedaemonians were wounded, and had to be
rescued by their fellows who, in turn, were forced to
abandon all their equipment. The Spartans dragged
their fallen comrades back to the gangway of their
ship; the discarded shields were seized as trophies by
the Athenians.

The attack got no farther on the land side. The
Lacedaemonians approached the berm with shields
locked, but could not keep the formation amid the

pilings and boulders strewn in their path. As the
Spartan line disintegrated, Athenian archery worked
its effect against their exposed flanks. The few of the
enemy who reached the top of the berm were met by
forty wild-eyed Messenian furies who fought with
clubs, shearing knives and, as necessary, teeth and
fingernails. For their part, the Lacedaemonians failed
to bring any archers or slingers to the battle, having
nothing but their usual contempt for missile troops.
A stalemate developed: the Lacedaemonians could
not take the barricade, but the Athenians and Messenians were too few to risk driving the enemy from the
field.

At length the Peloponnesian captains untangled
their vessels. The attackers came in waves against the
stockade, one ship at a time, each one using the same
tactic with fresh troops. Demosthenes coped as best
he could by rotating his reserves into the defense; the
battle dragged on through the morning, and then into
the afternoon, as the exhausted Athenians fought
with tongues swollen from thirst. At last, as the sun
descended over the island, the afternoon winds
swirled, and the placid surface of the bay broke into
a herringbone pattern of contrary waves. The enemy
triremes struggled to avoid each other and the rocks
beneath Koryphasion; the Lacedaemonians, landlubbers at heart, hung worried at the rails, and began to
gaze longingly at their camp across the bay. They
broke off the assault with an hour left of daylight.

The manner of the fighting had kept casualties
light on both sides. At the barricade, just a few of the
Messenians were down, mostly due to their own reck-
lessness, and the Lacedaemonians suffered mostly
nonlethal arrow wounds. In the water, no Athenians
were killed, and the enemy lost a handful due to spear

thrusts and drowning. The Athenians, delirious with this success, danced on the beach, holding aloft the captured shields with their crimson lambdas showing clear and dark against the flashing bronze. The Spartan troops watching from the heights of Sphacteria turned away in disgust.

At first Demosthenes could not help but share the elation of his men. But his downcast turn of mind soon asserted itself, and he found himself reflecting on the comparative childishness of the Athenians, celebrating the end of what was just an indecisive skirmish. The Lacedaemonians, in contrast, had the same expressions on their faces when they rowed away as when they had rowed in to attack. They never showed outward triumph or disappointment on the battlefield—victories, for them, were to be expected, and their reverses only transient conditions. They were never in a rush to redeem their setbacks, and the only ardor they ever showed lay in their conspicuous acts of piety.

When the next day dawned as calm as the last, the bulk of the Peloponnesian fleet came across the bay again. With typical persistence, they attacked in exactly the same way, with the ships coming in in virtually the same order. Demosthenes had seen this bloody-mindedness before, this conviction that their cause would prevail not through pretty tactics or innovation, but by virtue of the fact that they were Spartans. But Demosthenes soon understood the method behind their approach: with the Athenian blocking triremes burned to the waterline, his men had to defend a wider front. From the land side, a corps of Lacedaemonian slingers had been hastily organized. Their skills were so primitive, however, that they could hit nothing except from very close in, well in range of his archers.

The impasse resumed, the waves of attackers ebbing and flowing, until Athenian sweat salted the water of the bay and the Peloponnesian rowers grew ragged in their strokes. The sun climbed and loomed pitiless over them all, blazing with such intensity that its mere reflection in sand and water blinded the helmeted men. Despite the vain cleverness of their commander, Athenians were beginning to fall under the blades of the enemy hoplites. Into Demosthenes' throat crept the same sense of futility that he felt in Aetolia—the suspicion of being overmatched, of holding back a crimson torrent with clenched fingers, of his arrogance to believe that mere strategy could stop men as determined as the Lacedaemonians. Though not a single Spartan had yet set foot on dry sand, he began to feel as good as defeated. The conviction settled like a boulder on his chest until he heard someone calling to him from far away.

The voices were those of his lookouts on the hill. His head pounding with heat and consternation, he watched with incredulity as his men leapt and pointed out to sea, to the southwest. In the noise of the fight he could not hear their voices; he began to suspect what they might be saying, and with that suspicion felt the boulder lift.

The Athenian fleet sailed into the bay like a squadron on review, in single file, through the narrow gap between the island and Little Sphacteria. Their attention having been focused on the main channels, the Peloponnesians seemed caught off guard by the maneuver. The Athenians had more than twenty ships in the bay before the enemy sallied out with fifteen. The fleets made for each other, rams gleaming in the sun, as the Athenians deftly arranged themselves in line abreast and the Peloponnesians dissolved into an ungainly mass.

The result was never in doubt. Attacking in synchrony, the Athenians rammed or sheared the oars off each enemy vessel in turn. The hindmost Peloponnesian ships didn't wait to be taken, but broke for shore. Some of these were rammed amidships as they turned, and the rest pursued into shallow water as the enemy hoplites waded as far as they dared to support them. Demosthenes scaled Koryphasion to watch the aftermath: half a dozen half-sunk Peloponnesian vessels, their crews scattered around them like chaff, were pulled in opposite directions by the Lacedaemonian hoplites and Athenian sailors.

The battle around the stockade ground to a halt as both sides became spectators. Demosthenes' men cheered as the rest of the Athenian fleet, twenty-five hulls strong, struck from the west and drove away the Peloponnesian vessels guarding the north channel. With that, the Lacedaemonians broke off their attack. Two more enemy ships were run down from behind as they tried to escape; the land forces withdrew in good order, enduring as they went the taunts of the Messenians atop the barricade.

Old Eurymedon came down the gangway with a frown on his face. Fixing his one good eye on Demosthenes, he disgorged a spitting torrent of curses before he was in earshot, and didn't finish until the other was standing right in front of him.

"You will explain, Demosthenes, your defiance of our agreement!" Eurymedon snarled, looking as if he would hit the other with his staff.

"What explanation is necessary for men to make,

when they mean only to defend themselves in a hostile place?"

"You insult all of us with your damnable arrogance! Why are you here at all, in this miserable trap, that you must force the entire fleet to come to your rescue?"

"Forgive my arrogance," Demosthenes replied in measured tones, "but it seems that it is the Lacedaemonians who are trapped now."

He was suddenly able to move again, as if blood had at last forced its way into the strangled vessels in his legs. Gifted now with a sudden fluidity, he wanted to dance the praises of Nike who had cured him. But no one danced before Eurymedon.

Across the strait, hundreds of Lacedaemonians stood on the high ground of Sphacteria. All around the island, meanwhile, the Athenian ships swarmed, driving every Peloponnesian vessel away from its shores. The enemy force that had landed there to help contain the Athenians instead found itself cut off.

Eurymedon stood with his mouth open, as if the implications of hundreds of marooned Spartiates took that long to sink into his mind. After some time, he spoke again.

"If this is what you had in mind . . . it is not worth risking the fall of Corcyra." And then, turning to the captain of his flagship, he issued the command Demosthenes longed to hear: "Organize a blockade of the island. Let no one get off or come to the Lacedaemonians' aid."

III
The Theory of Joy

1.

Twenty-eight years earlier, Stone, Frog, Redhead, and Cricket left the herd of young boys to enter the most junior of the single age-classes—a pack made up solely of youths who had started their education in the same year. Antalcidas had already learned much in the half decade since leaving home. Along with Tyrtaeus, he knew great swaths of Homer, and most of the basic marching songs such as "Castor's Air." He had his letters, and soon would be literate enough to decipher the simple battlefield dispatches that constituted the only proper reading of the Spartan male. And though he had not yet practiced marching in formation, he already knew the steps of the Pyrrhic dance, which included most of the dodging, thrusting, and turning movements he would need in battle.

Survival out of doors, in all seasons, became second nature to him. He was proud of the engrained dirt on his knees and elbows, and the calluses that clad his feet. After his boyhood tunic was taken away, replaced only by a single cloak issued to him each year, he grew to despise the wearing of any clothes. Noble Thibron looked with approval on anyone who went around in defiant nakedness, standing up straight in front of the girls as they whispered and pointed in the streets. To Antalcidas they would exclaim, "There goes the boy who throws stones!" and laugh in mockery until, despite himself, he blushed in his hurt. Caring what females thought was one weakness he had not yet conquered.

To be sure, in their time the girls had also come in for derision. With their homebound diets, most of them had grown taller and stronger than the boys, and liked to show off the strength of their legs by gathering their tunics in bustles above their waists. Yet in their pride they would reveal exactly what they lacked. Antalcidas was much amused one day when, on the banks of the Eurotas, he spied three girls trying to piss standing up. They made such a mess of it, wetting themselves more than the ground, that he and his packmates fell out of the weeds laughing at them.

With the passage of years the attitudes of the adults hardened toward the boys. Every grown male in Laconia seemed to have a stake in their proper instruction, even to the extent of applying discipline. Boys who went around with eyes up or arms sticking out of their cloaks were rebuked in the street. Redhead and Cricket earned worse after an evening foray into Limnae, where they were caught taking cheeses from a storage pit. They were beaten first by the owner of the pit, who worked the lash with such skill that the boys' cries were heard as far as Kynosoura three stades away. When they were let go, another man, a complete stranger but an Equal, seized them by the arms.

"Are you the brats who were beaten for stealing cheeses?" he asked them.

"Yes."

The man struck him on the shoulder with his walking stick, then tried to kick Cricket in the rear end.

"By the gods, what was that for?"

"That's for being clumsy enough to get caught!" the stranger cried.

Most of his time in the villages was spent in the gymnasia, where supplies like olive oil, wrestling powder, and sporting equipment were made available free to youngsters of both sexes. The most popular game was called, simply, "wall ball": the boys would collect in a mob in front of a stone wall, against which one of them would serve a hard leather ball. The object for the receivers was to catch the ball on the fly. This had to be done with the competition doing everything it could to interfere, including pushing, punching, and tackling. The thrower served the ball as many times as he could, as long as no one caught it cleanly.

Antalcidas got to be very good at this game, standing in against boys much older and larger than himself. He had perfected a particular technique of his own, using the bodies of the competition to push off at just the right moment to receive the ball. As he showed off this skill one day, he noticed an old Spartiate sitting with Endius, resting his chin on the handle of his staff as he watched the boys exercise. Without making it too obvious, Antalcidas tried to read their lips as the men exchanged comments about this or that youth, saying things like "magnificent" or "an earthy break." Other remarks—such as "nice, tight ring"—seemed so cryptic that he thought he must have misunderstood their words. But there was no mistaking his meaning when Endius called Antalcidas over to meet his guest.

"So I hear they call you Stone, young man. Can you tell me why?"

The old man's glance flitted down Antalcidas' oiled flanks, his eyes shaking slightly in their veiny whites as they lingered on the patch of his adolescent down.

"It is just a name," the boy replied.

"What an admirable economy of words!" the old man exclaimed. "It would be a pleasure indeed to help cultivate such good instincts."

Antalcidas yawned. The old man gave Endius a significant look. The latter, as if by some prior arrangement, rose and took the boy by the arm.

"Do you know to whom you are speaking?" asked the boy-herd in a confidential tone. When Antalcidas shrugged, he went on, "You must remember the campaign of Nicodemus the Regent, several years ago. He marched with two battalions of the army and ten thousand allies to succor our friends in Thebes. Our former allies in Athens, who were still smarting after the kings dismissed them from Ithome, tried to oppose his return over the Isthmus. Nicodemus met fourteen thousand Athenians at Tanagra and made them learn the price of their folly. Zeuxippos commanded the allied left wing."

The old man did not feign modesty as he was so flatteringly introduced. Instead, he used his staff to leverage himself to his feet and placed a hand on Antalcidas' shoulder. As he came close, the boy could smell the smoke of a thousand campfires in his beard, and the vinegar from a thousand bowls of black broth seeping through the pores of his sagging skin. "It's been quite a long time since I've offered my sponsorship," he said.

"You could not ask for a steadier hand," pressed Endius.

To attract the attention of an elder sponsor was a requisite part of the Rearing. What Antalcidas had not expected was to be approached by so old a Spartiate.

Most mentors were young men in their twenties, barely out of the Rearing themselves, who tutored with one eye on their pupils and the other on the elders who judged them in turn. Who would supervise a man as distinguished as Zeuxippos?

"Maybe I should seek my father's counsel. . . ." he suggested.

"Zeuxippos is your father. As am I, and every Equal alive or dead, all of whom would have been pleased to learn at the knee of such a teacher . . ."

"Really, dear Endius, there is no need to force the issue!" said Zeuxippos. "Let the boy take counsel with anyone he wants. I trust he will not be disappointed at what he learns."

In fact, Antalcidas had glimpsed his father only once since leaving home. Molobrus' battalion was marching over the Eurotas bridge, on their way to stiffen the backs of the Megarians and Corinthians in yet another face-off with Athens. From the roadside the boys watched them, the great crimson line, setting out as they had for centuries with spearheads up and voices raised in song. Ahead went the fire-carriers bearing embers from the altar of Zeus-the-Leader in clay vessels suspended from poles. Behind the right shoulder of each hoplite followed his personal attendant in a white tunic edged with red, packing his master's helmet, shield, and camp equipment. It was widely understood among the boys, thanks to rumors deliberately spread by Endius, that Lacedaemonian servants marched better than the elite infantry of other Greek cities. Beyond the façade of well-heeled gentlemen-soldiers, much of the rank and file in the Athenian or Theban or Argive armies bore inferior panoplies and were almost random in their footwork. Among the Lacedaemonians, however, everyone had the bearing of a gentleman, and no man was ever on the wrong foot.

And then, abruptly, Antalcidas saw his father in the line. Molobrus marched with his cap pushed back on his head, his face open and smiling as he sang the praises of Apollo. Antalcidas could feel the warmth of his humor like the heat of a bonfire as he stood nearby. His father was relaxed, good-humored, kidding with his comrades in a way he never did at home. Antalcidas only saw his father for a moment. But that brief glimpse froze him, because he recognized nothing about the man. It was as if the person he had once known was a mere ghost of this, the true Molobrus, who existed only in a place where Antalcidas must be absent. Molobrus' eyes swept over the crowd as the paean reached its climax; his eyes passed over his son without a flicker of recognition.

Some time later he saw Zeuxippos again. The old man was approaching the grove where the Gerousia would meet that morning, while Antalcidas' pack was on its way into Mesoa to take instruction in the chorus. Zeuxippos called to him, "O Stone, what did your father advise?"

Antalcidas presented himself without shyness or shame.

"You and my father are wise men, so you should know what he said."

"Just as I thought," Zeuxippos replied. Placing two fingers under Antalcidas' chin, he raised the boy's face to the light. "Your features are coarse, but in spirit and body you have promise. I accept the burden. You will be instructed in tactics, government, diplomacy, how to resist the temptations of gold, women, and foreigners. Above all, you will learn the two skills essential to our life: how to take orders, and how to give them to other men. With your trust—do I have your trust?—I will make your mind worthy of your magnificence."

Antalcidas allowed himself to be inspected a bit longer than modesty dictated, gazing off into the dying mist until he became aware of his packmates whispering furiously behind him. In truth, he had as much reason to trust Zeuxippos as he did any prospective patron. Yet, in a way he could not have understood, his mother's wounds had done their part in shaping his fears. He returned to the pack as the other boys regarded him with ill-concealed envy.

"Maybe if we ask him nicely, Stone will let us play with his knucklebones!" shouted Frog. This was the worst kind of insult, because only girls played with knucklebones in Sparta. But by the same token only girls were too proud to take a joke. Men of virtue were supposed to accept the ridicule of their fellows with equanimity. Antalcidas might have expected better from Frog, having saved him from a worse beating at the hands of the older boys, but he showed nothing but a smile. After all, was he not magnificent?

2.

The late summer festival coincided that year with a wave of torrid weather. As the crops baked amber in the heat and the green wall of Taygetus appeared to flutter in the distance, the Eurotas seemed to flow with a viscous reticence, as if saving strength for its run to the sea. Festival-goers converged on the city in much the same way, laboring but perennial. In covered wagons, on horses and donkeys, or straggling in on foot, they came from the towns of Gytheion and

Pellene, Sellasia and Helos, and regions as far afield as Thyreatis and Messenia and Triphylia, and a thousand remote valleys in between that were too small to have names. They were Spartiates on respite from their estates, and Nigh-dwellers from their workshops, and helots—a few from Messenia and most native Laconians—to attend their masters. These arrivals made the Festival of the Flocks one of a handful of times each year when Sparta ceased to be an agglomeration of sleepy villages, but a bustling center of conviviality. Many a pilgrim from other cities, such as Athens or Corinth, came to Laconia with set notions of what to expect of the dour natives, supposing them devoted to whipping each other and niggling matters of soul-deadening precedent. Instead, the visitors would be surprised by what the Laconians always knew: their city was the place to find the best dancers, the shortest skirts, and the finest men.

For nine days Antalcidas wandered wide-eyed through his transformed city. Where ordinarily the verses of no one but Homer, Tyrtaeus, or Alcman were ever heard, poets from all over the Peloponnese converged to present works composed for the occasion, very often during informal recitals in the Persian Stoa or atop the foundations of unreconstructed houses. He stopped to listen to a wild-eyed poet from the depths of Arcadia sing an encomium to Panic as he accompanied himself on the lyre. He watched a chorus of twenty-four maidens from Sciritis dance for Artemis; in short tunics and hunting shoes, their bodies turned so rapidly their hair never rested on their backs.

The people watching these performances were turned out in old-style girdleless chitons, hanging loosely with gleaming stickpins at the shoulders. Puzzlingly, some of them carried small model boats in their hands, or wore little boats on their heads like hats, or bore tiny vessels upright on handles. He wanted to ask Zeuxippos about these boats, but the old man was busy dressing down Frog and Rehash for some infraction Antalcidas had not seen.

"No reason can justify quarreling in front of the helots," he told them. "Equals may disagree, but no difference between you is worth emboldening your enemies . . . !"

The center of the marketplace had been converted into a military camp, festooned with colored pennants and devices of the tribal phratries. Nine men were housed in each of nine tents for the entire nine day duration of the festival. The tents had three sides, with the fourth closed to the outside by a rope. During the nine days every aspect of the men's lives was regulated by the calls of a crier, who announced their activities to the spectators who gathered to peer into the tents.

"Why do they make camp, when the making of war is forbidden during the festival?" Antalcidas asked.

Zeuxippos smiled and nodded, as if savoring the innocence of this question.

"It is not always given to us to understand such things," he replied. "Still, I would tell you that there is a hidden premise in your question, that we make camp in order to fight wars. The festival camp shows us the very opposite: we succeed in war because of the things we value, such as discipline."

"And the meaning of the boats?"

"The boats represent the ancient journey of the Heraclidae from Naupactus to the Peloponnese, upon the first conquest of Laconia from the Achaeans. The children of Herakles, as you know, were vagabonds after being deprived of their lands by the treachery of Eurystheus, king of Mycenae. In their first attempt to reclaim their birthright, Eurystheus was slain, and the Heraclidae were obliged to take refuge in Thessaly. There they became allied with Aegimius, king of the Dorians, whom Herakles had once aided in their fight against the Lapiths. Aegimius adopted Hyllus, the eldest Heraclid, who in time became king of the Dorians upon Aegimius' death.

"Before resuming the war against the house of Mycenae, Hyllus sought guidance from the Delphic oracle. He was told that his campaign would succeed if the Heraclidae waited until the ripening of the third harvest, and if they invaded the Peloponnese by a narrow channel. Hyllus took 'the third harvest' to mean the third year, and 'the narrow channel' a land attack across the Isthmus of Corinth. But when he resumed the war after three years, the expedition again failed, this time with the death of Hyllus himself. Only then did the Heraclidae understand that 'the third harvest' was not by count of seasons, but of generations, and that 'the narrow channel' meant an invasion over the straits at the mouth of the Gulf of Corinth. One hundred years later, their descendants sailed in boats from Naupactus to Rhion. As the Pythia had foretold, they defeated and slew Tisamenus, son of Orestes, and became lords of the all the lands of the Achaeans, including Laconia."

"So I have heard," said Antalcidas absently, his attention straying to a young girl nearby. She stood in a girdleless tunic dyed purple, as if she had just stepped off the choral stage. Her coloring was of that striking blond, almost white, often seen among slaves from the north. But there was nothing slavish about her as she stood there, her head crowned with laurel, her hair slung over her shoulder in a queue braided with flax stalks. She was looking at him with large eyes filled with frank fascination. He turned around to see if she was looking at someone behind him, but when he looked back she was gone.

"Never mind the girls," Zeuxippos said with some annoyance. "There is something here you must see. . . ."

He led Antalcidas to the running track west of the marketplace. A huge crowd surrounded the place. Pushing their way to the front, Antalcidas saw the object of the gathering: a young man, probably just old enough to have completed the Rearing, was pouring a libation to the Dioscuri, then to Lycurgus the Lawgiver, then to Zeus, Turner-of-Cowards, then to Artemis-the-Leader, then Eileithyia, and then of course to Apollo-of-the-Flocks, patron of the festival. This man was dressed very curiously, in animal skins bound with woolen straps that ran from his breastbone all the way down to his thighs. Around him three others, naked, were bending and limbering up, as if preparing for a race. Zeuxippos leaned toward Antalcidas, arm around his waist, his mouth almost touching his ear as he spoke.

"The celebration goes back to the ancients, to before the Dorians reached these lands. Karneios was a harvest god of the Achaeans, among whom he was called Karneios-of-the-House. Can you tell me why the Lacedaemonians carry on the tradition?"

Antalcidas was still thinking about the girl he had seen. And though he knew that a prospective Equal must show piety, he never had much of a head for the old stories, the sheer multitude of which never failed to confuse him. He shook his head.

"When the Dorians conquered Laconia, they killed by accident a seer of old Karneios," the old man continued. "Fearing the pollution caused by the act, our ancestors propitiated the god—listen here, boy, because this is important—propitiated the god by observing all the honors due him. One of these was a rite of pursuit conducted around the time of reaping. So that the gods of the Dorians would not themselves be slighted, the festival was named for their god of all diviners and seers, who is our Apollo. . . ."

The libations completed, the man in the woolen fillets took his place in the starting position. The three other runners, after consecration by a trio of temple magistrates, lined up behind him. Turning his head, Antalcidas could see the goal of the contest: a crude wooden statue erected at the far side of the track, set on the stone altar and decked with flowers.

"Is that Karneios?" he asked.

Zeuxippos nodded. "The rite of the Hunt goes back beyond the original conquest. The Ram will run out ahead of the three hunters. If he reaches the image of the god at the end of the track before he is caught, disaster will befall the city; if they catch him, it portends good fortune."

It occurred to Antalcidas that the prevalence of the number three in the rites may have something to do with the three ancient tribes of the Dorians: Hylleis, Dymanes and Pamphyli. He would have asked Zeuxippos—if he wasn't afraid the old man might actually give him the entire dull story.

"The hunters we call the Grape-Bunch Runners—a name which might put you in mind of Dionysus, but that would be a misconception. . . ."

And then, before Antalcidas anticipated it, the race was on. The Ram ran down the track between the accumulated throngs. The spectators, male and female, screamed and held out their hands to the Grape-Bunch Runners, imploring them to join the pursuit. But those boys were cocky, standing around until it seemed certain that the prey would reach the finish line. At last they turned serious; coiling their finely oiled bodies at the gates, they launched themselves down the track to the thunderous delight of the crowd.

Their start seemed well timed to magnify the suspense. The pursuers were well behind, but the Ram's thighs were clad in woolen straps, which prevented him from taking full strides. But then, to the general mortification, the straps worked loose. The Ram accelerated to the sound of ripping and tearing, now only a few strides from his goal.

The fastest hunter charged and launched himself in the air. He caught his quarry by the foot, tripping him to the ground as the other kicked back at him. The Ram tore himself loose and crawled forward on his knees. At last, seemingly within arm's length of the altar, the other two hunters pulled him back by the arms. The three fell in a heap. When they rose again, their oiled faces and bodies were coated in the fine dust of the track, but the Ram was fully in their control. Triumphantly, elbows and knees battered, the three led their trophy on the long walk back to the start as the spectators cheered and danced around them.

"We are in luck this year, it seems," Zeuxippos said.

"Have they ever failed to catch him?"

"Once, not too many years ago, the Ram was well ahead but tripped over his own feet. Some say he would have reached the end if Apollo had not interceded. That was the festival just before the Great Earthquake. . . ."

The Runners presented their captive to the magistrates. At once, the crowd fell silent, and over the buzz of children and cicadas rose the thin voice of the Ram.

"The glad-tiding, the all-seeing, cultivator of spears, bearer of horns, Karneios-of-the-House, having seen the worth of the men of the city, here and for the year extends and avouches his forgiveness for the sins of the Dorians, and by such dispels the pollution of the murder of the seer Krios, his loyal servant, and releases his suppliants to practice sacraments of war for one year, until and unless the citizens assemble again in his sight, in the fashion handed down by their fathers, to plight their virtue as they must in their bloodguilt, on the fifteenth day of the month Karneia, next year."

With this blessing and the promise to earn it again next year, the Lacedaemonians received permission to be themselves again. A pair of belaureled priests took their places before the figure of Karneios. A real ram was then led before them with horns gilded and fleece festooned with crimson ribbons, followed by a maiden dressed in spotless white, bearing a basket. Her linen folds, freshly pleated, fell as straight and regularly as the flutes of a stone column. Priests, maiden, and animal processed around the image to the sound of the pipes, and then received the ablution—the humans with water on their hands, the ram with drops sprinkled on its head. The animal's head remained still. The priest poured out more water, this time flicking it more forcefully at the ram's eyes. It startled, jerking its head backward. This was good enough to resemble a nod by the ram, giving its permission to be sacrificed.

The basket was opened, the barley cakes inside shared out and consumed. The exposure of the knife produced a gasp in the crowd as if nothing of the kind had ever been seen before. With the cutting of a vessel in the animal's neck, a strong stream of blood projected onto the side of the altar, which was stained black with the residue of a hundred previous sacrifices. As the ram poured out its life, the women in the crowd raised their hands and ululated—a sound that always sent chills up Antalcìdas' neck.

"In my sixty-two years I've never seen the rites done better," avowed Zeuxippos, with a formulaic tone that suggested he said the very same thing every year.

The competitions in music and dance resumed, including a choral hymn by twenty-four maidens in purple. They stood at first in four lines of six, stepping in time to the verses, their swaying alternately exposing and hiding the nakedness between the ungirt sides of their tunics. They sang:

*In the center of Delphic Pytho, navel of the world, divine
    Phoebus
Touches the strings of his hollow kithara, sending its sweet
    ring
Over the rocky heights of Parnassus, beloved of the Muses.
But faster than the glint of light from his golden plectrum,
He flies to the mansions of Olympus, aerie of Zeus the
    Orderer.
There he diverts the gathered immortals, pleased to hear
    the son
Of fair-haired Leto play in honeyed notes, and step in
    radiance*

For the Graces so finely tressed, and Artemis pourer of
arrows,
And his sister, sea-born Aphrodite, who dance with hands
entwined,
As the Hours sing of the love of the gods, that gift to
mortal men
In their short, feeble spans, where there is no recourse from
decay,
No reprieve from death . . .

The blonde he had seen before was there, on the left end of the third rank. She danced and recited with her brow furrowed in concentration, lifting and placing her sandaled feet, kicking out with filleted ankles, grasping an invisible bow with the evocation of Artemis. In unison, the girls fell into a circle with each grasping the wrist of the dancer beside her, their turnings livened by ample flashing of shins and buttocks. At the quality of their extremities Antalcidas was compelled to stare: unscarred, round, softly glowing in the light as if covered with velvet. The knees of Spartan women, on the other hand, cut like swords. They were slightly discolored with the dirt of the gymnasium, or as foreign men liked to believe, in the kneeling service of their lovers. Antalcidas became so excited by these sights that he was compelled to run away without warning Zeuxippos.

"Where are you going?" the old man called after him. "We must tour the encampment!"

Antalcidas ran into the fields and found a grove of apple trees. Picking a fruit with a color as hale as the girl's thighs, he retreated to a private place and began to kiss the smooth surface of it, using his lips in ways that increased his frenzy. His kisses became nibbles, then bites, exposing the flesh, drawing the juice through his toothmarks, driving himself to bore at the bitter center of her, splitting the whole against his cheeks, reducing seeds and rind until all that was left was—nothing.

3.

On his fourteenth birthday Antalcidas moved on to the age-class of the *propaides*. He was mostly beyond the rigors of outdoor life, having long since become a thief with the skills to appropriate food, water, and shelter from helots or, if possible, from the unguarded estates of Equals. Unwary weaklings and youngsters supplied the rest, including the fawning respect due to their superiors. On the negative side of the ledger, he was under increasing responsibility to educate the boys beneath him, even as he continued to receive punitive thrashings from the three age-classes above. Being both men and boys, authorities and subordinates, propaides like him were caught in the middle.

This dilemma became more acute when, upon a raid on an olive grove, he stumbled on a brawl between two younger boys. Thibron and another Firstie sat watching the fight from a log as they passed a canteen between them. The boys dueled with iron sickles, lunging awkwardly at each other. The spectators shouted encouragements, spurring them to soldier on despite their exhaustion.

"Are you finished, girls?" asked Thibron. "Didn't your boy-herd teach you that a Spartan never raises a hand in surrender?"

"Look at the way he stares at you! Will you let him get away with that?" exclaimed the other.

The boys dutifully went at each other again, their blades flashing as they cut the air. When the taller antagonist stepped into a column of sunlight, Antalcidas was stunned to see the face of Epitadas.

He had not glimpsed his brother in many years, yet he recognized him instantly. He knew that Epitadas would have been a year behind him in the Rearing; in his idle moments, as when he lay awake on his nest of rushes at night, Antalcidas wondered where Epitadas' pack must be. Had they been on the same mountain before, out of sight of each other around some impassable outcrop? How many times had his brother taken cover when Antalcidas' group passed him, just as Antalcidas' had once fled at the sight of older boys?

The fight, it seemed, had not been bloodless. Epitadas had a cut over his eye, and his opponent was bleeding from a slashing wound on his upper left arm. Both were too tired to hold up their weapons, but just circled each other out of arm's length, darting in to attack when they saw an opening. More disturbing, neither of the adults present seemed to be interested in keeping the boys from harm.

"Honored fathers!" Antalcidas addressed them. "Do you wish me to take spotting position, or to confiscate their weapons—*as custom demands*?"

This sudden interference, and his particular emphasis on established custom, got the men's attention. Thibron turned to him with a mouth full of wine, surprised; his companion frowned.

"Who the fuck are you?"

This exchange distracted Epitadas, who swiveled his head around, gaped—and took a blow from a sickle handle in the temple. He collapsed, dropping his weapon.

"There, it's finally over."

Epitadas' opponent, a scrawny youth who had bitten down so hard on his lower lip that his incisors were lodged there, moved in. Laying the chipped edge of his blade against Epitadas' neck, he waited as the latter groaned and wiped the blood from his eyes.

"Give up now," he commanded.

Epitadas focused on his enemy above him, saying nothing.

"I said, yield to your master."

A bolus of blood-soaked spittle rolled from his perforated lips onto Epitadas' cheek. The sickle blade was pressed harder against his throat.

"That's enough, young man," said Thibron, who rose and scratched his balls as if after a long afternoon at the theater.

"Yes, a boy needs to learn when it's worth it, does he not?" chimed his comrade.

Having lost interest, the Firsties departed. Antalcidas rushed to remove the weapons, which the victor released with what appeared to be decided relief. Epitadas, for his part, glared at his opponent and didn't look at Antalcidas at all. His face betrayed nothing but a sullen, smoldering hatred.

The other boy, whose name and affiliation Antalcidas never learned, turned and walked away. There was a moment while the adults were still in sight and Epitadas climbed to his feet. And then, before Antalcidas could move to stop him, Epitadas pursued his enemy into the woods, running at him with admirable stealth.

Antalcidas followed with a mounting sense of dread. He was just in time to see his brother insert the point of the sickle into the center of the boy's back. It was a pitiless blow, inflicted with no warning or hesitation on a defenseless opponent. Epitadas watched with faint curiosity as his enemy, eyes gaping white, spun around, trying to reach the handle behind him.

As this went on for some time Epitadas smiled, clapping his hands as if watching a dance. Blood poured trembling from the crook of the blade, spattering the amber carpet of pine needles. When the boy fell at last, it was on that soft bed. Epitadas crouched to watch his face as he went still.

"What have you done, Brother?" Antalcidas asked. Epitadas narrowed his eyes.

"So it *is* you."

They watched as a blood-colored bubble appeared at the victim's left nostril. It seemed to grow forever until it burst and was replaced by another. A curious gurgling sound came from the vicinity of the wound.

"You're not as tall as I imagined, stone-thrower," Epitadas remarked.

Stepping across the prone body, he extracted the sickle and tossed it into the brush. Then he approached Antalcidas, coming to within inches of his face, looking down on him despite being eleven months his junior.

"You were saying something back there, distracting me when I had matters in hand. . . ."

"Epitadas."

"Never interfere again. Understand? *Never.*"

"Brother, listen—"

"I'll take that as your word."

The reunion over, Epitadas made off in the direction of the river. When he was gone, Antalcidas flew to Mesoa for help. As he ran, the odd thought occurred to him that Thibron, handsome and ingenious Thibron, so square-jawed and ideal, might be in trouble with his elders like any other boy. He also wondered just how many of the people of Sparta knew about the incident of the stone-throwing. What would his mother say?

Epitadas' victim was not quite dead. As the craft of medicine still bore a whiff of foreignness for the Lacedaemonians, and was therefore regarded with suspicion, no physician attended to the boy. Instead, two veteran Spartiates put him on a table in a nearby house and applied a field dressing. This stopped the external bleeding but accomplished nothing more. The boy's abdomen continued to fill with blood.

To inflict a mortal injury on a peer, even in the guise of training, was a crime in Sparta. Isidas the Ephor was summoned, along with five of the knights to apprehend the accused. Draping the gray locks of his beard back over his shoulder, Isidas leaned down to talk to the boy.

"Who did this to you, son?"

The other looked up at him with studied fortitude in his eyes.

"Am I hurt, father? I can't feel it."

"You are hurt. Who did it?"

The boy smiled. "I know what you're doing, elder. This is a test. You want to see if I will bear the wound."

The ephor squeezed his hand. "It is not a test."

"There is no crime to avenge—I would have done the same to him if I had the chance."

Isidas went on trying to convince the boy to name his murderer until he stopped giving replies. His last words were about going to tell his parents he had passed "the trial." The ephor stood, a crease of regret crossing on his face.

"A shame to lose a boy like that," he said to the knights. "And I believe his father now has nothing but girls."

He turned and saw Antalcidas standing there.

"You—I understand you like to throw stones."

Antalcidas shifted nervously, not knowing how to reply.

"Yes, elder."

"I know you were there, son. Speak freely—no one will hurt you. You have my promise."

Antalcidas took care to look the ephor in the eye as he answered, and to use as few words as possible.

"It was Thibron," he said.

4.

The testimony of the son of a free-born Spartiate, and the fact that the dead boy was under Thibron's supervision, were enough to bring an indictment. The Gerousia met to hear the evidence. In his defense, Thibron made a brief account of his service to the army and to the boy-herd. And while no one could dispute his record of excellence, a certain reputation for mischief—and rumors of private drinking—weighed against him in the elders' minds. Isidas, who still had a bald spot where one of Thibron's protégés had shaved hairs from his leg, was most adamant for the prosecution. In the end they voted twenty-six to four to convict, with both kings voting guilty.

Discussion over punishment ran well into the night. The prescribed penalty was death, but in light of the defendant's distinguished pedigree, King Archidamus moved for permanent exile. There was no consensus when the elders broke up at last to make their way home, torchless, over the empty paths. The final vote was a contentious sixteen to fourteen for banishment. On pain of execution, Thibron was obliged to cross the boundaries of Laconia by the following nightfall. In such cases this meant the convicted had to leave right away, without a pause to

collect his personal property or bid his messmates
farewell.

Thibron's trial and disappearance preoccupied
public discussion for days. That Antalcidas, son of
Molobrus gave the decisive testimony was the object
of much comment, for his mother's prediction that
her son would grow up to be "the shame of Sparta"
was not forgotten. The ruin of a young man as promising at Thibron, who came from one of the most ancient Heraclid families, might have qualified as such a
disgrace. Questioned about this by Lampito in front of
witnesses, Damatria neither confirmed nor denied the
fulfillment of her prophecy. She still had plans for her
eldest son.

Antalcidas took a big step toward that future with
his appearance in the Plane Stand. It began with a
chance encounter on the Eurotas, when his pack and a
rival gang of sixteen-year-old Yearlings met on the
shoreline path and refused to give way to each other.
The customary manner of resolving such conflicts was
to fight it out in a special arena: an artificial island
ringed with plane trees and a moat, with wooden
bridges on opposing sides. From time immemorial
Spartan boys had settled their differences there, under
the eyes of Herakles and Lycurgus, in any manner
short of the use of weapons. Many a hardened Spartiate, if asked how he had earned that gouged-out eye
or torn, fishhooked mouth, would boast that he had
not received it on the battlefield but, in fact, in a boyhood scrimmage on the Plane Stand. Every young
man was expected to fight there sooner or later.

The Lacedaemonians tempered the passions of the
moment with a heavy dose of procedure. As leader,
Stone was expected to conduct the sacrifice of a
puppy to Ares Enyalios at his shrine near the village

of Therapne. The animal had to be perfectly black, with no spots or imperfections; a regular part of the ritual was for each antagonist to disparage the other's offering as unworthy. His counterpart, a small-bodied but bigmouthed character named Gylippus, made much of a few gray hairs on the underside of the puppy Antalcidas had stolen from a yard in Limnae.

"Seems like a simple thing to me, to find a black dog," crowed Gylippus. "Maybe all our friend Antalcidas is good for is selling out his teachers!"

To invoke the fate of Thibron in the service of a petty squabble was to slap Antalcidas in the face. He didn't answer, but swore inwardly to make Gylippus pay for this remark.

The next preliminary was a fight between wild boars specially kept for the purpose. These animals were brought out by a deputation of Spartiates who seemed to relish the chore. Their eyes shined with amusement when, after Antalcidas and Gylippus cast lots, Gylippus won and picked the larger boar to represent his pack. The root of their humor became clear when the boys assembled to watch the animals square off: after trading snorts, Gylippus' champion turned rump and wriggled through the boys' legs to escape. Antalcidas led his pack in a cheer, for the affiliation of the boar that kept the field portended victory on the Plane Stand.

The next day, the sides cast lots to determine by which route each pack would take the field. Gylippus won again and chose the Herakles bridge. As the opponents gathered on the far side of the moat, the perimeter became crowded with spectators from every age-class, from Grubs to Yearlings to Cows to Firsties, as well as many full-grown Spartiates and women. The mood was one of anticipation but not quite joy: if the combatants fought as they were expected, some would watch their children maimed that morning. Conspicuous injuries on the Plane Stand, like death in war, were supposed to be grounds for celebration for the patrons and families of the wounded. In practice, those who gave damage were more genuinely cheered than those who took it.

The teams, Herakles versus Lycurgus, filed across to the island. Endius taught that the victory was decided by divine favor, bestowed on the pack that displayed the most manly excellence. There was therefore no huddling or cheerleading once the boys stepped on that sacred ground—inventive tactics, if attempted at all, were repugnant in Ares' sight. As he mouthed the ancient prayers in a voice too low for Antalcidas to hear, Alcander the Elder poured a libation to the god into the moat. With that, he sat on a field stool and raised his hand for the contest to begin.

The opponents formed up in single-rank phalanxes, their arms linked, and charged at each other across the pitch. They met in the center with a crash of unprotected ribs, heads butting, chest-to-chest. There was a murmur of approval from the Spartiates as both phalanxes remained intact after the shock.

The boys strove to push their opponents off the island, legs and backs bent to the task. The lines undulated as segments of each gained and gave ground. With flanks pouring with sweat, the antagonists began to slip past each other, straining against the linked arms before them. Antalcidas, struggling in the center of his line, found good footing in the ruts left by his ancestors. With a shout, he drove forward, ignoring the stabs to his feet from generations of teeth and severed toenails lodged in the dirt.

Gylippus's front broke. Encouraged, the Lycurgus

pack shoved them backward, step by begrudging step, until they were mere yards from the moat. Facing defeat, the enemy unlinked their arms to scratch and bite and rip. Cricket suffered a split nostril, and Antalcidas was unnerved to feel someone's fingers snaking into his mouth to administer the fishhook. He bit back, his teeth sinking straight through the ligaments. Gylippus screamed and fell back into the water with blood shooting from the stumps of his fingers. The rest of Herakles joined him in rout; Antalcidas' phalanx, meanwhile, had never been broken, though many of his mates were bloodied from gouges and bites.

The verdict among the spectators was that the melee was a qualified success. Gylippus's humiliation was aggravated by the fact that he had cried out with the pain of his wound. Antalcidas, fortunately, saved the dignity of the occasion by making no vulgar celebration. Instead, he spat Gylippus's fingertips out of his mouth and extended a hand to help him out of the water. As the other turned away in his shame, Stone overheard some of what the Spartiates were saying about his performance:

". . . never seen it done so fast . . ."

". . . that face with such a body . . . !"

"He seems pretty enough to me now!"

"Say what you will about him, but the boy *absorbs*."

The last voice belonged to Zeuxippos. As befitted any patron on such an occasion, with his peers lining up to shake his hand, he basked in the reflected glory of his protégé.

But it was a figure that said nothing at all that drew Antalcidas' attention: a thin female with her back to him, her head tilted slightly to the left. After nine years, he could still recognize that receding form. He felt an impulse to run after her, to seize her in some single manner that would express the totality of his feelings. Instead, he found himself surrounded by the faces of his packmates, assaulting him with the force of their admiration. When he looked again for his mother, she was gone.

His showing on the Plane Stand landed him in the front row of the minor chorus during the year's Festival of the Unarmed Boys. The day of his choral performance was not as hot as during the Flocks, but it was cloudless and the sun strong as it bore down on the dirt of the dancing circle in the marketplace. Except for the tasseled wreaths around their heads, Antalcidas and his packmates took the stage naked. The dance began as a simple march that grew into a complicated series of steps particular to his age-class. As he concentrated on the dancing, he had to remember the words of the paean to be sung, and endure the taunts of the older men as they scrutinized the boys for every imperfection in physique or conduct. At certain points in the performance the boys, in unison, had to stop, raise their fists, and proclaim, "By the glory of the Muses, we will be braver than our fathers!" The crowd would roar back, and the dance begin anew, only faster.

On and on it went, as the hours passed and the sun soared midway between Parnon and Taygetus. By then the temperature was irrelevant: all the performers gleamed with sweat and swooned with exhaustion as the audience only seemed to get bigger, more delightedly hostile. By the nineteenth round some of the boys could barely stand, and their promise to exceed their fathers had a decidedly uncertain ring. By the twenty-sixth the dancers in the back row collapsed. By the thirty-fifth, Antalcidas had stopped

caring whether the words or the steps were correct,
but thought only of the joints in his legs screaming,
and the pounding on the balls of his feet, and the sensation like the tip of a knife searching the clefts in the
back of his skull. He stopped, raised his arm, and declared nothing at all as his voice betrayed him.
Coughing up the dust of the marketplace, he croaked
the declaration as the adult faces seemed focused only
on him, on his failure. Despite himself, he felt the rising of tears in his eyes. He commenced the marching
step again, balancing himself on the insensate clubs
of his extremities. But Endius and Zeuxippos were beside him then, holding him by either arm, as the
sound of distant applause rose around them.

"It's over, my boy," Endius was saying. "You can
stop moving your feet. . . ."

"They say many see great Phoebus for the first time
during the minor chorus," asked Zeuxippos. "Can we
hope you were so lucky?" Antalcidas saw his lips
move, heard his voice, but could only stare back without understanding. If Apollo had truly come to him
during the ordeal, he would not have understood a
word the god said.

5.

Zeuxippos perpetuated his approval of Antalcidas
that night by buggering him at last. The old man
sought nothing untoward in this: the strength to rule
and be ruled, physically and otherwise, was the aim
of a Spartan male's education, and to that end it was
not unusual to mix a little intimacy with lessons in
politics and history. And so Antalcidas found himself
on his stomach on the bug-infested cot where Zeuxippos took his sleep. The old man was kneeling above

him, going on about the nobility of the Spartan rec-
tum, as he seemed to wrestle with the gnarled root between his fingers.

"Give me the honest ordure of a Lacedaemonian
crotch anyday!" he said. "The Tegeans are as dry as
crones, and the Corinthians—great Aphrodite's tits!—
they grease themselves so much with unguents they
might as well be women! In Athens they do it like
they do everything else, with their great yapping
mouths. But our Spartan diet produces shit as wholesome as butter, and an asshole so soft and sweet it
practically winks at you!"

Perhaps as inspired by his own words as by any
winks Antalcidas might have given, Zeuxippos
pressed down on him with his boney frame. His cock
snaked its way into whatever crevice it could find, settling at last into a refuge between the boy's thighs. He
was well wide of the mark, bobbing up and down like
the head of some agitated lizard, but Antalcidas felt
no urge to direct him.

There were other occasions for pride in his two
years in the Rearing. By the end of his time as a Yearling he took part in the rites of Artemis Orthia, at-
tempting to steal cloth-wrapped cheeses from the
altar of the goddess' sanctuary. Firsties with whips
guarded the altar as the priestess of the temple stood
by with a wooden image of the goddess in her arms.
If the guards spared the back of a thief, the priestess
would shout that the image was getting heavy with
the displeasure of Orthia-the-Willow-Borne. By the
time Antalcidas darted in for the last ball of cheese,
the priestess screamed that she could bear the weight
no longer. A grim-faced Firstie brought the switch
down on Stone's back with such force that it cleared a
furrow in his back he carried for the rest of his life.

He fell. The tormentors converged, laying into him as he writhed in every direction. The pain slashed through his mind as the snapping ends of the whips cut his skin. Yet at some point, as the blows all seemed to merge into a single molten core of agony, he could no longer distinguish between that torment and the sensation of a frigid wind cutting his skin during some cold night on Taygetus. Screwing his eyes shut, he saw what he took to be a blade of light piercing the darkness behind his eyelids. And just as he thought to himself, "Is this it? Is it He?", the heavenly knife flashed again, and again, until the Firsties over him were astonished to see a smile come over him, and the women in the audience, awed, gave indecent, animal cries.

By now even the priestess of Orthia was satisfied. Antalcidas was pulled to his feet, and his right arm raised for the crowd to see. Despite it all, he had never let go of that last ball of cheese. The Lacedaemonians, thrilled by the uncanny as much as by courage, hailed him—until some spoilsport cried, "Remember Thibron!" The crowd then fell into a confused cacophony of cheers and jeers.

Zeuxippos came to him after this with pride pouring from every bristly orifice in his face. "You must tell me now," he said, grasping his hand with womanly earnestness. "Did you see Him? Did you at last see the Shining One?"

"I think so," he replied, not too flush with pain and excitement to forget what he was expected to say.

With that, Endius suddenly appeared on his other shoulder. "Now you know the other answer to the question I once asked you, about the purpose of the Rearing," the boy-herd said. "The purpose is *joy*."

"Joy, yes," Antalcides repeated.

"Let the foreigners and fools call it cruelty. Today you join the ranks of men who know better."

Laying his hands on either side of the boy's head, Endius placed a tender kiss on his brow. Zeuxippos, meanwhile, threw his own cloak across the boy's slashed back and led him away to rest.

Antalcidas took a week to recover. When he was up again, he learned that his triumph had earned him an invitation to one of most eminent messes in the city. This was the so-called Spit Companions, otherwise known as Nuts of the Boar, among whom even royalty was known to sit. Zeuxippos was elevated to its membership more than forty years before. In that time, he boasted, neither the quarters nor the menu had ever changed, so that the members knew that they lay before the very same serving table, eating the very same food that King Leonidas did the night before he departed for Thermopylae. There was, Antalcidas expected, a story to be told for every scratch in the cushionless benches where cups clanked and swords dangled. But as much as he was there to learn from his surroundings, he was also on display, for it was for his elders to determine that night whether he deserved full membership in that or any mess.

"Sit in the proper spot, eat up, and bring honor on yourself," Zeuxippos instructed him. "But most of all, don't embarrass me. You'll get a thrashing if you do!"

By his eighteenth year Antalcidas had fulfilled the promise of his boyhood beauty. His limbs, once sleek, now bore sinews under skin pitted and broiled red by the Laconian sun; he stood a head taller than his contemporaries, with long, knot-knuckled fingers that seemed made to grasp the spear. His features, to be sure, still had a thick, coarse quality, with eyes half-lidded and vague. But attractiveness of face was only important for boys. Men were expected to grow beards at their earliest opportunity. The members of the Spit Companions therefore looked on him with approval as they came in out of the dark and took their places.

There were fourteen of them around the tables, not counting Antalcidas. Among them he recognized Damonon, son of Ischagoras, and Herippidas, son of Lysander, and Ariston, who distinguished himself in the conquest of Delphi before the Athenians took it back. There was Dorieus, son of Alcidas, and Iphitus, son of Periclidas (the admiral, not the governor). Eudamidas, who led the center at Tanagra, was there, as was Antepicydas, son of Epicydas and Edicus, son of Nabis, both Heraclids. Near the head of the table was Zeuxippos, and Isidas who was by that time an exephor. First in honor that evening, with a chair set out for his use, was the Agiad king himself, Pleistoanax, son of Pausanias.

They all stood as they waited for Pleistoanax to arrive. Light came from a single brazier in the center, which cast flicking shadows of the diners and the helot attendants along the walls. Antalcidas was set at the far left corner from the king's vantage, in the position formally reserved for guests. Zeuxippos watched him there, narrowing his eyes in rebuke when he seemed too comfortable, or too standoffish, until Antalcidas had no idea how he should behave.

The king arrived with an escort of two knights. Unlike commoners, who were discouraged the use of fire to accustom them to travel by night, Spartan crown princes were not obligated to undertake the Rearing. Pleistoanax therefore came in with attendants bearing torches. What little conversation preceded his arrival stopped as the king removed his woolen overcloak and fur boots. Free of this gear, he revealed himself to be a pale, rather stout figure who more resembled the aristocracy of other Greek cities. His shaved upper lip and long, forked beard were typically Spartiate, however.

Pleistoanax nodded to each of the diners in turn, mouthing their names inaudibly as he went around the room. Antalcidas was surprised when the king seemed to recognize him, muttering his name without hesitation or prompting. This honor caused Zeuxippos to fairly swell with gratification.

With Pleistoanax settled in his chair, the rest threw themselves on the benches. A helot entered with the meal's first course—a massive loaf of barley bread and a crock of black broth. Conversation among the Spartiates commenced as if picking up from where it had left off the previous evening:

"I have heard of the excellence of a comb none of you have mentioned, the one made of human bone," said Dorieus as he tore off a hunk of bread and passed the loaf.

"It is perhaps unmentioned, but not forgotten," replied Herippidas, "for I carry one with me all the time. . . ."

He pulled the comb from a fold in his tunic: a rough-hewn thing with sharp, uneven teeth that were indeed the color of bone. Isidas tugged at his beard as he regarded it.

"It's said that a comb made of man is most consonant with the properties of human hair."

"That is true, as I have never found it to pull or tangle."

"It will still tangle if you wash in ditch water."

"Of course. Only river water is fit for washing."

"But even then, the hairs might split," said

Dorieus, "unless they are treated first with rendered pork fat."

Eudamidas snorted at this, crying "What a keen grasp of the obvious you have, Dorieus! Now tell us the color of black broth!"

The company had a good laugh at the expense of Dorieus, who was piqued but went along with it because Spartiates are supposed to be thick-skinned. Thick-skinned, that is, at least in front of the king.

The broth was served on deep wooden trenchers. Though it was the staple dish of the mess, boys undergoing the Rearing had little opportunity to sample it until they were invited to a men's board.

Antalcidas stared at his portion as a metallic odor struck him. Black broth was pork meat boiled so thoroughly in its own blood that the flesh fell off the bone. The cooked blood, which had a flavor like salted saliva, was improved by a copious seasoning of vinegar. Depending on how long the broth was simmered, the color of it ranged from rust to inky black, and the consistency from soupy to stewlike. Most of the Spit Companions appeared to prefer it quite thick as they raised their trenchers to their mouths and slurped. A few others, including Zeuxippos and the king, made satisfied noises but buffered the taste with fresh lupine greens or chunks of barley bread. Pleistoanax, as king, got his served in a earthenware bowl with a spoon, and was entitled to a double portion. Having eaten less than half of it, though, he passed the rest to his chamberlain, saying, "Share this among the helots, as a gift from their masters." The servants blanched at his generosity.

Tasting it, Antalcidas willed himself to swallow. He at last understood the response of a certain ambassador from Sybaris who, being anxious to sample the

celebrated dish of the Lacedaemonians, bid his servants to bring him a bowl; after spitting it out in disgust, the Sybarite remarked, "Now I know why the
Spartans are so willing to die."

Antalcidas grew impatient as the meal progressed.
Lying out in the woods during frigid winter nights, he
had warmed himself by dreaming that his membership in a prestigious mess would open a whole world
of significance to him—a world of mythic personali-
ties, grand strategy, concentrated wisdom. But instead, the table talk continued to consist of petty
insults and matters of hygiene, and not even orotund
Zeuxippos seemed to be behaving like himself. Indeed, there seemed to be an unspoken agreement
among the members not to treat a subject of any importance. Lying there, his shrunken stomach recoiling
from its fill of pig blood, Antalcidas resolved that he
would see his expectations realized, even if it cost him
any prospect of membership later.

"But what of Athens?" he blurted. "I hear that they
have a strong leader in this man Pericles—a leader
who knows how to fight. They are building an empire
out of reach of any army, at sea. How shall we meet
such a challenge?"

All eyes turned to the young guest. After an awkward instant, Damonon and Herippidas laughed out
loud, and Isidas smiled into his cup. "It seems that the
boy has some interest in diplomacy!" he exclaimed.
Zeuxippos glared at Antalcidas, furious.

"If you please," said the helot server, "Polynicus regrets he cannot attend the king tonight because he is
on the hunt. In his place, he bids you to enjoy the gift
he had sent to the table. . . ."

The waiters brought out a brace of roasted hares.
Pleistoanax, looking much relieved, cleared a place in

front of himself. "Let us then remember our friend, the Equal Polynicus, as we envy his good fortune on the hunt."

And so Antalcidas' question was answered only by the sound of ripping tendons, decanted wine, and the clink of sucked-clean bones dropped on plates. Antalcidas, as he gnawed at a stringy foreleg, had all but given up on the prospect of edifying talk. Then old Isidas leaned back with his wine cup and made a clicking sound with his tongue.

"An interesting question the boy raises. It is all unclear, it seems. Very unclear."

"Athens is run by an ignorant, womanish mob!" cried Damonon with sudden vehemence. "They have a few ships, I grant you, but who mans them? Filth and locusts! That rabble will break with the first hint of real opposition, I promise you."

"Oh, I'd not be so sure about that. If you'd seen their fleet . . ." began Iphitus, the admiral.

"Our mistake was to have let them rebuild their fortifications after we chased the Persians out!" Eudamidas interjected. "Without artillery, we might as well piss on those walls as attack them. If only someone had seen through that cocksucker Themistocles, with all his smooth talk!"

Pleistoanax slammed his cup. "I would think Equals would better govern their tongues in front of the boy. And not let their fears overthrow their reason. What the Athenians don't know, after all, is that this Pericles, son of Xanthippus, is Sparta's man."

Antalcidas shook his head. "Our man?"

"The houses of King Archidamus and Pericles have long shared mutual sponsorship in their respective cities," explained Pleistoanax. "For that reason, there

will be no war. In fact, we are on the verge of a treaty
of peace."

There was another lapse in talk as the helots
brought out plates of dried figs and green cheese. As
an ex-ephor and soon-to-be member of the Gerousia,
Isidas had a special privilege to contradict the king.
The others therefore seemed to brace themselves
when the elder broke the silence.

"What you say must be true, Highness: our differences will certainly be resolved in peace, or end us all
in war. Or do I show too much of a grasp of the obvious, my dear Eudamidas?"

6.

Molobrus did his part to bring honor to his family by
dying in battle. It happened a few miles to the west of
old Lerna, in a clash with a battalion from Argos. The
Lacedaemonians were withdrawing south in the
wake of the new thirty-year peace treaty between
Sparta and Athens; the Argives, ever eager to exact a
toll in blood for the traverse of their territory, blocked
their progress. The enemies formed opposing lines
and performed their respective sacrifices. Molobrus,
to his credit, was in the first rank of the phalanx when
the pipes sounded the advance.

Spartan attacks were grindingly gradual things,
with coherence and precision valued over momentum. With plenty of time to watch the approach of the
crimson juggernaut, Sparta's enemies often broke before they were touched. But the Argives, still nursing
their ancient grudge against the Lacedaemonians,
stood their ground with locked shields.

"Argos never yields to the Lacedaemonians because she has never forgotten the Battle of Champions

in Thyreatis," Zeuxippos once told Antalcidas. "A century ago, after many battles for the domination of the Peloponnese, we met the Argives outside of Hysiae for a final reckoning. This time we agreed to settle matters the old-fashioned way, with a contest of three hundred handpicked champions from each side. The battle was fought for an entire day in every way possible, from serried phalanxes to individual duels by sword, knife, and bare knuckles. When it was over, divine Hesperus rose over a field with 597 corpses and three survivors, two Argive and one Spartan. The latter could barely stand because of spear wounds to the leg. Yet steadfast and true to his legacy, he offered battle. The Argives laughed at him and went off to their camp to celebrate what they took to be their triumph.

"The drunken Argives returned to consecrate their victory with a trophy. But they were too late: the Spartan had, all by himself, constructed one of his own out of upturned spears and abandoned Argive arms. They sent heralds in protest, demanding he take it down. But the Agiad king, Anaxandridas, ruled that his champion had indeed been left in sole possession of the field, and was by custom entitled to the victory. The Argives blustered, threatening to tear the trophy down, but in the end dared not, for fear of the gods. Since that day the battle has stuck like a bone in the Argive throat—and the Lacedaemonians have never lost a battle."

This story was told to youths to teach them the need to finish a task once begun. His father's end was not quite so glorious. As the phalanx advanced on the enemy, Molobrus had the misfortune to stumble on a stone and go down. The Lacedaemonians, trained to avoid at all cost breaks in their lines, could do nothing other than close the gap and march over him. After the first seven ranks had passed, the rear guard felt nothing of him but an indistinct softness in the place where he had fallen. In driving the Argives from the field, the Lacedaemonians suffered only a handful of casualties. One of these was Molobrus, whose crushed remains were identified from the wooden dogtags pounded into the mud.

By all accounts Damatria took the news exceptionally well. A wife of Sparta was not expected to tear out her hair, slash her face, rend her clothes, or engage in any of the other acts of conspicuous grief indulged by women of other cities. Instead, she was expected to take news of her husband's death in battle as the highest sort of honor. Damatria accordingly went around with her finest clothes and a smile on her face. The neighborhood children festooned her house with wild anemones and roses from the meadows around the city; in return, she had her servants deliver gifts of sweets door-to-door. For its part, the state contributed an honor unique to fallen veterans: the dead man's family had the right to inscribe his name on his tombstone.

Damatria did not have to pretend to be in good humor. To be spared her husband's interference in her domestic affairs, not to mention his permanent absence from her bed, were blessings too delicious to contemplate. Molobrus had at last contrived to make himself useful. Still, Damatria spared no expense on his grave, nor on the regular observances there, such as libations with precious oils. That she could afford to do so was beyond question, as she was able to produce a written contract between Molobrus and herself stipulating that all his property, including his share of the ancient portion granted his family by Lycurgus himself, went to her alone. To the annoyance of Lampito and her relatives, the agreement was duly witnessed by three citizen adults, and therefore perfectly legal.

Being still of childbearing age, she remarried with what all agreed was patriotic speed. The owner of the estate bordering hers, Dorcis, son of Nicolochus, had been Molobrus' patron when he was a Yearling. As a widower nearing the end of his years of active service in the army, Dorcis had frequent occasion to be home and watch this one-eyed beauty march around her property in her sun hat, declaiming commands to gangs of terrified helots. He sent her a stream of gifts—a dressed wild boar, a cutting from a rare apple tree from Asia that produced fruits with golden skin and red flesh, a fine wine jug from Athens covered with painted lovers—that made plain his admiration.

While Molobrus lived she did nothing to encourage him. In this she was somewhat unusual: extramarital couplings that enhanced the chances for procreation—legitimate preferred, illegitimate if necessary—were more than tolerated in Sparta. And if the long-absent husband gave his consent to share his young wife with an older man, such as his childhood patron, the act was not thought adulterous at all, but more properly a stroke of civic philanthropy. Damatria had seen them herself, those patriotic wives with compliant husbands, making their pious rounds of the temples with rouged faces and a swing in their hips. With her experience limited to a rape and the oafish pokings of her husband, she found it all incomprehensible.

Molobrus' death, and her wealth that followed, changed her view. The estate she inherited was only a fair one, sufficient to feed the household and pay Epitadas' mess one day. Dorcis' holdings were more impressive, including twice the land and steady income from several potteries and shipping interests out of Gytheion. Combining their properties would make the largest estate in Kynosoura. Accordingly, when Dorcis came to visit bearing a cart full of jars of imported Thasian black wine, she allowed him to tap one of the vessels to share a taste. As they drank together in the glow of the evening, Damatria let her eye wander over the rim of her cup and linger on his.

The next month they were married.

Their honeymoon was a revelation. Dorcis was nearing sixty but was left with all the appetites of a boy a third his age. With his unctuous smile and full head of hair, he presented a tempting prospect for lonely women all over the village. For the first time in her life Damatria experienced a degree of satisfaction in the bedroom—and a girlish possessiveness she would never have expected in herself.

"You're not betraying me with that slut Gyrtias, are you?" she asked him one day when he came home with a faintly fucked-out look.

"Certainly not," he replied, reaching down to adjust himself down there.

"Good. Because if you're lying, you'll lose those balls."

Dorcis believed she was serious, but couldn't help himself. With her conquest his enthusiasm for his new wife was flagging. Damatria kissed like a teenager who had never learned how, and her empty eye socket, which she hid under a patch during their courtship, was now too often on display for his comfort. He credited himself, though, for telling the literal truth about their married neighbor, Gyrtias.

His taste ran instead to pretty helots who worked

in his kitchen and gardens. Erinna, an eighteen-year-old, was unusual among the Messenian girls for her shameless gaze. She shot him with it when she carried baskets of figs across his path, and she shot him again when she fetched water. She challenged him until, during a rushed knee-benders in the root cellar, with his face in hair stinking sweetly of mint and sheep manure, he ground the pride out of her. The other girls were aware of it all, either not meeting his eyes or going out of their way to do so, and Dorcis was so flush with his mastery that he grew indiscreet enough to make a gift to his nymph in sackcloth. It was just a bit of lacework from the cargo of one of his Cretan freighters. But when Erinna wore the cloth on her head one day, Damatria needed nothing more to guess the truth.

She confronted him that very night. "Do you deny it?" was the first thing she asked, too furious even to say the words that made up her accusation.

"Hmm?" he responded as he unwrapped his cloak, knowing full well what she meant.

"You don't deny it. You can't. I only wish that the gods will strike me dead for being so foolish as to attach myself to you!"

She gave pious punctuation to this statement by spitting into a fold in her frock. He eyed her, tempted to insist on a denial, but strangely encouraged by the speed at which she had diverted her anger at herself. He frowned.

"All right, what of it? She is only a helot. Besides, am I expected to change overnight? You must have known about me already."

"I knew nothing. I don't talk to anybody."

With a shrug that he intended to be rueful, he turned to unlace his riding shoes. Damatria chewed a finger as he left, looking confused, and then with a certain coolness reached out to slash his eyes with her nails. He caught her easily, spinning her around and pinning her arms. She then felt, with a frisson of disgust, his erect manhood pressing against the small of her back.

"Accuser, be sure thou do not offend," he said, resting the pad of his left thumb against her surviving eyeball. He pressed until she gasped. "Do you understand? Say something. Shake your head."

She shook her head for yes—she understood.

He shoved her to the floor. Surprised, humiliated, Damatria looked up at him in frank disbelief.

"See the ephor if you want to make something of this," he finally told her. "But I think not. You may have been ignorant of me, but I know about you. What you really want has always been clear."

Thus Damatria learned the true nature of the creature she had married. It was a bitter lesson, invited by the tenderness she had foolishly shown him. It was not a mistake she would ever repeat.

Dorcis thereafter made no effort to hide his infidelities. At night Erinna's voice—or the voice of a woman she took to be Erinna, for she had never heard her speak—was audible through the floor of her upstairs apartment. The next morning Dorcis would speak to Damatria in a friendly way, as if nothing had happened. This seemed to be his way of suggesting that his betrayal bore no significance to him, and therefore shouldn't to her.

At this point Damatria did what any practically minded Greek wife would do. Seizing a lead tablet, she pried the metal out of its wooden frame and, by bending one end back and forth, came away with the strip about three inches wide by six long. She then took her bronze stylus in hand and etched onto the lead every malicious hope she could imagine for Dorcis and his helot whore:

Bôrphorbabarborphorbabarborphorbabarborphorbabaie. O divine
Hekate under the earth, bind Dorcis whose mother is Leonis, and
Erinna whom he beds, so that their ardor goes as cold as this lead,
and that his penis may droop, and her vagina go as dry as the earth
that covers this prayer to you, and to you, O Meliouchos Marmaraôth.
May they be bound, that Dorcis may burn only for Damatria, who
desires him not, and Erinna burn only for that which is shown
by the pulled-back foreskin of the he-goat, so that they forget each other,
and share passion no more.

It wasn't enough just to compose such a curse, fold it up, fix it with a nail, and drop in some well to send it on its way to the goddess. Though she judged her letters to be good, and her use of the charmed formulae adequate, she would enhance her chances for success by finding a magician to pronounce the right words at the time of its deposition. For that she would have to make her inquiries around the marketplace, and so was obliged to nurse her fury through to the morning.

She had a dream that night about three girls traveling to the Apollo sanctuary at Amyclae in a carriage wreathed with carnations. All of the youngsters, who had all just been cropped for their wedding night, laughed like drunks with every dip of the carriage wheels on the road. In their hands they bore their own shorn hair, the locks they had been growing since infancy, gathered tenderly in brushes that were fastened at the center with iron rings. In the sanctuary, under the great columnar image of the god, Damatria consecrated these remnants of the girlhood that would end with the mystery they all blushed about, but already understood. Her hands shook as she put her offering in the ground and buried it. Then she dreamed that she sang, in a voice of such ingenue purity that she shed tears in her sleep, the maiden song of the virgin bride.

She was jerked awake by the fear that she had made a terrible mistake. Lighting a lamp, she picked up the lead again and added a line to the curse:

And may any other women he desires or will desire be thusly bound.

7.

Damatria soon learned that the hearts of men, fathomless as they are, cannot match the inscrutability of the gods. Her fitful sleep caused her to rise late the next morning. Before she left for the market, she was informed that Dorcis had to be carried home from his morning ride.

"Why has he been brought back?"

"It seems he has suffered a grave accident—" began the slave.

And so she heard, as she stood with her binding spell still undelivered in the fold of her cloak, that her husband had been badly hurt when his horse, at a gallop, put a hoof through a rabbit hole. The horse did not go down, but Dorcis was thrown face-first into the ground with his hands still tangled in the reins. Of the extent of his injuries the slave was unprepared to say. Damatria rushed down the corridor to his quarters, making a show of the appropriate concern, but inwardly wondering why her prayer had such good effect before the goddess received it. Had someone else cursed him first? If so, was it another lover she had yet to learn about?

The figure on the couch had a face like a boxer's after some endless, evenly matched bout. The brow was bloated and split like a rotten fruit showing its pulp, the mouth caked with the lees of dried blood flecked with dirt. When he cracked his bluish, raked lips, there was nothing hanging from his upper gums but sharp little serpent's tongues of enamel. The rest of his teeth were left behind where they had implanted in the ground. The orbits of his eyes were stuffed with pinkish bulbs swollen enough to hide all but the tips of the lashes. When she saw him, Damatria could not help but pull up short and, in her shock, make a small, sharp inhalation. And though Dorcis' face could hardly form an expression that was recognizably human, he gave a little turn of the head as he heard and recognized her through his cauliflower ears.

She ordered all the servants to leave. Removing her street cloak, she stood over him with a wet cloth in her hands, struggling to decide where to begin cleaning him. Except for that single movement of his head, Dorcis lay so passively that it was hard to tell if he was awake. She wrung out the cloth in the bowl and wet it again, at last going to work on the skein of scratches that ran from his solar plexus to the bottom of his chin. That was when he spoke at last through his broken teeth, his voice wheezing, childish.

"I see one of us here is happy."

Damatria said nothing, determined to show neither satisfaction nor hysteria at his misfortune.

"Why have you tied me down?" he asked. As she began to wipe the blood from his mouth, she glanced down at his body: he was naked except for a breech-cloth, and there was nothing at all holding him down.

"By Herakles loosen the bonds, woman! I can't budge my arms or legs!" he cried.

In the coming days his condition did not improve. He could not move any of his limbs, though he did have feelings of pinching, twisting, and burning in them. She summoned what passed for a physician in Sparta, who could only say that the accident had damaged her husband's spine. A foreign doctor, a visitor from Elis who happened to be in the city, came, poked and prodded, and made his diagnosis: the injury had blocked the circulation of phlegm from the torso to the brain.

"Have you seen this before?" Damatria asked.

"Oh yes. It is not unknown after certain falls."

"Can you cure him?"

"By mortal arts, no. I suggest you pursue other remedies. Perhaps, if you can move him, Asclepius will manifest the correct course in his sanctuary. . . ."

"But if he can't move, how can he observe the rites? The ablutions . . . the sacrifice?"

The Elean shrugged.

Had Damatria been inclined, she might have taken advantage of Dorcis' helplessness to punish his treachery. Instead, she made a decision that surprised the household: she reassigned Erinna from the kitchen to be Dorcis' personal attendant.

By the expression on the helot's face it seemed that she believed her new duty would be easy, even pleasurable work. Believing at first that his condition was due only to lack of stimulation, she would strip slowly for him. With sluttish expertise, she unfurled her hair, leaned over his bed with breast in hand, and fed her aureole to him like a grape. Damatria watched this comedy through the window, enjoying it right down to the bitter end when the girl exhausted herself with all her useless yanking and blowing.

Damatria knew better. Tending to the invalid for a mere two weeks—cleaning his every inch, checking every crevice for dried feces, directing the flow from his torpid penis into the pan—reduced her to despair in a way unknown since her first days with Antalcidas. She particularly came to hate those random occasions when his penis came to life, for there was no way then to contain the ragged stream of urine that spurted onto his chest, his bedclothes, or in the air. Erinna, too, came to show that same panic in her eyes as the repulsiveness of her lover wore on her. Dorcis had gone overnight from a powerful lord to an incontinent, mewling shell, the odor of old age permeating him. Damatria walked in on them once as rigid Dorcis bewailed his fate, vowing never to eat again, and Erinna stood with her arms and hands drenched in piss, crying, "Then be a man! Stop eating and die already!"

Damatria closed the door, taking with her a certain satisfaction. She had, after all, taken no petty revenge, but only given her husband exactly what he wanted.

With Dorcis indisposed, his wife was now in complete control of his estate. Giving orders in his name, she commenced to reorder her universe according to her tastes. The straggling grove with his family's ancient olives came down first. The trees, after all, barely produced fruit anymore, and she needed the land to extend the wagon trail to service the most remote of her helot tenants. She likewise disposed of the vineyard. There was far more potential profit, she believed, in growing wheat for a market increasingly weary of barley bread. This gamble paid off the next season, when her grain sales and exports swelled her accounts. With this enhanced credit she purchased more land, more ships, until her estate was not only the largest in Kynosoura, but in all of Laconia.

Dorcis was not pleased with her management. To keep him occupied, Erinna would prop him up in front of the window, allowing him to witness the subversion of his legacy. At the destruction of his vineyard he screamed in impotent rage; with the demise of his ancestral olives he seemed to swoon, giving Erinna hope that he had at last dropped dead. He recovered, demanding in vain to see his wife. But Damatria's days of jumping at the summons of men were over.

Her commercial success was only a means to a greater end. With scores of helot families paying their allotments to her, she could afford to make donations of wheat bread to all the preeminent mess tables, taking care to inform the Spartiates that the gifts were from "Damatria, daughter of Evagoras, mother of Epitadas." The more traditional of the clubs returned the loaves, ostensibly because they would not give up their barley bread. More likely they simply resented the largesse of a woman. But enough of them accepted them to make her confident that her dear Epitadas would, in due time, be elected to one of the better messes.

8.

When Antalcidas' year as a Firstie ended, the city turned out at the Sanctuary of Artemis to honor his age-class. It was then that those who had distinguished themselves in the Orthian rites received their rewards: the boy who had seized the highest number of cheeses overall from the altar got a reserved place in the ranks of the Knights, the elite guard of three hundred who protected the king in battle. The champions of the individual packs got a marble plaque with his name, birth-year, and paternity inscribed around an iron sickle embedded in the stone. To receive this honor before the entire city filled Antalcidas with a simple filial pleasure, that unquestioned love of land and countrymen, that was always the true object of the Rearing. He also hoped he was well on his way toward burying forever the prophecy that he would be "the shame of Sparta." Yet even this, the very moment of his triumph, was almost ruined.

Since young graduates owned no walls on which to display their trophies, their plaques were handed over to their fathers. If the father was dead, the line of succession ran from the paternal grandfather through the eldest uncle to the youngest uncle to, finally, the mother. In Antalcidas' case only Damatria was left, and when she didn't appear at the ceremony he was left with the awkward task of carrying his own plaque around. Talk of the boy's abandonment spread quickly among the people, for the Lacedaemonians—despite their reputation for reticence—lived and died by personal reputation, and were therefore obliged to be irrepressible gossips. Antalcidas felt all eyes on him, and the words "Thibron" and "shame" hovering in the air, until the scandal of this humiliation threat-

ened to overshadow the achievement that brought
him the honor in the first place.

At last his mother appeared. Damatria was standing at the edge of the crowd, looking both familiar
and utterly unlike his memory of her. She was familiar in the way she stood slightly back on her heels, as
if trying to appear more imposing—and the way she
held her head, favoring her sighted side; unfamiliar,
in the way her scar had thrown out a web of premature wrinkles that spread beyond her patch and over
her left cheek, like ejecta from some ancient eruption.
She was also dressed in more ostentatious style than
most Spartan matrons, with an ankle-length linen
tunic of blinding white, a wide sky blue girdle, and a
cloak folded and draped around her shoulders. Her
ears shed pendants of gold hanging from filigreed
rosettes. It was the kind of kit designed to arrogate all
the attention to herself, provoking furtive glances
from the Spartan men and outright hostility from the
women.

"I suppose you'll want to give that to me," she said
to him in lieu of a greeting. It was the first time he
heard her voice in years.

"I think so."

"Come walk with me," she said, taking the plaque
under her arm. "I have something to tell you."

As she led him away from the sanctuary, he saw
that she wasn't alone. Two helots—one female and
one male—detached themselves from the background
to follow them. The latter, who was dressed in a short
household tunic with one shoulder bare, revealed his
curiosity with nervous, darting glances from the
ground to Antalcidas and back again. The female was
dressed to match her mistress, though with only a thin
girdle and no cloak, and had perfected the ancient

helot art of being physically available while mentally elsewhere.

When they were well outside the village, Damatria ordered the servants out of earshot. Turning to Antalcidas, she said nothing at first as she regarded his naked body from head to toe, then reached out to feel the veneer of olive oil applied to his skin for the ceremony. Damatria had not planned to touch him; it was an act done out of impulse, sparked perhaps by surprise at his unexpected maturity. She never lost track of how old he was, of course—that was difficult in a city divided into age-classes. But that knowledge counted little against her recollection of the small boy she had given up eleven years before. In the end she allowed her face to reflect her approval. Despite the coarseness of his face, he had grown up well.

"I am going to say something to you, and I want you to keep your peace until I am finished."

He kept his peace.

"Well then . . ." she began, now tempted to delay despite the importance of her charge. "You should know first that you have fulfilled your duty so far. Molobrus would have been pleased. . . ."

He glanced down at the plaque at her side. It occurred to him that she had yet to as much as glance at the inscription.

"What pride you must have! What vindication against your cold, uncaring mother! Yes I think you must feel that, though that all may change when I tell you something that will . . . surprise you. Understand that I say this not to diminish what you've done. If it is worth diminishing, that is for you to decide. I tell you because, as you know, an Equal must always look truth in the face."

He wondered if she took him for a weakling. For

why else would she hesitate? When have mere words ever harmed a man of any courage? He opened his mouth to interject, but she cut him off.

"You are not of Molobrus' blood. That is something not even he knew."

She paused to watch him. In his detestable, servile face, that reflection of an original that still came to her in her nightmares, she saw nothing but a brief flash of confusion, a momentary flickering in his eyes. His mouth softened, as if something mildly foul had passed down his throat.

"I can't tell you who your father was. All you need to know is that he was a helot, and that he is dead. What matters more now, I think, is what you choose to do with this knowledge."

Despite the years of training, the relentless drumbeat of injunctions to honor his gods, his ancestors, and his elders, Antalcidas felt the impulse to mock the stranger standing before him. The impulse manifested in a mildly ironic edge to his voice:

"So tell me, what would you say I do with this?"

"Don't take that tone, boy! If I tell you the truth it doesn't make *me* the fraud. Nor does it undo all that you have done—necessarily."

"Does anyone else know?"

"Not yet. But how long do you believe it would take for it to become obvious? Aren't there reasons why Spartiates rule helots—reasons that show in their quality as men?"

He shook his head. "I don't know if it would show. Maybe not for a long time . . . maybe never."

"And even if you manage to hide it, how long would you force me to keep your secret? What a cruel thing to expect of me, to go on lying in this way!"

She lifted her hand to wipe away a well-timed tear.

"Like I said, that is your decision to make. Endius tells me you have a good mind, so you must already see your choices."

All he could see at that moment was the web of creases, spread over the left side of her face, marring what was still a formidable beauty. It was the beauty seen on the faces of cult statues, Athena-the-Protectoress or Aphrodite-the-Warlike or Artemis-the-Right-Way. He was fortunate that she had only one eye, because he could not bear the scrutiny of another.

"You might sacrifice yourself," she continued. "In truth, that is a course that would reflect well on you."

Though he could not believe his ears, she appeared to be speaking in all seriousness.

"How you do it is your business. You could accomplish it in the field, against our enemies. You know now that you cannot become a true Spartiate, though you might learn to act like one. That would probably be best. . . ."

"Who are you?" he asked her. "Is this the way a mother speaks?"

"Is this how a son honors his mother, with interruptions? If you kept silent, you would hear another option that may please you more. Do you want to hear it?"

He shook his head, the accumulating absurdities beginning to crack his reserve. Sweat was beginning to mix with the oil on his skin.

"You should know that your brother Epitadas is properly the son of Molobrus. For some time now I have been arranging for his advancement. I won't say how, but you may well guess. What I suggest is that you become my partner in this task."

"Your partner?"

"I want you to support him, to do all you can to ad-

vance his interests. Devote yourself to his success. I
would think that would hardly be a burden at all for
a brother! Do what you would do anyway."

"What can I do for him? I hardly know him."

"I trust that you'll know what to do when the time
comes."

"And what of the secret that is too terrible for you
to keep?"

She smiled. "I'm asking you to serve, which should
be entirely in your nature. As for myself—knowledge
of Epitadas' safety would come as a great relief—if
you take my meaning."

Her meaning, to exchange her silence for his support of Epitadas, was clear. What was also clear was
her ignorance of the fact that, of his own free will,
Antalcidas had already done his fraternal duty to
Epitadas by covering for him in the Thibron affair.

For Damatria's part, she could see from the dys-
peptic expression on his face that he needed to hear
nothing more. She wondered what he was thinking,
but decided that beyond assuring that he did as she
asked, it didn't matter. She turned to the helots.

"You! Come here."

The male came forward.

"Should you choose what is best for your family,
your family has a gift for you," she said to Antalcidas.
"Now that you have finished the Rearing, you may
have your first attendant. Helot, introduce yourself."

The helot lifted his eyes only long enough to pronounce his name, "Doulos." Antalcidas looked at him:
he was young, perhaps no older than himself, and he
was short and thin, with the pale skin and soft hands
of someone who had never driven plow or spear.

"There's not much to the boy, I agree," said Damatria. "But you'll see that he has certain talents . . . that

is, if you agree to my proposal. Should he stay with you, then?"

Now both his mother and the helot were looking at him. Under the circumstances Antalcidas thought it was absurd to expect him to agree to anything. He heaved his shoulders in a gesture as much of despair as of assent. Pleased, Damatria held out the back of her hand to him.

"Good! Now give your mother a kiss."

Looking at her standing there, so splendid and terrible, his urge to perversity mastered him at last. Her assurance maddened him; he wanted to spring a striking revelation of his own, though he had none to make. Instead of kissing her, he spat on those shapely knuckles and golden rings. Doulos' eyes widened in panic. Damatria, however, kept her smile as she retrieved her hand and wiped it on the back of her cloak.

"Lovely," she said.

"For the sake of my young brother, who is innocent in this, you have my word that I will do as you ask," pronounced Antalcidas. "But even in Sparta, as we honor our elders, every woman is bound to honor the Equals. The words you have spoken to me here today, woman, show me no respect as a man. This will therefore be the last time we speak at all. Now get out of my sight."

Turning his back to her, he ignored her reply by focusing his attention on the sound of the cicadas in the trees around them. Rising to a crescendo, the cacophony lapsed, then began again in a different key. Other random insignificances preoccupied him: on the breeze he detected the tinkle of bells from the nearby altar of Aphrodite-in-Fetters, and the fragrance of myrtle. It occurred to him how little he cared to encounter Zeuxippos again, who would see the dejection on his face and chide him for feminine moodiness. When he finally looked back, his mother and her servant were gone; only Doulos was left beside him. His posture was akimbo, inquisitive.

The helot was puzzled further when his new master sat on the ground. Was he expected to sit too? He would have asked to take his burdens on his back, if Antalcidas had been carrying anything. As the time of his idleness stretched on, Doulos fidgeted, then felt an overwhelming compassion for this cross-legged young man in the weeds. And so he did sit down, and looking into the other's face, cleared his throat. Antalcidas regarded him as one would examine a puzzling blemish.

"It is the fate of even great men to be ruled by their juniors," Doulos ventured. He paused to see if the boss would thrash him or demand his silence, then completed his thought: "Themistocles the Athenian, architect of the victory at Salamis, once claimed that his son was the most powerful of the Greeks. The Greeks, he said, were led by Athens, and Athens by Themistocles, who was in turn ruled by his wife. And the one who ruled his wife was his son."

Antalcidas narrowed his eyes. "What do you mean?"

"I mean, you have pledged to serve your younger brother, just as Themistocles—"

"Not that! What do you mean, 'the Greeks were led by Athens'? The Greeks have always been led by Spartiates. Even at Salamis."

"With respect, master, that is not how the Athenians remember it."

"Just because the Athenians lie does not oblige us to believe them."

"Without question. But I submit that they don't perceive their version as a lie. . . ."

Getting to their feet, they went on arguing like this for some time, shoulder to shoulder, as they walked back to the village.

9.

In their twentieth year the young candidates for citizenship were cast back into a state of transition. They were not considered children anymore, but would not count as Spartiates until they were granted property and admitted to a dining group. For some, the anxiety of this passage was the hardest of all to cope with, as it seemed to wipe away whatever record of achievement they had compiled over the years of the Rearing. This was, in fact, one of the prime purposes of this time, to level the proud before they could carry their bad habits into the citizenry with them.

After their years of military training the recruits were ready for promotion into the ranks of the army. They were not placed in regular service at first, but consigned to a reserve force that kept watch on foreigners at Gytheion and the shrines, or patrolled the boundaries with Pisatis, Arcadia, and the Argolid. It was on one of these excursions that Antalcidas, with Doulos carrying his field kit and shield, penetrated as far as the river Alpheus and followed it downstream to Olympia. Indulging his curiosity, he went as far as a hill overlooking the Altis and peered through the oaks at the marble-girt sanctuary. There were no games that day—there would not be for several years—but the helot was determined to show his excitement.

"Pindar wrote of tradition that is both deeply

rooted and always ripening. Can we agree now his wisdom must have been divinely inspired?"

"I see only vanities," his master replied, nodding his head at the red-tiled edifices below. "The gods do not need fancy buildings."

"Vanity, or the glory of the Thunderer? The poet wrote:

Water exceeds all, and gold, like a blaze of fire in the night, is monarch of all varieties of wealth. But if, my heart, you wish to praise contests, seek not in vain some star warmer than the sun, shining by day through the heavenly vault, nor let us not pretend any contest is greater than
  Olympia . . .

"Helots read, men *do*," Antalcidas said.

Like any good Spartan boy, Stone was indifferent to any poets other than Homer or Tyrtaeus. He did have one thought of his own that verged on the Pindaric: of all the foreign places he had seen, the green vale of Zeus reminded him the most of Laconia.

At last the season arrived when the dining groups voted on whether to admit recent graduates of the Rearing. Mess membership was necessary for full citizenship, and demanded in turn the payment of monthly dues—in the form of produce or wild game—that approximated what the member consumed. For this purpose the graduates received farmland from their families and helots from the state to work it; elder patrons did their part too, helping to set up the households of the young men they had mentored. Damatria gave Antalcidas a corner of her property situated on a west-facing slope, with a modest farmhouse and a view of the mountains. Zeuxippos contributed a suite of furniture, including a sleeping

couch, linens chest, and a fine wrought-iron brazier.
These were the first significant possessions he owned
since he gave up his toys in boyhood. Still, as he was
in training or patrol for most of his time, and would
be obliged to sleep in the public barracks until he was
thirty, his domestic property would stand unused by
anyone—with the possible exception of his partner in
an early marriage.

The most immediately useful of Zeuxippos' gifts
was a full panoply of arms and armor. At last, he was
free to stop drilling with a blunt-ended pole and
wooden training sword. Instead, he was now the
proud custodian of an ash-wood spear, about eight
feet long, with a iron point and bronze butt-spike. The
spear was a veteran, Zeuxippos said, having served in
the line at Plataea and during the last helot revolt. A
tear swelled in the old man's eye as he said this, which
Antalcidas took to mean that the spear was carried by
the young Zeuxippos himself. The sword, with its iron
blade shaped like an olive leaf, seemed of similar vin-
tage. Like all Lacedaemonian swords, it was no longer
than a man's forearm, and therefore useful only for the
kind of close-in fighting fit for a Lacedaemonian. He
also received an old-style muscle-cuirass and greaves,
but no one wore such encumbrances on the battlefield
anymore.

Instead, the modern Spartan warrior relied for protection on the shields of his countrymen. Zeuxippos
gave him a newly fashioned design—three feet wide,
with a prestressed hardwood core and a front of
beaten bronze. While it was still common in those
years to see individual insignias on shields, Antalcidas' new model bore the emerging standard for the
Spartan army, the bold red Λ, for "Lacedaemon." His
patron never explained why he could bear to part

with his old spear and sword but not his original shield, but Antalcidas could well guess the reason: as the shield was worn on the left arm, it was designed to protect not only the wearer but also his immediate neighbor on the left. More than any other piece of equipment, then, the shield represented the sacred compact of each warrior with his comrades in the line. In Spartan houses it was not uncommon to find a sword used for gutting fish or a spear stuck in the ground to hold open a door. An old warrior's shield, however, was always proudly displayed over the hearth.

Voting for new members of a dining group occurred after the meal but before the wine flowed. Those wishing to advocate for or against the applicant were asked to state their case. Then bread was distributed to the diners, with a helot assigned to walk around the room with a bowl. Those voting for admission tossed one piece of bread into the vessel; those casting a veto squeezed the bread before dropping it. By the end, if there was even one pinched piece in the bowl the candidate was rejected—or in the vernacular, he was "bread-bowled." The confidentiality of the voting varied from group to group, with some encouraging all to speak openly about their preferences, and others going so far to assure secrecy that they made the helot go around with the bowl balanced on her head, so no one could see the ballots already in it. A young man could stand for membership in as many messes as he cared, though news of rejection tended to get around, damaging his prospects elsewhere.

Antalcidas had just returned from maneuvers in Messenia when he was surprised to learn that the Spit Companions had already voted on him. He was bread-bowled by a single ballot. Zeuxippos was more angry about the slight than Antalcidas, for he had sponsored his candidacy and spoken in favor of him before the vote.

"Mark my words, if it's the last thing I'll do I'll find out who insulted you!" the old man raged.

Antalcidas' knowledge of his servile origins had the effect of tempering his expectations. "No need," he said.

"I can't think it was Isidas, or the king," Zeuxippos went on, oblivious to Antalcidas' presence. "Eudamidas owes me for admitting Herippidas. So it must have been Damonon, that little climber!"

"No matter."

"Did you know that Damonon had been promised Thibron's cousin? I only heard about it after you came to the table. But the veto is not supposed to be used for settling petty scores! Really, it is a scandal! What is this city coming to, I ask you, when our traditions are abused in this way?"

"I see," replied Antalcidas, unable to rouse himself to disappointment. Nor did he feel any particular sense of alarm, considering that the Companions was the only group to invite him as a guest. His indifference melted only later, when Zeuxippos told him the results of another vote: it seems that Isidas, Damonon, Eudamidas, and Co. did see fit to admit an old acquaintance of his. It was Frog—stupid, hapless Frog from his boyhood pack—that merited a place at that eminent table.

Without membership in a dining group Antalcidas could not be nominated for the King's Knights. He was likewise passed over for service in the Hidden Service, though the idea of creeping around by night for the privilege of ambushing helots never held much appeal for him. The possibility that he might unknowingly eliminate a member of his father's family filled him with painful ambivalence.

At this point Zeuxippos promised to find him another mess, but Antalcidas preferred to hear nothing more about it. He found himself daydreaming instead about life as a mercenary, traveling to Asia and Africa, hiring himself out to kings and tyrants to bring Lacedaemonian-style discipline to the foreigners. In his more grandiose moments he even imagined bringing his troops back to invade Laconia, at long last seizing the respect his countrymen begrudged him. No one would laugh then at his questions about diplomacy; Thibron's exile would be a faint memory, and they would never, ever call him "Stone."

10.

Scant weeks later he saw his first combat on the borders of Arcadia. That rustic backwater, situated in the heart of the Peloponnese, had long been dangerous ground for the armies of civilized Greeks. The Lacedaemonians maintained a string of satellite towns, such as in Sciritis and Thyreatis, that acted as buffers against incursions by Arcadian raiders. These places were populated by noncitizen Nigh-dwellers who kept their local autonomy in exchange for their military service. In the last two centuries or so, which counted as "recently" in the Spartan mind, a policy took shape that sought to reduce Arcadia, like Messenia, to a helotized province. This ambition was never a matter of open discussion in the Gerousia or in the elite messes—the campaign just seemed to gather momentum on its own, as ambitious Spartiates were

drawn north to take part in the manifest destiny of
their people.

But Arcadia did not resemble the gently rolling
arable of Messenia. Its periphery was torturous, with
mountains stacked shoulder to shoulder, slashing and
unpredictable rivers, and winding valleys so steep
they seemed submerged in perpetual shadow. It was
a place where to take a wrong turn on a path was like
sinking in the sea; over the years entire columns of
Spartiates and Nigh-dwellers had gone down certain
tracks, never to be heard from again. Inside its sen-
tinel peaks the Arcadian landscape was lush, sun-
dappled, somnolent. The meadows were innocent of
buildings or the plow, the grottoes fathomless and
haunted, the old trees decorated with frightful faces
by anonymous carvers. It was confidently held that
tribes of talking wolves dwelled there, and Amazons,
and Centaurs; some said that goat-footed Pan, ever
ready to afflict intruders with lust or terror, still gathered reeds for his beloved syrinx along Arcadian
streams.

The Arcadians themselves were notorious for their
independence. It never seemed to occur to them to
concede defeat when armies came to burn their settlements; their talent for treachery made all invaders
feel perpetually surrounded. The few individuals the
Lacedaemonians managed to helotize turned out to
be liabilities, either running away or inciting the
Messenians to defiance. It was fortunate for those
Spartiates who coveted estates in Arcadia that their
plan of conquest was never officially debated. If it
had, it would have become obvious how bad the idea
was.

Antalcidas was blooded at last in a haphazard action in the north of Sciritis. He was part of a border

patrol of thirty-two other recent graduates of the
Rearing that included, by chance, his old packmates
Redhead and Cheese. In command was a young Spartiate named Praxitas who was anxious to make his
reputation on the frontier, but whose single accom-
plishment so far was to grow his beard to a precocious
length. Antalcidas, by contrast, had a growth of only
a few fingerwidths, and had yet to be elected to a dining group.

A messenger from the Sciritan town of Asea encountered them on the road. Someone had stolen a
dozen head of oxen from the pastures. When the
Nigh-dwellers set out to find them, they were am-
bushed by Arcadians with slings. A handful of Sciritai
were killed, and the thieves were still in the vicinity.

"How many are there?" Praxitas asked.

"I don't know."

"Where are they now?"

"I couldn't say for sure."

"Sounds like a job we can handle," Praxitas concluded.

As the Arcadians had not even bothered to remove
the cowbells from the rustled oxen, they were not
hard to find. They were making their way up a narrow track into the mountains. The ragged group of
twenty or so, dressed in everything from goatskins
to stolen tunics of the Nigh-dwellers, seemed high-
spirited as they turned to defend the herd. The dis-
tinctive crimson and bronze of the Lacedaemonians
did nothing to faze them. Praxitas, who had led the
patrol so far with a look of iron determination, was
somehow surprised as the Arcadians took up positions to use their slings. It fell to Antalcidas to summon the attendants to bring up the troops' shields and
spears. Doulos, who seemed a full foot shorter than

any of the other helots, straggled to deliver his master's panoply.

"By the gods you are slow!" Antalcidas chided him as he took up his arms. The logical rejoinder, of course, was that hoplites had attendants precisely because it was a burden to carry the equipment for long distances. But helots, alas, did not make rejoinders.

Antalcidas had just fitted his headgear, a conical bronze helmet of the "pilos" shape, when the first shots from the Arcadian slings flew past his ear. The Lacedaemonians instantly assembled in close order, locking their shields to present an unbroken front of metal. The slingers concentrated on this target, popping stones off the yard-wide faces of bronze like raindrops in a summer downpour. Crouching behind, the hoplites looked to Praxitas, who issued no orders but stared into the cave of his shield as if expecting a voice to emanate from it.

"Praxitas, what's the plan?" asked the shakey-voiced Redhead.

"Stay here, until they run out of stones."

Redhead looked to Antalcidas, who said nothing. It was obvious to all—except Praxitas—that the hill the Arcadians held was carpeted with a supply of smooth rocks perfect for slinging. To directly contradict a commander in the field, however, was a grave offense that, in the chaos it invited, brought deeper shame than losing the battle.

All this suddenly changed when a stone cracked through Praxitas' shield. The shot only just penetrated, and bounced weakly off the horsehair brush of his helmet. The shock, though, seemed to sink their commander deeper into a state of immobility. Antalcidas risked a peek around his shield: one slinger had fired at them from twenty yards, and more were edg-

ing closer. In a few minutes their shields would be of
no use.

"Praxitas, what do we do?" a man asked from the
end of the line.

"Should we attack?" asked another.

"Don't be a fool! Any closer and the stones will go
right through!" snapped a third.

"If we wait any longer they will anyway!" Cheese
retorted.

"Praxitas!"

Fragments of wood and metal flew from the rims of
their shields. Antalcidas looked to Praxitas, who had
opened his mouth like someone trying to remember a
long-forgotten tune. Without thinking, saying nothing
but a short prayer to the Twins, Antalcidas burst out
the line and charged with spear lowered at the nearest
Arcadian. The slinger, who was dressed in a goatskin
tunic festooned with freshly severed human ears, was
winding up his next throw when he saw Antalcidas.
He fired a low shot that Stone somehow anticipated
and hurdled. As the other slingers stood frozen, unwilling to shoot so close to their comrade, Antalcidas
closed and buried his spear in the slinger's chest.

There was a pause on both sides as the tableau lingered: the slinger run through, his weapon hung
limply at his side, as Antalcidas stood there, perfect in
his thrusting form. With his eyes locked on the terrified, flashing whites of his victim, he gave the requisite twist of the spearhead, which made a sound like
the crack of walnut shells as the metal tore gut and
tendon. Antalcidas heard distant cheers, and the
whistle around him of more stones from the Arcadians. Nothing hit him as the rest of the Lacedaemonians followed up his attack, forcing the enemy to fire
from on the run.

They took down a second Arcadian who stumbled over a rock. The rest escaped, but it hardly mattered—all the cattle were recovered, and the patrol could display two dead thieves for the satisfaction of the Nigh-dwellers of Asea.

Antalcidas had long imagined how he would feel after he had taken his first adversary in battle. The achievement left him more puzzled than thrilled: in killing his man, he had snuffed out a life with as much claim to air and water and the light of the sun as his own. And yet there were no trumpets, no exultancy, no feasting on the soul of the vanquished. The moment lacked even the occult electricity of animal sacrifice, pregnant with mystery. Killing a man, he found, was hard work, like slaughtering an ox, but without the reward of yielding a good meal in the end.

The other young men, with the exception of Praxitas, stood around eyeing Antalcidas in sidelong fashion. Their expressions were of bemused wonder, as if they had seen a lesson in training perfectly and unexpectedly proven useful in real life. A rush on the double, after all, was the standard counterstroke to a missile attack. They had heard this tactic described during the Rearing many times, but in the instant it was most necessary only one of them, Antalcidas, remembered it.

Yet when they got back to the city, the agreed version had somehow changed. Their examiner was Alcander, the elder who had, years before, joined his colleagues to save the infant Antalcidas from the Taygetos gorge. As the old man peered over the top of his staff, Praxitas described how, after his shield was holed, it was none other than Praxitas himself who ordered the slingers charged on the double. His platoon-mates stayed silent, but Alcander must have sensed their discomfort. He spoke for the first time, asking, "Antalcidas, son of Molobrus, tell me: do you agree with Praxitas' version?"

Suspecting betrayal, Praxitas stared hard at Stone. For unless someone had fed the truth to Alcander before the examination, why would the old man invite Antalcidas, in particular, to confirm his story?

Antalcidas stepped forward at attention. His eyes shifting to Praxitas and back, he gave his unswerving reply:

"I support my commander's account."

"But is it true?" the other pressed.

"It is true."

To which Alcander smiled, but said nothing more.

On those rare occasions when he was not training or on the march, Antalcidas visited his homestead. It was not in him to wax sentimental for pretty landscapes as such; the pastoralism of the citified Romans was still far in the future, and modern romanticism centuries beyond. Still, he felt a certain reassurance in the placement of a great oak on the south wall of the house, where it cast a cooling shadow and, as necessary, presented a more inviting target for the Thunderer than his thatched roof. The line of cypresses along the ridge suggested the comforting image of a mightly phalanx on the march. Though the lands were not extensive, he had an unusual variety of flora on them. In addition to the grain fields, there were stands of palm, pomegranate, myrtle, poplar, and laurel; the scents of basil, purple thyme, and rosemary wafting from the hillside, oleander from the stream bottoms and, in between, acanthus lofting their spires like upturned spears.

As the manager of the property lived in the helot village beyond the hill, no one was staying in the farmhouse. Antalcidas found himself wandering through its rooms, inwardly decorating it with a wife and children. His spouse was the blond girl he had glimpsed in the festival chorus—though it had been so long, and his look at her so brief, that he could not be sure his image was more invention than reality. The effort to conjure her appearance frustrated him; what perishable things, he found, were memories of faces.

As he came out into the daylight he saw, in the distance, a litter borne by four helots. This was certainly his mother on an inspection tour of her estate. Since the testy encounter at Orthia they had not spoken; their only communication was to pass legal documents for the gift of his portion, and over the state registration of Doulos' transfer to his use. And while what she had told him of his parentage was never far from his mind, it didn't preoccupy him. As all Lacedaemonians were taught, such things were in the nature of unalterable facts that, like Fate itself, were profitless to dwell upon.

He did wonder about his mother's influence when he was finally elected to a mess. He was admitted to the Hill Wolves, a club of deep antiquity that was long past the height of its prestige. Still, it did boast one recent member of great renown: Pausanias, son of Cleombrotus, hero of the battle against the Persians at Plataea. To be sure, this man later fell in with barbarian ways, and so disgraced himself that he was forced to take refuge from punishment in the Brazen House. The ephors, unwilling to violate the sanctuary, ordered him walled into the temple alive. So momentous was Pausanias' victory at Plataea, however, that he was posthumously rehabilitated and given a fine, named tomb.

If Damatria had anything to do with Antalcidas'

election, it could not have been due to her alone. One of the better known of the Wolves was Alcander—the elder who had questioned him after the Arcadian affair. On his first night as a member, Antalcidas was embarrassed when Alcander retold the story in terms favorable to him. Meanwhile he could not help but notice that Praxitas, for one reason or another, was never granted another unsupervised command.

These were the thoughts that immersed him as he walked along the road to the army's encampment. At first he didn't notice a solitary figure waiting for him at the wayside, leaning against a tree. Antalcidas' hand found its way to his sword as the stranger, dressed in the billowing black cloak, stepped out of the shadows.

"Antalcidas," the other said.

The voice, though deepened with age, was unmistakable.

"What do you want?"

"Is that any way for an Equal to greet a brother?"

"I'm not an Equal yet."

Epitadas flicked his head sideways as if to say that his elevation was only a formality. And in fact, with Antalcidas' membership in the Hill Wolves, he was right.

"Isn't this a time when we should be getting to know each other, with you on your way and me about to finish the Rearing? The time may come, you know, when we must serve together."

Antalcidas looked at him. Epitadas had grown up the handsomer of the brothers, with the tall frame and lean, quick features of the ideal Lacedaemonian warrior. He also had the longest beard—almost half a foot long—of any pregraduate he had ever seen. Even so, there was a look in his eyes, some mixture of fraternal admiration and jealousy, that struck Antalcidas as childlike still.

"I think you must be thinking of what happened to Thibron," Epitadas went on. "For what it is worth, I should give you what was due a long time ago, Brother—my thanks."

Surprising him, Epitadas then grasped his hand, and when that was done, pulled them together for an embrace. With this display Antalcidas lost his diffidence.

"I wasn't expecting your gratitude," he said.

"You have it anyway. And my confidence that we will always support each other, will we not?"

"We will."

11.

As difficult as Damatria's younger years had been, her maturity was a succession of personal triumphs. In business she was indomitable: when she set her sights on acquiring or altering a piece of property, nothing could stop her. The Equals were as innocent as children about matters of finance, caring only about keeping score in the ways Lacedaemonians had for centuries. They had no conception of how the world had changed—of how the pressures of population and political unrest were filling Greece with thousands of unemployed mercenaries. Power in the very near future would not be measured in terms of who could mobilize the most citizens, but of who spent most wisely within the rising empire of money. The small sack of foreign staters she had once begrudged herself had now grown into a treasure chest bursting with cash.

Her greatest competition in this came not from

among the men, but from their wives. With the helots employed in the tasks left to wives of other cities, the good women of Sparta were free to sample many of the delights abjured by their dutiful husbands. As their spouses dined on bitter bread and pork blood, the wives grew plump on delicacies imported from the islands, Sicily, and beyond; while the men made do with tunics of crimson sackcloth, their women went around the markets in Egyptian linen and Persian silk. In their fortunate idleness, the wives had opportunity to learn much about the value of wealth.

Damatria managed to enlarge her holdings at the expense of her neighbors, as well as acquire other estates in Messenia and on the island of Cythera. Her moneylending interests at the port attracted applicants from as far as Samos, until she owned a piece of virtually every ship plying the Aegean from Gytheion to Asia. Her gamble on the production of wheat had paid off so handsomely that she was providing bread for half the messes in the city. She even tried her hand, in partnership with Isidas, at bankrolling a four-horse chariot team for the games of the 85th Olympiad; in a suspicious decision, her team was awarded second place after crossing the line dead even with a chariot sponsored by none other than one of the Olympic judges. Barring scandal, whatever she put her mind to seemed destined for success.

Yet as she grew wealthier Damatria grew less happy. With her husband under her strict control and his lover grown ugly under her burden, she had no enemies left to defeat. In the void that was left she had much time to consider the errors of her past ways— particularly the injustice she had done to her eldest son. For what had Antalcidas done to deserve the resentment she had heaped on him? With what, except the love of a devoted son, had he ever repaid her? Indeed, what was her rape next to the pain of a mother like poor Gyrtias, who had lost four sons not in glorious battle, but to disease? In the pit of the night, when she thought with fondness of the times when a small voice called out to her, she was filled with regret at how she had behaved. "If only you could come to me now, my dear baby!" she would say to her empty bedroom, her arms extended in the dark. But Antalcidas was gone then, on campaign beyond the mountains in Thyreatis, Doris, the Megarid, and the time when her self-reproach could mean anything to him was long past.

Epitadas broke her heart in his own way. The fact that she had showered him with advantages had the effect of teaching him to expect her devotion. In those times when she was of no use to him—which were increasingly frequent—he seemed to regard her with the respect due to a used napkin. When she spoke to him, his face showed his impatience; when she sent him gifts of food he was known to give them away to helots and dogs. Salvaging her pride, she came to him and demanded the deference befitting a mother of Spartiates. Epitadas laughed, embraced her in a way that was faintly mocking, and asked what gifts she had brought him.

And so, for different reasons, she could only rejoice at a distance at the success of her two sons. Thanks to her patronage, Epitadas was welcomed into the Spit Companions, and in the ensuing years became one of the most sought-after bachelors in the city. Antalcidas emerged as an able field commander in small engagements with Arcadians, Argives, and Phocians. He then surprised her by making a fine marriage with a Heraclid heiress named Andreia. This girl was too precious for her taste—all blond hair and girlish calves and a supercilious attitude—but Damatria cultivated her strenuously since their marriage in the hopes of another chance with Antalcidas. Iris oil from Ionia was a particular favorite of the girl's. Damatria had just received another shipment of the stuff from Caria, packed in a darling little alabaster flask, when news reached the city that joined her to Andreia in a way she had not anticipated.

Under normal circumstances, measures were taken to assure that brothers did not serve in the same units of the Spartan army. They had lately ended up together, though, when soldiers were chosen by lot for a special garrison duty. Now it appeared that the brothers were on an island, and furthermore that their garrison would be there for some time. Damatria turned to Dorcis' old shipping maps to check the location. Was it a big island like Zacynthus or Leukas? A mere rock like little Prote? She sent her chamberlain back to the agora for more details. He returned an hour later with bad news: the Lacedaemonians were blockaded by a large Athenian fleet, with no supplies or reinforcements getting through. The sound of the island's name, *Sphacteria*, suggested to Damatria the course of a blunt knife tearing a throat.

IV
The Terror

1.

The island's appearance varied with the hours. Late in the afternoon it was a featureless undulation, low-slung and stealthy like a surfacing submarine contoured to evade detection. With the morning light at his back, the observer faced a two-color composition of hardscrabble and scrub green that, even from far across the bay, looked pitted from numberless insults. A string of low pinnacles formed a jagged line off the south end, culminating in a flat-topped butte—Little Sphacteria—that seemed to follow its consort like a lifeboat. Both islands are great concretions of marine detritus, alternately squeezed and lifted, their bodies rent by fissures, dimpled by sinkholes, tortured by the sea.

The land bears scars of its own violent legacy. The western reaches of Messenia were once protected by three thousand foot limestone ramparts, including Sphacteria, more ancient than the gods. The wall was wracked along the fault lines that invested it, until it was finally breached. The soft, near-shore soils were then exposed to the assault of wind and water, resulting in the largest stretch of protected anchorage in Greece.

The surface calm still hides the conflict of titanic forces. The commerce of centuries, including Athenian triremes, Turkish galleys, and modern excursion boats, has plied these waters oblivious to the dramatic, earthquake-riven landscapes beneath. Less than a mile from Sphacteria's west coast the sea floor plunges to seven hundred feet; a few dozen miles farther out lies an abyss deep enough that if Mount Blanc were dropped inside, its summit would be submerged a depth of one thousand feet.

On this particular day, inside a pointed archway punched through the mass of Little Sphacteria, the rising sun revealed the gleaming ram of a warship. A good pair of eyes might have seen the white tunics of the ship's senior crew atop the rock, looking north at the prison they'd made for the Lacedaemonians. A few moments later another trireme of the Athenian fleet rounded the island. It was one of two vessels Demosthenes kept in constant orbit around Sphacteria, traveling in opposite directions, day and night, in all weather. The blockade had been underway for a week.

The trireme *Terror* arrived with Eurymedon's rescue force from Zacynthus and alternated on blockade duty ever since. Over the eight hours of its watch it had circled the island in a counterclockwise direction, proceeding at a steady pace that brought it around twice. By the end of the last hour the rowers were tired: the blades of their oars no longer cleared the water by much on the backstroke, and the piper was forced to slow the cadence. The men were looking forward to a meal and a rest—though with the Peloponnesians in control of both the island and the mainland coast there was not much land for them to dry their hulls. The only safe spot was Demosthenes' little stockade on the beach near the Sikia Channel. This had grown over the week into a busy little port, with more than fifty Athenian vessels lining up offshore, waiting their turns for their crews to pull out, eat, and snatch whatever sleep they could in the sand. The prolonged monotony took its toll: there were affirming murmurs all around when Patronices, the eldest of the oarsmen at fifty years old, spat from the starboard outrigger and grumbled, "I say we've got ourselves under siege, not the Lacedaemonians!"

The mood was much the same as it had been in Athens two months earlier. The year's campaign was the seventh consecutive summer of war against the Peloponnesians. The Lacedaemonian land army had not yet arrived in Attica that summer, but inevitably would come. The enemy would then settle in for a season of economic devastation—burning houses, upending crops, razing trees. The Athenians, meanwhile, would watch ruefully from the tops of their city walls as the works of their fathers went up in flames. That all this was stipulated in Pericles' grand strategy—that the entire population of Attica would withdraw safely behind the city walls, supplied by the navy while the invincible Spartans raged outside—did little to relieve the general dejection. Pericles had, after all, not anticipated the outbreak of plague in the second year of the war that would kill so many thousands, including himself. Now all that was left of noble Pericles was his tomb, a few pretty buildings, and his strategy.

The crowding inside the walls, and the threat of a new outbreak of plague, made it easy to recruit crews for the triremes. What else was there to do, except to take any opportunity to work their revenge against the enemy? And so it was with the usual combination of anticipation and unease that nearly seven thousand dispossessed citizens, resident aliens, and slaves took the oars of the fleet under Eurymedon.

The sun cleared the mass of Mount Hymettos to reveal forty ships gathered off Piraeus. As the crews and captains sat with their heads bowed, and thousands more of their relatives gathered on the shore, a herald led them in prayers to Athena-the-Guardian, Enyalios, and the other gods of the city. At a signal, libations of wine in silver cups were poured in unison from the bows of every ship, and from golden bowls by the priests on land. At last the assembled citizens, ashore and afloat, sang in praise of Poseidon as Eurymedon ordered the vanguard to pull out to the cadence of the hymn. Tears standing on their cheeks, those left behind sang out as the voices of their fathers and brothers faded on the water, the line of their sails sinking into the mists around Aegina.

The crew of the *Terror* had special incentive to reach the theater of war. Their town, Acharnae, was set in the plains northwest of the Cephisus river, six miles north of Athens. Nearly every summer for seven years their land had been sacked by the enemy. Having been evacuated within the walls of Athens, the Acharnians were in excellent position to witness the plumes of smoke rise from their homes, fields, and vineyards.

The Lacedaemonians added insult to injury by making the place their preferred spot to camp for the season. Thanks to the proximity of the forests of Mount Parnes, Acharnae was a center for the production of charcoal; the particular sweet odor of burning coal was as familiar to Acharnian children as the scent of their mothers' hair. It was therefore with particular bitterness that the exiles smelled the fruit of their labor on the wind from the Spartan campfires. But despite the wailing of the women and the young warriors' demands to punish the invaders right away, the Athenian generals would allow no piecemeal attack.

The frustration of the Acharnians made them the most hawkish of all, opposed to any accommodation with the enemy. The playwright Aristophanes exploited their almost pathological jingoism to the hilt in his comedies. The Acharnians, in return, thought little of wits like Aristophanes.

Fortunately for the town's partisans, the richest man in Acharnae, Philemon, son of Hippias, saw fit to spend ten thousand drachmas to outfit a warship. The *Terror's* hull was of a typical trireme design, forty yards in length and five across at her widest. One hundred seventy rowers were packed inside in stacked triplets rising from near the keel to the outriggers built atop her bulwarks. The *Terror* was fast because she was unstable: like her fleetmates, she was fast in calm water but so slender abeam as to be a menace to her crew in rough seas. For this reason she hardly ever sailed out of sight of land, and spent her nights beached.

The *Terror* was exceptional for certain other reasons. Philemon, as the vessel's sponsor, was nominally its captain but in practice functioned more like poorly stowed ballast. His girth made it difficult for him to move unassisted even on land; at sea, where the proper distribution of weight was particularly important, Philemon seldom dared leave the little cabin he had built for himself on the top deck. If it had not been for his fear of the plague in Athens he would never had gone to sea at all. As it was he kept to his couch, diverting himself with plates of relish he could never keep down when the ship moved. When he was glimpsed, it was to empty his bucket. When the crew heard his voice, it was to make noises of authority from behind a curtain that the crew, over time, had learned to ignore.

As poor a sailor as Philemon was, he was an excellent delegator. His hired captain, Xeuthes, son of Cratinus, was a veteran of a hundred actions from Cyprus to Sicily. Born within spitting distance of the strand at Munychia, his first memory was the spectacle of the Athenian navy smashing the Persians at Salamis. His father, Cratinus, piloted a trireme during the battle, and kept Xeuthes at his side through many of the campaigns that followed in Ionia and among the islands. As he came of age he became the living image of his father, down to the flat nose, sunblasted skin, and salt irremediably ingrained in his beard.

With so many ships fitting out in Athens during those years, it was difficult to find a decent helmsman. Xeuthes scored a coup, then, when he brought aboard an old comrade, Sphaerus of Anaphlystus. This character was of such indeterminate antiquity that he called Xeuthes "sonny"; he seemed to have firsthand experience of Artemisium, a battle fought fifty-five years earlier. There was some concern all around when Sphaerus had to be physically led to the helmsman's position on deck, between the two rudders mounted on either side of the hull. They had to guide his hands to the raked tillers as if he could see nothing at all.

The oarsmen below decks were the hardest of the hard core of Acharnian patriots. Some, such as Dicaearchus, son of Erasinus, were rich men before the Lacedaemonians sacked their estates. Others, like Cleinias, son of Menanthus, and Timon, son of nobody-knows, were dirt poor laborers from the charcoal works to whom the rowers' salary of one drachma a day was a considerable windfall. All were landlubbers from a place as distant from the sea as any in Attica. Yet together they constituted one of the best crews in the fleet, working together so well that they once almost beat the state flagship, *Salaminia*, from Piraeus to Aegina. This feat was all the more remarkable because the *Terror*'s gang of riffraff matched the *Salaminia*'s crew of professionals stroke for stroke.

On their first trip around the Peloponnese they sailed in the company of nineteen other ships under the admiral Phormio. This voyage was as gratifying as any campaign the Acharnians had ever seen on land or sea—with the Peloponnesian ships afraid to engage them, the entire enemy coast was open to attack. The Athenians paused where they pleased to burn towns just as the Lacedaemonians did in Attica; when they landed their ships for the night they were free to liberate all the provisions they needed from nearby farms, including cattle and pigs. To the relief of the oarsmen—and the delight of Philemon—the men of the *Terror* ate better and got better air and water on campaign than they ever had in overcrowded, plague-ridden, bug-infested Athens.

The only cloud on their horizon was Xeuthes' mania for equalizing the oar power of the ship. It was not unusual for the port or starboard side to be stronger because, by chance, one or the other team of rowers had more strength or superior technique. Yet producing balanced teams was not as easy as simply commanding the oarsmen to swap benches. There was a clear heirarchy in the positions of the rowers, with those seated atop the outriggers, the so-called "beam men," getting the most fresh air and the best view of the action outside. Below them were those in seats mounted on the middeck (the "deck men"), and lowest of all those laboring belowdecks, or the "hold men." The deck men could see little of the outside world and depended on the beam men for guidance, but their position was still infinitely preferable to being in the lowest rank. With their benches mounted barely above water level, the hold men worked in a sunken stall of wood and flesh. If the ship was flooded they were least likely of all to escape with their lives. On a long voyage the atmosphere could be stifling, as they pitched blindly in their warrens, the stench of bilgewater rising from below while an unrelenting flow of sweat, urine, or worse flowed down from the crewmen above. To ask the beam man Patronices to exchange seats with a hold man like Timon was, therefore, as good as to invite Patronices to riot. In the end, Xeuthes had to match the power on each beam by exchanging men of equal rank only—a puzzle that took days to sort out.

The wisdom of the captain's preparations paid off during their very first battle. In the third summer of the war, Phormio based his little fleet at Naupactus, on the Crisaean Gulf athwart the shipping lanes of Sparta's ally, Corinth. The Peloponnesians had sent a fleet of forty-seven ships under their admiral Machaon to support an attack on Athens' allies in Acarnania. Though he had fewer than half Machaon's force, Phormio shadowed the Corinthians. Supposing that they would try to slip by him in the predawn darkness, he then positioned his fleet to catch them on open water.

The enemy, having more troop carriers than triremes, adopted a defensive circle with their rams facing out. If Machaon's men had been Athenians, there would have been little chance of breaking into their formation. But the Corinthian crews were not nearly so disciplined. Phormio's ships encouraged their disorder by rowing around them in a circle, sometimes passing close enough to brush against their rams. As the sun rose and the wind freshened, the enemy ring became a lozenge, then a confused tangle of prows and oars. Judging that moment to be most opportune, Phormio released his fleet to attack.

Sphaerus had by this time done as little steering as necessary. At the captain's signal, the old man worked the rudders to make a sharp portside turn, then shot into a gap between two Corinthians with their oar-blades ensnared. In that single maneuver, the *Terror* sheared off the oars of both ships, then went on to ram Machaon's ship beyond them. Witnesses in the other Athenian ships cheered; the men of the *Terror* endured a few breathless moments as Xeuthes ordered them to extend their oars back into the water and row for their lives in reverse. But Sphaerus had not doomed them by planting their ram in an irretrievable spot. Their ram pulled away easily, opening a hole in the enemy flagship that sank it to its top rails in minutes.

By the battle's end the Athenians scattered a superior fleet and captured twelve vessels. The *Terror*, having disabled three vessels all on her own, distinguished herself most of all. In the seasons that followed she was not always on the winning side; on a number of occasions she survived only by running away. But there was no doubting her value on difficult voyages far from home—including, in the war's seventh summer, blockade duty around a desert island, with a precarious base of supply and no end in sight.

2.

When Demosthenes presented the Athenians with an opportunity to entrap hundreds of Spartiates, his superiors could hardly deny him. Yet Eurymedon still wouldn't give up his plans to sail on for Corcyra. He subsequently left with half the fleet, leaving Demosthenes in command with barely enough ships to blockade the island and defend the straits into the bay. Just two ships were enough to keep watch on the enemy during daylight. But after dark, and particularly on the moonless nights toward the beginning of the siege, there was danger that the Lacedaemonians would send small boats or swimmers to help their countrymen, or that the members of the garrison would try to swim for shore. This made it necessary for Demosthenes' entire fleet to anchor at even intervals around the circumference of Sphacteria. The oarsmen, who were already hungry, overworked, and bored, were forced to take whatever rest they could sitting upright on their benches. Falling over each other in their exhaustion, most gave up sleep altogether. On the *Terror*, the nocturnal watch therefore became an occasion for lively discussion, whispered but lively over the lap of nighttime swells against the wales.

"Just for your information, you little sprats, do you know why you're all here, breaking your health in this miserable tub?" asked Patronices.

Dicaearchus, a beam man, had removed the sheepskin cover from his seat and folded it against a bulwark for a pillow. "Of course. It's because someone decided that the Athenians must have an empire, but did not think of the jealousy it would cause among the Peloponnesians."

"Wrong! That it exactly what certain people want you to believe, but it isn't the real truth. . . ."

"It's a matter of geopolitics, idiot. Nothing more and nothing less."

"I have heard," chimed Cleinias from the deck,

"that it had to do with the Corinthians encouraging one of our allies to revolt."

"No, the war is over the way we helped Corcyra in their war with Corinth," said someone else from the shadows.

"Again, all wrong. What a sad thing it is, to see citizens of Athens giving up their lives for a cause they don't understand!" declared Patronices.

"All right, slick," Dicaearchus said as he closed his eyes. "Why don't you tell us why we're all here?"

Patronices wiped his face with his oarcloth, for they were stuck in the lee of the island on as stifling a night as he had known in thirty years afloat. "We're here," he began, "because of *whores*. To be more accurate, because of whores of whores. Have any of you spent any time in Megara, among the lovely ladies behind the Temple of Asclepius?"

"All right now, don't show off. . . ."

"If you'd been there not very long ago, you might have met a girl named Anyte. She plied her trade right at the gate. She was a good-looking girl for that business—I mean soft, plump thighs, hair black and long as the night, tits like scoops of cream. Maybe too good-looking: she had the kind of face you could fall in love with if you forgot yourself. Best of all, she didn't stink of garlic like every other Megarian, or try to steal your money. For two obols she'd make an honest go of sucking your balls straight out the end of your cock. For three you'd get acquainted with her pink piggy. . . ."

"And nine months later you popped out—end of story!" shouted Cleinias.

"Not hardly! Yes, Anyte hung out with Asclepius, and like him she was good for what ailed you! She was so good at her job, really, that she fell in with some operators who put her into the high-end trade—entertaining rich pricks at their wine parties, if you know what I mean. It was around this time that she changed her name to the exotic, the erotic, the untouchable—Simaétha! Now does that ring any bells?"

Dicaearchus jerked awake. "By Zeus, it does! He's not kidding, boys: that girl's legs cut papyrus."

"I see our friend Dicaearchus is a fan of good flute playing! And so we get to the truly interesting part of our story: seven years ago two purple-faced ne'er-do-wells from Muses Hill, let's call 'em Frick and Frack, decide to do a little slumming in Megara. They ride over there with their tender rumps on horses, and after throwing their silver around, they get the best room at the inn and order out for some entertainment. . . ."

"Is that the best you can do, 'Frick and Frack'?"

"Shut up and learn something!" Patronices went on, waving his arms in the constricted space of his station. "So, after a little drinking, a little fish relish without bread, they bring in Simaétha for dessert. And she really wows 'em, friends—by the end of the stripdown they're sitting with their tongues out, and when she gets down to business Frack is so taken with her that he won't let Frick get his share! I mean, can you imagine? Frick objects, and Frack tells him to go to his mother in Hades. So the friends get to fighting with knives, with Simaétha screaming, but nobody comes to break it up because they're thinking there's nothing wrong, it's just a lively party.

"When it's over, Frick's on the floor, cut up, and Frack is so out of his mind he believes he can't live without his dear Simaétha. So what does he do? He smuggles her back to Athens wrapped in a blanket! And how do the Megarians react? Like their kind always does, of course—they figure, as the aggrieved party, they might as well take advantage of the situation to . . . what's the expression? . . . *trade up*. So instead of tracking down the man who stole their property, they head straight to the cathouse run by Pericles' chippy, Aspasia. Next day her squeeze, old squinchhead, the captain of all our fates, Lord High Pericles Himself is running around the Council House with his hair on fire, denouncing the treachery of Megarians. It seems that not one, but two of Aspasia's best girls were smuggled off during the night!

"Now not even Pericles, with that honeyed voice of his, can quite convince the whole city to go to war over this. What he proposes instead is a boycott of all Megarian goods within the boundaries of Attica. And so much are the people willing to be fools for him, they actually go for it. Megara, naturally, protests—first to the Assembly, which is useless, and then to the Peloponnesians, who are just waiting for any excuse to clip Pericles' wings. And the rest, dear friends, we all know, to our sorrow."

Dicaearchus shook his head. "I may have heard of your Simaétha, but that story is a pack of lies! You've been humping an oar too long if you think all this is over a bunch of stolen whores. . . ."

"I disagree! All the really important wars have been over girls, have they not? Remember your Homer."

"The Romans have a story about how their ancestors stole women from their neighbors, the Sabines," Cleinias volunteered.

"Romans? Never heard of them."

"Oh shut up, Timon."

"Shut up yourself!"

"Oreus, punish him for me."

Cleinias' friend Oreus, who had the deck seat over Timon, slapped the latter on top of his head.

"On my father's name I swear you'll pay for that, Oreus . . . !"

"All of you, keep quiet down there!" growled the bosun, Stilbides, through the hatch in the topdeck.

"Just your fellow citizens discussing matters of state . . ." said Patronices.

"If I have to come down there, fellow citizen, you'll spend the next three months up to your balls in bilgewater!"

3.

It was the *Terror*'s turn on roving blockade the next day. After a four hour rest and a breakfast of tired, cankered onions, the crew was prepared to go out for a clockwise round. As they set oars to water, Xeuthes was surprised to hear Demosthenes request permission to come aboard.

"Thank you, Captain. . . ." the general said as he wove a zigzag course on the unstable deck. Xeuthes extended a hand to steady him.

"If you'll take my seat at the center, General, I think you'll be more comfortable."

"Of course," replied Demosthenes, who made his career campaigning overseas but resented every minute he was forced to spend afloat. He looked at Sphaerus, the old pilot, and inclined his head at him, but got no response as the old man stared ahead.

Xeuthes settled in a crouching position at the ladderway just above Stilbiades. For the next four hours, as the piper sounded a cruising cadence and the swallows bowed and flitted in the cliffs, he had an opportunity to inspect the general as the general inspected the island.

Demosthenes spared few words as they circled that blasted shore. Instead, his sharp-beaked, birdlike features seemed to respond to every cut and thrust of Sphacteria's profile. What he would never say, but what Xeuthes might have suspected, is that the disaster at Aetolia had taught the general how topography itself could be turned against him. Here, the island was a prison for the Lacedaemonians, but it was also a kind of fortress protecting them.

He scowled at the island's highest ground to the north—a gray eminence of bare, deeply incised stone, as high as the crag of old Pylos across the strait. The enemy, however numerous they were, would adopt that mount as their defensive stronghold. As the ship proceeded, there seemed precious few safe places to land troops: the shoreline was either too steep, or full of rocks worn by the swirling water into a riot of bowls, arches, ruts, and crags. The water seemed to leap out of the bay to lash the stone, traceries of silver-white filling the runnels in the backwash. Near the southeast flank the ground set down into a low, pebbly strand before sweeping up toward the flat-topped southern headland. That spot seemed a serviceable landing place, but as the island's only real beach it would undoubtedly be guarded, and require his men to clamber over the scree to reach the interior.

The *Terror* threaded through the strait between the big island and Little Sphacteria. The general perked up as a towering cleft appeared in the island's mass. It was not deep enough to count as a cavern, but it cut some distance inward, and the higher reaches of the cleft rose near to ground level above.

Demosthenes turned to Xeuthes for the first time in an hour. "If there's a way to reach the surface through there, we could land without being seen."

"The crews lie in that hollow to rest or make repairs," said Xeuthes. "I've looked at the roof of it myself—there doesn't seem to be any way up."

"Take me closer."

They were now pushing up the seaward side of the island. Prospects for a landing seemed even worse there, with swells from the Ionian Sea rolling in broadside against the rocks. The trireme rocked sickeningly from beam to beam, the leather oar sleeves of the lowest bank disappearing under the surface with each pitch. Xeuthes thought nothing of it, but Demosthenes had not been on open water since he first arrived at Pylos.

"If you focus your eyes on the horizon, sir, or on the island."

"Yes, Captain, I know. . . ."

His voice trailed off as he saw something appear on the heights. Following his gaze, Xeuthes saw what he did: a solitary figure standing above them, silhouetted against the ascending sun. He was carrying a spear and a shield, the insignia and the color of his cloak concealed in shadow. The face of the Lacedaemonian lookout was too far away to see, but Xeuthes could feel him staring down on the *Terror*, impassive, as stolidly immobile as a natural feature of the landscape.

"We see them like that sometimes," said Xeuthes. "They come out to eye us, those fearless Spartans— but never within bow range."

Demosthenes kept his eyes on the Lacedaemonian until he was hidden behind the brow of rising ground to the north.

"If you might, I'd like you to drop me off at the stockade before you make your second round."

4.

Spartan warriors were among the best amateur podiatrists in Greece. This was because, notwithstanding Napoleon's famous dictum, an army marched on its feet, not its stomach. Lacedaemonians therefore lavished a quantity of time on their soles and toes that was second only to that spent on their hair.

In this regard the topography of Sphacteria presented special problems. The Lacedaemonians had landed on the island with the bare minimum: spears, shields, and the clothes on their backs. The expectation had been that there would be plenty of time to supply them later. But when the Athenians turned the tables, the lack of certain equipment, such as nail files, became urgent. The island bristled with bramble fields and rocks that were either cracked or sculpted into razorlike corrugations. Slashed arches and bloody heels were epidemic; the irritation of broken, overgrown nails drove the soldiers to carve away at them with their sword points, causing as much damage as they relieved. Feet everywhere were caked with suppurating cuts that never had a chance to close; by night, their toes were covered with gnats that feasted on the blood.

The Lacedaemonians signaled their predicament by flashing messages on a polished shield to their superiors on the coast. Though little was getting through the Athenian blockade, Antalcidas pressed his brother to add a request for buskins. Epitadas refused; such a request would only disgrace him in the eyes of the generals. His estimate of Spartan empathy turned out to be dismally accurate: when the first helot swimmer got through from the mainland on the eighth day, he bore nothing—no food, no spare flints for fire-making—except a coded message. These dispatches, which looked like random marks at the edge of strips of parchment, were decoded by winding them around a wooden rod of a standard size. In this case Epitadas found the marks aligned into an aphorism: "Enemy skins make good buskins."

If it ever rained on Sphacteria, Antalcidas saw no evidence of it. Dry leaves shed like the molt of reptiles from buckthorn and cistus; the grasses growing between the eruptions of rock bristled like broom heads. The only tolerable opportunity to chew thyme leaves was just after dawn, when the proportion of dew and salt spray was on the sweeter side. There were brambles in the hollows, and arbutus on the heights, and pine trees where the soil would take them. Here and there were a few spiny, spindly oaks, but these were dwarfed by the constant wind and offered little shade. And everywhere wafted the tendrils of broken spiderwebs, finding their way inevitably into eyes and mouths and beards. The spiders themselves seemed to have decamped for better quarters.

There were 420 Lacedaemonians on the island, including more than 200 Spartiates and an equal number of Nigh-Dwellers chosen by lot from all the battalions of the army. Helot retainers came to attend the citizens. This temporary population of more than six hundred made their base at an ancient redoubt on the northern summit. The fort lay in a shambles, the outline of its square tower barely discernible, its blocks stacked nowhere higher than six courses. Once, in the time of warlords and charioteers, it must have

served as old King Nestor's outpost against pirates.
Now it barely cast a useful shadow.

There was a single source of water on Sphacteria,
down on the flats in the center of the island. With
the intervention of the Athenian fleet, Epitadas cut the
water ration by half, and then halved it again as the
surface of the water receded into the depths of the well.
The food situation was dire: with no grain getting
through and no significant game on the island, the
troops were reduced to throwing rocks at birds, or
scaling down the cliffs to collect eggs. The rocky soil
begrudged them only a few insects.

The extreme exposure of their position, on a sunblasted rock with no heavy timber available and little
soil to dig into, took its toll. A wet wind from the sea
beset them at night; Epitadas forbade the setting of
campfires lest the Athenians use them to guess their
numbers. The men were forced to take what shelter
they could on the lee sides of boulders, under shrubs,
or curled up in shallow nests with their cloaks thrown
over them. The sea spray reversed years of patient
work on the Spartiates' glossy locks, with the strands
becoming so caked with salt that they refused to take
the comb. The proud crimson of their uniforms began
to fade to mottled gray.

Antalcidas's thoughts were far from these priva-
tions as he stood his watch. For what was the Rearing,
after all, but to prepare him for just this situation? As
he faced west, he concentrated instead on the golden
lay of Andreia's glory around the horizon of their
bedclothes. Rising up next to her, he regarded the pool
of sweat in the cleft of her neck, and as he tasted it, the
scent of iris oil on her skin. From that close her laughter was an indistinct piping from far away. When he
opened his eyes he realized that the pipes were com-

ing from a trireme on patrol below him, and the taste
of salt on his tongue from the trail of perspiration over
his parted lips. The monotony of the siege had left
him more than typically ruminative for a Spartiate.

Most of the others assigned to the island were from
age-classes much younger than his thirty-eight years.
He knew many of them only by sight. The presence of
Frog, clopping around the stones with a ridiculous
pair of incised greaves, his beard neatly combed
down to conceal his grotesque necklessness, came as
an unwelcome surprise. Antalcidas, being constantly
aware of the delicacy of his position, couldn't afford
to betray his real opinion of his former packmate; instead, he stood on a bluff over the bay and shared
with him what in Sparta they called "intelligence,"
but other Greeks called "gossip." He learned that
Beast and Redhead were with King Agis in Attica,
hacking down orchards. Cheese had helped to found
the garrison city of Heraclea-in-Trachis, to assure
Peloponnesian control of the pass at Thermopylae.
Rehash fell near Naupactus in the battle with
Phormio's fleet, while Gylippus, whom Antalcidas
had once defeated at the Plane Stand, had distinguished himself on Zacynthus.

"And where have you been?" asked Frog, apparently unable to resist letting the superiority of his
mess membership show on his face.

"The Isthmus. The Megarid. Attica once, under
Archidamus. And you?"

"The Argolid and Lesbos. Tell me, Stone, what do
you think of serving under a younger man?"

This was not an innocent question. Looking
around, he noted that Frog asked it with no one else
in earshot.

"It is not for me to have an opinion."

"It is good that Epitadas invokes Enyalios," said the other, "though I wonder if it is adequate for the occasion."

Frog removed his cap, fiddled with the material, and set it back on his swelled head. His opinion of serving under Antalcidas' brother was clear enough: as his senior by one year, and one of the Spit Companions, he believed he deserved the command more than Epitadas. He continued, "Of course it is not your brother's fault we are trapped here. I have no use for rumors like that. But this matter of the invocation . . . it is most serious to get such things right."

At dawn on the third day of the siege Epitadas convened an assembly of all the Lacedaemonians on the island. The Athenians were bold when wet, he told them, but would never challenge the Lacedaemonians to a contest of virtue on land. Their best chance to prevail, then, was to outlast the enemy:

"Look around you!" he commanded. "Every inch of the coast, except for that little stretch near Koryphasion, is under our control. The Athenians can barely take their ships out of the water! They cannot resupply themselves from Messenia, which we own, so they must bring everything they need by sea. When foul weather comes they will have to withdraw—they cannot avoid it."

He paused to let this point sink in.

"I keep hearing talk of trying to escape by swimming to the bay. Let no one deny it—you have made it obvious! But these waters are not the Eurotas; the currents are swift. The shortest swim is across the channel at the north end, where the Athenians would await you on the beaches. To the south it is at least a mile to land. The enemy navy is keeping its closest watch on just that narrowest stretch, and while you might dog paddle with the best of the hounds, I have not heard yet of a man who could outswim a ship!

"The Athenians want us to panic. All we must do, though, is control this island until the fall storms come. That will be a matter of a few weeks . . . maybe less. Do you doubt that we can win a contest of endurance with the Athenians? Who is more prepared to live off the land than we are? It is our key advantage, that we are Lacedaemonians—the only advantage that we need, granted us in the wisdom of our elders. Go now! Stand your watches with every confidence that time is on our side! Let us prevail by being ourselves."

Epitadas gave daily speeches to fortify morale, but in Antalcidas' view all that was unnecessary. As the sun climbed up to banish the ground mist from their sleeping holes, the young citizens around him looked to their commander with an innocence that verged on the bovine. The notion that their elders had not anticipated everything was inconceivable to them. All except for Frog, that is—he did not rise to stand his post but stayed behind with a troubled look on his face. Antalcidas paused to hear what he had to say.

"Is something on your mind, elder?" Epitadas asked. He instilled the word "elder" with a certain mocking overemphasis.

"We'll need to do more than 'be ourselves' if they come after us with archers."

"They won't. They have few places to land, and they don't know our numbers. If we show ourselves all over the island, they'll think we have thousands."

"I understand that. But in case of something unexpected, would it not make sense to prepare some cover? Trenches on the fortress hill?"

Ill at ease, Epitadas shifted his eyes to Antalcidas.

Frog was also nervous: some of the younger troops were lingering to hear the exchange, and it was not thought honorable to question the commander's thinking so publicly.

"The soil is too thin for trenches," Antalcidas ventured.

"Yes, it is thin," agreed Epitadas. "And would we have Spartans cower in holes because of a few Athenians with bows? Your concern is worthwhile, *elder*, but it is a danger we need not face if we keep watch on the landing places."

Under the combined scrutiny of the two brothers and the gathering audience, Frog beat a tactical retreat. "Yes, of course! How wise. Mere worries should not distract us from a forward strategy."

With that, he turned and descended the hill with his greaves clanking. Epitadas stared after him, then cast an appreciative eye on Antalcidas. The latter held his gaze for a moment, then departed for his post on the west cliffs of the island. There would be time yet to grant that Frog had a point.

5.

The attendants of the Spartiates lacked the status of soldiers but bore some of the same responsibilities. After sleeping in cold, craggy holes beside their masters, they stood watches on windswept rocks. Their standard ration was one half a soldier's dole, which corresponded to expending half their effort to find berries and insects for the Equals. Although all helots were, by law, considered as much enemies of the Spartan state as the Athenians, their loyalty was expected. To discourage any possibility of revolt, their social intercourse was regulated, with congregations of more than two helots in any one place forbidden on pain of flogging.

Doulos had come to Antalcidas with no training as a shieldbearer. His tender hands and feet testified to a relatively soft existence on kitchen duty or prone on his master's bed—Antalcidas had never asked which. He was ignorant of how to handle the panoply. Antalcidas had to show him how to use the cords pegged to the reverse of the shield to sling it across his back. Doulos responded by clapping his hands in childish delight and exclaiming, "At last I appreciate the scenes on certain red-figure wares! Especially kraters and cups by masters like Psiax, Makron, Euphronios. Recall Menelaus and Hector fighting over the fallen body of Euphorbos—Achilles and Ajax taking their ease over the gaming table, the shields slung over their shoulders! The leave-taking of armed Memnon. Yes, thank you for teaching me this, my lord!"

"I showed you to save your strength on the march, you fool."

"Oh that—well of course. But a cramped arm is worth learning something about the noble arts of war, is it not?"

Antalcidas turned away with the requisite scorn. Inwardly, he was amused by the boy's combination of uselessness and expertise. Since the day he left the Rearing he had had trouble finding the will to put the lash to Doulos' back. The thought of how he had tormented helots in his youth caused Antalcidas to flush with regret.

Epitadas came to him after watching the discussion about the proper way to haul a shield. "The way your slave disputes with you," he said, "sets a bad example."

"He's my business," replied Antalcidas.

"Wrong, Brother. It's all my business now."

The next day was overcast, with a solid dome of clouds stretching from Mount Mathion in the east to the slate gray edge of the western horizon. The respite from the sun made the twin aches of hunger and thirst seem more manageable; the prospect of rainfall filled the garrison with a subtle excitement. Meanwhile, a storm far out at sea sent high swells barreling into the island's flank. To escape taking the waves broadside as they proceeded along the coast, the Athenians were forced to tack east and west. The pitching and rolling of their hulls was harrowing just to watch. When the Athenians tacked inshore, sentries standing downwind of them could detect the faint odor of vomit.

During daylight the Lacedaemonians did their best to keep hidden. Overt maneuvers were restricted to dawn and day's end, when the twilight hid their movements. On the ninth day of the blockade Antalcidas made his way at dusk to check their positions at the south end of the island. There he found the guard in that area, an under-thirty named Namertes, lying on his belly as he peered over the cliff's edge. Antalcidas crept around: the boy was looking straight down on an Athenian trireme resting in the calm water of a deep rift in the rock. Hacking up a gob of phlegm—the lack of fresh water made spitting a challenge—Namertes let the wad gather on his lower lip for a long moment, then let it drop on the deck below. It hit an Athenian bowman in the back of his neck. Reaching back to wipe it, the man gazed at the sky as if checking for rain.

Antalcidas cleared his throat. The young man leapt to attention.

"Excuse me, elder. I didn't hear you."

"Of course you didn't. You were busy."

Namertes blushed. "I was watching the enemy."

"Speak plainly, boy! You were insulting him, though without much effect. And what if their archers reply by putting a bolt through your eye?"

The other tossed his head as if to deny he could ever fall to something as womanly as an arrow. He was a handsome lad, with a firm, straight brow over deep-set eyes. The coating of dirt on the front of his tunic made him seem more the rambunctious school-boy than a soldier.

"I wanted to use something heavier, but I couldn't manage it alone," he said. He indicated a small boul-der at his side. It was roughly spherical, about three feet in diameter, resting in a notch less than two yards from the edge of the precipice. Antalcidas looked from the boulder to the ship and back again. The thing probably weighed as much as five men, and if it were pushed over the side would drop something like a hundred feet to the sea. The idea intrigued him.

"Who's your platoon leader, son?"

"Arcesus, son of Sphodrias."

"Of Amyclae?"

"Of Limnae."

"I see." Antalcidas dropped his shield and spear and threw the front of his cloak over his left shoulder. "Well, what are you waiting for? Are you going to help me?"

Namertes smiled. By rocking the boulder back and forth they muscled it out of its notch, but because of its irregular shape they had to struggle to get it to roll farther. Once they forced it free, the partners had to re-verse themselves to keep it from going over the side. When the rock was finally in position, Antalcidas wedged a flat stone behind it to stop it rolling back-ward. The trap was set now, a rude Sword of Damocles. Antalcidas peeked over the ledge at their target; the Athenian ship was backing water now, ready to resume its patrol. From the disposition of the figures on the top deck it seemed that they had neither seen nor heard the Lacedaemonians above them.

"Looks like we've lost our chance for now."

"They'll be back," said Namertes. "I've been here five straight days and they come here every morning—one ship or another."

"Then I will see you this time tomorrow."

Antalcidas retrieved his equipment and walked away. Namertes gazed after him with admiration, but wiped it off his face when the other suddenly turned.

"Do I have to remind you to keep this between us?"

Antalcidas, whose enemies needed little encouragement to call him "Stone" to his face, stared into the younger man's eyes.

"I'll say nothing," pledged Namertes.

6.

In the months since he left on campaign he hadn't thought much about home. He might have said it was because he was engrossed in fighting the war, but that would have been fooling himself. Demosthenes preferred not to think about Athens. He was visibly pained when her memory crossed his mind. To dwell on the place was to be reminded of what she had become over the course of seven disastrous years.

He had once owned a town house pleasantly situated on the Hill of the Nymphs. A lifetime before, when the wind was right, he could sit in his parlor, sip good wine from a silver cup, and listen to the tinkling of the cymbals at the still-uncompleted Sanctuary of Hephaestus. When he couldn't sleep, he need only

look out his window and be lulled by the dimming of
the cressets on the renovated Acropolis. On festival
days, after a morning at the theater watching some offering from Sophocles or Aristarchus or Ion, he would
round the sacred mount and stop in the marketplace
to check the catch of the day. Sometimes he would
pause, the fish under his arm, to laugh at a comic in-
terview between Socrates and some self-important big
dome. He was a nodding acquaintance of Pericles on
his rounds of the city, though it was always sad to see
the great man hounded by a train of unwashed, unemployed Furies, remonstrating with him as they
hinted that a three-obol loan would fill their bellies
nicely.

He would sometimes linger too long at these er-
rands, arriving home with the fish going stiff in its
sack. Ianthe would give it to him then, a bolt of black
hair loosed over her eye, wagging her head as she did
at his irresponsibility, to be wasting his time listening
to those fools downtown. Demosthenes smiled as he
did when she railed, taking her soft face in his hands
to cover it with kisses, and more kisses after that, until
she would look at him and ask if he'd been drinking.
He would exclaim, "Only the nectar of your gaze!"
The fish landed on the table, the lovers in their room.
Demosthenes' smile soured on his lips as he remembered that table where, come the plague, he was destined to sit by his dear, dead Ianthe, moving neither to
eat nor wash, for all the days it took to wring out the
last of his tears.

It was not the same city anymore. Thousands of the
displaced had set up shanties in the narrow area between the north and south long walls to Piraeus. Their
cooking fires sent up a haze of smoke that put the city
under a pall thicker than usual; the enormous pits

dug for their sewage overflowed with the winter
rains, spreading their filth and foul odor over the
roads. Other refugees found shelter where they could,
in doorways and porticoes, laid up with reeking blankets in the stoas. Panhandlers waited around every
corner, hands out, never sparing a harsh word for fellow citizens who hurried past, their heads buried in
their cloaks. Demosthenes had once ascended the
Acropolis to deposit a contract; on his way out, he
saw a man show his regard for Pericles by squatting
by his Maiden Temple, staining the freshly hewn marble with his shit.

Worse than this physical degradation was the
steady sapping of the people's spirit. By unspoken
mutual consent, the wars of the past had always been
quick affairs; even the Great Wars against the Persians
had been forced to a conclusion in only a few years.
Now, in the face of this endless conflict, faces everywhere were stricken, unable to believe what their eyes
told them. Lively public debate had been replaced
with the useless clash of irreconcilable dogmas. Make
peace! Stay the course! How dull it all was! The summer invasions had slipped Athens from her moorings,
cutting her off from the country around her, making
the city seem no more than a vessel adrift, shorn of its
oarbanks. To think that the rich used to scorn the simple Attic wines, the plain homegrown olives or figs
that were now such sentimental luxuries! Under the
circumstances, even the gods suffered: the loss of pil-
grims from half of Greece made for empty seats in the
theater during the Festival of Dionysus. Like many
others, he could hardly remember how the Eleusinian
Mysteries were conducted in peacetime, before the
Lacedaemonians cut the way to the sanctuary. Instead, celebrants had to content themselves with an

austere procession by sea, without the joy of the traditional roadside offerings and choruses. The unceasing obsession with security obliged the bodies of loved ones who died in summer—like his beloved Ianthe—to wander like shades in Hades. Instead of going to their rest, they were temporarily buried inside the walls, then exhumed and moved, half-corrupted, to the outside graveyards after the invaders were gone.

Despite himself, Demosthenes sat in his little command tent on the beach at Pylos and brooded over these things. He was encouraged now only by the possibility that the Lacedaemonians would understand that they must make terms to save their men on Sphacteria. He had seen some reason lately to believe they would send emissaries. First, although it was an exhausting task, the blockade was working—little more than the occasional swimmer was reaching the island. Quite a few of those had been picked up, lugging behind them such meager supplies as poppy seeds fixed in blocks of solid honey, or sacks of unshelled nuts. Others were found facedown in the bay, drowned. His spies in Messenia told him that the Peloponnesians on the mainland would not even launch their ships. This had forced the Spartans to offer freedom to any helot who reached the island with a boat; some of these might even have slipped through the screen at night or in foul weather. A few fishing boats were seen wrecked on the shore after thunderstorms. But these never seemed numerous enough to amount to a serious problem.

Second, word had arrived from home that the army of King Agis was rushing to Pylos. News that the annual invasion of Attica was abandoned after only two weeks must have been received with jubilation in the city. What other evidence was necessary to prove that the Spartans were worried? The troops on the island, after all, represented one tenth of their entire citizen army. While fools who knew nothing of war took the Lacedaemonians to be indomitable, Demosthenes knew firsthand how reluctant they were to sacrifice their precious Spartiates. The possibility that the Athenians' little stockade would become the nucleus of a new Messenian revolt must also have weighed on their enemies' minds. He could only hope that these developments would strengthen the hand of the peace faction over the warmongers in the Assembly. By seizing this insignificant piece of Messenia, the Athenians stood to force concessions from the enemy that a dozen naval victories couldn't achieve—if only they agreed to negotiate in good faith.

All uncertainty on this score was dispelled when Leochares brought him a letter from home. It was brought in by supply ship in the form of a short scroll. Demosthenes was about to break the seal when he looked up and saw Leochares was still standing there, his curiosity having overwhelmed his tact.

"I'll tell you what it says, my friend," the general said, "but for now let's observe the formalities."

Leochares blushed to his ears. "Yes, of course," he said, backing out. Demosthenes watched him go. This man, one of the best officers he had ever served with, had learned that both his elder brothers had been killed in the fighting, one off Sicily, the other in the Chalcidike. Since then his face had taken on that ashen cast often seen among the Athenians in those days. He performed his duties well, of course—but it was competence rooted in obligation, in the fact that there was little else he could do.

Demosthenes broke the seal and scanned the first lines of the letter:

To Demosthenes, son of Alcisthenes, citizen of the deme of Colonus Agoraeus, General-select of the Ægeides tribe, from his friend and colleague in the People's service, Cleon, son of Cleaenetus, felicities and greetings. The People rejoice at the news of your recent victory over the Spartans in Messenia. Please understand that this comes as no surprise to your friends here in the Assembly,· who have had nothing but the highest regard for your talents. . . .

Even without the salutation Demosthenes would have known the author was Cleon. Only the demagogue would arrogate upon himself the right to speak for "the People." The sole question in his mind was whether Cleon had the sophistication to draft his own letters: it was well known that he was the scion of a low-born family in the skinning trade. The fact that old Cleaenetus had made a lot of money as a tanner, and then discarded his former friends to consort exclusively with the nobles, only seemed to amplify his absurdity, like a manure carter who collected droppings from only the best homes. The son had at least charted his own course—Cleon was now a shit peddler of a different stripe, devoting his energy to flattering the scum and layabouts who dominated the Assembly.

We have learned further that your forces have trapped a large number of Spartiates on a mountain [sic]. This achievement greatly pleases the People, for it affords the opportunity now to exact terms from the enemy that are right and proportionate to their in-

*jury. And while we have every confidence that it is
not necessary to say so, we expect that you will not
fall prey to misplaced compassion, but allow the assault to proceed apace, so that the Lacedaemonians
will understand that time is not on their side. We
therefore write to you now with the understanding
that no unauthorized accommodations will be made
before the People have had their chance to dictate
terms. The Assembly expects that peace emissaries
with plenary powers will arrive in Athens as this letter reaches you. And so your friends bid you continued good fortune in your campaigns, and that you
will continue to prove ever a faithful servant of the
public good, as those who await your return endeavor
themselves, until victory crowns the efforts of all of
us who keep the People's trust. . . .*

Demosthenes threw the scroll across the tent. The
People's trustkeeper, it seemed, had decided to "dictate" terms that were "right and proportionate to their
injury." Would that "the People" have understood the
true precariousness of their position! The wind-lashed
ramparts of the island prevented a landing in force in
all but a few easily guarded places. To attack with infantry, on ground covered with thickets, against an
enemy who undoubtedly knew the field better than
anyone, would risk having his troops scattered and
annihilated. And while he could maintain the blockade for the present, his long supply line back to Piraeus would be cut with the arrival of the fall storms.
By then the fleet would have to leave, whether the
Sphacteria garrison had surrendered or not. These
were facts even a tanner's son should have been able
to grasp.

The letter had unrolled flat in its flight across the

tent. Retrieving it, Demosthenes saw it had a post-script:

> *P.S. As we are most interested in assuring solidarity with our friend Demosthenes, we have instructed the courier to delay his return to await his answer to our message.*

So much for the People's confidence in him! Rolling up the scroll, he called for Leochares. The latter stuck in his head with scarcely a moment's delay.

"Yes?"

"Tell the guards I'll see the Spartan emissaries now. And tell the steward to bring a wine jug—the good Chian white, perhaps—and three cups."

"Yes, sir!"

Back at his desk, Demosthenes searched for his stylus under the mountain of tablets and dispatches. As a third of his mind cursed his disorder, and a second third Cleon's presumption, the remainder was busy composing his response:

> *Greetings to Cleon, son of Cleaenetus, from Demosthenes of Colonus. Only now being in receipt of your most recent letter, I must first express my thanks for your confidence in my modest efforts in Messenia. As you must know, there is none among us who would rather see the Lacedaemonians defeated unconditionally. I must report, however, that the military situation here has already obligated me to conclude a truce with the enemy that is, of course, on the most favorable terms to Athens. If you will indulge me, I will explain the tactical problems that led me to believe that a cease-fire will be in our long-term interests. . . .*

7.

The next day the sea was too high for the Athenian ships to rest in the cleft. For three days after that Namertes was assigned elsewhere; since Antalcidas couldn't budge the stone by himself, their attack would have to wait. It wasn't until the fifth day, with the wind blowing from the east, under a sky filled with plump clouds in slowly drifting archipelagoes, that conditions seemed right for the attack.

He found Namertes in the same posture as before, peeping down on the Athenians. When the younger man heard him come up he greeted him in a loud voice, prompting Antalcidas to silence him abruptly. There was no way to know how much the enemy could hear from below.

Antalcidas looked down: the lithe vessel had only just cocked her oars, the oblong blades alive with the glint of shedding droplets. The peculiar pattern of the current in that spot made the cleft a perfect vortex, holding the hull in a state of almost imperceptible rotation. Just then the bow turned through the imaginary bull's eye where the boulder would strike the water. Antalcidas summoned Namertes to take his position behind the rock; in a few moments the stern would come around and they must be ready. The time passed reluctantly, and Antalcidas thought what a miserable kind of warfare this was, to hide and watch the unsuspecting movements of men doomed to die. It was not out of pity for the Athenians that he thought this—a Spartiate could feel no sadness for the enemy archers carousing there, laughing, passing a

canteen of water between them in what they believed
to be a moment of peace. Nor could he feel much empathy for the helmsman, an ancient man with a pate
flecked with the liver spots, as he released his oar to
spread sweat over his scalp with a slow, spiraling
movement of his hand. Antalcidas was restive, instead, because he was a mere man in a position that
was proper only to the immortal Fates. Such presumption was ruinous to the order of the world. Yet to
forsake an opportunity to kill his adversaries, while
they were in Lacedaemonian territory, was just as
surely a sin against his ancestors. There was nothing
else he could do.

He braced himself behind the boulder, envisioning
the turning of the ship in the water. Locking eyes with
Namertes, he pushed forward to relieve the weight on
the braking stone, then kicked it away. The whole
mass of the boulder was bearing down on them now.
Antalcidas, his heart leaping in his chest, squared his
shoulders and drove toward the cliff.

"Now, boy! Push!"

The rock seemed to have settled in that precarious
spot, stuck as if glued there, but after they managed to
roll it the last few inches to the edge, it seemed to
shoot out of their hands. Antalcidas fell forward with
his own momentum; he saw the boulder tumble over
as it fell, revealing more of the Athenian deck as it receded. In the instant before it hit he didn't think to
notice who was standing under it, but only lay gri-
macing, his gut filled with disgust and suspense.

Their aim was perfect: the rock's arcing path took it
down amidships, to strike the body of the trireme not
with a crash, but with a discrete, hollow sound, like
the slamming of a door on an empty room. The ship
recoiled on itself just before the first screams went up.

It reminded Antalcidas of what a man's body did when he took a spear on the run, the point sinking straight through to his spine.

The aftermath was like the frenzy of a disturbed anthill. The Athenians scrambled as if they were not sure where the blow had come from. The old helmsman, who wasn't injured, swore before the gods that they had not run aground, as the oars lost all semblance of order, falling across each other as their operators struggled to flee the ship. It seemed as if no one was in charge; some men were diving into the water to save their lives, others falling as the top deck pitched in the chaos. Antalcidas and Namertes had no need to hide themselves because no one thought to look up.

Before long the ship began to sink. Swells broke over the wales, forcing the last of the topsiders into the water. The shoreline in that area was pitted but sheer, leaving them no place to swim for refuge. The survivors, who seemed to number more than a hundred, clung around the waterlogged hull on broken strakes, oars, and each other. It would have been easy to kill a few more of them with another rock, but there were no more sizable ones at hand. Antalcidas noticed that several other Lacedaemonians were watching the commotion from a vantage up the coast.

Namertes nudged him and pointed south: a second Athenian vessel was rounding the point. As it came closer, Antalcidas saw that the archers on that ship were looking right at him, arrows slung in their bows. A grayheaded figure whom he took to be the captain was standing on the bow, his hands cupped to his mouth.

"This is Xeuthes of the *Terror*! Who is that?"

"Isocrates of the *Sounion*," replied a voice from the water. "Our keel is broken, *Terror*!"

"So I see. You are still in danger."

Xeuthes pointed to the top of the cliff. A hundred pairs of eyes turned up at Antalcidas and Namertes, who reflexively withdrew. As they struck inland they heard a few desultory bow shots from the *Terror* fall around them, striking sparks as they hit the rocks. This was the first time Antalcidas saw the Athenians waste arrows in this way.

The two men separated on the high ground along the spine of the island, clasping hands but not looking into each other's eyes. They never indulged in whoops of triumph; they never exchanged congratulations. Their attack evidenced more cleverness than virtue, and was by their mutual reckoning only marginally honorable. The whole regrettable business was the Athenians' fault, Antalcidas told himself, because they had been so foolish to place themselves in danger. Though they were on a small island, he hoped never to see Namertes again.

The unapproachable shore prevented the Lacedaemonians from seizing the waterlogged hulk as a prize. Instead, after a transport ship arrived to rescue the crew, Xeuthes had a bowline rigged to tow the *Sounion* into the prevailing northerly current. The garrison watched as the *Terror* labored nearly the entire length of Sphacteria, not reaching the Sikia Channel until the sun sank into the sea. It hardly seemed possible that the enemy would refloat the wreck. Then again, they would need all their ships to defend their position and keep up the blockade. If nothing else, these Athenians had proved themselves a tireless people.

Antalcidas reached the summit fort just in time to

hear Frog speaking. Long before he could make out his words he could discern his tone: mocking. His brother was listening to him but not responding, his eyes turned away to face the dying day. The rest of the garrison was spread over the slope, clearly as uncomfortable with the argument as children before their bickering parents.

"So *this* is your victor's strategy, Epitadas? Spartiates reduced to behaving like Arcadian hillmen, toppling rocks on people? My, my, what would Leonidas have accomplished at Thermopylae if he'd just rolled a few stones! I guess both you and your brother are just chips off the old block!"

"How do you know it was Antalcidas?" Doulos demanded. "What proof do you present?"

Hand on his sword hilt, Frog gaped in the direction of the helot as if a worm or a weed had spoken. Then he turned back to Epitadas.

"We may well ask whether you have control over your brother. After all, he is the elder between you!"

"No one controls me!" Antalcidas declared. "And I affirm before the gods that the attack was mine alone. My brother had nothing to do with it."

This admission caused a pained expression to wash over Epitadas' face. Frog smiled.

"There was never any doubt of that, *Stone*."

Antalcidas loomed over him. "Would you care to see my skill with the sword?"

The other turned to face him. A rare moment followed—one that was not lived like most others, with the next moment much like the last, but where a thousand possible fates ramified from the smallest choice. Antalcidas slipped his sword from its sheath.

Epitadas rushed in to interpose himself between them. "How happy the Athenians would be, to see

Spartiates quarreling like their democratic rabble! Both of you, stand down."

"Yes, stand down, Antalcidas!" cried Frog. "Can't you see that your little brother will always defend your dishonor for you?"

He opened his mouth to reply, but Epitadas broke in first, saying, "Dishonor? Not at all! Our duty is to kill the enemy—Antalcidas killed them. There is nothing for him to defend."

Frog scowled and spat at his feet. Antalcidas waited until he turned away to replace his sword. Epitadas ignored Frog and watched his brother; there was a commander's fixity in his eyes, a determination to fight by his side if necessary. But not far beneath it was a plaintive, almost womanish hurt—the question, *why do you test me this way?* Antalcidas felt compelled to explain himself.

"Brother, I . . ."

"No need!" Epitadas cut in. "I suppose we know now why they discourage relatives from serving together. Our ancestors were wise."

He found Doulos preparing his sleeping hole for the night—removing stray burrs and rocks, laying down his chiton as a liner. Antalcidas dropped his shield at the helot's feet.

"Frog would have been within his rights to run you through, the way you disrespected him."

"So be it," said Doulos. "I recall my Ibycus: 'An argument needs no reason, nor does a friendship.' "

"If you must. But remember, our enemies have friends of their own."

The dispute between Epitadas and Frog left an ugly cloud over the island. There was little chatter as the men gathered in their hillside rookery to comb their hair and bind their lacerated feet with strips of fabric blackened with old blood. Lacedaemonians were used to short campaigns and clear lines of command—circumstances that were not in evidence as the siege wore on. But just before the day ended, as the last rays of the sun reddened the highlands, the mainland army flashed a message across the bay. The Spartiates gathered on the summit to read the news.

A truce had been negotiated with the Athenians. The next day, a Peloponnesian ship would arrive to feed the garrison.

V
She-of-the-Tapering-Ankles

1.

He guarded his target with a militant ardor. As the helot paced his little patch of earth Epitadas lay watching, drinking in every detail of the way he moved. He chose him like an admirer would, as the most appealing of his type, and having marked him he would allow no one else to encroach. One day, as the helot stripped his clothes to haul a large stone from the path of his plow blade, Epitadas spied another young member of the Hidden Service crouching behind a hedge of wild plane. He allowed the newcomer to stay for the show—the sweat of honest labor, the pursing of buttocks, the unfurling of magnificent muscles—but after the helot removed the stone Epitadas ejected his rival with a whistle and a jerk of his head. The other turned in his direction with the promise of challenge in his eyes, but when he saw who claimed this helot, his resistance died. He slunk away. Epitadas, meanwhile, found a way to creep still closer, his eyes full of lust for the culmination that must come.

If the helot had been of any other race he would have been handsome. The brow was high and straight, undergirded by a fine, chiseled ridge that, in turn, sheltered eyes that twinkled through its shadow. Long hair was denied his class, but what remained was black and glossy with the humors of genuine, unwashed poverty. His short beard was as red as a freshly quenched blade in the armorer's shop. Yet what was most impressive of all about him was his confidence: everything he did, from handling his plow ox to planting a hand on his wife's wide rump, was done with the grace of effortless virility. He stooped when Spartiates were near, of course, eyes downcast, denying the mark of his natural aristocracy. But Epitadas saw what happened after, when the Spartiates were gone and the helot unreeled his spine to its superior height. He would have towered over his masters.

The helots had learned from bitter experience that the Hidden Service struck mainly at night. They therefore avoided the dark, and if forced to travel, went around in groups. Paths through forest were absolutely shunned; stockpens were abandoned to jackals and children undergoing the Rearing. Epitadas would therefore need some luck and a lot of patience to take his prey.

In the long hours of waiting Epitadas worked himself into a lather of indignation at the presumption of the helots. As descendants of Herakles, the Spartiates had always owned Laconia by birthright. This right had been contravened for centuries as his ancestors wandered the north, but now they had returned for good. Every hour this helot, this detested descendant of a race of squatters, strode those furrows constituted an affront to his blood overlordship. This was a claim that transcended mere legality—it was divinely sanctioned and was its own justification for everything that must follow. That the helots were permitted to be useful to the Lacedaemonians was a conditional privilege whose alternatives were dispossession or, if necessary, annihilation. How this tall helot had the temerity to thrive on his plot of borrowed land was a conundrum only the gods were sufficient to unravel. In the meantime, Epitadas was obliged to carry on the war.

The helot youngsters, less careful, were easier to put under the knife. He knew one man, a highly respected Spartiate on the brink of election to the Gerousia, who specialized in killing children. Epitadas did not exactly disapprove of this practice: in this generational struggle, a dead boy was as good as a dead warrior. Those with their hearts in the right place must be excused their enthusiasm. For his part, Epitadas had many opportunities to take the youngest son of the farmer he coveted. The boy, who was as thin and downy as a yearling swan, was kept home long after the age when the Lacedaemonian masters went to the Rearing. The helots, in their moral squalor, did not understand that boys must be parented by the city. They were also ignorant of the importance of older men's intimacy. The boy belonged solely to his parents, beloved, stroked, cooed at to a sickening extreme.

On the son's eighth birthday his father gave him a ewe to tend. In the stubble of the fields he would drive the sheep back and forth with a little ashwood stick, tapping her lightly on the flanks as his father had taught him, never straying far from the house. The ewe bleated, ears twitching, whites showing around the barred slits of its eyes. Epitadas could have taken the boy on any of a dozen occasions when his mother, standing at the window, shifted her attention to her housework.

But the taking of small children held no interest. Those who knew Epitadas knew his defining quality to be *impatience*—he was in a hurry to achieve the destiny envisioned for him. In this regard he saw no impropriety in the way his mother had provisioned him during the Rearing: she was only speeding him toward the success he would have taken for himself. Other mothers fed their children too, but none of his rivals had grown so strong, so quickly. Should a colt destined to take the olive wreath be forced to grow on inferior fodder?

The night came when the boy left his pet tied outside. Epitadas descended from the hillside, sensing an opportunity. He was not alone: the single wolf was visible by its eyeshine, crouching behind the rungs of the drying rack. The ewe, perceiving the threat, jerked its tether. Her bell sounded in a way the helots understood. Epitadas heard a commotion within the house, saw the door open, and the lank figure of the father framed against the glow of the hearth fire.

Men's eyes also shine when they observe a lighted place from a dark one—Spartiates were taught to conceal this by focusing their gaze on a point slightly away from their object. The helot strode into the yard grasping a flaming brand, his pace slowing as he searched the dark. Epitadas watched sidelong with wide, unwavering eyes, his black pupils reflecting nothing. The ewe lowed; nearby, a lazy blink briefly eclipsed the blazing stars of the wolf.

The ethos of the Hidden Service called for using the smallest, dullest knife that would do the job. Epitadas liked to think he outdid the others with a weapon that was a piece of shop discard, an iron prong no more substantial than a belt buckle. From behind, it entered the helot's neck with a slapping sound, followed by a wet, farting exhalation as he drew the thing across the windpipe. Epitadas had to reach up to make the kill;

he laid the helot on the ground with the satisfaction of
rendering him not so tall after all.

He would be long gone when the men of the village
found the body. As he ascended the hill, with his
brother the wolf bounding not far behind, the cries of
the helot women would waft up behind him like
plumes of curing smoke from a very good hunt.

2.

In the opening year of the war, six campaign seasons
before the siege of Sphacteria, the Dog Tail Battalion,
having suffered no combat casualties, returned from
the first invasion of Attica. The only deaths were by
misadventure: a Nigh-Dweller was crushed under an
apple tree he had cut down with too much zeal, and a
low-caste Spartiate, relegated to the shame of riding
with the cavalry, fell from his mount onto a fence of
sharpened logs. Though King Archidamos proceeded
slowly, making clear his army's position each day, the
Athenians stayed snug inside their fortifications and
would not fight. As the season wore on, the king had
the Lacedaemonians march under the Long Walls
with their heads exposed, spears on their shoulders,
shields lowered. The guards on the Athenian ramparts, selected by Pericles himself for their coolhead-
edness, looked down on this challenge with perfect
equanimity, as if observing a migration of sea turtles.
The monotony of a whole season consumed by burning fields and felling trees left the Lacedaemonians
desperate to risk their lives in battle.

Antalcidas was thirty-two years old when he at last
contemplated taking a wife, but he seemed younger.
He was then part of a dwindling cohort of unmarried
males over thirty. Zeuxippos, who was by then too

frail for anything but giving advice, reminded him that his responsibility lay in taking on a young protégé of his own. As his hair grew out and the lines on his face deepened, Antalcidas became an object for furtive glances from the new propaides, who leaned to their fellows to inquire what mess he attended. But he never felt up to the task of mentoring. By his own reckoning, he had yet barely proved himself on the battlefield, while knowledge of the helot blood in his veins did nothing for his self-confidence. To be exposed for a fraud would dishonor not only himself, but anyone he took under his wing.

Something similar applied to the prospect of his marriage. Damatria did what her station demanded, sending his way the daughters of Spartiates who would think well of attaching them to the largest estate in Laconia. Ever gallant, he entertained these women, though they all left him cold.

"What was wrong with gentle Elephantis," his mother asked him in a letter cut in wax, "that you would treat her with such little regard? I thought her teats worth the liability of her face. And think of the expense you'd save on a wet nurse . . . !"

Grinding his teeth, he rubbed out her message and sent the tablet back without inscribing a reply.

On those occasions when he was in the city he found his thoughts going back half a lifetime, to the girl in the chorus at the Harvest Festival. Sparta was not a big place—in time nearly every face became familiar in form if not by name. Yet in all those years he never saw her. Was it a peculiar kind of fate that kept them strangers? Or was she outwardly so changed by the intervening time that he had seen her already, but not recognized her? He was not under the impression girls changed that much in their maidenhood—or did they? Was she married? Honored in death from child-bearing? A figment lasting only a day in the spell of his devotional enthusiasm? These thoughts occurred to him.

And then, just when he had stopped looking for her, they met on the path between the villages of Mesoa and Pitana. It was early in the new year, just after the Festival of the Unmarrieds, when bachelors like himself did penance for their childlessness by performing choral dances in the freezing marketplace. After, with the sun showing weakly through the trembling poplars, reefs of dark cloud fled over the olive terraces to drop their burdens of snow on the mountainsides. He was concealed from the chin down by the military cloak wrapped around his body and she with her himation fashioned into a hood to cover her ears. Still, a look of recognition came over both as they approached each other.

"So there you are," she said, matter-of-factly.

Though Antalcidas knew exactly who she was, he was momentarily embarrassed by the force of his own reaction. He nodded his head in mute denial.

"No? Forgive me then, elder. . . ."

He searched her face as she moved to pass him by. The years had drawn her face longer, with care lines parenthesizing her eyes. She was still fair, but the sweep of hair beneath her hood had turned amber as she passed into mature adulthood. Yet this was undeniably the same face that lived in his memory—the same eyes, wide-set around the same thin, straight nose, the painted lips above a chin whose upper line bowed oddly, like a shallow omega. Her eyebrows were neatly plucked lines as liquidly expressive as the ripples on a pond. As she slipped past, the end of her left brow seemed to meander, dangling and inquiring, above the corner of her eye.

"Wait," he said, suddenly afraid he would lose her again. "What's your name?"

"What an impertinent question! Have you told me yours, Antalcidas?"

Too distracted to take her joke, he stood with his mouth open. She read his lapse as if he had taken affront. Leaning forward, she laid a reassuring hand on his elbow as she said, "Andreia, of Pitana." Her voice was pitched girlishly high, but rang like a well-cast bell; the slight pressure of her breath stirred his beard hairs as if a sparrow had flown under his chin.

"Of course I know your name," she continued. "You are Antalcidas, son of Molobrus and Damatria, also known as Stone, one-time eromenos of Zeuxippos the Ephor. You testified against Thibron in the trial that led to his exile—out of jealousy according to some, for the sake of the truth according to others. Your first action was in Sciritis, where you charged alone against a gang of Arcadian slingers. After you set the Arcadians to flight, you let your leader, Praxitas, steal the glory of your victory, but no one believes him now. Today you command a platoon in the Dog Tail Battalion. You have a strong javelin throw and fair skill with the sword. But you truly excel with the spear."

She looked at him with obvious self-satisfaction. "How do I know all this? If you men only knew! We girls know everything about the city's warriors. Lots and lots of details about every one of you!"

Confounded, he could think of nothing more to do except to point his chin ahead. "I am going to Mesoa."

"Extraordinary news! Good day, then."

"Good day."

She seemed to take a perverse pleasure in the awkwardness of their parting, as if it had gone exactly as she had imagined it would. Antalcidas walked on, not quite sure if he had enjoyed the encounter. Into his head rushed all the things he might have said to her instead; it occurred to him that he had appeared the fool, and that he might never redeem himself. He must ask Doulos for advice on what to say to women. Some Greeks had made studies of such matters.

In the next days he found many more occasions to walk between Mesoa and Pitana. As Andreia did not appear, he was left to the kind of thoughts that often preoccupy young men in his position: imagining what his life would be like with this particular woman at his side. The images were trivial and profound, and came hurtling upon each other. In the Kynosoura house, he stares at her at her reading, the end of her tongue showing as she concentrates; their arms brushing as they walk, they promenade into the market with smiles on their faces, well aware of the other Spartiates staring; after she is *here,* retying her girdle with fingers sticky from pomegranate juice, she is *there,* writhing in the pool of her own water as she delivers him a purple, pucker-lipped infant.

He was activated three days later, when half his battalion was garrisoned in Corinthia to dissuade the Athenians from mischief on the Isthmus. In the spring the troops returned to Laconia for only a short time before the summer invasion of Attica was to be launched. These periods of idleness when he was neither training nor on campaign wore heavily on him. Apart from his board with the Hill Wolves, he was mostly alone because he had cultivated no genuine friends in the city. He was too proud to see his mother because of her disrespect, yet too insecure in his ori-

gins to mix easily with anyone else. If his loneliness
did not kill him, he reasoned, it would only make him
stronger.

In the spring the verges grew wildflowers, the air
so redolent with the scent of violets that Persephone
would have blanched. He was on the Pitana road
again, but walked in such a state of perfumed distrac-
tion that he forgot to expect Andreia. She was almost
upon him when he recognized her. This time she was
bareheaded and wore a short tunic that showed her
arms and legs—the limbs he had once watched, fretting with lust, as they bent in tribute to Phoebus. So
busy was he in staring at these tapering stems that he
made no greeting.

Her eyebrow afloat, she said, "I see you're on your
way to Mesoa again."

Antalcidas looked up to reply, but his tongue could
only flop in his mouth like a landed fish. Now that she
was hoodless, he saw that she had the long hair of an
unmarried woman.

As if reading his thoughts, she reached up to twist
the blond ends around her finger.

"Shall we walk for a while?" she asked. Hollowed
by disappointment, an endless expanse of black broth
and inanity stretching before him, he could only nod
and follow her.

3.

They took one of the cart roads toward the foothills of
Taygetus, picking their way around the wheel ruts.
On the estates around them the helot sharecroppers
tramped behind their plows, drove their wains of manure, or stood curious, swabbing their foreheads as
they regarded the odd pair walking west from the city.

Unlike in certain other parts of Greece, strolling was not a typical pastime in Laconia.

Andreia was indeed unmarried. Her mother had died trying to give her husband a second son. Her father, Ramphias, son of Clearidas, was only a few years older than Antalcidas, but had already risen to the position of Spartiate judge on the Nigh-Dweller island of Cythera, off Laconia's south coast. He had gone there at the beginning of the new year, and would stay until the next. In a tone more rueful than self-pitying, she granted that she walked a lot because Pitana was full of Ramphias' relatives, some of whom claimed the right to keep watch over her. Certain others, including some of the males, asserted rights even more presumptuous.

"All that would be more bearable if Sparta offered any diversion at all," she said.

"There are festivals," he replied. "There are parades."

"Oh yes, we Lacedaemonians love our parades! It seems we are always either preparing to march, marching, or returning home from a march, year in and year out. And we never find it tiresome, do we?"

This struck Antalcidas as a strange thing for the daughter of a prominent Spartiate to say. Reading him, she explained that while she had the typical upbringing of a Spartan girl, her tastes were corrupted by her father's Athenian guest-friend, who often came to Laconia on state business. During those visits he would describe to her the charms of his native city.

"The music! The paintings! The drama! When he invited us to travel back with him, I longed to go, but my father took my eldest brother instead. When he returned, do you think he described one temple to me, or a single sculpture? No—his only response was to sneer, and tell me that I was fortunate not to go, because Spartan ways are best!"

"They are," he said.

"But of course . . . it goes without saying. So why say it? Why should our superiority drive us to sneer and not to understand? Why are we so content to be so ignorant?"

Such confusion! Looking at her, Antalcidas believed he could perceive her sickness of spirit in those tremulous features, that threadbare beauty that seemed barely to cover her mortal bones. She shared with sophists and children the fault of posing too many questions. Insofar as doubt was the undoing of man, she was dying as surely as any hoplite facedown on the battlefield. And yet . . . what would so utterly disqualify the woman in the eyes of most eligible Spartiates filled him with a powerful impulse to save her. To that end—as much as his lust—he followed as the conversation waned and they passed on to roads that narrowed to tracks, and then to mere paths sloping up between stands of arbutus and pine. Goats milled under the boughs, either flicking their ears in idle contentment or rearing up on their hind legs to reach the spring buds. They turned to the intruders, with eyes as opaque as pans of milk, staring as if whatever might happen held no significance, something common in the world, and therefore innocent in its inevitability. He would kiss her and yes, they would commence their sorrow. A love, like any other new bud, to unfurl and be nipped.

Her lips were softer than her face promised. Nothing was angular about them, nothing hard beyond but the teeth that opened to reveal what he did not yet know how to fill. With his nostrils at her cheek, he smelled iris; with the passage of what could have been hours, he opened one eye and saw a honeyed emerald peeping back. Her lips pulled into a smile.

Out of curiosity, he had kissed some of the women his mother had delivered to him. After a handful of these experiences he presumed that he had mastered the skill; it struck him as marginally of interest, more appealing in the anticipation than the doing. Yet with Andreia he realized he knew nothing. A kiss, he learned, could become like drinking seawater, each drop urging the consumption of another. What had barely seemed consequential before now seemed to have a deep, indescribable meaning. He meant to ask her what she was smiling about, but found his mind emptied by the prospect of tasting the neck she presented to him. When they pulled apart an amount of time had vanished that he was not aware; they were standing in a spot a hundred feet from where they had begun, the dirt in between marked by the course of their footprints spiraling around each other.

They were fortunate not to be seen. The theory in Laconia was that familiarity breeds contempt, and contempt sickly children, so the bride and bridegroom in a Lacedaemonian marriage were not supposed to be acquainted. The Spartan male's most important spouse, the one to which he gave the first thirty years of his life, was the state. The betrayal of this matron was necessary to propagate the citizenry, but was not to be taken lightly.

Until her father returned no formal arrangments were possible. Over the next months he and Andreia were obliged to be discreet, stealing time together in his empty farmhouse. Dramatic, she dropped her clothes on the beaten floor and stepped free like Aphrodite striding from the surf. She was pale and thin for a Laconian girl, with the breasts of an adolescent, but when he took her in his arms her forehead rested flush into the crook of his neck, and his fingers precisely encompassed the angles of her shoulder blades. Smelling her, he felt a sensation within like a sweetness on his tongue that could never melt, the dripping of a fluidity into his core—impressions, he had to grant, that bore advantages over lying with old Zeuxippos.

She stripped him with impatience and swung astride, raking his chest with dirt-flecked nails and an expression of feline voracity on her face. He watched her with her eyes screwed shut, face turned up, away, anywhere but facing him. It struck him that giving this performance was somehow more comfortable for her than the act of looking into his eyes. When she was done, which was often before he was, she took the reclining posture of a symposiast and tried to ensnare him in discussions of politics and philosophy.

"You have been farther abroad than me, so please tell me—for what are the ways of the Spartans?"

Having been prepared for this question during the Rearing, he replied with all the confidence of the best student in the class: "Freedom, of course. And joy."

She laughed. "You recite that as if the boy-herd taught it to you!"

"He did. What of it?"

"What of it, dear Antalcidas?" she exclaimed, then kissed every one of the knuckles on his right hand before she added, "Look at us here, hiding in this house. Are we free?"

"We are, in the ways that are proper to mortals."

She shook her head as if bidding him to explain. For anyone else, he wouldn't have tried.

"For those as imperfect as men, there is only a choice of miseries. But so far as it takes nothing to excess, the Lacedaemonian system is the envy of all the Greeks. Our aristocracy has stood for a thousand years without tending to tyranny. Every one of our citizens may vote in the Assembly; anyone can become an ephor or earn a place on the Gerousia. What, then, can the rantings of democrats teach us? All states will pass away in their time—some sooner than others. But I promise you that men will always look back on the Spartan constitution with wonder."

She was looking at him agape. It was the longest contiguous string of words he had yet produced in her presence.

"The one you should speak to is Doulos. . . ." he concluded. "The boy is very content to waste his time in debate."

She laughed. "Doulos, your helot? I wonder what freedom he claims."

"Is it so bad to have his fate? What helot ever starved, or was ever denied mastery over his own house?"

"You seem so confident you know what the helots want!"

"Why didn't your father take you with him to Cythera?" he asked, bidding against hope to change the subject.

She sat up, grasping her knees against her chest. "I don't know . . . except maybe that he never trusted a Nigh-Dweller in his life. He probably believed there was no more wholesome place for me than here. . . ."

As if to add perversity to irony, she ran her fingertips up the inside thigh of her lover-not-her-husband.

"You sound alike, you and my father. So certain of yourselves, when you've seen nothing else of the world!"

"And your precious Athenians, with their mobs

and demagogues. Is that what you want to praise?
Come, be plain!"

Standing, he pulled her to her feet and into his
arms. Electing to be languid again, she let her head
fall to the right and exposed her neck. Antalcidas
jerked her back to attention; meeting his eyes for only
an instant, she slid off to the left. He pushed her back
to front and center—face to face at last, she stared at
him with an expression of gathering fright.

"What is it?" he asked.

She shuddered, jumped up, and ran from the room
without pausing to retrieve her clothes. He went to
the door to watch her go: stitchless, she walked down
the road, straight toward an old man in a hay cart. As
Andreia threw back her shoulders in determined non-
chalance, the old man did not turn his head at first,
waiting until she was past to take in the view of what
followed.

4.

Mystified by her behavior, he made no move in the
next few days to find her. After that he was in the field
training for a week, preparing for the next invasion of
Attica under King Archidamus. Experts from Syracuse were brought in to demonstrate the craft of sapping fortifications. The Lacedaemonian army was
brought up by battalions to watch the Syracusans un-
dermine a makeshift wall erected out of old ashlar
blocks. Though their techniques worked well enough,
the mood in the ranks was contemptuous. Digging in
the dirt was for slaves and barbarians. Nor did the
Syracusans show how they might bring down Athens'
Long Walls with the enemy raining arrows down on
the sappers.

When he returned, his idle time wore heavier on his hands than ever. The table conversation among the Hill Wolves struck him as more than typically inane—it centered not on whether Athens would be defeated, but how long it would take. The diners reasoned that if the enemy wanted to stay inside their walls it was a sign that they were desperate. It was further held that if the Athenians came out to fight it was also evidence of desperation. Antalcidas thought that even in Lacedaemon there must be some rule against accepting two mutually exclusive propositions at the same time. Or was he infected by Doulos, prattling on about the sophists and their logic?

Andreia was waiting for him in the farmhouse. When he took her, she seemed to go to pieces in his arms, this part shaking with desire, that aquiver with loathing. He tried to soothe her by stroking her cheek like Zeuxippos had once done for him, when he was despondent for losing a footrace. But this tenderness only unnerved her further. "Don't do that!" she cried. "Don't ever do that!" Then she retreated to the far corner of the room to bury her face in her hands.

How to question a woman about her feelings was not part of the kit of Spartan manly virtues. Antalcidas did his best, though, by declining to give up on her. Taking her upset to be like an elusive sort of animal, he decided to wait until it broke cover. The vigil went on and on—she did not look up until the turtle-doves fell silent in the eaves and the bats began to stir. When she spoke her voice was calm, as if she had been marshaling her words for a long time.

"I don't know why you must look at me like that."

"Like what?" he asked.

"If you would only have me without looking at me, without touching. You'd think you'd never had a woman before, the way you use your eyes to look at me!"

"What else should I do?"

"What everyone else does. It is not for the men of Sparta to see so much, to touch me like you do! To fuck and be fucked—that I understand. Want to take me like one of your boys? I expect that. But all this sweet gazing, this patience, these whispers in my ear that I love so much . . ."

Her voice unsteadied. Collecting herself, she finished:

"I can't help but think of it all as . . . indecent."

Antalcidas laughed out loud at her. And so because the Lacedaemonians were not known for making tender love to their women, she was unnerved at his devotion? How ridiculous! So at last she stood exposed as all noncomformists must be—conventional to her core.

He seized an ankle and dragged her across the floor to him. On her face was an expression halfway between weeping and relief; when he came close to kiss her again, as dearly this time as he'd seen his mother caress Epitadas, she shed blissful tears that streaked both their faces.

"Don't laugh at me," she said, blushing as he set back on his haunches to admire her. "It's easy for someone like you to break the rules—a Spartiate through and through."

"Is that what I am?"

She leaned forward to shove him.

"You're cruel!"

5.

The hunters bounded through the undergrowth in breechcloths and buskins, their eyes showing the

same lethal fixity Lacedaemonians always brought to
the killing business. The boar, which had been on the
run for more than an hour, had tried to slip away into
a thyme thicket. The scent raised by its movements
betrayed its position to the other hunters standing
downwind, their spears ready. Whooping and clapping slats of wood together, pulling their line together
into a moving wedge that would further confine their
prey, the helot beaters drove the animal downhill.

A gloom fell as a storm front rose over Taygetus,
frowned, and loosed a steady rain on the foothills.
The hunters waited visorless, drying their eyes with
forearms spotted with blood drawn by brambles and
the resinous bark of pines. Epitadas listened to the cacophony descending toward him, with the boar somewhere ahead. A willow nearby caught the edge of the
unsettled air and seemed to sigh over the bloodletting
to come.

"Epitadas, take my shield side," commanded Ramphias, though he held no shield and Epitadas was not
obliged to follow his commands. With his deep, stentorian voice and round-faced jollity, the old governor
had the charm of everyone's favorite uncle. Epitadas
took position on his left.

"But where is my future son-in-law?" Ramphias
asked.

"Antalcidas follows his own commands."

The governor had organized the hunt to acquaint
himself with the family of his daughter's betrothal.
With the patriarch an invalid, he paid his respects to
the widow with mixed feelings: the lady Damatria
controlled a vast estate, but there was also something
not quite couth about her, with her unflinching gaze
and her Asian embarrassment of jewels. Oddly, she
confessed to know nothing of Antalcidas' intentions,

yet she was far from irate at her ignorance. She showed only the most perfunctory interest in the qualities of the woman who would share her son's house. Her biggest concern, it seemed, was over whether Ramphias had any other daughters who might suit her youngest.

The brother struck him as exactly the kind of young man of which the city needed more. Good-looking, fearless by all accounts, and hungry for approval, Epitadas already understood all the code words of Spartan political discourse, such as "security" (domination), "piety" (license), and "patriotism" (when to shut up). He knew how to laugh at the right jokes, and wink at the wrong ones. Truth be told, he wished Andreia was worthy of a groom of his quality, but when it came to disposing of daughters, one couldn't be particular.

His first impressions were not changed by their experience on the hunt. Epitadas knew how to flatter and how to accept the generosity of his betters. He knew to stay on the shield side of his host, and would certainly allow the older man the honor of the kill. Antalcidas, by contrast, was a cipher; at the campfire he said nothing, and on the trail he tended to wander off with no warning. Ramphias had heard that he had acquitted himself well in battle. If this was the best of the new generation, the governor thought, then Lacedaemon was in serious trouble.

He heard a commotion in the buckthorn above; something was charging, heavy-footed but fast, up the slope. In the instant before they charged after it, he met eyes with Epitadas: both knew that the boar was backtracking on the beaters, who had begun to scatter in fear. In another moment the animal would break through their line and escape.

Ramphias followed the younger man over a goat trail in the direction of the melee. The noise reached a climax just as Epitadas glimpsed a gathering of helots through the brush. Bushwhacking, it seemed to take an eternity as the action unfolded in obscurity ahead of them. "Stand fast, boys!" the governor cried as he tore his spear from vines that seemed to reach out to entangle the point. "Don't let him through! We're coming!"

They broke into a small clearing ringed with vertical cypress. Like the trees, the beaters were standing quietly in a circle. Epitadas stopped, allowing his host to take command of his servants; Ramphias plunged ahead, expecting to hear excuses about how the boar was allowed to slip away. But when the helots parted for him he saw the boar was not gone, but lying dead at Antalcidas' feet.

"What happened?" the governor asked, his voice laced with more disappointment than he could help.

This man who would marry his daughter was in the center, still out of breath, with the ashwood shaft of his spear—the one Zeuxippos had given him—broken in his right hand. The rest of the weapon was sunk into the neck of the boar, which lay in a slick of its own blood like a great ship aground on the rocks. Its mouth was open in midgasp; the tongue a wine-colored bulb, tusks gleaming, great ears spread wide like the wings of some bristle-haired bird. The boar's legs, meanwhile, were bent in an almost delicate posture, as if he had just stooped to nuzzle some tender morsel in the dirt.

Ramphias regarded Antalcidas. The latter was still out of breath, his eyes flashing white as his excitement ebbed. The governor could see that he was clenching his left hand in a fist, and that it was bleeding—probably because the boy had gripped the spear too far up the shaft as the boar thrashed on the point. But such injuries were part of the reward for hunting boar on foot. It was a good kill, it seemed; one he would have been glad to witness.

They agreed that it would be best to send the boar to the table of the Eurypontid king as he prepared to lead the invasion of Attica. Ramphias' servants had brought in enough other game to sustain them in camp: a dozen hares, a red deer fawn, and a stork. As the three of them sat around the fire, metalware chimed from the governor's tent as the valet made the preparations, Antalcidas looked up and saw the glow of a half dozen Spartiate camps scattered across the lap of Taygetus. A constellation of five more twinkled on Parnes across the valley. A twelfth flame, a reflection of their own, danced in the eyes of the boar as it hung otherwise invisible in the gloom.

"Crowded up here tonight," Ramphias remarked at the distant fires. Indeed, there seemed to be more citizens in the mountains than in the city, which looked dark by comparison. But Antalcidas knew that this was an illusion; the cressets on the ridge of the Acropolis were only obscured by trees, and the wives of Laconia were almost certainly not idle that hour. In all, the view comforted him—a Spartan cosmos to mirror the immortal one above.

They served the stork first, roasted with a sauce of rue, pepper, raisins, and honey. This was a finer sort of dining than he had ever known in the city—so good that, in other contexts, it would qualify as subversive. Yet it was not uncommon for Spartiates to eat better on the trail than at home. It was the guilty little secret behind their passion for hunting.

After stripping the bones Ramphias and Epitadas

discussed another sort of gratification. The governor's second wife, it seemed, was quite a bit younger than he, yet had failed to bless his house with a boy. Proceeding elliptically, as if he was stalking a large bear, Ramphias worked his way around to a proposition:

". . . If you value your manhood you should avoid the trap of bureaucracy. . . . With every dispatch I write I can feel my balls shrinking. . . . The Cytherans are on the sea-lanes, so they are too close to the Asians. . . . I've heard it on good authority that they prefer to chew their wives' privates . . . climate most dispiriting . . . we need a little new blood in the house. . . ."

As he took the governor's meaning, Antalcidas felt an impulse to recede into the darkness. Ramphias, misreading him, raised a hand to reassure him. "Not that I wouldn't ask you to stand in for me, dear son . . . though we feel you are already a part of the family, so you can understand, I think!"

"What is your wife called?" Epitadas asked.

"Areté—and I think you will find her quality befits the name. She came to me genuinely spotless."

Epitadas looked into the fire, betraying no sense of surprise or anticipation, his perfect ease saving the moment from awkwardness. It was as if the governor had asked him to borrow his sharpening stone. In fact, his cocksmanship had become something of legend among the older Spartiates, many of whom turned to their younger countrymen as need arose. Epitadas' looks and connections made him a popular choice.

"As for your elder brother here, I say we can expect great things. Don't worry about losing that old spear, my boy—I'll find you a better one from my own collection. One that has pierced the hides of a few helots over the years, you can be sure!"

He clapped a hand on Antalcidas' shoulder, meaning to praise him honestly. Yet as Ramphias rhapsodized over the old-fashioned helot-hunting that was once so popular, a vault seemed to be sealed behind the young man's eyes. It was too late—as the excitement of his kill receded, he faded beyond reach again. Ramphias then understood, as surely as he knew anything, that while he and Antalcidas might become aligned by marriage, it would never be as friends.

6.

On the appointed day Andreia consecrated her shorn locks and all her girlhood dolls to Artemis; the bride's procession led to the fountain of the Temple of Aphrodite-in-Fetters, where Andreia purified herself with her marriage shift billowing in the water around her like a saffron cloud. Antalcidas likewise performed all the rituals expected of him—the ritual bath, accepting the insults of his messmates—until the time came for the banquet at Ramphias' house. As Damatria would be there, he made only the briefest of appearances, excusing himself right after the sesame cakes were distributed. He declared his virtue according to the formula, "I have forsworn the good and found the better," and made his escape as his mother made her approach. From her expression it seemed she wanted to tell him something, but he didn't wait to hear her out.

The traditional moment of possession came when the bride, hair dressed like a new recruit, wearing a man's work shirt, waited in the groom's bed to be "taken." On this wedding night the newlyweds, who were already more than familiar, did more mocking than lovemaking. By the light of the handmaid's torches, Antalcidas watched Andreia turn buttock to him. "Elder, teach me," she begged in the piping voice of a schoolboy; he, sharing the joke, replied in the oro-tund style of Zeuxippos, "What a fine, tight ring!" The eavesdroppers outside, whose presence was as tradi-tional as the wedding dress and sesame cakes, were very confused by what they heard.

With Andreia's arrival the Kynosoura farmhouse at last came to life. The gifts from Damatria and Zeuxip-pos came out of storage and were carefully placed; the bride's trousseau required three men to lift it to her women's quarters upstairs. When he left for the sum-mer invasion there was a thick carpet of bear's foot growing outside the door. On his return it had all been replaced by a kitchen garden of basil, marjoram, mus-tard, and woody thyme, fringed with beds of cham-omile, pennyroyal, sage, and other medicinal herbs he did not recognize. After weeks invested in chopping and burning the fields of Attica, he dropped his spear and fell to his knees in his own yard, admiring each tender shoot raised by her hand. She came out to greet him with the fragrance of mint leaves on her breath and a new fullness around her hips. He asked the question with his eyes, and she answered by grasping her breasts through her chiton and saying to him, in a voice pregnant with happiness, that her breasts had begun to fill.

Their first child was born during the second winter of the war. Andreia suffered through the delivery, but was rewarded with a daughter who did not cry at the world but arrived instead with a look of quiet aston-ishment. Ramphias consoled Antalcidas for the mis-fortune of siring a girl; the new father, charmed by the glow of reddish down on her smooth head, was de-lighted. A daughter, he knew, could never earn citizenship and so could not be sanctioned with betrayal of her grandfather's helotry. Provided she married respectably, her descendants would be forever safe from his shame.

In their happiness, they called her Melitta—a name unheard of among the women of Laconia. It was only the beginning of their exceptionalism. In a thousand ways, from the way Andreia chose to grow her hair long, to the scrolls of foreign writings they collected, to their pledge to permit Doulos to educate Melitta in the classics, they sought to find new ways to be Spartan.

"Let this house be an island of philosophy in a complacent sea!" Andreia declaimed to the hills, with her hand in his and their daughter at her side. It was a metaphor that would come to seem prescient to him when, years later, on another island miles to the west, loneliness and boredom drove him to savor the memory again.

7.

A few weeks after Antalcidas and Doulos left for Attica, Andreia received a guest at their house. Damatria came over the hill from her estate without attendants, dressed in a simple linen chiton with her hair bound in woolen fillets, like a farmgirl. She carried a flat harvesting basket, and in the basket was a bouquet of wildflowers. Despite her humble getup there was nothing common about her: Damatria's gray-frosted hair had been washed and arranged with a dresser's skill, and she traveled in a cloud of imported perfume. Andreia recognized her only by sight, never having spoken to her mother-in-law in person. Antalcidas had long ago pointed her out from their upper story window, concealing his bitterness under a curious tone, as if he was indicating some rare kind of bird. Andreia detected the anger beneath his jauntiness, and the sadness beneath the anger.

"Hello. I am your mother," Damatria said.

"I know who you are."

"If that's so, then you might offer a couch to your elder."

Andreia took the flowers and hosted her elder guest the way a good Lacedaemonian wife ought. Damatria looked around at what had become of the little farmhouse at the edge of her domain: Andreia had turned it into a modest but fine home, with furniture unscuffed and beaten floor meticulously swept. A subtle bubbling sound emanated from the iron cauldron on the hearth. Through an open door to the husband's parlor, Damatria could see a small girl, no more than a toddler, lying asleep at an odd angle on the drinking couch.

"My husband is gone," Andreia hastened, reddening.

"No need to explain," replied Damatria. "I used to let my boys sleep in the men's rooms in my time. It's better than running up the stairs to check on them."

Her reassurance was kind, but Andreia's embarrassment only deepened. She had no idea why this lady had come; courtesy was expected in such instances, yet she could not shake a nagging sense of disloyalty to her husband.

"Can I offer you something? Water? Something to eat?"

Damatria was staring at her now. "You are fair, aren't you? Fair but pretty. The young men love that."

"Do you like almonds? They're last year's, I'm afraid."

The other smiled. Rising, she wandered to the hearth and snatched up a rag to lift the hot lid of the cookpot.

"Barley soup?"

"With narthex."

"Dried?"

"Fresh. They sprout early on the south-facing slope."

Damatria stirred the mixture and tested its scent. "You used a vinegar fish sauce. Try an oil-based; the soup comes out thicker, and the men get so sick of vinegar from the mess."

Andreia tried to look her most demure, eyes down. "I have tried it—he doesn't like the oil."

Lips tightening, Damatria replaced the lid. Was the girl trying to make her feel guilty, telling her something she might have known about her own son? No, look at her: she's never had a devious thought in her life. Did he choose her as some kind of living reproof against his mother?

"There must be something I can show you that you don't know yet. Do you use asafoetida?"

"I've only heard of it."

"There must be some growing around here. . . . Shall we look?"

The girl hesitated, looking toward the parlor.

"Your little one should be all right," said Damatria. "We shouldn't be gone long."

"No, I'll take her."

And so they went out beyond the kitchen garden, Andreia with Melitta clinging to her side, Damatria in her faux-peasant costume. It was a cool day for early summer, with high, serrated clouds above and a hint of vernal green lingering in the foothills. As Damatria showed Andreia how to recognize the resin-bearing plants, she glanced at the girl asleep with her face buried against her mother's neck. The sight filled her with a vague warmth; forgetting her age, she momentarily contemplated becoming a mother again. It wouldn't be by Dorcis, of course, who had grown comfortably flaccid in his paralysis. He was Erinna's husband now in every sense but the legal one.

Melitta stirred, yawning. As the child turned away from the warmth of Andreia's neck, Damatria, trembling, got her first good look at her features. The face she dreaded was reflected there, but—thankfully—it was softened by Andreia's delicacy and the tenderness of early girlhood. If she unfocused her eyes, she might even obscure the resemblance. Could she spend half a lifetime looking with her eyes crossed at her granddaughter?

"You take the stems here," she was saying, "and pound them to render the resin, except you shouldn't use a wooden mallet, unless you want it to forever smell of garlic. . . ."

Back at the house the women stood side by side at the cook table. Though Damatria knew more about the preparation of asafoetida, her proficiency in the kitchen suffered from dependence on servants. Andreia, meanwhile, undertook the lesson with the confidence of knowing virtually everything else. Before long the younger woman had matched the elder's skill; she had been at her pounding for some time before she realized that Damatria had withdrawn some distance away to watch her.

"What? Am I doing it right?"

"Does he know?" Damatria's eyes flitted down to the slight hunch in Andreia's abdomen.

Andreia took a few more swings of the mallet,

brushed her hair out of her eyes with her wrist. "No. He left before I was sure."

"He'll be pleased it's a boy."

Andreia smiled. "How can you know that?"

"From how it lies in you. Remember, I've borne a few sons in my time."

The other, not knowing whether to believe Damatria's judgment or, more deeply, her intentions, said nothing. Damatria approached again and leaned forward, pausing only to say, "Congratulations are due." Then she delivered a kiss on Andreia's cheek that burned with such ambiguity that she felt it for hours to come.

VI
The Squeezing Place

1.

The hill the Athenians called "the Squeezing Place" had a fine view of what was at stake in the deliberations there. Below the rock-cut dais, the Assembly of citizens packed shoulder to shoulder onto the sloping ground; when the speakers took the rostrum, the west face of the Acropolis stood on their right, the blue and dusty outlines of its temples looming against the ascending sun. To the left spread the smoky quarter of the marketplace, whose stallfronts and urinals were the usual venues for political discussion when the Assembly was not in weekly session. Under normal circumstances the city constables would have to literally rope the populace to the hill—a ship's hawser, covered with red paint, was stretched across the square and swept in the direction of the meeting place. Anyone marked with the paint was liable for a fine if they did not turn up for their civic duty. Wise idlers learned to avoid the market altogether on Assembly days.

This morning, under dawn's indigo skies, some twenty thousand male citizens—a fair majority of the public eligible to vote—were gathered into the confines of the sacred precinct. No one this time was filing up the slope late, and no one was smeared with red paint. In the seventh year of a conflict unprecedented in its bitterness, a war that divided the public down the middle, few wanted to miss the day's debate. It was rumored that the Lacedaemonians had at last come to discuss peace.

In the best of times the crowd sorted itself in a patchwork of political affiliations. People from the interior of Attica separated themselves from the coastal people; rich citizens stood apart from poor ones, who were further divided into those who worked the land and those in the trades. Controversy over the war accounted for another division between those who wanted a negotiated peace and those who didn't. The Acharnians, a nation unto themselves, formed the core of the militant bloc on the far right of the crowd.

Along the edges of the throng was perhaps the greatest concentration of genius yet known to history— Socrates, the father of philosophy, absently picking his nose; Alcibiades, the prodigy, silk-clad and hungover; Nicias, the reluctant general, quietly hopeful for peace; the historian Thucydides, angrily scribbling notes; the dramatists Sophocles and Euripides; Aristophanes, the comedian, enjoying the spectacle of Socrates' slovenliness. All were there; all had their views. But it would be the fools who would speak loudest that day.

The proceedings began with an invocation and sacrifice to the city gods on the altar behind the rostrum. Blood from the pigs was collected in clay pots, which were carried to the corners of the enclosure. As the crier promised the collective wrath of Athena-the-Protectoress, and of Aglauros, Hestia, Enyo, Ares Enyalios, Thallo, Auxo, Hegemone, and Herakles against anyone who spoke crookedly, the blood was poured in a ring around the assembled.

The solemnities were conducted above the buzz of conversation among the citizens, the chat of the magistrates in their front row seats, and the hawking of the bread- and cheese-sellers as they rushed to complete their sales before the blood circle was closed. The crimson trio of Spartan emissaries, grim-faced, grasping their staffs in identically diffident fashion, sat silent, making strict observance even to the rites of their enemies.

The preliminaries done, a banner of plain white was run up the staff at the crest of the hill. With this sign, the excluded part of the city's population—that is, most of it—was made aware that debate was underway. The president of the Assembly asked the crier to recite the agenda, which had only one item that day: to hear the Lacedaemonians plead their case before the people. The motion to hear the emissaries passed by a show of hands. The herald, with the speaker's myrtle-leaf crown on his head, rose to invite the Spartans to make their presentation.

All private chatter ceased as Isidas, son of Agesidas took the rostrum. There was a pause as he took the wreath from the herald and set it cautiously on his head, as if afraid to muss his dressed locks. The sprinkling of laughter was heard in the crowd—Lacedaemonians were well known for their vanity. Like a teacher before a class of unruly children, Isidas stood stone-faced, his staff planted on the platform, until the crowd settled. When his angular features at last cracked to speak, his voice was like the clatter of an old drum tumbling down an endless, boulder-strewn slope.

"O Athenians, we are not ones to address crowds. Those of our city, being more or less of one mind in matters as fundamental as war, have no need of such skills. Our craft is soldiering, and as such we are used to speaking plainly. We were sent here by our elders to be nothing other but plainspoken, and to give you the soldiers' truth. Having been nominated to speak for my colleagues, I will say nothing more than what I must. My language will be simple, and the argument, by your standards, unadorned. I will not take much of your time."

At this, Cleon, son of Cleaenetus, jerked his upper torso backward, as if struck bodily by the speaker's absurdity. He was, as usual, in the front of the standing crowd, his bullish face marked by great, half-moon circles under his eyes. The feature made him seem perpetually exhausted, but he was in fact one of the most energetic men in Athens. As the emissary spoke, his eyes never stopped moving, flashing knowing glances at his friends, observing the mood of the crowd, regarding the Spartan up and down like some freakish spawn of Pan from the deepest backwoods of Arcadia.

"If nothing else," Isidas went on, "we can agree together that this is an important moment in the course of the war. The truce arranged by our commanders in Pylos has held for two weeks. By its terms, the Lacedaemonians have agreed not to attack the illegal fortification your army has built in our territory. We have also restored to you, on a provisional basis, all warships that have been captured in actions around the Peloponnese. For his part, your general Demosthenes has undertaken no assault on our men on the island, and has allowed the delivery of such food, such as milled grain, as may not be stockpiled by the garrison. Apart from whatever we accomplish by this embassy, by hewing to this agreement both sides have shown themselves capable of restraint. It is our hope that the opportunity presented by these acts will not be wasted."

Isidas' eyes fell briefly on Nicias, son of Niceratus, who was seated on a bench before the arm of the Assembly dominated by the peace party. The latter returned his gaze, but only briefly, for his enemy Cleon employed sycophants who urged prosecutions on the basis of gestures as minor as a look. In any case, Nicias was not known for meeting the eyes of others: though he was one of city's most talented generals, a leading citizen and natural heir to noble Pericles, he had little of his predecessor's highborn bearing.

Since the war he had dwindled to just a gray-haired wisp of a man, his skin a cadaverous green, his gaze fugitive. The dolefulness of his temperament was legendary: several years earlier, after he returned from victory over the Megarians on the island of Minoa, Nicias moped his camp as if his father had died. After plague struck the city, he spent a considerable amount of his own wealth to rededicate the island of Delos to divine Apollo, assembling a fleet of gold-encrusted boats for the procession to the island, and raising a palm tree of solid bronze in honor of the god. Yet even as he led the splendid choruses over the water, witnesses reported that Nicias seemed spent, as if weighed down by the burden of his own benefaction. There was a similar look on his face that morning, as all the hopes of the peace party fell on his shoulders.

Isidas continued, "I have promised to speak plainly, and so I will: the goddess Fortune has done you a great favor with the entrapment of our sons. Even for men such as ourselves, who spend their lives making war, the goddess has much to do with the success of our efforts. It has been a hard lesson for us to learn this time, for we have had more than our share of her blessings in the past.

"Yet you Athenians have a decision in store that

will be equally difficult: you must decide what to do with your good fortune. Yes, there will be voices among you that will urge all kinds of extravagant demands, to force a settlement favorable to yourselves that they imagine will be permanent. They will say that the Lacedaemonians are desperate, and that instead of accepting a just peace, you should take this opportunity to reach for something more. These men look at what is obvious to the rest of us—that the mighty one day may be laid low the next—and take a lesson that is directly opposite the truth. I don't say this because I presume to lecture you on such things; I only say what even a simple soldier may understand.

"Other voices, perhaps not as seductive, certainly not as loud, will tell you that your gains must by necessity be fleeting. For this reason, this is the best possible moment to accept our invitation, and to make the kind of peace between us that will assure our joint hegemony. For when Athens and Lacedaemon work in accord, what state in Greece may stand against us?

"You may trust our word, for there is no more compelling debt than that of generosity owed an adversary who has put aside his own temporary advantage. So much the more, now that the contest has reached this point, where the end cannot be known to either of us, and no offense done by either side that yet makes peace impossible. And even as you make your advantage permanent in a more creditable form, think of the glory that will attend your name when you claim the gratitude of the Greeks for ending this war. What a lesson it would be, for the city some think the most grasping to pause here, on this precipice we all find ourselves, and redeem her reputation for wisdom!

"On the other hand, think what precedent will be

set if you miss this opportunity. What lesson may the Peloponnesians take from a refusal of our offer? Grind us into the dirt, break our olive branch, and what can the Athenians expect of us when Fortune withholds her smile from you, as she inevitably will? Think hard on this when the chicken hawks come to perch on your shoulders, put their beaks to your ears, and whisper of reaching for something more. You know of whom I speak. . . ."

At this, Cleon put his head back and gave his audience the benefit of his laughter.

"Allow us to suggest the following terms, then: the forces of both sides, and their allies, will relinquish all occupied territories. In cases over which the parties disagree, forces will remain deployed but undertake no action. All prisoners and captured ships will be repatriated without exception or condition. When these measures have been taken, the governments of our respective cities will enter into negotiation over the disposition of all remaining disputes, and over the terms of a new alliance between our two great peoples.

"That said, I feel chagrined to stand before you now. I know your Athenian speakers are capable of going on for hours, but you have already seen the extent of my skills. To those who have come for a rhetorical exhibition, I must concede defeat at the outset: they will talk rings around me. But to those who have come to decide matters of substance, consider me an ally in the common struggle, that good sense and our mutual interest may, even now, carry the day."

2.

Isidas surrendered the myrtle to the herald. With that, he and his companions were escorted out by the fur-trimmed Scythian bailiffs. Emissaries of enemy powers were not permitted to hear Assembly debates in such dangerous times.

The herald looked out over the mob, waiting a few moments as waves of unease rolled through it. The Lacedaemonian's speech was refreshingly brief, palate-cleansing in its clarity, perhaps even persuasive. If pressed, some listeners would confess that they preferred its taste to the cloying bonbons to which Attic rhetoric had lately descended. Fortunately for the hawks, the old menu would soon be served again in the form of Cleon.

But not before Nicias came up to say his piece. Donning the wreath, he turned his rheumy eyes on the people, whose reactions ranged from applause to polite silence. His services to the city had already been too great to permit undisguised hostility. Still, there were anonymous whistles from the vicinity of the Acharnians, who mistrusted the depth of his zeal.

"Gentlemen, I leave it to you to decide this day on the question of war or peace," Nicias began. "I have my view, as you all know, but in our democracy that opinion does not—*should* not—count for anything more than that of any of you, my fellow citizens. By the same token, of course, we should expect the opinions of those who may disagree with us to weigh no more and no less in these deliberations. Under this white banner, we stand equal in our obligation to serve the city.

"Rather than persuasion, my aim today is simply to confirm certain facts of which we should all be aware. . . ." The general paused as he withdrew a small wax tablet from a fold in his tunic. He didn't look at it yet, but its appearance in his hand now compelled the attention of forty thousand eyes.

"According to the accepted figures, which were confirmed for me last night by the treasurers, when the war began the Athenians had six thousand talents of coined silver stored in the sacred precinct. The city has use of additional incomes, in the amount of one thousand talents per year from the mines at Mount Laurion, about six hundred talents per year in dues from our partners in the Aegean commonwealth, two hundred talents from the war tax, and five hundred more from exceptional sources. An additional forty talents may be obtained, in desperate circumstances, by stripping the temples of their gold. These monies, you will agree, represent the bulk of the wealth of the state, notwithstanding the mandate of additional liturgies, which in my view seems unlikely given the existing burden.

"It also cannot be denied that some of this revenue will not be realized as income from year to year. The presence of the enemy in Attica has had a disrupting effect on operations at Laurion. The stream of money or ships from certain of our partners can be broken by the vicissitudes of war, such as we saw in the late, almost tragic case of Mytilene. It must be acknowledged, then, that the figures I have listed represent our assets in the best of circumstances, and do not take account of anything our adversaries might do to affect them.

"Now let us consider the other side of the ledger. Without going into the details, the navy costs no less than 500 talents *per month*, assuming we man and supply a fleet of two hundred ships—a figure you will agree to be conservative in these times. This estimate takes no account of special circumstances, such as the cost of maintaining what sieges may be necessary, or for chartering supply ships for Demosthenes at Pylos.

It also does not account for replacement costs for vessels lost due to weather, mishap, or enemy action. Admittedly, not all ships are deployed at all times during the campaign season, though most are for at least several months each year. For the sake of illustration, then, we may stipulate that the annual maintenance of our navy costs the treasury some 1,000 to 2,000 talents. Please note, then, that this expense alone consumes all our income from the Laurion mines, dues from allies, and the war tax.

"As for the army, the arithmetic is no less inescapable. To field a levy of thirteen thousand hoplites, compensated at two drachmas a day, costs more than 4 talents per day, 30 talents per week, or more than 120 talents per month. The pattern of future deployments cannot be predicted for certain, but we may assume that we will be looking after our interests in the Megarid, in Chalcidice, Euboea, Acarnania, Leucas, Magna Grecia, Corcyra, Cythera, the Hellespont, and certain other places. Over the last seven years, maintenance of the army has cost—" he glanced at the tablet—"in excess of 600 talents a year. This is, again, more than the total of what our allies pay to the treasury toward their defense.

"I pass now to the expenses associated with the maintenance of our passive defenses, such as the Long Walls, the harbor, as well as those necessary for the normal operations of the government, which on no account may be called discretionary. . . ."

Nicias spoke like this for almost an hour, deliberately setting out the figures that drove home his bleak prediction: despite the vastness of her resources, despite all her victories and the fact that, the plague notwithstanding, Pericles' strategy had more or less worked, the city must soon be finally, inevitably, and utterly broke. When he was finished, the Assembly neither applauded nor jeered; his facts were not new, and his conclusion not very controversial. The lack of response was, in the end, bound up with the strangeness of thinking in terms of thousands and tens of thousands—figures that bore very little relevance to the Athenians in their daily lives. The argument struck the assemblymen as some thing more than hypothetical, but less than real.

"Anyone else?" asked the herald. He looked to Cleon as he said this, but the latter only stood there with arms crossed, making no move toward the rostrum. The air of ambivalence that followed Nicias began to crackle with energy; assemblymen turned to each other with the same question on their lips, until the questions merged into an indistinct buzz of anticipation. The all-important issue had abruptly changed: it was no longer "Should Athens accept the Spartan peace offer?" but "Will Cleon accept the wreath?"

Moments like this are living things, maturing and dying in their time. Exploiting them required a knack for knowing when such opportunities were about to reach their prime. Just as the uncertainty verged on the discordant, Cleon uncrossed his arms.

3.

"O Athenians, know that I came here today without the intention of saying a word. . . ."

Cleon said this with complete awareness of its absurdity, and got the calculated response: an outburst of laughter so explosive that it reverberated back from the slopes of Hymettos. Housewives miles away heard the commotion, and knowing that Cleon must just then be speaking, bent back to their washing. On the Acropolis, a temple slave brushed a weevil off a leaf on Athena's sacred olive tree, heard the distant peals, and smiled.

The people were not unanimous in their opinion of him. Some took him for Athens' most trustworthy defender, others as a harmless clown. Still others regarded him as a dangerous running sore on the backside of the democracy. Virtually everyone, however, was entertained by Cleon, and looked forward to what might issue from his mouth next.

"It troubles me, though, to stand in this consecrated place and hear our ancestors insulted, our traditions despised. Indeed, I would expect the same response from any of you if I stood up here, giving the Athenians such bad advice! I would expect all of you to rise in a body and say 'no!' to the naysayers, 'no!' to the rationalizers, to the sophistic apologists. If I ever argue so badly to this body, let me be forever barred from attending her deliberations. Make an alien of me, declare me no son of Erechtheus! And let this standard apply right now, to what I say today and whatever the others may say in rebuttal. I, for one, would gladly stand for such a test.

"Hearken now! We have heard this morning from noble Nicias. For myself, I will never allow it to be said that this general has not done his duty for the Athenians. He is a good man, a moderate man, and his words merit all due attention. And yet, I submit to you now that these times do not require moderate men! Was it not Pericles himself who warned us that this will be a unique war, one that would demand new tactics? For these are not the set-piece battles of the past, with armies lined up on the field of honor, each committed to forcing a resolution in a single day.

No! This is a war for our very existence, fought against an enemy with contempt for our democracy—an enemy who thinks nothing of making war against the land itself! And so while we esteem Nicias, we must acknowledge as well that his experience may provide no guide. There are no experts in this kind of struggle! Instead, we seek our answers in the collective wisdom of the people.

"What concerns me first is the suggestion that we cannot afford to protect ourselves. Since when have the Athenians measured what is possible by the contents of the treasury? Shall we make bean counters our generals? When all of us claimed our birthright as citizens, a pledge was implicit: we will bear any cost to defend this city, even unto death. In any case, I believe that if our fate hung on it, the sailors and hoplites would be content—glad, in fact!—to serve without recompense. Before Salamis, did Themistocles question how many obols would purchase salvation from the barbarian? Not at all! Nicias is not unique in the sincerity of his patriotism. If I did not know better, I would say he's insulted all of us with his self-serving calculations! You there, wouldn't you serve without pay?"

Cleon was pointing at a fellow assemblyman in the front row. The stubble-cheeked man, who seemed hardly out of his twenties, was struck dumb by all the attention suddenly focused on him. Opening his mouth, he stammered. Cleon clasped his hands together in a mock imploring gesture that could be read from the back of the crowd.

"Come now, my friend! Don't make a liar of me!"

"Of course I would serve!" the young man finally cried.

"Good boy!" Cleon winked. "Magistrates, dock his

salary next time he's in uniform. . . . What's a few lost drachmas for a man so rich in patriotism?"

More gales of laughter. Cleon was in good form that day. Meanwhile, Nicias scowled, pulling his head down in a manner that made his ears level with his shoulders.

"Yes, perhaps the day will come when men measure out all that is valuable in gold and silver. How convenient it would be, to search our hearts for virtue and know where to look—in the columns and figures of men like Nicias! Perhaps that day will come at last, long after the beating heart of Athens is stilled, when her legacy is scattered, and these stones bleached and cold. But by the looks on your faces now, my fellow citizens, I can tell that day is not here yet!"

He had the whole crowd now, from one side of the precinct to the other. As standing silent then, glowering, would have been less than politic, Nicias and his coterie joined in the ovation.

"As for the Lacedaemonians . . ." Cleon began, but stopped when jeers erupted from the vicinity of the Acharnians. "As for the Lacedaemonians . . . I tell you that what I feel toward them this morning is not the rage I expected. No, my friends, I feel instead a deep sadness for them, as I would feel for any Greeks who struggle with an implacable enemy. For I tell you that the real enemy of the Spartans is not Athens. . . ."

He was interrupted again by voices from the right, crying "no!"; others showed their dissent by whistling and clapping their hands over their ears. The rest of the crowd was variously amused and annoyed by the partisans. Cleon raised his hand for quiet.

"No, their real foe is not Athens at all. Rather, it is the affliction of their own overwhelming arrogance! For how else may we understand what pours from the

mouth of Isidas? Listen to him when he lectures us,
'that the mighty one day may be laid low the next.' In
what other way may free people hear this than as a
veiled threat? Yes, Isidas, Fortune has a way of shifting allegiance, but she favors us today, not you! It is
our boot that presses the neck of your men on the island. For this reason, by the gods, you will treat with
us now, and spare us your bullying!"

He paused to invite the Assembly to cheer. A large
proportion did, as they typically did for self-gratifying
bluster.

"Equally as telling, recall when he said that 'with
Athens and Lacedaemon in accord, what state in
Greece may stand against us?' That he happened to
speak correctly in that instance is immaterial—skilled
liars know how to bend the occasional truth to their
purposes. What should concern us all, rather, is the
ambition it implies, that the Spartans clearly wish to
dominate Greece and, incidentally, that Athens might
figure as junior partner in their plans. Is this not the
kind of arrogance we would expect from these
Lacedaemonians who, alone among the Greeks, offend the gods by enslaving other Greeks? We might
well ask the good men of Messenia how the fetters of
Spartan hegemony feel on their wrists . . . !"

Cleon had begun now to use his trademark the-
atrics—screeching, raising both arms in supplication,
grasping the tufts of hair that remained on his head.
The crowd watched for the appearance of these like
the return of long-lost friends.

". . . We might ask the Laconian helots, who have
been slaves so long they have forgotten to aspire to
freedom! Are men such as Isidas in any position to advise the people of Athens, who sprung from this
ground as free men and forsake it only when they re-

turn to it as dust, what the wisdom of free men should lead us to do!"—Cleon flailed his thigh—"What does a hungry cur stalking the barrens know of the heart of a noble eagle?"—Cleon stalked jackal-like across the rostrum, then ripped open his tunic to bare his freedom-loving breast—"Nothing, I say! And again, I tell you, nothing! And a third time, I deny them the right to speak for me!" With escalating force, Cleon pounded his chest with his fist.

He had by now titillated the Assembly into a state of precarious complacence. Like a crowd filing past an overturned carriage on the road or someone else's botched blood sacrifice, it felt both superior to the danger and direly sensitive to its sting. The question of what to do with this paradoxical tension could only be answered by what Cleon would say next.

"If we understand all this, what need have we of Isidas' estimate of what Fortune has in store? Little, if anything, I say! The Lacedaemonians, of all people, who have offended the gods so thoroughly, have no right to expect a reversal of Fortune anytime soon. *Be humble, Athenians,* they say—*don't dare reach for something more.* How easy it is for them to dispense advice, with their homes intact, their fields and orchards unburned! Before we avail ourselves of their sagacity, let us seek counsel with the Decelean children, the widows of Thriasia, the piteous Acharnians . . . !"

The response from the right made it impossible for Cleon to be heard. As he waited for the Acharnians to subside, he stood with head slightly bent, glowering from under his eyebrows.

"Grasp for something more? I say, why not? For just as we will bear any price to prevail, we will never stint on securing the best for our children. For their blood on the field, for their suffering from plague, for their freedom, the Athenians should accept the following terms and nothing less. . . ."

Someone in the front row handed him a scroll. He unrolled it, but his eyes never looked down as he recited the terms he had so evidently memorized.

"First demand: the warships released by the Lacedaemonians for the period of the current truce will belong forthwith to Athens. Second demand: the entire garrison on the island of Sphacteria must surrender themselves into our custody. These will be held as hostages for the third stipulation, which is the return of certain territories, including the cities of Pegae, Nisaea, Troezen, and the treaty lands in Achaea. Finally, the enemy will then agree to embark on good-faith negotiations over a permanent settlement, which must in any case leave intact our hegemony in the Aegean. Only at that point, when the treaty is in effect and all Peloponnesian forces have withdrawn from the vicinity of Pylos, will the Athenians relinquish their position there and return the captives.

"It may seem to some that this is a lengthy set of conditions for peace. To those people I say—what is the alternative? Shall we give away all advantage at the outset, before we have gained anything from the considerable expense we have already incurred? Is that any way to negotiate? I have been in contact by letter with our general in Pylos, Demosthenes, who assures me that our position there is strong. Let us therefore dare to be worthy of our soldiers' audacity! Let us have the courage to allow freedom to triumph! On such faith, the gods cannot fail to look with favor."

4.

For the conclusion of his speech Cleon had gradually moderated his volume, bringing the Assembly down from frenzy to merely a heightened state of apprehension. A motion was put forth to approve Cleon's demands for presentation to the envoys. It passed by acclamation, with massive support from the right and the middle, and sullen acquiescence on the left.

The envoys were escorted back to hear the terms of the Athenians. These were read by the herald in the same order that Cleon proposed them. Isidas, impassive, looked at neither Cleon nor Nicias, and didn't take the wreath when the herald offered it. Instead, a parade of irate speakers took the rostrum, demanding that the Lacedaemonians not withdraw to confer, but make their reply right away. The clamor rose steadily, until Isidas looked at his colleagues with resignation: though the terms were impossible, they would have to say something or risk failure by their silence.

Isidas called for the myrtle.

"Gentlemen, you place us in a difficult position today. We would like nothing better than to reach some agreement, but we were not prepared for an offer of such . . . comprehensiveness. Allow us therefore to suggest that representatives of the Athenians be appointed to discuss terms with us. You have my pledge as a Spartiate that we will give each point due consideration."

At which Cleon charged the rostrum again and snatched the floor. "Can you see now the machinations of tyranny?" he cried. "Instead of discussing the peace in the open, before the People, our friends ask to scurry away to collude in secret! Is this your good faith, Isidas? If the Lacedaemonians are sincere in their desire for peace, let them prove it now, in front of the Assembly! We will agree to hear them out. . . ."

The crowd agreed with a thunderous roar that drowned out the rest of Cleon's statement. Holding out the wreath to the Spartiate seated on the far end of the dais, he then turned to the foreigners, a determined smile on his lips. When the envoy turned it down, he proceeded to the next one, and finally, as the roar mounted, to Isidas. The old man looked forward without lifting a finger; Cleon offered the myrtle again. Isidas tossed his head. A third time, with the people in a frenzy behind him, Cleon dangled the wreath until Isidas raised a hand to refuse it. The gesture—the Spartan warding off the myrtle—became frozen in the minds of the onlookers, destined to be described and redescribed up and down the drinking halls and alleys and fountainhouses of Athens.

VII
Cyclops' Spectacles

1.

The Athenians kept up their double patrols around the island during the period of the truce. By this time, forty days into the siege, the constant sound of the pipes playing the cadence for the oarsmen had worked its way into the blood of the Spartans. It became the unconscious rhythm in their breathing and walking. They heard the sound in their dreams, and after the deliveries of food resumed—when they felt the need to squat again—they moved their bowels in time to it.

With the peace, Epitadas excused the Spartiates from guard duty. The under-thirties continued to stand their posts, while the helots were put to work looking for a new source of sweet water. The first problem—where to dig—was solved by a helot farmer with some experience as a dowser. Instead of a divining rod, he used a round pebble dropped in the back of a shield. He spent a morning pacing, plow-ox style, up and down the center of the island, as he propelled the pebble around the shield's cave with gentle swirling movements. When the pebble at last lodged in the center, the helot declared that water lay beneath his feet. He was standing virtually at the top of the island's highest peak, near the remains of Nestor's fort.

"How far down?" Epitadas asked as he eyed the beaten soil.

"That, only the gods know."

A gang of twenty helots were assigned to the digging, with Doulos taking it upon himself to lead them. As none of the Spartiates would risk blunting a sword among the rocks, the workers went at it with spear butts and bare hands. Pebbles and soil were hauled away in rucksacks and dumped on the cesspit. The Lacedaemonians, meanwhile, indulged their birthright to sit around and watch the helots work, all the while believing that they could do a superior job if their station didn't preclude soiling their hands with anything but blood.

By the terms of the truce, the Peloponnesians were allowed to dispatch one unarmed vessel to the island each day. An Athenian warship could accompany it, but could carry no archers and had to remain offshore while the food and water were off-loaded on the little beach on the southeast quarter of the island. The Lacedaemonians could not come down to claim the supplies until the sailors who delivered them had returned to their ship. This no-contact condition had been hatched by Demosthenes, who realized that the Lacedaemonians might try to escape by secretly switching places with the supply crew. In truth, the notion that they would save their skins by impersonating seamen was so distasteful to the Spartiates that it was never entertained.

The menu was designed to discourage hoarding; the grain, usually barley, was sifted in advance so it spoiled if not used right away. Each Lacedaemonian also received a single piece of goat or lamb, which was delivered just at the edge of turning foul. The Athenians, anticipating that the enemy might try to use their rations of wine to preserve the meat, had their jars severely watered down. Despite these mea-

sures Epitadas ordered his men to put aside half their
rations. To eat cankered, maggot-ridden meat and
fungal grain every other day was a small price to pay
to stretch their resources.

To aid preservation, one of the helots, a cook, suggested they obtain salt by evaporating seawater in the
soldiers' upturned shields. Epitadas and Frog, in a
rare show of concord, agreed that using a hundred
Lacedaemonian shields as salt pans had a vague un-
seemliness. Still, they did nothing to prevent it. It took
days to collect enough salt to be useful.

After a full day of digging, Doulos' team penetrated Sphacteria's tough hide to a depth of three feet.
Antalcidas squatted at the edge of the pit to watch the
work: he saw that the shaft was oblong and irregular,
having been dug around immovable boulders. The
soil looked different the deeper they went, appearing
darker, richer, like the loam of a proper garden.

"The dirt may appear that way," said Doulos,
scooping up a handful, "but it is an illusion due to the
moisture in it. Look here as it is exposed. . . ."

True enough, the little pile gave off a curl of steam
as it lay in the sun. In a few moments it dried to the
color of straw, as powdery and lifeless as the contents
of a funeral jar.

"Does that mean water is close?" asked Antalcidas.

"It may."

Soon they began to find things made by human
hands: bronze dressing pins, broken and corroded;
shattered terra-cotta roof tiles; tiny clay figures of
women, rudely wrought, with profiles that resembled
the letters Φ and Ψ. When the dirt was rubbed off, the
figures showed fine incised ponytails, breasts, priestly
sashes. As the workmen handed them over, Doulos
laid them on the ground with a care that promised he

would rebury them all in due course. This reverence did not satisfy Frog.

"This mucking around is going to offend somebody," he warned.

"Our ancestors are pleased to sacrifice in their children's emergency," replied Epitadas.

"The ancestors of helots?"

"The makers of these things," Doulos interjected, "were born the brothers and sons of old King Nestor, in the time when Messenians and Lacedaemonians joined as partners to topple the city of Troy."

"Who asked you, you little shit?" cried Frog. "Stone, you'd better shut your shieldbearer's mouth or he'll end up buried in that hole!"

Antalcidas smiled. "What he will say, I can no more predict than what comes out of you."

Frog waved him off and clambered down the slope. Antalcidas, meanwhile, caught a gratified gleam in Epitadas' eye as he turned away. It was the first hint of good humor he had seen on his brother in many weeks.

The next morning Antalcidas perched on an oblique ledge on the east side of the island. Sphacteria's bay side, being more sheltered from the sea wind, supported a variety of weeds common in the mountains of Laconia: grayish asphodel in tiny phalanxes, bristling acanthus, a patch or two of wild garlic at his elbow. Looking at the bay, he was surprised at the water's changeability—at the way it reflected the mood of the sky, at how he could anticipate a shift in the wind by watching the pattern of ripples in the distance. Like most natives of landlocked Sparta, he was naïve to the attractions of the sea. When the breeze was in his face he could hear seals barking on the little island in the center of the bay. Dolphins

paced the Athenian triremes as they made their
rounds, breaching just ahead of the metal rams as if
fascinated by their gleam.

He was startled to perceive Doulos crouching beside him.

"What is it?"

"We've found something you should see," said the
helot in a soft voice.

"Water?"

"Come and look."

The helot work crew was above ground when Antalcidas arrived. All of them—and the few Spartiates
who had bothered to come—stood around in pensive
silence, looking down at something in the pit. Not a
few seemed genuinely disturbed, as if some dire portent had manifested.

Antalcidas pushed his way to the front, grumbling at
Doulos and his taste for trivialities. "What is it you've
found now? More hairpins and tiny princesses . . . ?"

His voice trailed off as he looked over the edge.

2.

They had unearthed a skull. Still only half-exposed, it
was of titanic proportions, stretching as far from chin
to crown as a man could reach with outstretched
arms. Unlike any other skull Antalcidas had seen, it
lacked forward-facing holes for the nose, but instead
had two widely spaced, downward-facing nostrils at
its base. What was most remarkable, though, was the
creature's single, cavernous eyehole, set right in the
center of its flat face.

"By the gods . . ." he muttered.

"Other giants have been discovered this way," explained Doulos. "There was the sea monster that

washed up at Sounion in the time of Solon, and the griffin dug up near the mines at Laurion, and Pelops' shoulder from the Trojan straits. But this is the first cyclops."

"No, Cleomenes once spoke of giant's bones he had seen in a dried-up riverbed in Achaea," said Epitadas.

"A cyclops was once born to a sheep on a farm in Amyclae, though it didn't live long," ventured Frog. "Its remains are in the sanctuary there."

Doulos shook his head. "I think we should make a distinction between those creatures who are *meant* to be titans, and those who only resemble them by some accident."

Though Doulos had contradicted Frog, the latter was too distracted by the spectacle below to object. In this the Spartiates and the helots were united, for they were confronted here by a vestige of a superior world, peopled by gods and giants, that had passed away long before the age of ordinary men.

More remains turned up. There were upper arm bones the length of men's legs, and ribs like the beams of roofs, and a line of vertebrae that, when fitted together, described the line of the cyclops' great, humped back. To Doulos, the latrinelike odor of the soil that entombed the titan suggested that he must have perished feet-down in some dismal pit. Pieces of chopped vegetation, like the stems of hard reeds, were scattered through the viscid mass. The titan's weapons—a pair of great, curved horns, possibly from some long-vanished line of colossal stags—were embedded in the mud nearby.

A further discovery suggested that the cyclops had died in battle. The tar-colored pelvis, wide enough for an armored man to wriggle through, was misshapen but intact; buried in its winglike extremity Doulos found a small, fine, flared point hewn from flawless, cream-colored flint. The point still had a bud of mastic stuck to its flat end, and to the mastic, the blackened stub of a wooden arrow shaft.

Frog extracted the point and held it up for the Lacedaemonians to see. Examining it solely as a piece of craft, Antalcidas recognized good work: the knapping scars were precise, symmetrical parabolas, all confidently struck; the surface of the flint still held a sheen that made it seem permanently wet. Yet what the find portended was troubling. The Lacedaemonians passed the arrowhead around, admiring the shining thing as they turned it over in their chapped hands, yet their faces showed no pleasure at all. For them, as for all Greeks, nothing appeared just by accident.

Frog said what the rest were thinking. "So we are not the first to fight on this island. And it seems that the bow decided the issue last time."

"Maybe for this one it did," replied Epitadas. "How can you be sure his comrades didn't win the battle?"

"Because the body was left to rot."

"Perhaps," said Doulos. "But can we presume on how his kind treated their dead? Some people bury their dead in pits, with their weapons. The Scythians, for example."

"Listen to him! When have you ever laid eyes on a Scythian grave, you dog?"

"Better to be a dog than a neckless serpent," Antalcidas interjected.

"So you take a helot's part against an Equal . . . ?" bristled Frog, his hand resting on the hilt of his sword.

"Calm yourselves, now," said Epitadas. "We can all agree that these are the remains of some ancient giant—there is no doubt of that. But what its fate means for us is not as clear. I say, then, that we not assume the worst."

"And how do we know that, *elder*? Stuck here like pets of the Athenians—with not a single goat or sheep—nothing to offer the gods except milled flour and bugs! How do you say we ascertain their will?"

"Maybe Frog will offer himself on our behalf," said Antalcidas.

There were subdued chuckles from somewhere deep in the crowd.

Frog drew himself up to his unimposing fullness of height. "How easy it is to joke when you hide behind your younger brother, Stone! But mark my words: we will all pay a price for ignoring this sign."

It took the rest of that day and part of the next to finish extracting the giant's bones. As the sun set on the second day Doulos was seen dragging the remains around the heights of Sphacteria, arranging them in their living order. All together they constituted a skeleton four times larger than a man's. That such a creature could be brought down by arrows seemed incredible. Then again, such people as the Indians and the Carthaginians were reputed to hunt wild elephants with spear and bow. Antalcidas tried to imagine the scene—the cyclops wading across the narrow channel to the north end of the island, the sea only wetting him to its knees, its great, solitary eye sweeping the heights as it brandished those enormous ivory scimitars. Maddened by blood fever, the giant tops the crest in pursuit—and meets a hail of missiles from its painted, feathered prey. Dauntless, it rushes forward until, like Polyphemus in the caves of Acis, it is rendered helpless by a bolt to the eye. . . .

Epitadas indulged Doulos' curiosity for a while,

but soon ordered him to get on with digging the well. For the moment the Athenians were still allowing food and water to get through. The air around the deliveries, though, had lately chilled: the warships were pressing within bow shot of the beach, and the enemy hoplites were more than watchful. Their purpose, it appeared, was to count the number of jars put ashore, in order to estimate the number of Lacedaemonians on the island. The truce was not made to last.

3.

A letter from Nicias reached Demosthenes. Withdrawing at once to his tent, the general broke the seal and scanned the lines, his expression darkening with each word:

> To Demosthenes, son of Alcisthenes, deme Colonus Agoraeus, General-select Ægeides, etc. etc., from his friend Nicias, son of Niceratus. The peace negotiations are over. The proposals of the Lacedaemonian envoys were not only rejected, but they were denied fair consideration by certain wrong-headed people. The emissaries themselves were most poorly treated. As they were escorted to the gates our mutual acquaintance— you know who—had them taken through one of the affected quarters of the city. While the plague itself has subsided for the present, the Spartans were given a good look at the looted houses. Meanwhile, they were jeered by the masses of exiled souls who have been forced by crowding to follow in death's wake—

So the fools meant to ruin him. For if there was anything that could end a career faster than losing a battle outright, it was squandering the promise of an easy victory. Nicias was an honorable fellow, Demosthenes thought, but he had no head for Assembly politics; of course "certain wrong-headed people" had opposed the peace! If Demosthenes took the island, Cleon would share the glory of advocating the decisive stroke. If, on the other hand, the siege failed, Demosthenes would be finished and Cleon would still benefit, having forced a rival into retirement. It was rather a beautiful piece of gamesmanship, in fact; he would almost have believed that Cleon had a future as a strategist.

Demosthenes again felt that heaviness in his legs. Bending one at the knee, the tendons seemed as brittle as desiccated sticks. No, he thought, he would not be hobbled in the very hour of his greatest test! He began to pound his thigh with his clenched fist, declaring, "Just flesh! Just flesh!"

A dispatch from the archons arrived on the next supply ship. The war must continue, they wrote, because of the intransigence of the Spartans. All deliveries of food would henceforth stop, and hostilities against the troops on the island commence at the commander's discretion. As for the matter of the ships captured by the Peloponnesians and returned to the Athenians as part of the truce—there was a peculiar sentence that might have been dictated by Cleon himself. It read: *The general is advised to release the ships in his custody back to the enemy if, in his judgment, they have adhered to the truce in spirit and in letter.* The implication could not have been clearer to him: it would be up to Demosthenes to find a pretext to keep the ships.

He sent for Leochares. The officer, who never seemed to stray far from his tent flap, arrived as Demosthenes reread the letter, and stood so quietly that the general was startled to look up and find him already there.

"You called for me, sir?"

Demosthenes looked into those gray eyes, so pale that they seemed to repel all light. How, he wondered, can a man stay so blanched after weeks of waiting on a beach?

"The truce is off," he said. "Prepare your men."

Leochares' face twisted into an unfamiliar configuration—a smile. For the first time since news of his brothers' deaths, his chance had come to kill Lacedaemonians. Demosthenes, perceiving this sudden enthusiasm, raised a finger in warning.

"You know your orders. Accomplish your goals, and take no unnecessary chances. Control the Messenians!"

The smile faded from Leochares' lips, but not from his eyes.

4.

Using an old trick, the party kept to the stony patches of the trail to avoid raising dust. Leochares went in front, furrows of worry besetting his brow as he tried all at once to take in the view both near and far; behind him, a trio of Athenian peltasts—light infantry—marched with their helmets off and the bronze parts of their shield faces covered with burlap. Farther back a dozen Messenian exiles, likewise draped so their equipment would not glint in the sun, proceeded up-country in reverent silence. For most of them, it was the first time they had walked free in the land of their ancestors.

The night before, the trireme dropped them off behind the Lacedaemonian lines. The vessel had gone on an overcast night without lanterns or pipes, feeling its way up the coast to a landing place scouted the day be-

fore. The steersman, whom Leochares had known only
from his muffled curses, was obliged to pick his way
north, guided by nothing but the sound of the waves
on the beach and the black profiles of the rocks against
the somewhat lighter gray of the water. At the worst
moment the forward oars to starboard crashed against
something submerged—probably more rocks—and
there was yelling as the boatswain ordered the blades
raised. For several anxious moments the vessel floated
free, every soul on it frozen in silence, as they waited
for the enemy lookouts to raise the alarm. But they
heard nothing.

They went ashore a few miles behind the enemy
positions north of old Pylos. About the location of the
helot village that had sent supplies to the Athenians,
Leochares could only guess: the boys who had first
visited the stockade had never specified it, and in fact
had forbidden the invaders from incriminating the
villagers by contacting them. With the end of the truce
all bets were off, however. To make mischief in
Lacedaemon's own backyard was an opportunity
both rare and irresistible, now that Messenian exiles
from Naupactus had arrived.

The exiles were the descendants of the Messenian
rebels who had, in the days of Cimon, held out against
the Spartan army on Mount Ithome. Lately they had
become little more than semi-civilized freebooters.
They came by their own initiative in a ship of thirty
oars, sporting shields, spears and cuirasses stripped
from victims all around the Corinthian gulf. Their
most valuable contribution lay not in their arms, however, but in their mouths: unlike the Athenians, they
stood a chance of convincing the local helots to revolt.
No self-respecting Messenian, after all, would believe
promises made in the mincing dialect of Attic

dandies. The exiles could speak to them in their native, barnyard Dorian. If they did manage to spark an uprising, and the unrest spread as it once had after the Great Earthquake, the Lacedaemonians would be so beset they would have to make peace on Athens' terms.

The party struck east through a scrubland of pine dwarfed by the breeze from the sea. As the water receded behind them, Leochares led them down to a stream bottom wet by a winding trickle and lined by oleanders. It was a fair guess that the helots sited their village near this rivulet; they would proceed along its bed until they found signs of a settlement. They had been walking a long time, though, when Leochares began to wonder just how far the Messenian boys could have lugged those sacks of meal and skins of wine.

Doubling back, he searched for the village, risking detection by sticking his head up over the crest of the slope. They had backtracked almost to their landing place when he was rewarded at last by a cluster of thatched roofs. The helots had placed their houses within a grove of broad cypress to moderate wind and sun. Coming closer, Leochares made out stockpens and wagons parked at the margins of the settlement, and crops marching in neat rows toward the eastern highlands.

He turned to the leader of the Messenian exiles, a rawboned giant with the charmingly Homeric name of Protesilaus. "We've found them. It's up to you, now."

The other never took his eyes off the line of roofs ahead. "I think not," was all he said.

Leochares snorted at this rustic bloody-mindedness. Perhaps the only charming thing about Protesilaus was his name. But as he came closer to the village he understood the Messenian's caution. Though the houses were intact, none of them showed smoke for cooking or cleaning. The black-faced sheep, which he thought would be driven up to pasture at that time of day, seemed to doze in their folds. And it seemed inconceivable that the Lacedaemonians would leave the place unguarded with the enemy so close by.

He had almost reached the rail of the enclosure when he saw that the sheep were not asleep, and did not have black faces. With muzzles pressed against the earth, their wool was stained by puddles of their own congealed blood.

"Take guarding positions!" commanded Leochares.

They entered the village in a defensive circle, with shields up and visors down. In this way, with their noses assaulted by the stench of slaughtered livestock, they inspected the settlement, peering into every house and granary. The place was emptied of people in a manner that hinted at some sudden evacuation. There were water jugs set next to half-filled cauldrons, abandoned in midpouring, and half-clad spindles left in stoolside baskets, and axes stuck midway through logs. A clay figure of a warrior lay in the dust of one threshold, as if it had been dropped by a child roughly snatched away.

"Stand down," Leochares said at last, and pointed at one of the other Messenians whose name he had never learned. "You there—get up on that hill and keep watch."

Closer examination did nothing to lift the mystery. They found no bodies and no sign of a struggle. None of the houses were damaged by fire. The people had gone in a hurry, but someone had taken the time to cut the throats of the larger animals. He looked to Protesilaus, who remained silent but offered a rueful expression.

"All right, then," Leochares addressed him. "Do you know what happened here?"

"What happened," the Messenian replied with weariness, "is what always happens, and what you Athenians should have expected. The Spartans have cleared the villages."

"Cleared them all? Can they do that?" asked one of the peltasts.

Protesilaus gazed pityingly at the man. He opened his mouth to say something, but closed it again, as if judging himself too perturbed to speak.

Leochares led a more thorough examination of the village to see if any of the helots had hidden away or been forgotten. They found not a living soul in the whole place, and indeed discovered that every possible source of food, down to the last piglet, had been destroyed. He was at a loss to decide where to go next when the lookout cried that he had seen something.

There was a large area of trampled grain a short distance to the east. When the lookout reported it, Leochares thought at first that someone must have camped there. But on investigation they found not a camp but a zone of disturbed soil with a mound in the center. It seemed that something had been buried underneath.

It took only a few minutes digging with knives and swords to find the first helot body. Brushing away the soil, Leochares was looking into a rot-blackened face, the maggots congregated around the soft tissues of the eye. The body was of a beardless young male. Fighting the sickening effect of the stench, the Messenians pushed this first corpse aside and dug deeper through dirt thick with the effluvia of the dead. The exiles were hip deep in their countrymen and standing on more when they pushed their spear butts down through the stinking mass.

"It's bodies all the way down," said Leochares.

"There's a story the Messenians remember in times like this," Protesilaus began, unprompted. "It was in my grandfather's time, in a town just a few miles east of here. The great revolt had already swept through most of the country, but in this one place the helots had stayed on the land. The Spartiates came one day with a proposal: if the fittest of the men agreed to serve garrison duty along the Arcadian borders, the state would emancipate them and their families. With the prospect of seeing their sons free, and the pledge that they would not be forced to fight their countrymen, 211 of the strongest, brightest, most hopeful Messenians of the town agreed to serve terms of seven years.

"The Lacedaemonians welcomed the helots into the army like long-lost brothers. All 211 were given crimson cloaks and shields, and led on a procession to make soldiers' dedications at the local shrines. After this they were feasted in the town crossroads in full view of their families. The wives wept to see their husbands treated like men at last, instead of like animals. The sons of the elect went about boasting that their fathers were warriors in the Spartan army. The next day they were formed into platoons and paraded out of town. They said they were going to receive their training in Laconia. The echo of their voices singing the marching song, 'Castor's Air,' was heard in the village for a long time after they were gone.

"Not one of those 211 Messenians was ever seen again. Some say all were killed in the mountains and tossed into a chasm; others that they were locked in a

pen and starved to death. What is very clear is this:
the Lacedaemonians feared these men, and lured
them out with challenges only the strongest would
accept. And when they had taken an oath before the
gods to serve their former masters loyally, these Spartans, these honorable and pious Spartans, had them
killed in secret. Not a pinch of ash or a fragment of
bone was left for their families to honor."

The Messenian turned to the peltast he had meant
to speak to before. "You ask, can they do that? The
Lacedaemonians have nothing if not long memories.
If Fortune is with us, they have only evacuated—not
killed—the women and children. But they'll slaughter
more than sheep to prevent another revolt."

Since a pyre would give away their presence,
Leochares forbade the exiles to give the victims the
proper rites. There were too many bodies, in any case,
to do anything more than cover them up and consign
them to Hades. That night, the party went upstream
as far as they dared, mounting hills and climbing trees
as occasion demanded, looking for any sign of human
habitation. Over the entire expanse from the Messenian highlands to the sea, not a single torch was burning except in the billets of the Lacedaemonians—no
hearths in the towns, no lamps in the farmhouses, not
the campfire of a solitary shepherd. When they had
gone their farthest east, Leochares thought he saw a
knot of lights twinkling in the foothills; in the moments when the night air settled, the luminous mass
sorted into a cluster of points too haphazard to be a
military camp. Had the surviving helots all been ban-
ished to that place, as far as possible from the corrupting influence of the Athenians?

The party had started on its way back when one of
the pickets heard a noise to the south. He ordered all

the exiles and peltasts to ground, signaling they should do nothing but hug the earth. More sounds: the snap of a fennel stalk, an exhalation that might have been the wind—or an outburst of whispered commands.

Nobody trained for night fighting like the Spartans; rivals all over Greece had learned to concede the dark to them. The suspicion that they were being stalked robbed the Messenians of all confidence. They jabbered at each other, rattling their panoplies in their alarm. Even with the burlap covers, the din of their shields against the rocks became truly alarming. Leochares turned back at them.

"Shut your traps you dogs! If you make me give away my position again—"

He meant to leave the threat unspecified, but the exiles only laughed.

"And you'll do what?" said a voice behind him.

Leochares responded in as deliberate a tone he could manage at a whisper: "I'll hobble you and leave you here."

The party retreated to the sea by the light of a low crescent moon that cast faint raking shadows on the ground. The sight of their own tramping silhouettes had the effect of accelerating their pace, until they were careening at a run, stumbling over rocks and their own feet. As the sound of the water rose to meet them Leochares thought he heard the thud of bare knees against stone. Someone cursed in what seemed like a Dorian drawl.

"They're behind us!" a peltast cried, practically running up his commander's back in his haste to escape.

Leochares thought of pausing to make sure one of his Messenians had not fallen, but was distracted by the sight of the warship riding offshore. Leochares gave the recognition signal, three cracks of his spear shaft against his shield, and listened for the response. He heard the voice of the boatswain ring out in much-welcome Attic, and the rip of oar blades in the water as the ship pressed inshore. His men couldn't wait: slinging their shields across their backs and dropping their spears, they hit the water en masse, reaching for the ship's stem, for oar shafts, for anything they could lay their hands on.

Then came the moment when Leochares, alone, watched from the beach as a knot of exiles accumulated on the ship's ram—a ball of panicked men clinging there like bees swarming on a tree—and the captain hissed for them to take turns lest they upset the ship on her keel. It was a moment in which he thought he glimpsed the end of a war that was for so long unimaginable. Athens would be defeated.

It was near dawn when they approached the stockade on the Sikia Channel. With distance from shadowy threats the men regained their composure; the captain had them divided in two groups now, squatting in balanced numbers along each rail. Casually, almost in boredom, Leochares counted the exiles and peltasts—and then, his alarm rising, counted them again.

"We left with sixteen, didn't we?" he asked Protesilaus.

"Fifteen plus yourself," came the answer, and after his eyes danced over the heads strung out behind him, the Messenian added, "Fourteen now. We've left someone behind, I think!"

5.

The Acharnians of the *Terror* took the oars the next day for their eighteenth circuit of Sphacteria—the most of any ship in the fleet. There were almost fifty other vessels at Demosthenes' disposal, but after two months it was clear which crews were good at blockading and which not so good. On none of its previous trips had the *Terror* run aground, gotten rocks dropped on it, or lost rowers to oar shafts snapped back by submerged obstacles. Sphaerus, the steersman, had neither orbited the island in wide, lazy circles, nor taken undue chances coming in close. The captain, Xeuthes, had not sought undue shore privileges, but had beached his vessel only as much as necessary.

Yet the effort was taking its toll on Philemon's investment. The limited laying-up time had saturated the hull's wood, causing leaks. What supplies they had shipped for repairs were long since gone, forcing the carpenters to beg for replacement blades, unsplit oar sleeves, and intact sheets from the rest of the fleet. "Don't look, but here come the Acharnians again!" the other captains would complain; though the quality of their patriotism was well-known, the fact earned them no sympathy from their fleetmates. All of them would ultimately confront a long voyage home, very likely out of fair-sailing season, when—if ever—the accursed siege ended.

Xeuthes was therefore in a foul mood as he watched the familiar serrations of the island slip by. He was tired of these waters and these rocks. He was tired of being tired. He had never lost a vessel in his time, but might yet see one rotted out from beneath him. And it was all on account of a pack of stubborn

Lacedaemonians who refused to accept they were beaten! In his gloom he could imagine his enemies starving themselves, eating dirt, consuming their dead companions—going to any extreme to outlast the summer, to see the Athenians scattered by the autumn storms. He envisioned them as grinning, cocksure skeletons, taunting him from the beach as the *Terror*, down to one bank of patched oars, waddled away on its waterlogged strakes.

Lately he was consumed by another peeve: with time ashore rationed among all the ships, he had been forced to take far too many meals afloat. No one was meant to eat on the water, he decided; there was a reason the gods had given mortals legs instead of flukes. Nor were men made to spend all their days packed like sprats in a jar, struggling to breathe in sweltering middecks or stockades strewn with filth. He summoned Stilbiades.

"By the gods," Xeuthes declared to the bosun, "we will eat our next meal on dry land!"

"Sir?"

"Stop the ship. Tell Sphaerus to find us a decent place to go ashore."

Stilbiades sucked in a breath like a drowning man breaking the surface at last. "But isn't that against orders? The Spartans—"

"Use your eyes, man! If we come ashore on this low section, we can see them coming from a long way off. I suspect they have no archers."

"I suspect you're right," the other replied, his wind-chapped face cracking into a grin. In fact, he longed for the Lacedaemonians to attack. Anything to force the issue at last.

The men of the *Terror* went to the island in relays. They had very little food with them—just a few sacks of half-rotten onions and whatever remained of the rationed flour. Yet these seemed like a kingly repast to those privileged to recline ashore, free to stretch every limb beside a fine, fragrant, sleep-inducing pinewood campfire. Patronices, the beam man, lay dozing, his head cradled on a rock that, by the peace that shone from his face, might as well have been a silken pillow.

"I wouldn't get too comfortable," Timon advised. "The longhairs will spot our smoke sooner or later."

"Let them come! They'll learn a lesson they'll never forget, coming between a sailor and his rest—"

Dicaearchus was sitting up, examining the soles of his bare feet. "These fucking rocks! I've never bled so much in seven years of war!"

"In seven years of war you've never stopped complaining."

"Look for yourself, then! Here, here, and *here* . . . !"

"I'd dance on razors not to have to walk on sand again," said Timon. "I believe my toes are permanently curled."

"So your boyfriend tells us," Patronices replied, the ends of his lips smugly twisted.

The next group to land included Xeuthes, Stilbiades, and the deck men Cleinias and Oreus. Old Sphaerus was invited as well, but refused. "Anyone who invites his enemy to dinner is a fool," he said in a voice so dripping with portent everyone had to laugh. Philemon, the trierarch, meanwhile, made one of his rare appearances outside his cabana, sticking his head out when the ship came to rest ashore.

"Is the siege over?" he asked.

They had three large fires going now, each loaded with sap-filled twigs that made much smoke and noise. *The Lacedaemonians obviously know we are here*, thought Xeuthes as he leaned against a boulder, his eyes fixed north; *if we bring enough men ashore that may be protection enough against an attack.* It made no sense for their adversaries to reveal their numbers before the real battle, he judged. Yet he was also beginning to suspect that he had been precipitate in declaring the beach safe. A third of his crew was now on their backs, snoozing or roasting little buff-colored lizards they had caught in the brush. If the enemy managed a sneak attack, most of his men would be cut down before they got to their feet.

"You there! Keep your traps shut!" the captain snapped at the archers posted on the *Terror*'s foredeck. The bowmen straightened up, ceased their chatter. They were, after all, supposed to give cover if the Lacedaemonians came. "Remind me to trade away those idlers when we get back," Xeuthes said to the bosun. Stilbiades agreed with a drowsy grunt.

The attack came just past noon. Before Xeuthes heard anyone cry out, arrows were whistling over his head. Scanning the hillside, he spotted them at last—not Spartans, but weird negative images of Spartans, with cloaks faded to gray and skins broiled red from the sun. They were spearless, swords in hand, zigging and zagging like oblong rocks bouncing down the slope to crush them. There seemed to be only a dozen—or in Lacedaemonian terms, there were only sixty Athenians to face twelve raging furies.

"They're here! They're here!" someone cried.

"Back to the ship!" Xeuthes commanded. "Archers . . . by the gods . . ."

They were shooting, but hitting nothing as the lead Spartan approached the edge of the camp. He struck down the first Athenian he met—a hold man named Lysimachus—with a precise economy of effort: just a brief pointing of the end of his blade, a stab to the soft

part of the throat, and on to the next one. Everything
was in an uproar now, his crew breaking frantically
for the water, the great crimson lambdas appearing
over the rocks; the *Terror*'s little corps of six hoplites,
having brought their armor with them, made a stand
with shields presented. Three Spartans raised their
own shields as they crashed against them, pushing
the Athenians backward over the broken ground until
the latter lost their footing. Five of Xeuthes' men were
killed where they lay; the last escaped by abandoning
his shield.

Stilbiades was yelling something as he shoved
Xeuthes back toward the gangplank. Philemon, for his
part, was running with impressive speed, his bulk
streaming back in great liquid waves across his torso.
With the Lacedaemonians closing behind him, he
seemed suddenly to be airborne, little feet churning
on pointe as his piercing scream rose to a funereal
crescendo.

Xeuthes was yelling at him, at the bosun, at everyone as he backed onto the plank. The archers seemed
not to have hit a single attacker. The enemy were at
last slowed down by the extraordinary efforts of a few
ordinary oarsmen who threw flaming boughs. The
smoking missiles seemed to give the Spartans
pause—one of them stood still long enough for an
archer to get a bead and put an arrow through his
shoulder. He was propelled sideways, toppling on his
side like a stone cairn blown down on a windy hillside. Two other Lacedaemonians converged to help
him; the oarsmen kept throwing their burning sticks
until they were distant enough to turn and run.

The crew took with them as many of their dead
comrades as they could. Yet, as the *Terror* pulled away
from the shore she abandoned ten bodies on the

beach. The captain had Sphaerus take them out into the bay and back again in a wide loop, to rest again near shore, ram-forward. Xeuthes then went up to the stem and did what custom demanded: he asked for quarter and the Lacedaemonians' permission to retrieve the dead.

The customary answer was to accede, but he got no answer from the island. Xeuthes repeated his plea, then turned to Stilbiades.

"Are those dogs ignoring me?"

"Feel that," said the other, raising his open palm to the shore. "There's quite a strong fire behind that smoke."

Xeuthes could feel the heat through his beard. The island, of course, was a tinderbox, but could the blaze have spread so fast? And what was the precedent for claiming the fallen from a burning battlefield when the victors have fled? Pondering these questions, he left his ship floating, with oars poised in midstroke, as the rising inferno melted the crystals of sea salt on his brow to stinging tears.

6.

The Lacedaemonian emissary arrived the very evening the truce lapsed. Demosthenes received the man in his tent before joining one of the ships that would guard the island that night. It had lately turned cold on the bay; a hint of fall, of snow on some Balkan mountain and leaves beginning to moulder, hung on the northwest breeze. On his field bed his valet had left his equipment for the night: a pack with some bread and cheese, a woolen cloak, a little scroll of light poetry to divert him, and if that failed, a set of well-worn worry beads. That his visitor would perceive

him to be a man willing to stand a post himself was all
to the good, he thought—but in retrospect he regret-
ted showing the beads.

This time they sent an old Spartiate named Zeuxippos. As he regarded the cadaverous fellow, the old
man's eyes shot back a look of mildly tempered amusement, as if the sight of anyone not Spartan bearing
arms seemed somehow absurd. Demosthenes responded with the condescension Athenians typically
reserved for Attic and Euboean hicks who came into
town on festival days. And why, wondered Demosthenes, did the longhairs always send a new man for
every errand? Was it something as straightforward as
not permitting any one person to become indispensa-
ble? After years of fighting the Lacedaemonians, he
suspected that the reason was both simpler and subtler:
they must believe that any one of them had to be com-
petent, by the mere fact that he was a Spartiate.

"By the terms of the truce, the Peloponnesians
handed over all the Athenian ships they had captured," Zeuxippos was saying. "Need we remind you
that with the resumption of the war, you are now
bound by oath to return our property to us?"

Demosthenes stuffed his beads into a fold in his
cloak. "Honored guest, what you say is correct—but
incomplete. By my understanding of the terms, the
smallest violation by either side nullifies the agreement."

"And how have the Lacedaemonians failed to keep
their oaths?"

"In what ignorance do the Spartans keep their elders! Nor am I obliged to tell you how you have
wronged us—though I will, just to show you how
Athenians value their agreements. A small party of
our allies was attacked during a foraging trip to the

north of Pylos. One man was killed. And so by the terms of the armistice, we are released from our obligation to return the ships."

Zeuxippos appeared ready either to laugh in Demosthenes' face or assault him with his veiny fists. "I think you speak of an invasion of our territory by bandits. The attempt was driven into the sea. Have I heard you rightly—did you say the Athenians were in league with these troublemakers? If so, the violation was on your part, not ours."

"It is my understanding, sir, that the Messenians are the rightful owners of this territory, and that it is therefore impossible for them to 'invade' what is already theirs."

"Take care, Demosthenes! We are not disputing in the stoa here. These are matters older than you know, and perhaps beyond your understanding. If you wish to speak of what is 'rightful,' know that the rabble you call your 'allies' swore before the gods never to return from exile."

"Their grandfathers did, perhaps," replied Demosthenes. "But that is nothing to us—they fight with us now, and as I have said, the smallest violation nullifies our commitment."

On schedule, Leochares begged to interrupt.

"General, the fleet is ready."

"So you see I must leave you now," said Demosthenes. When Zeuxippos said nothing, he could not resist adding, "If you wish anything to eat or drink before you leave—wine, fruit—please ask the steward. We are very well provisioned here."

Zeuxippos turned himself around. Before he left, he leaned hard on his staff and addressed Demosthenes over his shoulder.

"I wonder if they will elect you general again,

Demosthenes, when you fail to learn the lessons of Aetolia."

It was a blow well struck. Demothenes colored despite himself, but could think of nothing to say. He was rescued when Leochares made an unexpected return.

"Begging your pardon, but we have word from our lookouts on Koryphasion."

"What is it? Have the Peloponnesians found the courage to attack?"

"No, General—it's the island. It's burning."

VIII
Dispatches

1.

Cleon had a sophisticated sense of which speakers to attend to and which to ignore. Just then there was a youngster from Scambonidae on the platform, probably some sweet-cheeked scion of a rich father too frightened to risk his own name in public, propounding the kind of moderation that lost wars. Cleon only heard one or two words at a time—a weakling verb, some overwatered adjective—but that was enough to know the speech wasn't worth his attention.

Instead, he focused on the message in front of him, written just days before by a Messenian informant outside of Pylos. Through his network of merchant guest-friends scattered from the far west to the borders of Attica, he got his information, delivered by mounted courier, days before the dispatch ships rounded the Peloponnese. In ordinary times this was a handy advantage; during crises like this, it would be decisive in the defeat of all his enemies, near and far.

> . . . As the fire was hidden from the Athenians by the high ground of the island, it was first seen from the glow it cast over the south end of Sphacteria. Some time later a ship returned from patrol with news of its outbreak in the dry brush of that area. Demosthenes was at first suspicious of this story, for the vessel was

*manned exclusively by Acharnians, who had been
known to exceed their orders in their zeal to harm the
enemy. At length the captain of the ship, Xeuthes, son
of Cratinus, convinced the general that the Lacedaemonians were themselves to blame, having foolishly allowed a campfire to go out of control. As
Xeuthes was prepared to swear by the name of his father, who fought the barbarian at Salamis, Demosthenes was convinced that no unmanly treachery had
been done on his account.*

*In the following days the fire spread to an extent that
amazed both Athenians and Peloponnesians. The
south was scorched overnight, and when dawn broke a
great tower of smoke was seen rising over the island.
The lookouts on the ships said they could follow the
progress of the blaze by the streams of embers, which
ignited the vegetation that was downwind and weak-
ened by drought. The crackling of the flames was
heard from the water; the explosion of certain tree
trunks made thunderclaps that echoed from one end of
the bay to the other. . . .*

He reached the last line of the message just as the
speaker concluded. From the left of the Assembly
came a smattering of applause which, by his internal
measuring stick, he judged to be of no threat to his interests. The herald, holding the myrtle at the end of
his outstretched arm, did not need to pose the question, "Who wishes to speak?" before a familiar face
made the slightest of affirmative gestures. The citizens
of Athens broke into an uproar as Cleon mounted the
rostrum. The dispatch he had been reading was now
safely inside a fold of his chiton, tucked reassuringly
next to his heart.

"Gentlemen, we have heard much today about what is advisable, just, or prudent about this war. I would not dare to impugn the motives of those who urge policies with which I disagree. For our system is unique in the freedom under which such debate is held, where any man, rich or poor, educated or ignorant, may have his say, and in so doing place his wisdom in the service of the state. Instead of demeaning these deliberations with the language of faction, I will therefore confine my remarks to the facts as we know them—and only to the facts."

The cacophony of cheers and catcalls died away, for they all recognized that Cleon had decided to explore a new key. Today, he would out-Nicias Nicias' calm, detached, measured drone.

"All can agree on how matters now stand. It is fifty days since the Lacedaemonians were trapped. The effort to reduce the island has been under the nominal command of our esteemed Nicias, though he has yet to leave the city to take direct control. That task he has left to his deputy on the scene, Demosthenes, son of Alcisthenes, which I agree to be only right and proper since Demosthenes not only conceived the operation, but has been in Pylos from the beginning. To this end a sum of three hundred talents has already been spent, with every reason to believe that significant further monies will be required. What, then, have we gained from this expenditure of time and resources?

"Since the end of the truce, we are told, no supplies have reached the garrison except what one man or a small boat may slip past our blockade. No blockade mounted so close to an enemy coast can be 'watertight,' the admirals say. Fair enough! But if that is so, to what degree can we expect this strategy of delay to ever achieve success? There is no sign that the Lacedaemonians are in desperate straits at the moment. Indeed, the Spartiates who once seemed so desperate to gain the return of their sons have never returned to the Assembly with better terms. How confident those old men of the Gerousia must be! How heartily they must be laughing at all of us!

"Please don't misunderstand me—I don't say these things to be provocative. I raise my concerns because I believe the People deserve to know what the prospects for success really are. And so the question must be put to our strategist-in-chief: with the Lacedaemonians lounging unconcerned on the beach, and our treasury running low, and the autumn storms bearing down on our brave sailors, what provision has he made to bring the siege to a prompt end?"

Having said not one word more than he believed necessary, Cleon surrendered the wreath. And while there were some titters around the sanctum when he claimed not to seek an argument, it was an uncannily statesmanlike performance for a man of Cleon's reputation.

Nicias, who was at the nearby house of a friend when his adversary had begun speaking, rushed back just in time to hear Cleon's final question. One of his allies filled him in on the rest as he came forward, his back bent like an old tree tormented by the wind. When Nicias reached the platform he seemed more than usually loathe to speak. It was a reticence that had served him well over the years: though he was one of the wealthiest men in Athens, his defenders came from all strata of fortune and penury, many out of simple pity for the civic burdens he so obviously bore.

"Cleon is a speaker," began Nicias. "I am not a speaker, but just a general. Perhaps Cleon will excuse me, then, for voicing an opinion on matters of my expertise during one of the rare moments when we are not enjoying his."

Laughter. Cleon bit his lip.

"I know that it seems that this affair has gone on for a long time. This should not be a surprise, considering that certain voices have been proclaiming victory since the first hours of the siege. In any case, I need not remind this Assembly of the magnitude of our task, both to maintain a blockade on a distant island and to defend our position there, deep in enemy territory. Many minds have been concerned so far with how to accomplish this—minds far more subtle than mine, grappling with problems many of us cannot begin to fathom. Through their efforts, we stand today on the brink of the victory so loudly anticipated by some. It is something to savor on its own, the nearness of our victory! That we cannot yet make a final celebration is unfortunate, perhaps, but hardly an emergency.

"But now we hear the question posed, I suspect more in impatience than in disrespect, of what plans we have to subdue the enemy before autumn. With equal respect, then, allow my reply to be just as abrupt—there are many plans. Plans, after all, are cheap; they cost nothing, and have no consequences. They are as plentiful as pebbles on a beach. What is rare, though, is the wisdom to know which plan to use.

"Allow me to answer the esteemed Cleon with another question: how many Spartans are on the island today? Or to put it another way, how much force need we apply to defeat them, without leaving the fleet too

weak to fight its way home? For surely, given our
friend's confident turn of rhetoric on this issue, he has
the kind of deep strategical knowledge to allay the
concerns of minds so much simpler than his! How
many Spartans, Cleon? The People want to know."

Nicias's sarcasm, so uncharacteristic of him, struck
the Assembly like a bolt of lightning, electrifying the
left and deadening the tongues of everyone else. But
in the midst of it all Cleon was calm, even amused.
With his right hand, he patted the place on his chiton
where he had tucked the dispatch. In the letter, his informant had described the final consequences of the
fire: with Sphacteria denuded of most vegetation, the
enemy was exposed to the Athenian lookouts on Koryphasion. There were precisely 582 Lacedaemonians
on the island. Of those, no more than 420 were hoplites, and the rest shieldbearers. This was a lower
number than anyone had supposed—and far too few
to defend an island twenty stades long.

"Nicias asks a question," Cleon replied. "Far be it
for me to deny our distinguished friend an answer,
fashioned in the same style with which he answered
mine! He wonders how many Spartans occupy the island. I say this is a strange thing for a commander to
ask a civilian! How many Spartans, Nicias? I tell you
I have no idea—and I say further that the real problem
lies not in my ignorance, but in yours! *Why don't you
know, Nicias?*"

Cleon had fallen into his signature mode now—his
tone rising, his right hand pounding his thigh. The assemblymen looked at each other with anticipation;
with any luck, Cleon would soon be running up and
down the sanctum, voice in a shriek, excoriating citizens at random as if each of them was Nicias.

"What fun our commander makes of the basic good

sense of the Athenians! While we all wonder why the Lacedaemonians are allowed to make fools of us month upon month, Nicias dares quibble over qualifications. As if only generals are permitted to take pride in the reputation of Athenian arms! As if honest citizens are not obliged to sniff out incompetence! Tell us, is this how little you think of us, Nicias? Tell us!"

A wave of sound, like one of the monstrous surges that pounded the coast after a storm at sea, rose from the back and broke over the front row where Nicias glowered.

"There have been a lot of questions posed today— questions that have gotten no good answers from either side. And so permit me to make not a question but a statement. I want to make a statement that is so simple, so self-evident, that even we, we unschooled Athenians, can understand it! Here it is. . . ."

2.

If twenty thousand pairs of ears made a sound as they pricked to attention, Cleon heard it. After the requisite pause, he opened his arms wide in a gesture of indiscriminate, encompassing, yet self-aggrandizing love.

"Neither Nicias nor I know the strength of the enemy—but I say now that should not matter! What care had the men who fought at Marathon for troop counts, Nicias? Or the citizens who took the oars at Salamis? The verdict of this war, and the future of the Athenians, depend on either routing the Lacedaemonians or taking them to ransom. For that reason the task must be done despite the odds. It must be done despite the excuses of topography, bad supplies, or interference from the enemy ships. It must be done despite fears for our personal reputation if we fail! For the Athenians can accept defeat—they can understand and forgive, as they have the valiant Demosthenes, who lost so many in Aetolia. What they cannot forgive, though, is the failure even to come to grips with the task—to flit and skulk and delay while the chance for victory slips away!

"Do I have your attention, Nicias? If I do, I call on you to avail us of the talent you showed so well against the Megarians. The moment you present yourself at Pylos, and redouble your efforts against them, the Lacedaemonians will fall in no more than twenty days. That is my prediction—you will bear them home in chains in twenty days. For I have faith in you, Nicias, if you do not!"

Cleon came down with his fellow citizens reduced to silence before him. Men came to the Assembly to hear him speak for many reasons; in a body that could only function in an air of mind-numbing decorum, they came for Cleon's histrionic excess, for his humor, for his talent of turning any debate, on any issue he chose, into an elemental struggle between light and darkness. He had often used the tactic of picking out one member of the opposition in the crowd, some specimen of his class, and blustering directly at him. But today another line had been crossed. Pericles, in a generation on the platform, rarely deigned to mention the name of any living man, let alone expose him to direct criticism. Cleon had dropped all such delicacy in his war against Nicias. A debate about policy had become, in his hands, a prosecution.

Nicias was obliged to defend himself, but he did not rise at first. Instead, he listened as his allies whispered into his ear, showing no reaction except a weary nod as the conferral ended. There was no evidence of anticipation, no joy in rhetorical combat on his face when he came forward. Offered the wreath, he didn't put it on his head, but held it in his hand, as if he expected to speak only a moment.

"To Cleon's rantings, I make no reply except this: if he would do better, I would be pleased to surrender my command to him—if the Assembly agrees."

The rancor gathered by degrees as Nicias withdrew. Citizens turned to complete strangers and argued with them; the place divided between those who denounced Nicias' offer as an abject surrender and those who saw it as a brilliant tactic. The latter observed that Cleon, who by upbringing knew leather making better than soldiering, would now be forced into a difficult choice: either accept nomination to lead a campaign with uncertain prospects, or refuse a command that he himself had claimed should be wrapped up in twenty days. Nonsense, replied the skeptics— Nicias' shame for abandoning his command would damage him more than any defeat would harm Cleon. Back and forth they went as the magistrate screamed for order, and the sun climbed higher, and the lunch vendors in the market looked up and wondered why the Assembly was taking so long that morning.

At length Cleon took the floor and raised his hands for quiet. The uproar died at once.

"Athenians," he said, "how have things come to this? The generals of our city now surrender their sacred responsibilities like fancy friends trading whores across the banquet table! Like all nobles with too much to lose, Nicias fears the consequences of defeat more than he craves the fruits of victory. In this hour of crisis, he therefore indulges in petty rhetorical ploys, hoping to confuse the People by shifting attention to his own indispensability. Nicias, your selfishness is showing! Very well, then, let us call this sad bluff! I accept your challenge, Nicias, if you truly are derelict enough to surrender your command. I have no faith in the depth of your sincerity!"

The herald accepted the wreath and looked again to Nicias. The latter did not rise to speak, but merely shook his assent. The herald looked to the president of the Assembly, who also shook his head.

"The measure is before the People," the herald announced, "to accept the resignation of Nicias and dispatch Cleon in his place."

A thunderous cheer went up that echoed back from the hills. But the tone was only half-serious: in these dismal times, it came as a fine joke, to replace Nicias with this windbag. It might even serve Cleon right, to get his hands dirty at last!

Cleon went white. He had not been thinking of the actual effect of his words, but only of scoring a victory over Nicias. Shaken, he demanded the myrtle from the herald, who ignored him. He tried to seize it; the herald, who was a much taller man, held it out of his reach. The spectacle became a burlesque: Cleon, desperate to take back his words, was reduced to hanging on the other's arm, trying to use his weight to pull down the hand that held the wreath. At last the herald relented. Cleon snatched the myrtle and unleashed a stentorian wail.

"O perfidy! O my dear Athenians! Don't let yourselves be fooled by the schemes of devious men! Perhaps I speak too earnestly in defense of my city; it is a tempting excess for me, I admit, but no vice! I say let Nicias show similar zeal as he prosecutes the war. If he had, we would not be in the position we are now, casting about for his replacement. . . ."

"WE WANT CLEON!" shouted a voice from the

left. The demand was followed by an outburst of guffaws from that side, which provoked the right to rise in indignation, crying, "YES, WE WANT CLEON!" The wings of the Assembly then became locked in a competition over who wanted Cleon more; the herald and then the president could scarcely be heard over the riot as they demanded order, and Cleon stood helpless, trying to fathom what was happening.

Looking down, he regarded Nicias, who avoided returning his gaze. Cleon believed he saw mirth in the manner of Nicias' furtiveness—some trace of smugness that boiled his blood. Cleon reached up and again felt the dispatch under the fabric of his chiton. The touch of it restored what had been shaken in him; if Nicias had known that the Spartans held the island with such a small force, he would never have surrendered his command. The advantage, then, was still with Cleon—if he had the courage to exploit it. He raised a hand for quiet.

"The measure is before us, and I say let us vote, gentlemen! Unlike Nicias, I am not afraid of the Lacedaemonians. True, I have not seen battle in decades, since my days as an ephebe. But because Athens trusts me, and I love Athens, I accept this challenge.

"Moreover, I will not strip Athens of defenders to guarantee my word. I will take only the foreigners who are in the city—the peltasts from Thracian Aenus, the men from the islands of Lemnos and Imbros—as well as a company or two of archers. With these few troops, and those under the command of Demosthenes, I pledge to accomplish what more experienced men have not. I will wipe the sneers from the Spartans' faces. I will capture them, or kill them where they stand. Twenty days from when I depart, it shall be done."

3.

Word of Zeuxippos' return from Messenia spread ahead of him through the villages of Laconia. Before it reached Kynosoura, Andreia could sense the tidings were not good. There was an air that filled Sparta with news of victories of the military or diplomatic kind—an air not of outright celebation, but of quiet reaffirmation of the expected order of things. In this world, the Lacedamonians got their way and foreigners yielded, and it would always be so until the day it wasn't. That air was absent the day of the old man's return. There was only a sense of cruel suspension, of a sword that had slipped a little from its tether but still hung over them all.

Zeuxippos would only come to her after he had reported to the ephors. She filled that time in the garden with her daughter, pulling out weeds from between the rows of onion and chickpea. As it was getting difficult to support herself bending over, she sat on a reed mat on the ground, directing the small girl to the places that were out of her reach. Towheaded Melitta, by now scarcely visible under a mop of fine curls, presented her mother with handfuls of stems and leaves.

"No, my silly one—take the weeds by the roots, like this—"

Melitta squealed and snapped her body around in a twist, costing herself her balance. Andreia, half in nervous suspense, made the mistake of laughing at the girl, who bloomed at this encouragement and found her feet to begin the maneuver again. "Silly one. Silly one!" she repeated in varying intonations, spinning.

With the sky threatening a storm that had still not come, she found herself eyeing the oily undersides of the clouds as they slipped by Taygetus. In fact she was indifferent to the prospect of rain. With the birth just weeks away, she would have stayed in her bed if the discomfort of lying down had not been as bad as sitting up. She had not been to the market in a month, sending instead the helot girl Damatria had lent to her. The girl was now overdue, and as her eyes rose to scan the path for her return, Andreia gave a short, involuntary gasp. Someone was approaching the house, but it was no maid. Instead, she recognized the thin form of Zeuxippos, swinging his staff ahead of him in that peculiar way he did, like a scythe.

"There is only a little I can tell you, for there may be informers about," he began in a conspiratorial hush.

"Of course, elder," Andreia replied, her head bowed.

"I can confirm that your husband is on the island. There is no question now. He is in good company, as the sons of many well-born families are there: Eudamos, grandson of Isidas; Areus, son of Damis; Epitadas, your brother-in-law. An entire generation of future leaders."

"So the elders will treat with the Athenians for their release?"

"We have treated with them. There was a truce, but it has failed."

"But won't they try again?"

"The Athenians are infatuated with glory. The Gerousia can offer nothing more. We anticipate an attack soon." He was blunt, but when he saw the effect of his words, he added, "You should prepare yourself."

He watched her absorb this with the courage appropriate to a Spartan wife. Inwardly, he mused over the ancient predicament of woman, prone on the ground with breasts teeming, body replete with the seed of beautiful men fated to die. He reached out to tousle the hair of little Melitta, bright and careless. Yet how soon would she, too, suffer the perennial sorrow of her sex? The thought gave him sentimental pleasure, like the memory of some long-done hurt. He moved to leave.

"My husband—" she said, halting. He paused, looking at her. "Can you get a message to him for me?"

Zeuxippos believed such a thing to be impossible. But what harm would it do to indulge her?

"I can try, though I promise nothing."

"Tell him—he has a son."

The old man smiled. It is somewhat premature, he thought, but it was a good message. He then bid her good-bye with a touch of his staff to his brow.

On his way back, Zeuxippos sighted the lady Damatria coming the other direction with a harvest basket on her arm. Curious, he paused to watch her make her way down to the farmhouse. Andreia, struggling on the balls of her feet, rose to greet her. The younger woman said something to Damatria, who stared back, regarding. Andreia fell into the other's arms, holding her so tightly that only their clothes distinguished daughter from elder. Zeuxippos sighed and thought how pretty, how reassuring, this sisterhood of shared grief. Among the Lacedaemonians, men were at war, boys growing, women weeping. May all be forever as it was!

As they embraced, the women thought of what each faced losing on the island. Damatria believed she could be forgiven for thinking of Epitadas, just as the other must worry for her beloved Antalcidas. Yet as Andreia wrung out tears on her shoulder, Damatria felt a certain awe in the trust she had earned. She had never favored women very much in her life, after all. There were few things in this world, she believed, that were more ignoble than woman. Yet now she found herself embracing another of her kind, close enough now to smell the dampness on her face, and feel both her trembling and the capsule of her womb, hard as a full wine sack, pressed against the pit of her abdomen.

Melitta, feeling left out, grasped the thighs of her mother and grandmother. Had he seen it, Zeuxippos would have approved the girl's early taste of the portion of mortal females. But he was already gone, down the path to mess with the Spit Companions.

IX
The Starlings

1.

They heard the flock before they saw it. The sound was like that of a second sea on the landward side—a rhythmic rising and falling of sibilant waves washing the island. When Antalcidas poked his head from beneath his cloak he saw a flickering cloud conceal the dawn. As the starlings came nearer, he made out their individual forms in the mass. Each was a black, pointed, busy thing, fluttering in synchronized fashion with the whole. Of their number he could not guess; the Lacedaemonians, who had little use for figures above ten thousand, could only look at the immensity and think, "Many birds."

The fire had burned for three days, scorching the island from end to end. The Spartans had lost no one to the flames, yet stood bereft of cover, pregnable, on a smoking spit of ash. The provisions they had hoarded from the truce were ruined, as were whatever shields, cloaks, and spears were left in the fire's path. As if smelling their vulnerability, the enemy ships made ever tighter circles around the island. Every man, from the youngest under-thirty to Epitadas himself, understood that the Athenians could now gauge their exact numbers from the heights of old Pylos. An attack would come soon.

But the misfortune of the Lacedaemonians presented an opportunity for the birds. Approaching in their hundreds of thousands, the starlings broke into two cohorts—one making for the vertical cliffs on the

lee shore, the other directly for the Spartan camp.
Along the cliffs, they intruded into the nesting holes
of the swallows and doves, stabbing at whatever
moved inside. The mothers fled by thousands into
the air, flying over the bay and wheeling around to
protest their nestlings' slaughter. But they were still
outnumbered by the frantic invaders, who flew in pat-
terns alternating between chaos and unity, tips of
beaks wet with blood, feathers gleaming an iridescent
purple-black like the carapaces of beetles.

"This kind of bird," observed Doulos, "is rare so far
south, over water."

"A foul portent," said Frog.

"Foul for the Athenians."

The starlings at the top of the island came to feast
on the seeds that littered the ground after fire. The
flock descended in a broad wedge, crowding onto the
ashes. The birds in the vanguard pecked as others
flew over them from the back, rushing for the uneaten
seeds a few inches ahead. In this way the mass resembled a liquid wave that rolled forward but never
broke. Now and again they would come upon some
insect or lizard baked in its tracks, and a knot of inky
opponents would gather around the carcass, picking
it apart as the great black wave rolled on, leaving
them behind until the contestants had split their prize.

The Lacedaemonians said nothing as the birds
worked their way down the slope. The visitors took
wing at last as they reached a line of sterile boulders,
forming themselves into a pliant cloud that seemed to
flash white and black as the birds, in choral unison, alternately exposed dark backs and pale bellies. Rising,
they merged with the other cohort ascending from the
cliff. The reunited host formed itself into a twisting
tower, then a sphere, then a flattened disk as it flitted

in indecision. By whatever reason moved them, the birds finally went south. A moment later they were over the Athenian base on Little Sphacteria. A pair of birds dove toward it, trailed by a game few, but when the majority refused to follow, the deviators reversed course and rejoined the mass. The flock was far over the water, halfway toward a double-humped mountain on the shore, when Antalcidas lost sight of it.

2.

"Epitadas, I would speak with you," said Frog as he planted his defiant squatness athwart the path. Epitadas, bending to the inevitable, turned an impassive face on the other; Frog had been insisting on yet another public confrontation since they had driven the enemy from the island, but had been frustrated so far. At least this time he chose a place away from the other men.

"I am concerned about the tactics we used against the Athenians from the ship," he stated.

Epitadas replied, "Do you mean the tactics we used with such success?"

"If we must call it that. I call it a foretaste of disaster. The threat of their archers—you have not solved it."

"I recall that they had archers last time."

"They came with only a handful. But ask your brother, who killed more than his share: did the arrows slow him down? Ask him."

Antalcidas stood nearby, blowing into his clenched hands. The days dawned colder now. He had been listening to the exchange between Epitadas and Frog, but chose this time to play the stolid Equal who responded to questions only when directly asked.

"Brother, were you bothered in the least by their arrows?"

"No."

"He's lying," asserted Frog. "I saw him shifting his feet to avoid them. And did he not have an arrow stuck in his helmet?"

"It barely went through."

"But it could have! These buckets will be useless if the Athenians shoot their arrows down on us. If they aim high—"

"If need be, we can fight without helmets at all," replied Epitadas. "Recall that is why our fathers invented boxing."

"Zeus save us, are you suggesting the Athenians want to *box* with us?"

"I am always amazed at those like you, *elder*, who can turn a success into a defeat for the sake of what might have been!"

Frog squared his shoulders, hand on swordhilt. "If we are fated to die—so be it. But it is not for us to throw our lives away for want of taking simple precautions—a few dozen slingers, for instance—"

"And where would you find anything to make slings, with everything burned?"

"I've thought of that. We can strip the carrying straps from the backs of a few shields. Slingers don't need shields anyway."

Epitadas strode up to Frog, staring down at him from a distance only slightly more than the length of his nose. With his arms hanging easily at his sides, he seemed unconcerned by Frog's hand on his sword.

"Hear me, *elder*. If I die, you can waste as many shields as you want. But not until then."

"I do believe Epitadas thinks he is Leonidas," Frog

said to no one in particular. "His own little Thermopylae—and we are his three hundred."

Epitadas smiled. "Say another word. Just one more
word."

Frog scowled, spat on the ground, but said nothing
more.

That evening the breeze freshened from the east.
The wind brought with it the smell of the live trees on
the hillsides. Only then did Antalcidas realize how the
odor of fire had come to permeate everything in his
world, from his clothes and beard to the hides of the
men around him and, of course, the still-smoking
ground. He was walking to the windward side of the
island, the fresher air attracting him, when he discovered Epitadas standing on a ledge above the cliff. He
had said nothing to him since the last confrontation
with Frog.

Antalcidas knew that the Neckless One was right:
the Athenians, when they came, would not risk a
shock attack against elite Spartiates. Instead, they
would land missile troops. Yet this, of all possible
truths, was the one most awkward for him to broach;
Epitadas would no doubt call him "Stone" again, saying he had spent too much time as a boy throwing
rocks at helots. He could have no more luck with his
brother than Frog had. Yet the voices of Andreia and
Melitta were talking to him now, as the time in the
siege grew late; their faces appeared to him nightly in
his dreams. Could he deny them a mere word in defense of their future? If it was so destined, could he
make his descent into Hades in good conscience,
without even making the attempt?

Epitadas was looking out at the campfires of the
Peloponnesians along the eastern limb of the bay.
They seemed close, and far more numerous than the

Athenian ones under Koryphasion. Yet in all those weeks they seemed as immovable as the stars. He was thinking, without resentment, that the men around those fires were painfully idle; he presumed that at least the hunting was good. There was a hint of roasting stag meat on the breeze. He had heard that Messenia, particularly around the deserted slopes of Mount Ithome, was still good country for red deer.

"Brother, Frog is a fool, but—" Antalcidas began. He let his words trail off, expecting that the other would interrupt him, but he did not. "Could it be so unwise to do as he suggests? Some of the shields were damaged in the fire."

"I know that," said Epitadas.

"We could designate two platoons of the under-thirties to be slingers, and give their shields to the Equals who have lost theirs."

"I suppose we could."

"Then . . . why . . ." Antalcidas shrugged, though his brother was facing away and could not see the gesture.

"The Athenians might try what Frog fears," Epitadas said, "but it is not so easy. The ground will make it hard for them to land, and break up their formations."

"Maybe."

"We can be among them in time—remember their faces when we attacked them on the beach? They're cowards—children. They will always run without a fight."

"Which of us are you trying to convince, Brother?"

For the first time since he saw Epitadas kill that boy in the olive grove, his brother turned to him with eyes full of suspicion.

"Do I need to remind you, Stone, of your promise to our mother?"

"No, you don't. But if you're wrong?"

"It will be decided as the gods will. But if I'm wrong—if the fight is decided by arrows and rocks—then I say it is not a battle worth winning."

3.

Cleon arrived in Pylos on the sixty-third day of the siege with a flotilla of ten ships and two hundred infantry. Demosthenes welcomed the ships and men, but could not fathom the Assembly's choice of Cleon to replace Nicias. Yet there he was, striding up the beach in a spotless kit of parade armor, in a closed helmet mounted with horsehair brush, gold shield with repousséd Gorgon head, and fancy-tooled muscle cuirass. It was the panoply of a man who knew everything about shopping and nothing about fighting.

Perhaps equally as bad, he was followed by an entourage of other would-be warriors from the merchant trades—men he recognized from the Assembly as pottery magnates, fishmongers, moneylenders, and purveyors of high-class female entertainment. How impressive, those armored pimps, those joint chiefs of gash coming down the gangplank! Demosthenes watched them approach with his arm extended, a farcical smile carved on his face. Cleon took the hand and ignored the mockery.

Demosthenes conferred in his tent with his new commander. The general demanded water. His steward delivered a cup; sampling it, Cleon bowed his head and spat on the ground. "This is brackish!" he declared.

Demosthenes, pulling a face full of threadbare rue,

explained that there were no sources of sweet water in the compound and deliveries from home were few. "Alas, it is what the People drink here," he said. Cleon, regretting himself, looked into his cup and tasted again.

"On second thought, it is not exactly brackish," he said. "Perhaps I meant to say it is hard—full of clay, I think."

"Better clay than sewage. We're short of space for those needs too."

Cleon frowned. "Then it is good that we have been sent to put an end to all this."

"That is also my hope."

Cleon gave Demosthenes a long look. The latter, recognizing that he had strayed too close to the edge of insult, buried his misgivings and launched into a review of the tactical situation. Cleon seemed to relax as the details washed over him, not the least because he was pleased to have most of that information already.

"With the addition of the ships you have brought, we can expect to reduce the smuggling still further. The garrison should be quite weak then—weak enough to take by assault in a short time."

"How much time?"

"Not long. Two weeks perhaps, or three."

"We will attack in two days," said Cleon.

Demosthenes stared at him.

"Perhaps . . . you did not hear me rightly. The Lacedaemonians are weakening, but we can make them weaker yet before risking an attack—"

"We will send a herald to enemy camp on the mainland tomorrow morning," Cleon went on. "The longhairs shall have until sunset the same day to make their decision."

"Knowing their numbers is not the same as knowing their disposition. There could be any number of traps on the heights we can't see from the water."

"Thereupon we will embark our forces at night and land them before first light on the second day."

"A defeat might leave us undermanned against another attack on the stockade, notwithstanding our superiority on the water—"

"Your misgivings are noted, Demosthenes!" Cleon shouted, waving his right hand with oratorical flourish. "But I rule in accord with the will of the Assembly."

In fact, storms had delayed Cleon on his trip around the Peloponnese—he needed to make up time if he was going to fulfill his promise to take the island in twenty days. If they could reduce the Lacedaemonians within the week there might be time to get word to Athens by mounted messenger, along his line of private contacts. It would be a shame to reveal this resource by bringing the news to town that way, but of course by then the issue would be decided and he would have won, so it would be a small sacrifice.

"I must urge you to consider again," Demosthenes shook his head, "before our position here is ruined."

"Demosthenes! Never let it be said that your efforts here have been unappreciated. What you have done here—Nicias, that dullard, would never have attempted it. You are the best we have—"

"I assure you that there's plenty of time yet to make an attack before foul weather sets in."

"—but if I need to pack you off for home, I will."

The threat stopped Demosthenes' tongue. Cleon continued, "Understand me, I would rather do this with you than without—but it will be done. Will I have your help?"

The Aetolians came down the slopes on both sides of the

canyon, letting loose their half-barbarian cries. Most of his men crumpled instead of fought, too exhausted by their tramp through strange country to raise a sword in defense. When they were finished the little stream ran red with Attic blood. Their bones are still there, scattered and sorted by the spring flood into little piles, like with like—arms here, the tiny bones of the hands and feet there, swept farther down the creekbed—

The commanders were overheard to argue for quite some time, with neither willing to shift his position. The final word belonged to Cleon. The other got small revenge, though, when Cleon asked where he and his companions might pitch their tents.

"General, we need every patch of sand here for the ships and men! Those in your staff are free to make whatever arrangements they can on the ships. You, of course, are welcome as my guest here—if that will suffice."

From the middle of their raccoon patches, Cleon's small eyes shifted over the cramped space of Demosthenes' tent, which smelled of salt, rotten seaweed, and the sweat of his host's feet. The circumstances would not suffice. The campaign would have to be a short one.

4.

As it became clear that an attack would come at any time, Epitadas decided that the Lacedaemonians should make a sacrifice to Artemis. There were no goats or pigs on the island, so they were at first stymied by the problem of what sort of beast they should offer. The gods soon provided what seemed like a miracle: a pair of storks came out of the south, and after wheeling for some time above the wondering Spartans, landed a short distance down the slope. Namertes, the under-thirty who had helped Antalcidas push a boulder on an Athenian ship, was on guard not far away. He brought one of the creatures down by hitting it in the wing with a rock. Namertes ran forward and took the bird, grasping it by its great beak and gangling feet. The other soldiers cheered as he held his prisoner up in triumph.

Such a handsome prize inspired them to make a lavish gesture. Epitadas ordered a rude altar built out of stones of the old fort, and a flame kindled out of embers left under the dirt by the fire. Epitadas conducted the ritual himself, spraying his bleached tunic with its blood as he sawed off the stork's head with his sword. Meanwhile, Frog stalked the back of the gathering, pacing stiff-backed like an effigy of himself, fretting over the propriety of offering a skinny bird to Artemis.

"The liver is without flaw," Epitadas declared.

"And how would we know how the liver of a stork must look?" sneered Frog.

They separated the edible parts from the rest of the carcass. The goddess got the bones and entrails in the form of smoke from the fire, while the morsels of meat were divided between the officers and elder Spartiates. These, as it turned out, included Frog. Antalcidas went up to him as he was licking stork grease from his fingers, looking at him as he would someone fatally ill.

"Your opinion would mean more here, if you didn't complain about everything."

Frog turned his back, saying over his shoulder "So would yours, if you didn't hide behind your brother."

To the end, the man had a petty nature, but Antalcidas would take no offense. More and more, he had come to agree with Frog's assessment of their predicament. To defy his brother was unthinkable—though not because of any private promises he had sworn to him or anyone else. For better or worse, a Spartan's personal honor bound him to his commander. Frog's honor, though, was not his concern. He resorted to an aphorism:

"The roused bull is better approached from the side."

Frog departed without giving any sign he had heard this.

Late in the morning the garrison raised a polished shield to flash what they took to be their last message to the mainland. It was a simple question: "What are your instructions?"

They had to wait until the last moments of daylight to get their answer. From the hills •over the bay, drenched in the blood-light of sunset, their superiors signaled back:

"The Spartans bid you to do what you think best, as long as it brings no dishonor."

5.

The *Terror* was held back from regular blockade duty that night. Several hours before daybreak, all but a handful of the Athenian ships were deployed in a double line around the stockade. Each took on a complement of landing troops—Attic slingers and archers, hoplites in their heavy gear, allied peltasts who, from their accents, Xeuthes took to be from some wind-lashed Thracian shithole. His vessel was assigned a platoon of Kephallenian archers who grasped their bows with white knuckles and grave expressions on their faces. Where land troops often resorted to jokes to cover their anxiety at sea, these men settled down wordlessly along the rails, somber in the face of the coming task. For this was daunting business, to hunt Spartans.

More orders from Demosthenes: for the battle each captain would land on the island all the men in his top two oarbanks, with the lowest bank left behind to mind the ship. To that end the youngest, most able-bodied rowers were assigned topside and the eldest, most experienced oarsmen to the holds. This reversal of the natural order, under most circumstances so galling in its implications, was sullenly accepted by Patronices and Dicaearchus on the eve of this, the final attack. For them, the worst part was not the loss of status or the stench of the hold, but the taunting grins of Cleinias, Timon, and other guttersnipes as the senior citizens went aboard first.

"Watch yourself, Timon, or I'll punch that face!" warned Patronices as he filed past.

"We'll try to keep the lice off your seat covers," replied Timon.

"Shut your traps, the lot of you!" Stilbiades roared. "You'll wish you were back in the hold today, Timon! I guarantee there's a Spartan spearhead out there with your name on it."

When it was time for the officers to take their places Xeuthes noticed that Philemon's cabin was empty. Searching the strand, he found the man soon enough, standing dry and safe on the sand with a wine cup in his hand. Philemon raised his drink as Stilbiades signaled that the ship was ready. Xeuthes saluted in response; his sponsor was a coward, of course, but he had sent the best part of himself—his money—into danger with his fellow citizens. It was

better, in any case, to go into battle without the trierarch slicking the deck with his vomit.

Each captain drew pebbles from a sack to determine his ship's place in the assault. Xeuthes got a
black rock—the *Terror* would join the north squadron
on the Ionian side. As Sphaerus' unerring oars steered
them through the Sikia Channel, Xeuthes looked out
first at the heights of Koryphasion on the right,
topped by the watch fires of the Athenian sentries.
The lookouts had assembled on the face of the
promontory closest to the channel, as if gathered to
discuss prospects for the attack. Turning left, he examined the opposing eminence of Sphacteria: it was a
great shoal of rock, ghastly white in the half moon-
light, that broke abruptly into a sheer cliff on the bay
side. This steepness barred any attack on the interior
from the north. Large numbers of Spartans had been
sighted up there during the day, with their main camp
on the flats beyond the rise. Unlike the Athenians, the
longhairs set no fires at night. The place seemed as
abandoned then as the city of old Nestor, but Xeuthes
believed he could sense them, sharpening their blades
or praying to Artemis or doing whatever they did on
the eve of bloodshed.

The *Terror* shifted a bit on her keel as Sphaerus
made southwest, burying her ram in the sea swells.
As the familiar pitching began and the cadence of the
oars lulled him, Xeuthes settled deeper into his chair
and closed his eyes. In a moment he was asleep.

6.

The moon was down and the sun still hidden behind
the bulk of Mount Mathion when the time came.
Overhead, the sky was a venous blue that grew red-

der to the east, until the few clouds heralding the ascent of Helios flared like kindling. In the moment of collective pause no sound rose—not the cooing of the wild pigeons in their holes, nor the usual murmur of the bay's waters, nor the chatter of nine thousand Athenians, suspended mutely in their beaked ships.

Demosthenes raised the signal pennant. As planned, his order was relayed around the south end of Sphacteria and around to the Ionian squadron. The troop carriers off the east and west shores of the island drove ashore and disgorged their contents: crack platoons of the Athenian hoplites in full panoply, assigned to set up a defensive perimeter around the landing places. After them would come the regular oarsmen equipped with spears and wickerwork shields, and finally the archers, who would form up in ranks to cover the push inland. If the whole operation went as planned, the Athenians would outnumber the Lacedaemonians on the island by a ratio of ten to one.

Resplendent as the dawn in his new armor and exhilarated by the spectacle, Cleon wore a proud, militant pout. Though he had contributed nothing to the attack but its timing, he clearly had the most to gain or lose from its outcome. The high personal stakes gave him a sense of ownership over the forces unleashed that morning; men were marching to war, he sensed, in the service of his destiny. So it was this, he thought, that made Nicias so enamored of the military life! Such had never figured in his plans, this kind of glory. But as the brave little bronze figures splashed ashore, and serried to his purpose, Cleon was thrilled by a world of possibilities. He could not help but wonder now, "Why not me?"

Demosthenes turned around. "Did you say something?"

"Nothing," he replied, still intrigued by the question. *Why not, indeed?*

From the water they could see only the east prong of the attack, but that seemed to be progressing well. The hoplites met no resistance at the beachhead, and as they pushed further up the broken ground, probing shadowed crevices with the points of their spears, it appeared as if the enemy had deserted the island. Time seemed to slow as Demosthenes awaited the key deployment; he envisioned his forces, before they organized and dispersed, suddenly swept onto the hardscrabble shore as if by some invisible force. For the first time in months he feared to unlock his knees, lest Cleon see his legs snap, and learn he was not a man but a two-stemmed figurine of clay and dirt. What business had his kind on the pitching deck of a ship? Was there any doubt that, when he failed, they would toss him over the side, like drunken merchants disposing of a spent wine jar at sea?

Less than a mile west, Xeuthes waited his turn to scramble through a jag on the island's seaward rampart. The point was narrow, a mere crenellation in the island's natural defense, and the Athenians found themselves bunched up along the gangway and back onto the deck.

"Keep moving, you women!" Leochares hissed from the shore, waving his hands like a chorus master exhorting his troupe. "This is no time to worry about soiling your skirts! I've seen girls file through a springhouse faster!"

"He's been in and done with a whore faster, too," cracked Timon, who waited in line a few places behind Xeuthes. Cleinias found the wind to laugh along, though his terror at the Lacedaemonians had left him without a trace of spit in his mouth. Under the circumstances, embarking through the passage in that dreary half light, it was as if they each awaited their turn at the gates of Hades.

When the men of the *Terror* reached the plateau they joined a force of four thousand others massing there. Space was still limited, and with most of the Athenians wearing old closed helmets with a limited field of vision and no earholes, many of them could neither see nor hear. Disgusted by the jostling, Leochares combed through the mass in a silent frenzy, sorting peltasts from archers, hauling the latter out by their leather corselets and into position. Time was running short: though the sun had still not showed itself from behind the mountain, the halo around its summit promised it would soon. With that, the possibility of surprise would be lost.

The first wave of light-armed troops charged inland. True to their reputation, the party included a disproportionate number of Acharnians. Scaling the spine of the island, Xeuthes, Timon, and Cleinias were slowed by boulders, hidden kettle holes, and the blackened skeletons of trees looming in the darkness. A man beside Xeuthes suddenly fell behind, clutching the back of his calf; Timon, his heart pounding, felt a tearing pain in his right big toe but ran on. Only later, when his excitement ebbed, would he realize that the toe was cut nearly in two as he stumbled over a sharp rock.

Xeuthes willed his old legs onward a few more steps. He was among the oldest in the attack, but felt his gaunt form renewed by it. To grasp the spear, to embody the will of his city with every stride, was a thrill rarely available to him anymore. As the first sunbeam broke over Mathion he felt a trickle of sweat course through the bristles at the back of his neck.

There was a square of fabric lying on the ground before him—a faded cloak with traces of crimson at the edges.

With Timon and Cleinias at his side, Xeuthes watched as something rustled under the cloak. A lump appeared, and a dirt-caked finger along the hem. When a fold of the cloak was suddenly flipped up, the Acharnians looked down on the face of a young Spartan.

Lips cracked with thirst, locks disheveled like a nest of snakes, Namertes squinted at the newcomers. He was still struggling to make out what he saw when Cleinias, in a sudden panic, lifted his spear and sank it through the cloak. Timon followed before Xeuthes could stop him. Six others converged, taking their chance to jab a vaunted Lacedaemonian. As he was attacked, the victim made only a single sound: a kind of startled grunt, like a man stubbing his toe.

"Stand down, you men!" shouted Xeuthes. "Cleon wants *prisoners*."

The Athenians laughed at this. Not that their captain had said it with much conviction—who ever heard of such a thing as a Spartan captive? Didn't the longhairs take pride in never raising a hand in surrender? Well, if someone was going to give himself up today, it wouldn't be this fellow!

The hold men perforated the corpse until they were exhausted. Xeuthes cast a reproving eye on them.

"Satisfied?"

Timon extracted the point from Namertes' backbone with a twisting motion. "No," he replied. "It seems they die just like other men."

7.

It was not long before Antalcidas understood the magnitude of their blunder. They had seen the fleet ring the island the night before, as usual. What no one among the Lacedaemonians had thought to do, though, was to count the number of vessels the Athenians had used in the blockade. If they had, they would have known that ten extra ships—together carrying as many as two thousand men—had taken up position around the south end of Sphacteria. There was now no doubt about their purpose.

Epitadas could spare no time on regrets. When the alarm went up, his first thought was to control the helots. Spartiates barked at their squires to fetch their shields and spears; the servants were then herded to one spot and two platoons of troops placed around them. It was the most he could spare in the face of the enemy attack. He assumed the latter would be driven off soon enough, but he feared what the helots might attempt in the interim. Defeat and death at the hands of the Athenians would be disappointing but creditable in the eyes of their elders. To be slaughtered from behind by unsecured helots, on the other hand, would be remembered as a true humiliation.

Epitadas summoned the captain of the guard and said—with no particular effort to conceal the threat— "If they so much as twitch, kill them."

The rest of the Spartiates and under-thirties assembled around the well at the center of the island. There were enough of them to form a phalanx forty files wide and eight shields deep. The platoon leaders were in the front rank, and the most experienced hands in the back to bar retreat. But when Epitadas inspected his men, he saw the impossibility of cowardice. Every spear was held straight and true, the blades aflame with 320 tiny, reflected dawns. The new-style helmets left their faces exposed, burning eyes fueled by steady rage, lordly jaws square with confidence. After all the weeks of privation, of impotent waiting, the Lacedaemonian machine, leveler of the proud, stood assembled. He stepped before them.

"This looks like the day we've seen coming, so I won't detain you with fancy talk. In Laconia we don't need rousing speeches to fight, but only our love of country, and the sense to follow our training. You all know we've met the Athenians before, and whipped them. We'll whip them here too, provided you each keep the line. They might try to use bows against us. I expect the under-thirties to do their duty in that case. . . ."

Frog, who was standing in the file next to Antalcidas', leaned toward him. "*Might* try to use archers? Doesn't he see the bowmen down there?"

"Tell him, not me, fool!" growled Antalcidas. "This is your last chance."

"We are three hundred today," Epitadas went on. "I probably don't need to remind you of the significance of that number. When our grandfathers stood against the barbarian at Thermopylae, he faced an army unglimpsed before or since in the history of men. It is said that they were so numerous that when they crossed into Greece, their host covered the plains of Thessaly, and the dust from their feet blocked the sun for three days. But despite such odds, despite the incompetence and betrayal of those they trusted, Leonidas and his three hundred were not diminished by their defeat. Instead, they gained everlasting fame.

"Today it is not Xerxes' thousand thousand before us. Instead, we face Athenians, in numbers just two or

three times our own. In these last months, in the time
I have been privileged to lead you, we have con-
tended with hunger, thirst, and fire. There have been
injuries, storms, plagues of birds. The enemy thinks
we are weak. He may even believe he has an advantage! But we know he is still overmatched when he
faces us. For we fight now not for some distant mountain pass, but for soil vouchsafed by our ancestors,
who long ago crossed high Taygetus to humble the
Messenians. With their conquest it became our
birthright—it became our life. I say to you, then, that
I don't expect we face Leonidas' fate here.

"Yet I also say that if it comes to that choice, to consecrate another three hundred to eternity, I will not
shrink! Nor will you, if my experience in these last
months is any guide. For that is the way for men bred
like us, for war. If we do our duty, if we fight as if the
shades of our fathers back us in the phalanx, we must
be victorious, either on the field this very day, or with
our willing deaths, in the hearts of our children. And
that, my companions, is all I have to say."

No one cheered. The Spartans, who understood the
importance of hearing orders above the roar of battle,
were fastidious in their silence. Instead, the men simply raised their spears, checked the fit on their helmets on their heads, and tightened up their ranks.
Epitadas, satisfied, turned to look down the hill at the
enemy's disposition.

What he saw encouraged him. The Athenians were
pouring onto the island and collecting in the center, in
the level area below the slope. His advance post, held
by thirty of the younger men, already appeared to be
overrun. Yet it seemed that the Athenians had landed
only a company-sized force of hoplites. Did they think
so few of their heavy troops, who were inferior to the

Lacedaemonians under the best of circumstances, would carry the field? There were others flitting about—peltasts taking up positions on the hill, archers beyond them—but Epitadas knew from experience to focus on the real threats—the hoplites—and ignore the auxiliaries.

He was startled by a voice beside him, saying, "Look how they occupy the high positions with their bowmen. They hope to catch us between fires."

Antalcidas was standing there, leaning into him as if to keep his counsel discreet. The presumption was galling.

"What are you doing here? Get back in line!" roared Epitadas.

The other hung his lower jaw for a moment before replying, "I just thought I would help."

"Don't presume upon my patience, Brother. And I'll thank you to leave the thinking to me!"

8.

It was testimony to Lacedaemonian discipline that they could march on Sphacteria at all. They had no pipers that day to govern their pace, and the irregularity of the ground made it impossible for them to keep their ranks straight as they descended the hill. The Athenians, to Epitadas' contempt, did not even try: Demosthenes had instructed them not to advance, but to stand still and let the archers and peltasts do the killing.

The Spartans came within bow shot. At first, their upturned spears knocked down a few of the arrows, until the archers found their range and the missiles began to drop vertically down on them. Antalcidas watched from the back as noble Spartiates were stuck with arrows straight through the crowns of their helmets. He could see a few of their faces as they twisted and fell—some dropped in their tracks like men struck by lightning; others stood for a long time with faces aghast, disbelieving, as if they had suffered a personal insult.

Peltasts pressed close on the left with their slings. Epitadas barked an order, sending two platoons of under-thirties out of the phalanx and after the peltasts. Antalcidas had seen this maneuver done better and faster elsewhere. The young men moved sluggishly, as if underwater; a good many ran as if bothered by wounds to their feet. The Athenians pulled up short, turned, and ran; being more lightly armed, most got away to slightly higher ground where the archers stood. Retreating, the under-thirties were then exposed to missiles both ahead and behind, from the bowmen shooting from the other side of the island. Half of the Lacedaemonians were wounded as they clambered back to the phalanx. A good many never made it back.

That was all Antalcidas needed to see. The enemy had demonstrated the principle behind his tactics—all that was left now was to let it succeed. With the Athenian hoplites unwilling to engage and their archers free to hit the phalanx from either flank, Epitadas could not grapple with the enemy anywhere. Nor could the Lacedaemonians survive in the open with their inadequate headgear.

Peltasts attacked from the right. Two fresh platoons bolted out to meet them. Same mistake, same result: the peltasts ran away, and the Spartans were plied with arrows. Antalcidas looked to Frog who, to his credit, seemed discomfited to be proven correct.

The stomping of thousands of feet stirred up the

freshly burned ground, sending up a curtain of fine, black dust. The Spartans could no longer see where the arrows were coming from. The slingers and peltasts, meanwhile, were growing bolder, appearing out of the gloom no more than a few yards away. On impulse, Antalcidas darted out at one of the attackers, approaching him from the blind side as he turned to use his sling: Antalcidas speared him with such force that the tip passed through the man's body and pierced his leather corselet from the inside. Stone tried in vain to extract his weapon intact as the enemy peltasts swarmed around him. "Use the cover!" he shouted to his brother as he planted his foot in the dead man's back and, pulling the spear right and left as blood arched from some torn vessel, snapped the ashwood shaft. "Use the dust to cover a withdrawal . . . !" Someone came at him through the gloom, swinging a sword. Antalcidas blocked a blow by driving forward with his shield. The assailant fell back, but there was no time to finish him. Antalcidas dropped the broken shaft and retreated back to the phalanx.

The dust had become a noxious cloud, coating their throats and stinging their eyes. The Lacedaemonians kept their silence, but the Athenian hoplites were hooting and shouting, and the peltasts screwing up their courage with wild cries as they pressed the attack. All the while the arrows kept dropping from above, the tumult muffling the snap of the bowstrings, the gloom hiding the volleys until they struck. Under the circumstances, even the Spartans, who credited themselves for their calm in the face of battlefield chaos, turned with worried eyes to Epitadas.

And still he did not concede. Instead, the phalanx was ordered forward at a half march, inching along like a man groping for something in the dark. The enemy hoplites were somewhere ahead—certainly as encumbered as the Lacedaemonians were, perhaps equally as contemptuous of men who fought at a distance. Perhaps they might meet in the center, and give each other someone to kill in the time-honored way. There was still a chance a battle might break out in the middle of the massacre.

But they never saw the Athenians. Though they marched for an eternity, the hoplites seemed to recede from them, as if Demosthenes had somehow compelled the island to serve his purpose by stretching longer. Antalcidas was now stepping on or over his comrades, the finest troops in the world, now reduced to gray lumps on the gray earth. As losses mounted and the men closed ranks, and the phalanx seemed to contract on itself, Antalcidas felt he could no longer keep silent. "Epitadas!" he shouted, packing the magnitude of his despair into the one, desperate word.

Through the haze he saw the shadow of a horsehair crest—the badge of his brother's office—turn toward him. Somewhere far beneath the unceasing clang of Attic vowels, he felt a Laconian marching command that he did not hear as much as feel in his bones. The order, relayed by the platoon leaders to all the men, reached him just as he saw the forward ranks pivot.

There was no time for fancy countermarches now, no stepping in place to wait for the officers to lead the way back. Everyone just spun on their heels and retreated up the hill. The reversal of direction was missed by the Athenian bowmen, who went on pouring arrows through the cloud to where the Spartans would have been. When the phalanx was spotted it was halfway up the slope and barely in range; as bad as the advance had been, Antalcidas saw no one fall during the retreat.

9.

The Lacedaemonians were safely inside the old fort when the sun was at its highest. With nostrils caked by dust and ashes, lungs burning, and wounds begging for care, they were desperate for water. The island's main well was, alas, now in Athenian hands. The new one by the fort, beyond the bones of the old cyclops, had so far produced little more than a trickle. Epitadas allowed the men to take turns crawling down to wet their lips.

The Athenians made another series of landings, swelling their contingent on the island. Xeuthes, Timon, and the rest of the crew from the *Terror* were on the left, having advanced as close to the Spartan lines as Demosthenes dared. The heat tortured them too, as months of confinement on ships and crowded beaches had ruined them for marching, and their commanders had not yet organized distribution of water to troops that far up the slope. They had hoped, after all, that the longhairs would be crushed on the flats, in the first hours of the battle. That the enemy had escaped to the high ground was the first thing to wipe the smile off Cleon's face that morning.

With almost a hundred well-born Spartiates lying dead below, it was already an expensive day. At that point, with more fighting ahead, it would have been unseemly to remind Epitadas of his misjudgments. Antalcidas made nothing of it, contributing only what he could to help secure the fort. At least a defense was feasible: with no way to approach the Spartan position except from the south, they could not be enveloped. The men guarding the helots also kept watch on the steep ground leading down to the Sikia Channel. So far the Athenians had made no attempt to land there, though they could easily have swum across the channel from Koryphasion.

Meanwhile, against widely held expectation, the helots took scant pleasure in their masters' difficulties. There was no cheering as they watched the disaster unfold before them, no uprising when the Spartans returned exhausted and fewer. Antalcidas caught Doulos' eye as he walked by on inspection: the latter smiled, as if glad to see his master alive. Something in Antalcidas' face caused his good feeling to fade, however. As a rule, Antalcidas was seldom aware of what expression was on his own face.

In a rare feat of personal discipline, Frog also kept his tongue. He would not meet Epitadas' eyes as the latter issued his orders for the defense of the fort; he was heard to mutter as he stalked between the old stones. Yet he made no outward challenge for the leadership. It was too late for that.

Epitadas made a final inspection of the defenses. They were safe from arrows and infantry where the walls remained intact up to three courses. Their remaining front against the enemy was short enough to place one man every few paces. If the attackers managed to drive his men off the blocks and clamber over, he kept a reserve squad of his best fighters, including Antalcidas, to deal with them.

Then they waited. From his vantage at the very top of the island, Antalcidas could look out at the Lacedaemonians on the other side of the bay. It was impossible they would not be aware of the Athenian attack, yet the allied ships remained stuck on the beach. Why?

As if overhearing this question, Epitadas appeared at his side. "No use looking for help over there. The Peloponnesians are too terrified to come out."

"Then they should let our men take the oars."

Epitadas laughed. "They need more reason than a few trapped Spartans for them to risk their precious ships!"

10.

By nightfall, the Lacedaemonians were still in possession of the heights. Demosthenes had sent his men up in continuous waves, hoping to wear out the defenders by weight of numbers. The Lacedaemonians fended them off with spears, and if those broke, with swords. Some lost their swords too, and fought with shields or stones; most had spent so much time striking at metal armor that, for hours after, their hands vibrated like struck bells.

At sundown Demosthenes called off the assault. He had already sacrificed more than a hundred men to inflict only a few enemy casualties. He couldn't use his archers when his infantry attacked the fort, and when they weren't attacking, Nestor's tough old walls gave the Lacedaemonians cover.

Cleon, unmussed and undaunted, demanded a night attack. Demosthenes restrained the temptation to laugh in his face, calmly explaining that the Spartans were masters of night fighting. "We have the advantage," he said, "and so we must have the strength to be patient."

"Then forgive my ignorance, my dear Demosthenes, but how do you propose to supply five thousand men for a patient siege on a barren island?"

Demosthenes dismissed him with a toss of his head. It was, however, the most perceptive question Cleon had asked since his arrival.

The captain of the Messenian exiles, Protesilaus,

came with an answer. Dressed in a set of armor that seemed thrown together from corpses found on a dozen battlefields, he towered over little Cleon, who had a reflexive mistrust of anyone he had to look up at. What the Messenian had to say, though, delighted him.

"The Lacedaemonians need incentive to give up. Give me fifty archers and you'll have their heads—or their surrender—by nightfall tomorrow."

"How do you propose to accomplish this?" asked Cleon.

"We'll circle around behind them. We can use that bunch of rocks to defend ourselves, then use the archers to make things hot for them."

Demosthenes glanced at Leochares, whom he understood to have some experience with the Messenian. But Leochares just shrugged.

"By what path," Demosthenes inquired, "do you think you'll 'circle around'?"

"There is no path," came the easy answer. "That's why they won't expect it. But we can scale around on the cliffs, just below where they can see us."

"In the dark? With equipment?"

"It can be done. We've done it before."

"You've done it here?"

"Not here. In Aetolia, Phocis, Achaea. Worse places."

"Perhaps. But as for my men, I won't risk—"

"Fifty archers are too many for you to defend," interrupted Cleon. "Can you manage with twenty-five?"

"If we must."

"Good. Then we expect to see you behind the fort by sunup tomorrow."

Protesilaus, exultant over his new prominence

in the campaign, flew away to assemble his party. Demosthenes could hardly look at Cleon. He wanted to knock the party-favor helmet off his head, smack the ignorant smile from his lips. But instead, he had to content himself with sarcasm.

"Yes, I see now how you trust my judgment," he said.

"I expect you want to hit me," Cleon replied, smiling. "But what is there for us to lose? At most, we're out a few archers and some bad-smelling pirates. Let him try."

Demosthenes' face cracked into a grimace.

Lost in the canyons, some of the Athenians tried to climb straight up the jagged walls. The ones that didn't plunge to their deaths were picked off by the Aetolian slingers, who made a game of it. He could hear his men scream until they hit bottom; their bodies made a wet, popping sound as they struck, exploding like overfilled wineskins.

Cleon clapped a reassuring arm around Demosthenes. "And don't look so sick, my friend! It is not for our sake that we take risks, but for the People. Athens demands action!"

11.

The Athenians slept huddled together on the ground. Though the air was no colder than in the stockade or on the ships, it felt more chill on the island at night, as if something in the rock sucked the heat from their bodies. That the Spartans had survived there for months, without shelter or fire, earned them more credit in Xeuthes' eyes than anything he'd seen them do on the battlefield.

They awoke to a surprising commotion. Raising his head, Xeuthes saw a fight had broken out behind the

Lacedaemonians. A raggedly dressed bunch, unmistakably Messenian, had taken up position on an outcrop at the very summit of the island. They were standing above the Spartans now, bringing clubs and swords down on them, as a platoon of shooting bowmen perched behind. Their volleys were disorganized, ugly—but none of that mattered. The Spartans huddled in the fort had no cover from them.

The Athenians cheered. Xeuthes slapped the shoulder of the man nearest to him, who slapped him back. "Those dogs have done it!" he cried. "Better pack up your things, boys! We've spent our last night on this dunghill!"

Antalcidas had also passed the night poorly, though not because of the cold. Something kept waking him up—something less than an overt sound, but more than a suspicion. He jerked awake at one point at a rustling he could not place. He woke again when he realized what it was: the whistle, familiar to all infantrymen, of a right arm being slipped among leather strap. It was the sound of a soldier slinging his shield across his back. Antalcidas looked around at the other Lacedaemonians. Most were asleep, and none were about to rig their shields for carrying. He made an examination of the ground between the fort and the enemy; the Athenians were quiet.

He closed his eyes. In what seemed like the next moment, an uproar broke out all around him. Men were discovering arrows stuck in their bodies. Antalcidas searched the morning sky over the Athenians—but saw no volleys in the air. He turned to the man closest to him.

"Where are they shooting from?" he demanded.

The other, who was hiding with head under his

shield, replied by pointing to the high outcrop behind the fort.

The Messenians had come up near the place where the guards were watching the helots. The exiles were among them before anyone could raise an alarm—no one expected that the enemy would somehow bypass the fort. The guards were killed where they slept, before they could arm themselves. Most of the helots, equally surprised, ran down to the fort where their masters might protect them. The confusion of the moment—and the fact that the exiles spoke the same dialect as the Messenian helots—led the soldiers to mistake their servants for the enemy. Dozens were struck down by the half-asleep Spartans before Epitadas called a halt to the killing. When dawn broke, the Lacedaemonians, uncomprehending, stood among the bloody remains of their squires.

But not all of the helots died in this way. A few, though as unarmed as newborn babes, tried to attack the Messenians as they emerged. The fighting was grim, with the helots using stones and fingernails against the exiles, who wondered if it was the Spartans themselves who had discovered them. When it was over the Messenians saw that it was not the Lacedaemonians they had slaughtered, but the very helots they had come to liberate. Protesilaus, puzzled, gazed pityingly at the faces of the fallen servants—his sweet, misguided countrymen. Then he ordered the archers to begin shooting into the fort.

Antalcidas found his brother barking commands from behind a stone lintel tumbled on end. "Give me the reserves," he told Epitadas, "and I'll clear the Messenians for you."

"No, not now. The Athenians might attack from below."

"We have no cover here."

A soldier nearby, an under-thirty, took an arrow in the leg. The boy suffered it well, making nothing but a baleful frown as the point split his tibia. Epitadas rushed to him, tearing off some of his cloak to help staunch the bleeding.

"Is this how Leonidas would have led his men?" pressed Antalcidas. "To have let them die at the hands of men with *spindles*?" And he used the old Dorian word for the bow, which was identical to the word for the tool helot women used to spin wool, to goad his brother.

"The gods curse you—keep your position!" Epitadas shouted back at him. Then he closed his ears to anything more Antalcidas would say.

The rest of the Lacedaemonians cast wary eyes on Antalcidas as he stalked around the fort, enraged and heedless of the arrows whistling down on him. After he did this for a time he came to where the bodies of the helots, killed in the first confused moments of the day, lay in a heap. Glancing idly at the faces there, his anger cleared long enough to remember Doulos.

He examined each body in the pile. Some were, in fact, not quite dead, but there was no chance to save them. By the time he was satisfied Doulos was not among them, the sun was well up and the Athenians below were still standing around like spectators. This, he decided, would be his only opportunity to go out and retrieve the boy. It was an act he knew was reckless, incomprehensible to his fellows. He would do it nonetheless, because that day, his last on the island, he was determined to do something that was not for Epitadas, his family, or his city.

He walked out helmetless. The Messenians, although gripping their spears, observed him with what seemed like mild amusement. Protesilaus stood on the tallest rock, regarding Antalcidas with the kind of icy disdain that men reserved for things that were implacably polluting, like parricides or menstruating women. Antalcidas stared through the exile as if he wasn't there.

He came within ten feet of Protesilaus—close enough for them to smell each other's stink, but just out of spear range. The latter was beginning to wonder if this Spartiate had lost his mind. "What do we have here, boys?" he asked. "A hero?"

Doulos had collapsed at the foot of the outcrop. Examining him, Antalcidas found he had taken a spear thrust in the chest. By this time the effluent had turned a thick black, pulsing weakly through the clotted wound. Antalcidas waved aside the gnats that had gathered on his flesh. One of the insects flew in a nervous, tightening spiral that ended on Doulos' closed left eye. The eyelid quivered, then opened. The helot fixed his gaze on Antalcidas—he was alive, though he showed no outward sign of recognizing his master. Antalcidas stripped off his cloak to protect him from the chill and the flies.

A Messenian came up to deliver Protesilaus a javelin. The commander took it, but did nothing. He was too engrossed in watching the spectacle before him—a Spartan taking the weight of a wounded helot on his noble back. Imagine it! Did this servant have some damning secret to tell? Was it a trick, or a joke? Was this a loyal soldier protecting state property? He handed the javelin back—he might as well let the Lacedaemonian go. There was nowhere for any of them to hide.

The Athenian archers kept shooting as Antalcidas reached the fort. His comrades looked at him warily;

violating orders for the purposes of gaining eternal
honor was one thing, but this stunt just embarrassed
them all. He ignored them, placing Doulos in the lee
of the tallest block he could find. Searching his body
for other wounds, he discovered that Doulos had lost
all the fingernails on his hands except one, which was
caught by its root at a right angle from his blood-
smeared thumb.

"You seem to have lost your cloak, my lord," Doulos suddenly said. Antalcidas looked up to find his
eyes open again. As he spoke, his voice was accompanied by a hiss of air from the hole in his chest. Antalcidas grasped his hand.

"You fool, it wasn't your business to fight like
that."

The helot smiled until the pain seemed to grasp
him, and he frowned.

"I'm sorry to miss your victory."

Antalcidas squeezed his hand.

"You haven't."

In the sight of his brother and the gods, he bent
down to kiss the helot on the lips. Then the Spartans
watched, gaping, as he reached for his sword; Antalcidas covered Doulos' eyes with his hand to shield
him from the sight of the blade. When he sank it
through his friend's left breast, the heart's last beats
made the hilt tremble. For all the men Antalcidas had
killed, it was something he had never noticed before.

12.

The Athenians pressed them again as the sun climbed
and the breeze faded. As if by prior arrangement, they
charged into the collapsed sections of the wall, forcing
the defenders to rise up and expose their backs to the

archers. Demosthenes forced his men to run risks: in the places where the Athenians filled the breaches they came within bow range themselves. Their helmets, which were of the archaic, closed style, sealed off their hearing and vision but protected them from arrows better than the Spartans'. No speeches were necessary to tell them how near the end lay. They fought that day with a hunger for victory that the Lacedaemonians had seldom encountered.

Epitadas, Antalcidas, and Frog defended their posts as if the arrows were mere raindrops. Still, the pain and bleeding of multiple wounds slowed them down, until it felt as if their arms and legs belonged to others, so sluggishly did they seem to move. Antalcidas broke his spear; he swung the buttspike like a club, spraying himself with shards of bone as he caught an Athenian full in the face. He spat the splinters at the next man, who came at him with the expression of someone urgently trying to find a seat at the theater. Antalcidas flailed with no technique, wasting precious sweat on overswings, until the force of his exertion made his desiccated tongue split like the skin of a grape.

He fought on as the boundaries of his vision seemed to collapse to a fog-fringed point. His arms still moved as they carried him to the rear; he watched as a circle of sky blue enlarged, broken now and then by the streaks of feathered shafts. The face of his brother appeared before him. Epitadas was no longer handsome—his eyes had sunken into bony wells, his cheek torn, corpuscular flesh within. His expression seemed to ask a wordless question—are you ready to lead? Antalcidas nodded. His brother bowed his head, revealing the arrow in the back of his neck, lodged in such a way that he could not even rest on his back. Antalcidas helped him to his stomach, but dared not remove the arrow.

When he was on his feet again the news spread through the fort—"Epitadas is wounded," "Antalcidas leads us!" Frog looked at him with ample contempt. Passed over again for command, he seemed to make no distinction between the men who obstructed him. "Yes, Antalcidas leads," he said. "How fortunate for Damatria and her wealth!" The struggle dragged on as before, with the Lacedaemonians dying in ones and twos, and the Athenians charging in inexhaustible supply, and the end always seeming near, until some Spartiate or under-thirty would, by some miraculous exertion, push the enemy out of the fort again.

Beset from all points, their position was ideal for martyrdom. If Antalcidas issued no orders at all, the day would end as Epitadas envisioned. When the Athenians swarmed over the top of the hill, and the Spartans across the bay saw it, they would send emissaries to acknowledge defeat and collect the bodies. The funeral rites would be on the beach; their bones, still steaming from the pyre, would be shoveled into a mound that would become their common grave. In years to come, they would erect some marker on them, some leonine cenotaph, which would become one of Messenia's "points of interest," a featured item in some future travelogue. Epitadas himself would get a bronze statue on the acropolis of Sparta. The old men would bring their boys to see the figure, and wonder if the living man really had such a fine, square chin. And then they would turn and go about their lives, never having heard the name "Antalcidas" because it appeared nowhere on the inscription.

The Spartan mind did not flirt with regrets. It

would have been easy for him to blame Epitadas and his flawed strategy. (The Athenians shifted to press en masse against Frog's men, trying to overwhelm them there. The defenders shifted with them, and the tactic failed.) Doubts notwithstanding, Antalcidas had made a thousand choices since the beginning—choices of when to fight and when not, when to speak or stay silent, that had made him complicit in everything that followed. (Frog took an arrow in the calf. He tore it out and jabbed the bloody point into an Athenian's neck.) These things he had done would make incomprehensible any change he might imagine now, pragmatic and sensible though it might be. True, there was many a Greek who would understand if he defied Epitadas now. Those Greeks were not Lacedaemonians, however, steeped in a tradition of loyalty that transcended reasonableness. To rule men and to be ruled: these were the things that were in the bones of every Spartan, well-born or half-helot. (An enemy peltast, bearing a wicker shield, pushed through the line.)

Before he was conscious of willing it, Antalcidas confronted the intruder. "You're a brave man to come here with a shield made of sticks!" he told the Athenian. Timon, looking at this spattered, wild-eyed Spartan bristling with arrows, took fright and ran. Antalcidas brought him down with a slashing attack to the tendons in his leg. He then slaughtered Timon as he would an animal, making a small slit in his throat to let his blood pour on the ground. "For the glory of the goddess, an offering," he said to the dying oarsman. "And for Doulos."

And then, with the sounding of horns, the Athenians pulled back. After a few more arrows fell, the archers behind them also stopped shooting. The cooing of the wild pigeons in the cliffs rose again over the abrupt silence. Suddenly bereft of opponents, the Lacedaemonians stood around, bewildered; by all honest account the day was nearly lost for them, yet the enemy had flinched. "Spartans, we've broken their nerve!" proclaimed Frog, waving his sword above his head. His companions cheered, but Antalcidas didn't believe it. Such a miracle could only be the work of Artemis Herself.

A more worldly explanation soon presented itself. A voice from behind the Athenian lines asked for a meeting between the captains of the two sides. It took a while for Antalcidas to register that they were calling for him, not Epitadas. As he went, Frog called out to him, saying, "Serve your men well by what you do, Antalcidas!"

13.

He emerged barehanded, helmet dimpled from glancing arrow hits, arms and legs smeared with blood, nose and eyes caked with the residue of fire. On his appearance the Athenians fell silent, staring wide-eyed at him as he strode from between the ramparts of enemy dead.

Demosthenes and Cleon, by contrast, looked as fresh as when the day began. The former had not wanted a parley at all; the notion that the Lacedaemonians would negotiate a surrender was absurd. Yet Cleon had insisted on it, thinking that the mere possibility of crowning his victory with captives was worth the attempt. Demosthenes indulged his foolishness as best he could—the men could at least be given water as the futile act was done.

The antagonists met midway. Antalcidas eyed the

Athenians with more than a crease of disdain. In victory or defeat, it would always be in his nature to despise foreigners. The squat one standing before him was shifty, with flesh as soft and flaccid as a woman's; he doubted the man had ever spent a day risking his life in the line. The taller man, whom he took to be Demosthenes, had a certain aristocratic severity, but his eyes betrayed the uncertainty in his mind. Antalcidas said nothing, allowing the Athenians to speak first.

Cleon was delighted with this display of laconic primitiveness. If it was up to him, Antalcidas would be brought back to Athens just as he was, elbow-deep in gore. What a trophy the rustic warrior would make! What a triumph awaited the People's champion!

"Do you know who I am?" asked Cleon.

"You are my enemy," replied Antalcidas.

The other smiled. "They say the Lacedaemonians are stupid, but I've never believed it. So I'll address you frankly—what is your name?"

"Antalcidas, son of Molobrus. But I'll thank you not to sully my father's name by speaking it."

"You must see that your position is desperate today. Though you have fought well, we both know the fate in store for you. I must tell you that many of the Athenians would just as well see you all slaughtered. But as we are all Greeks here, I have prevailed on them to allow me to make this offer: surrender yourselves and your arms now. You will be well treated. Provided your masters behave responsibly, you will live to see home again.

"Now I know all about you Lacedaemonians and your lust for death. You all see yourselves as part of the gallant Three Hundred, itching to die to defend the pass from the barbarians. But understand this, my friend: we are not barbarians, and you are not Leonidas. You were beaten here today not by Asian profligacy with lives, but by the superior leadership of fellow Greeks. I suspect that even Spartans must give up their childish fantasies one day; they must confront facts just like the rest of us do. I implore you, then, with respect—think of your men. Think of your wives and children. Consider our offer."

Antalcidas looked at him as if expecting him to say more. When Cleon didn't, he raised an eyebrow. "I think you must be right. I must be stupid, because unlike you wise Athenians, I cannot see the difference between surrender and humiliation. So if that is all you have to say—"

He turned to walk back to the fort. Cleon looked to Demosthenes with alarm. The latter, for his part, would have been glad to see the conference end. In his experience, addressing a Spartan was as useless as talking to a rock; he had once heard Aristophanes quip that although Athenians and Lacedaemonians had Greek in common, they used opposite halves of the language.

"Before you go," Demosthenes spoke up, "you should know something."

Antalcidas paused.

"Be aware that your masters have been treating with our Assembly very hard for an end to the siege. So it seems that a few hundred dead Spartiates is a matter of some concern in Sparta. They want you back alive, not dead and covered in glory. Personally, I'm happy the negotiations have failed. I have not worked these months for you to walk free of here—I'd prefer to see you humbled, once and for all. But even if I care not a spit for you or the wishes of your elders, perhaps you should."

Antalcidas regarded Demosthenes with something close to approval. "So it seems that some Athenians are capable of speaking plainly," he said. "It is good to know. As for what you say—it is your ignorance to suppose that Spartan mothers do not care for their sons. And so, because you are a soldier, and have spoken honestly, I'll make you an offer: allow us to send a messenger to our superiors ashore. If they order us to surrender our arms, I will not disobey them."

Cleon was about to agree, but Demosthenes spoke first. "We have no objection. But we will deliver the message for you—none of you will leave this island."

The truce persisted for several more hours as the Lacedaemonians consulted. As they waited, Antalcidas checked on Epitadas' condition: with the arrow still lodged near his spine, he had lost a lot of blood, which in addition to his dehydration kept him sunk in semi-consciousness. If they didn't soon find a way to remove the arrow safely, he would die. Then again, was that not the fate to which he was resigned for some time now?

Antalcidas did not think the ephors would give the Athenians the satisfaction of a speedy reply. He was therefore surprised when the Athenian ship soon returned with a message, shut with string and a wax seal with the mark of Zeuxippos. Unscrolling it, he found a single, uncoded line, unmistakably in his old mentor's hand. It read:

ὁ τοῦ Ἀνταλκιδου τράφεται

The message pleased and puzzled him in equal measure. It was the first word he had heard of Andreia in months, and it was good. No Lacedaemonian could receive news that he had fathered a son and be displeased.

And yet—what did it mean? Were his superiors inviting him to return home, without prejudice, and raise his son? Or did they wish to imply that, with his legacy assured, he should see now to preserving the honor of his name?

The son of Antalcidas grows.

The Athenian generals watched as he stood there, reading the line again and again. Cleon immediately discerned the uncertainty on his adversary's face. "Does the answer surprise you?" he asked.

Antalcidas ignored him. He had been too long away from Laconia—that Zeuxippos could expect anything else than the traditional sacrifice was unlikely. What proof did he have that Demosthenes was telling the truth, that the ephors had bargained hard for the garrison's release? Nothing more than his word. And what was the word of an Athenian worth, when they dispensed so many of them, to such little effect?

He rolled up the message. "The answer is clear," Antalcidas replied. "It is what we all expected. I bid you return to your men now, and ready your arms— for the Lacedaemonians choose to die."

14.

The scroll was still in Antalcidas' hand when he returned to the ruins. All the surviving Spartiates glanced down at it, as if curious over what it said, but too proud to ask outright.

Frog had no such trouble. "So what do our elders require of us?"

Antalcidas gave it to him. Reading the words, Frog grimaced.

"What does this mean?" he asked. "Is it some kind of code?"

"The men will prepare themselves for the attack."

Pushing their helmets down low on their heads, the men settled down in their positions. Antalcidas saw that a few had used the reprieve to stack several small blocks at the back of the fort, making a small stretch of cover from the bowmen behind them. But this position offered no refuge from arrows shot from the other side.

Frog had not finished his interrogation. "Tell me, Antalcidas, why are you so sure they expect a sacrifice?"

"I'm not sure. When in doubt, the Spartiate will always make the most honorable choice."

"There are many good men here," the other persisted. "If there's a chance to them to serve again in the line—we should be sure. You might petition the ephors to clarify."

Antalcidas rounded on him, sneering, "Would that make your father proud? For us to prattle back and forth like women? No—I will not embarrass our elders by begging them to make our choice for us. If you must know, that is the duty of the command you wanted so desperately. Now leave me alone."

Frog stared at him with eyes wide. Then he bent at the waist in a mocking bow.

"Well, then! Let us all hail our lord Antalcidas, third king of the Spartans!"

Before the other could straighten up again, Antalcidas shoved him to the ground. Looking back, Frog

wore a face of such undiluted hatred that it might as
well have been a theatrical mask.

"You've made a mistake, Antalcidas."

Antalcidas reached for his sword. "And you've
plagued your commanders for the last time. Get up."

Frog rolled to his feet, his blade at the ready. Facing
each other, a fight was inevitable, with Frog whipping
himself up into an emotional froth and Antalcidas
staring back, expressionless but with every intention
of making the other suffer before he died. He had not
fought another Lacedaemonian since that day on the
Plane Stand, and never killed one. He found himself
strangely attracted to the prospect: his love of country,
which was unshakable, had somehow made him
more contemptuous of certain Spartans than he knew.
It was nothing so simple as resenting those of modest
talent but legitimate birth. Instead, he felt a powerful
need to purify and ennoble his love by removing irri-
tants like Frog from the life of his city.

Suddenly the scream of wind through bowfeath-
ers descended on them. Antalcidas looked up—and
saw the sky again filled with Athenian arrows. He
and Frog crouched together next to a wall as the volley hit the ground; neither of them was struck, but a
handful of the other men were caught in the open
without their shields.

"You men get your equipment!" Antalcidas cried.
"Forward positions, prepare to receive the enemy—"

But the Athenians had changed tactics. The
wounded Lacedaemonians were limping and crawling to where their shields lay, or injuring themselves
further by ripping the arrowpoints from their flesh,
when another volley came on. More went down as
missiles tore through their flimsy piloi. Desperate,

some of the Spartans darted out to strip a few of the heavier, closed helmets from the Athenian dead.

Demosthenes had decided to send no more human waves against the breaches: he would no longer gratify the Spartans by offering them the sort of death they preferred. The conference with Antalcidas, whom Demosthenes took to be a petulant fool, had relieved him of all chivalric scruples. He would now grind the Lacedaemonians down constantly, mercilessly, and from a distance.

Reading this fury, Cleon saw there was no longer any chance for live prisoners. Looking to sea, he visualized bringing a severed human head—perhaps Antalcidas'—to the Squeezing Place. No, the institution's traditional decorum would never allow it. Yet would they not talk about that day forever, when Cleon brought such vivid evidence of his newfound military prowess?

"The archers are running out of arrows," Leochares reported.

Cleon supposed that this was bad news. He looked to Demosthenes, who spared him only a glance before turning to Leochares.

"Tell the line officers that a ship is already on its way from the stockade," he said. He then added—more to gall Cleon that to inform Leochares—"I called for resupply hours ago."

15.

The bombardment went on as dark clouds appeared over the Ionian and spread east, glowering over Sphacteria. Showing bottoms of grayish purple, the clouds seemed to groan with moisture; Doulos would have called their arrival the best evidence of rain in months. Sure enough, a thin, desultory mist fell, increasing the Spartans' misery as they clung to whatever crevices gave them refuge. The mist became a downpour; rivulets formed immediately in the thin soil, scattering the cyclops bones Doulos had so carefully fit together. Meanwhile, some of the men removed their helmets, so useless against the arrows, and used them to collect precious rainwater. Antalcidas didn't bother. For rain to fall now, when their fate was sealed, could only be some sort of divine joke at his expense.

The Athenian bowmen kept shooting. Those arrows that didn't hit a Spartan were now sticking upright in the mud; looking at one of these, Antalcidas noticed that a message had been cut into the wooden shaft. It read, in clumsy letters, *For the Acharnians, against the Lak—*. The writer appeared to have run out of room before he could finish the taunt.

"Is this your virtuous stand, Antalcidas?" Frog called through the storm. "Tell us, do you feel like Leonidas now?"

"Shut up, trembler!"

"I'll show you," replied the other. "You and your brother have insulted me for the last time. I'll show you. . . ."

The rain fell for only a brief time. Soon an uncertain sun shone through, making the water beads gleam on the masonry and the ground with slicks of blood-soaked mud. A cry went up behind the Athenian lines, answered by another from the Messenians. Antalcidas did not always understand the Attic lingo, but the command sounded like an order to stop shooting.

The volleys ceased. A voice came to them then from below—one he did not recognize as belonging to either Cleon or Demosthenes.

"Lacedaemonians, this is your last chance!" the voice cried. "Surrender now, and we will let you carry your shields to the ships."

So they would allow the Spartans to go down with their shields, thought Antalcidas. How desperate they must be to make trophies of us! And yet, how long before they confiscate those arms as they push us into the hold? He looked to the under-thirty who shared cover with him behind a block. He was making a brave face of it, but his fear was there to see, in the subtle trembling of his lips.

"Take heart, son," Antalcidas told him. "It will be over soon . . . and your family will have the honor of cutting your name into your tombstone."

There was more murmuring from behind the enemy line. He heard the archers draw back their bowstrings—an act that was individually silent, but when done in numbers made a distinct sound, like a sharp intake of breath. Antalcidas put a reassuring hand on the under-thirty's back: this, at last, would be it.

A memory seemed to seep out from within, from the core of his bones. Antalcidas was alone, hungry, trapped between blackness and a damp rigidity pressing against him. His brothers and sisters were whispering to him now from their stony cradles, dressed in only bits of scalp, fine hair, residues of blood scattered across the gorge. As their mothers lived their days on the plain, weaving their shrouds of forgetting, the children of Sparta collected in rising numbers against that hard teat. . . .

Frog's detested voice suddenly called out again.

"By the gods, Antalcidas, must all the Spartans die for your vanity?"

Then Frog did the inconceivable: breaking cover before the arrows flew, he waved his arms and

shouted, "The Lacedaemónians will bear their
shields!" The words pierced Antalcidas deeper than
any arrow. Yet he did nothing at first, preferring to believe that he had misheard. There was also the possibility, as sweet as the memory of Andreia's face, that
the Athenians would do them all the favor of shooting
Frog down.

There was no snap of the bowstrings. Instead, the
other Spartiates around Frog gave up too, and more
around the fort, until the post dissolved in confusion,
with some of the men wandering around the ruins
and asking, "Have we surrendered?" and others not
waiting for confirmation, but throwing up their hands
unsolicited. Before long most of the garrison had
stood up, exposed in a way that made the Athenians
stare up at them, openmouthed.

From their position on the left, Xeuthes and
Cleinias looked at each other, captain and oarsman
united in mutual amazement. Neither had to ask if the
other had seen the Lacedaemonians behave in such
disorder, so *ordinarily*, in a set-piece battle. Was it not
common knowledge that Spartans never raise their
hands in surrender?

Antalcidas burst from his hiding place, spear lev-
eled at no one in particular. "Don't listen to that man!"
he cried. "All of you put your hands down! I'll kill the
next man who disgraces us . . . !"

But Frog had already let the Athenian hoplites inside the fort. There was a sharp struggle, metal
crunching against metal, as Antalcidas and a handful
of other diehards clashed with them. As the sound
reached Cleon, he became alarmed, thinking perhaps
that the enemy had drawn the Athenians into a trap.
Demosthenes, on the other hand, was serene—his
troops were now pouring into the fort, and most of

the Spartans had already thrown their spears to the ground. The end was foregone.

It was the sixteenth day since Cleon made his promise to the Assembly. If he got word north to Elis by the next evening, he could have runners deliver the news to the archons before his twenty days were up.

The solution presented itself. Of course he would not do anything as crude as display the heads of fallen Spartiates. Instead, he would take the platform with a round object wrapped in burlap. He would defy expectation by refusing the wreath, and refusing it again, until the cumulative buzz over what he carried hit a fever peak, and he tore the burlap cover away. The captured Lacedaemonian shield would blaze in the rising sun, shining as a Spartan shield ought, the great crimson lambda splashed like blood against the polished metal. He would hold it over his head for all the time it took for the waves of acclaim to roll through the Assembly, and wash over him as they chanted his name—"Cleon, CLEON, *CLEON* . . ." Victory would then wing her way down from the clouds, bearing a crown of olive leaves for setting upon his head. Nike had the face of the little brunette chippy from the Chersonese who served the relish at his drinking parties; her feathers were dark too, like raven's wings, and her chiton thinner, almost like a whisper, pressed down so flat by the wind that it cratered within that little dimple at her midriff. The goddess would give him that same little fetching smile the slave gave him when she finished blowing on his stubby flute. . . .

His assurance restored, he turned to Demosthenes.

"As I told you, dear Demosthenes," he said, "the Lacedaemonians have seen it our way."

16.

The 292 Lacedaemonian survivors, including 120 Spartiates, marched down the hill between the divided halves of Demosthenes' army. Epitadas, who had been unconscious through the final assault, was carried to the shore on a litter rigged out of two spears and some sailcloth. Antalcidas went by his side, not looking at the Athenians around him. Since he had been the recalcitrant face of the Lacedaemonians earlier that day, the Athenians focused their scorn on him, staring with smug grins, whistling and hissing at him as they would to some down-at-heels tart in the street. In their shame, the Spartans marched with their shields reversed, crimson lambdas hidden.

Frog, who went behind, was still not satisfied with his day's work. It struck him as unfair that Antalcidas would receive all the notoriety for leading the Spartans; the decision to surrender, after all, was his. His only gratification came late in the day, when he was about to join Altalcidas and Epitadas in the hold of the fleet's fastest ship, the *Terror.* Just before he ducked into his new prison, Patronices, the deck man, shouted out an impertinent question to him.

"Capitulators! Shall we suppose your dead comrades are the real Spartans?"

Frog stopped, and with barely a moment to consider an answer, replied, "Athenian arrows would be wiser than the Athenians, if they could choose to fall on good men instead of cowards."

Frog and six others were shackled to separate posts in the bowels of the ship. The holds of Athenian triremes were not capacious, with the most clearance available atop the keel, between the rows of the bottommost oarsmen. If there was a place on a ship more disagreeable than the seats of the hold men, it was where the Lacedaemonians were imprisoned: a mere crawl space, with no more than three feet of head-room, among stinking blocks of cobble ballast and the unkempt feet of sixty exhausted, sweating men. Nor were their miseries private ones, with those in the lowest stratum of Athenian society able to peep down between the thwarts at the conceited Spartans, free to try out all the insults their frustration had inspired over seven years of war.

The hold rode well below the waterline, so Antalci-das could see nothing of the outside world but the glow of reflected daylight from between the oars-men's seats. A scratching sound along the keel told him when the ship reached ground at Koryphasion. The Athenian oarsmen, who never seemed to shut their mouths, complained about the miserable meal they were about to eat, as they disembarked by sec-tions.

From his vantage in the semidarkness, Antalcidas watched as an Athenian doctor came down the lad-der. When they learned that the original commander of the Spartans was not dead but only wounded, the Athenians spared no effort in making certain their ad-versary reached Athens alive. Cleon's personal doctor had extracted the arrow and cleaned the wound be-fore they left the island. When he came down to in-spect Epitadas' dressings, Antalcidas addressed him, saying, "You would be better off letting him die, friend."

Scratching his bearded neck, the doctor spared him barely a glance before vanishing up the ladder. His charge, apparently, did not include tending the wounds of the other Lacedaemonians.

The Athenians seemed to be in a hurry. After only

a few hours the hull was refloated and the oarsmen, only half-rested, filed back to their seats. There was much noise on the deck as the masts were stepped and sails bent on them. Soon they set off again; the ship adopted a rocking motion that suggested they had entered open water. It was then that Stilbiades, the bosun, served the prisoners their first meal in days: a husk of bread and one half-blackened onion for each man, and a sip of water from a common canteen. As Frog's lips touched the water before Antalcidas', the latter refused to touch it, though he was cotton-mouthed with thirst.

Frog produced a bitter smile. "So I see we should add spitefulness to Stone's list of faults."

Antalcidas ignored him. He had nothing to offer tremblers but his scorn.

Epitadas roused sometime during the first day at sea. He tested his shackles, then took a long look at his new surroundings.

"Is this Hades?" he asked.

"Not yet, Brother."

He stared in Antalcidas' direction, his expression blank, as if he could not recognize the figure sitting there. "You sound like my brother," he said. "But that can't be true. Antalcidas affirmed his loyalty to his family upon his honor as a Spartiate, and so must be among the virtuous dead in battle, not chained like a dog."

The words cut deep into Antalcidas. Closing his eyes, he replied, "By the gods, I swear that I kept my word. It is not my choice that we are here."

Frog perked up at this exchange, anxious once again that his role not be overlooked. "I can barely see you, Epitadas, but your ignorance marks you well enough."

"I don't remember leaving Frog in command, but you, Brother," said Epitadas.

"I was in command."

"Then the fault is yours. There is nothing more to say."

"No, keep talking!" interjected Cleinias, the hold man, who was listening the whole time. To hear dissension among Spartans was most entertaining during long, dull days at sea.

Antalcidas tried to appeal to Epitadas through the day and later that night, when the ship was beached southeast of Methone and the prisoners were unshackled for a brief turn on the top deck. Epitadas did not rise when Stilbiades removed his chains; after trying to rouse him with his boot, the bosun said, "Suit yourself," and shackled him again. In his haste to escape the stench, Stilbiades missed the six-inch long shard of wood Epitadas had torn from the post during the few moments when his hands were free.

The next day his brother's silence began to weigh on Antalcidas. He spoke to him in monologues, hoping he might stumble on some combination of words that would unstick Epitadas' tongue. He tried reminiscing about good things, such as the beauties of Laconia, better days on the battlefield, stories from the Rearing, and the joy of festival days. But as time passed, and Epitadas persisted in his silence, Antalcidas' tone became more bitter. At last, when he thought he could stand it no longer, he flung the rebuke he had longed to make for more than twenty years:

"So this is the thanks you give for the favor I did you!" he cried. When Epitadas' eyes shifted to him at last, he went on, "Yes, you remember, don't you? The way you killed that other boy, and how you got away with it because Thibron took the blame. And why was he exiled? It was on my word!"

The other gave nothing but a sour smile and a chuckle, a little contemptuous hack, as he turned his face away.

"As you sit there you may ask yourself how many brothers would take such a risk. And yet here you are, stinking with a murderer's pollution, presuming to pass judgment on other men! Isn't it you who should feel shame, Epitadas?"

Frog jerked his chains with his excitement. "Yes, I had always wondered about that story! So Thibron was innocent, was he? Poor fellow!"

The oarsman, Cleinias, stuck his face down below his seat again, declaring, "Betrayal, recriminations, regrets . . . this stuff is precious! Pure gold!"

Epitadas was dwelling on his shame, to be sure, but not over Thibron. He was mulling instead over the fate of old Cleomenes I, the Agiad king from before the time of the Persian Wars. Cleomenes was one of the great kings in Spartan history—the scourge of the Argives at Tiryns, shrewd manipulator of Lacedaemon's enemies. When Darius of Persia demanded tokens of earth and water to signal Sparta's submission, Cleomenes had the Persian emissaries thrown in a pit, bidding them find their earth and water there. The king suffered his downfall shortly after, when he bribed the Delphic oracle to proclaim illegitimate his rival, the Eurypontid king Demaratus. When the sacrilege was uncovered, he fled the country and attempted to organize the Arcadians against Sparta; word of the revolt moved the Gerousia to invite Cleomenes back, but a life of intrigue had already taken a toll on his mind. The king went mad, lashing out with his staff at anyone he could reach. His family was at last compelled to imprison him.

Cleomenes decided he could not live with his shame. He was guarded by a helot with a knife. The king, using his natural talents of command, compelled the weak-minded man to hand it over. After ordering the helot from the room, he used the blade to flay himself alive, cutting the skin from his legs, working his way up his body until he carved bolts of flesh from his abdomen. When he had half disemboweled himself, Cleomenes called the guard back, returned his knife, and died.

Cleomenes' end was a popular story among the boys of the Rearing, presenting as it did both a gory tale and an implicit challenge: under similar circumstances, would any of them have the courage to make his end just as emphatic? Epitadas had always declared that he had. Branded now by defeat, locked in the bowels of an enemy ship, surrounded by tremblers and low-caste Athenians, his time now seemed at hand.

He grasped the wooden stake in his sweaty palm, cherishing the prospect of his release. Until then, he would refuse every comfort, shut his ears to the words of friend and foe, and wait for the dark to prove his virtue.

X

Ekphora

1.

No effort of Cleon's was necessary to spread word of the surrender at Sphacteria. It swept by horseback over the breadth of the Peloponnese, by foot messenger, and donkey deep into the roadless hills of Phocis, Aetolia, and Epirus, and by ship all the way to Italy, the islands, and Asia Minor. Wherever Greeks lived, men stood in the marketplaces and shook their heads—how could such a thing happen? Laconian wet nurses, who were popular amongst the nobility everywhere, were summoned to explain the news to their puzzled masters; where the Lacedaemonians fought the allies of Athens, such as in Thrace and Sicily, they found renewed spirit on the part of their enemies, who now saw them as fallible, even beatable. Some dismissed the story, preferring to believe it was Athenian propaganda. But the skeptics were hard put to explain how, if the story was a lie, Cleon was in a position to dedicate thirty full Lacedaemonian panoplies—a tenth of the spoils—to Apollo at his sanctuary in Delphi, and another thirty to Zeus at Olympia.

In Laconia, word of the disaster plunged the people into a common funk. The quiet orderliness of Sparta became a stifling silence, as if a great, invisible blanket had been laid on everything. The Gerousia met in emergency session, but no resolutions were passed, and no word of the deliberations leaked out. The

Spartiates, meanwhile, kept watch on the helots, anxious for any sign of revolt. But most of the helots knew better than to display their true feelings. Instead, among those with a temperament for it, there was a deep, hidden flush of spiteful satisfaction.

Matters took a bizarre turn when a foreign trireme approached the Spartan port at Gytheion, its sail bearing the insignia of the Athenians, ΑΘΗ. The sight of it pulling into the roads sent the town into a panic. Had the enemy decided to capitalize on their victory at Pylos by burning down the port? The population—composed of mostly Nigh-dwellers and helots—rushed to find any Spartiate from whom to take instructions.

But it soon became clear that this was no invasion; the trireme was not the vanguard of a fleet, but came alone. Closer, and a flag of truce could be seen flying from a jackstaff. The helmsman worked the tillers with an expertise rare among the Peloponnesians, picking his way through the crowd of merchantmen and pentecontels, turning the hull broadside just as the crew withdrew their oars from the water. By force of momentum, the ship came to rest against the wharf with a gentle bump.

The Acharnians on the *Terror*'s outriggers kept their seats, eyeing the Lacedaemonians with smoldering contempt. The latter glowered back, hands on their spears and swords, until their attention was diverted to activity on the deck. Xeuthes leapt ashore first, wearing a leather corselet and boots but weaponless. After surveying the crowd around him, he turned to receive the handles of a stretcher that had been carried up from the hold. The stretcher had the figure of something like a man on it, covered with a blanket soaked through with blood.

With Stilbiades handling the other end, they bore the stretcher down from the deck and lowered it gently to the wharf. The Nigh-Dwellers' eyes followed every movement, their curiosity beginning to outweigh their hostility. Xeuthes faced them.

"Tell your masters that we declare, by the gods, that we did this man no harm."

He held up the splinter—a stake, really—that Epitadas had used to cut himself. It was dyed now with the purplish blue of congealed blood, with strings of skin and muscle still embedded in it. Xeuthes placed it on the blanket as he would the sword of a gallant warrior beside his corpse. Then he turned to Stilbiades, whispering, "We should go while they're preoccupied."

As the crowd closed around the stretcher, Patronices the beam man, gazed out at the town. "It's the port of Sparta, boys! Take a good look now—we'll never see it again."

"Speak for yourself, defeatist!" countered Dicaearchus.

"Suit yourself . . . while you're busy here your mother will be playing my flute."

"I'm just happy to get that carcass off the ship," said Oreus from the deck. "The way that Spartan went—that kind of thing can spoil everything."

On that none would disagree. That evening, after grounding the ship on a sandy beach at Cythera, the crew performed the ablutions that would purify it, scrubbing the decks with sand and seawater just like a family cleansing their house after a relative had died. The griffin figurehead was likewise washed, and the very bodies of the crewmen, all of whom were every bit as polluted by Epitadas' act.

Lastly, the Spartan prisoners were tossed rags with

which to clean themselves. Frog and the others complied, but Antalcidas did nothing, having yet to banish the stupefying image that had met his eyes when he woke that morning. He ignored Stilbiades' order to wash, and Xeuthes' as well, until the captain ordered a gang of oarsmen to bathe him forcibly. They set upon him while his arms were shackled, scouring his skin with dry sand until he bled. He then sat in the hold, covered with a cement of sand and dried blood, for the rest of the trip to the Piraeus.

It was some time before the first Spartiate arrived to take charge in Gytheion—a junior officer who had been hunting in the hills above the town. Looking down at the mass that had once been Epitadas, Rehash commanded, "Get away from him, you dogs!" He then re-covered the body, which had been exposed by the curious onlookers, with a tenderness worthy of a true hero—for anyone who had gone through the Rearing could recognize at once a death befitting the legend of Cleomenes.

Patronices was not entirely correct. A decade later, some of the men of the *Terror* would look out from their seats and glimpse the Spartan port again, albeit at a great distance. They would see it as part of a force of forty thousand men and two hundred ships, on their way west for Alcibiades' great, doomed expedition against the city of Syracuse.

2.

A deputation of Spartiates came to Kynosoura to inform Damatria of the death of her son. It was the moment a noblewoman prepared for all her life—the culmination of her son's education, in a sense, and the apogee of her personal honor. The fact that he appeared to take his own life gave her pause, to be sure, but like the other Spartiates she understood and accepted the special circumstances of Epitadas' case. The death of a man who preferred self-mutilation to confinement, who would make a spectacle of himself before the Athenians could do it for him, was a model for the generations.

The mother of the heroic dead was expected to reflect the magnitude of her good fortune. She displayed the remains of her son, anointed with imported oil, dressed in a linen chiton of purest white, on a flowered bier in the men's quarters of her house. For two days Damatria sat next to him in a condition of carefully arranged dishevelment: fingers stripped of all but one fine gold ring, ashes demurely scattered in her finely combed hair, a single picturesque scratch scoring her alabaster cheek. The male relatives of Dorcis came to her in cheerful procession, bearing congratulations. Their wives and daughters came in somewhat smaller numbers, but with plates of honey cake, making the customary pleas for the bereaved to eat, to sustain herself. At the proper intervals, and with conspicuous preliminaries (for she loved this part), Damatria would let loose a piteous shriek. The guests would stand around her, admiring the perfection of her mourning, looking as if they might burst into applause. On the last day even Dorcis was carted into public view for the first time in years—fatter, as helpless as ever, but beaming in the reflected glory of his son-in-law's honor.

Two hours before dawn of the third day, they carried Epitadas out the door, feet first. The cortege lined up behind the wagon carrying the bier, with the relatives walking behind Damatria and the helot mourners and flute players going last. The streets were more than typically full at that hour: it was well known in the city that the only hero of Sphacteria would be honored that morning. As the retinue passed and the pipers played, soldiers stood and saluted; from the road around the base of the Acropolis, Damatria saw the caretakers dim the lamps of the Brazen House.

The pyre flared to its full magnificence just as the sun rose over Parnes. Curiously, it was at that point, as the body neared consumption and the flames began to wane, that Damatria felt her first stab of genuine grief. For the burial ground was one of the places where she had met her son in secret, during his first years in the Rearing, to deliver him extra food. She would see him in the twilight, stepping out of the forest and wearing nothing but grime and a ravenous look on his face; he would make no greeting as he snatched the bread from her hands, his hunger as elementary as a newborn baby's. The tracks of real tears creased her soot-caked cheeks as they wrapped his bones in his chiton, and the last libation was poured on the ground. They buried the remains under a handsome marble stone she had commissioned in his honor. Unlike most of the other stelae around it, his grave bore a personal inscription: ΕΠΙΤΑΔΑΣ.

By consensus it was the finest funeral seen in Laconia for some years. Though there was some concern that Damatria's ostentatious ways would spoil the event, her taste this time was impeccable, her conduct beyond reproach. She gave all the requisite feasts on the third and thirteenth days after the ceremony. Best of all, she did not embarrass the Spartans by breathing the name of her other son.

Epitadas was held exempt from the general decree that stripped the capitulators of Sphacteria of their status as Spartiates. The prisoners in Athens, who

were now publicly known as "tremblers," were denounced in absentia by their dining clubs. If they ever
returned from their captivity they would find their
legal rights to land and helots curtailed. Those they
left behind in the city, such as wives and daughters,
were no longer welcome to participate in the festival
choruses, or become betrothed to boys of respectable
families. The trembler and his family were required to
give way to other pedestrians in the streets, and forbidden to wear bright or conspicuous clothes. That a
trembler or his wife would smile or otherwise show
good humor in public was inconceivable, for such a
miserable fate could leave them nothing to be happy
about.

With the prisoners on their way to captivity, little
came back to Sparta about the circumstances of the
disaster. At some point Cleon and Demosthenes
would testify before the Assembly, of whose deliberations the Peloponnesians received regular reports
from their paid informants. Until then, gossips spoke
of an uncoded message sent to Antalcidas from
Zeuxippos, regarding the existence of an unborn son.
Zeuxippos' rivals among the Spit Companions
brought the story up at the mess, hinting that the
message might explain the surrender of his former
protégé.

The old man rose from his bench, and with an expression more sad than indignant, said, "Gentlemen,
if you wish to suggest that I would do anything to
make the boy behave disgracefully, I believe you already have my answer. The message was sent out of
compassion for the wife, who wished to reassure her
husband that his line would live on, regardless of
what Fortune had in store for him.

"For my own part, it pains me to know that I will

not live long enough to learn what really happened on the island. But I am more troubled to see the direction of this discussion, which seems designed to blacken the name of a young man who has been noted for his fighting skill. In the past, it was the virtue of the Lacedaemonians not to assassinate without cause the characters of decent men. I see now that I no longer live in the city I once loved. And so, for the first time in a half century, I must surrender my spot on this board—the one I remind you was once occupied by Eudamos, son of Styphon, who died with Leonidas at Thermopylae. Good night."

With that, Zeuxippos removed his chiton and overcloak, left his staff leaning against the wall, and strode out of the mess wearing nothing but a breechcloth. Later, a helot reported seeing a bony figure walking into the forest, toward the moonlit wall of Taygetus. The old man was never seen alive again.

3.

Though she dreaded it, Andreia was prepared for word of her husband's death. But what was she to do with news that he was a prisoner?

The helots were removed from her household the day after the Gerousia demoted Antalcidas. She was eight months pregnant and already quite large; being reluctant to leave Melitta alone in the house, she fretted over what to do with the child when she went to the springhouse or on market days. But the girl, who was perceptive beyond her few years, laid a small hand on her mother's arm and begged, "Let me carry too!"

At the market, Andreia felt a sharp plunge in the social temperature. She overheard snatches of whispered conversation around her—phrases like "poor Thibron," "he stole the credit from Praxitas," and, of course, the epithet Antalcidas' own mother had once used against him, "the shame of Sparta." Some voices were less subtle: under-thirties felt license to murmur lewd insults as they passed, and her bread-seller made her burn with humiliation by proclaiming, loudly enough for all to hear, that he didn't sell to the families of tremblers.

She wrote to her father for advice. Ramphias, who usually replied to her letters in rapid order, took a week to respond, and then only by sending her two of his own helots to keep her house. "Has he given you any message for me?" she asked them. The helots shook their heads.

Her consignment to oblivion took time to sink in, and had a curious effect when it did. For all her years she had looked with ambivalence at her membership in the community. To be a Spartan seemed something petty, parochial. Of her fellow Lacedaemonians, her feelings had always been divided between pity and contempt; when she learned of the civilized pursuits of Athens or Thebes, she was convinced that she was literally mislaid by Fortune—born into a tribe for which she was not intended. Antalcidas, who accepted her as she was, would listen to her opinions and look at her as if she had dropped out of the sky. Would it ever occur to him to feel so detached from his people? She thought not.

Yet, to be a true outsider was something for which she was completely unprepared. When she appeared in the street and was made to feel like nothing more than a ghost, she shed tears like a young girl shunned by her schoolmates. She conceived an irrational attachment to roads, buildings, and statues she had

barely looked at before. Avoided by all those she respected, she found herself respecting everyone. She
fell to such depths that she worried for the son within
her, thinking that he might somehow partake of her
sadness, and be tormented by low feelings for the rest
of his life.

She knew only one person who might have influence over the powers that had condemned her husband. When she left to find Damatria, she considered
leaving Melitta behind, but thought the girl's presence could only help her suit. And so they went off
together just after sunup, in overcloaks with heads
wrapped, as an autumn haze lay over the fallow
fields. It was a short walk to her mother-in-law's
house—just out to the wagon road, over a small hill,
and right at the cobbled way. As she made her way
slowly, rehearsing in her mind what she might say,
she saw a group of six young women approach from
the other direction.

They all seemed to be late teenagers, barefooted,
dressed in short tunics and hair tied back with fillets,
as if on their way to exercise in the gymnasium. As the
distance closed between them, Andreia perceived the
exact moment when they recognized her: she saw that
look, that resentment of her existence on the public
roads, that she had seen in the faces of a hundred others. Partly out of shame, partly to save herself the
pain, she had learned to avert her eyes. Yet something
made her keep staring back this time—something
about Melitta's presence, perhaps, that made Andreia
slow to abase herself. She locked eyes with the evident leader of the group, the tall, long-faced, sharp-
kneed girl around whom the others seemed to orbit.
The face-off continued until they were abreast of each
other.

"What are you looking at, coward's wife?" the leader asked.

Andreia, startled at such brazen disrespect, could say nothing at first. One of the other girls, whose features hinted that she might be the leader's sister, put a hand on the other's arm.

"Leonis, let's go."

"Shame on you, Gorgo!" said Leonis. "Don't you want to know why a breeder of tremblers goes around with her head up?"

Andreia was so furious that she forgot her circumstances. "How dare you address your elder so impertinently!" she snapped. "What kind of mother raised you?"

"A mother of brave Spartiates raised me, whore."

Without thinking, Andreia slapped the girl across the left cheek. "That's for showing disrespect in front of my daughter," she said.

Leonis turned to give her sister a single glance. Gorgo reacted with dread, as if having seen this look before.

The girl's fist landed on Andreia's temple, knocking her backward. Andreia fell hard, landing with a sharp rock square in her back. Through the pain, a memory flashed before her: an incident many years before, when she was beaten in the gymnasium by a girl one year her senior. Spartan schoolgirls were not encouraged to brawl by their elders—it was something they seemed to do because they wanted to. Just like in school, the other girls gathered around in a circle, their purpose as much to screen the fight from view as to watch it. Only Gorgo hung back.

Leonis was kicking Andreia indiscriminately around the neck and face. Melitta, frightened, let loose a scream. Between blows Andreia begged, "Hold my child! Don't hurt my child!" Gorgo picked up Melitta and walked some distance away, holding the girl's face away from the spectacle.

Leonis cried, "Bitch of a trembler, beg my pardon!"

Andreia uncovered her face, and fixing her eyes on Leonis again, made clear she would not beg. Meanwhile, the other girls shouted out encouragements to Leonis—"In the belly! Hit her in the belly!" Leonis reared back and kicked Andreia hard in her swollen abdomen. Having underestimated the toughness of it, her bare foot recoiled hard from the blow. She planted herself and tried again, striking just under the navel. The impact seemed to reverberate through Andreia's insides; she soiled herself as her bladder gave way. Then Leonis hit her again, and again, until it felt as if her baby's body was spinning within her, trying in his own way to avoid the blows. Melitta was still screaming in Gorgo's arms as Gorgo begged her sister to stop; couldn't she see that the woman was pregnant? Leonis shifted her wrath back at Andreia's face, landing a kick that cut her cheek and broke her nose.

A pair of eyes stared at the melee through cracked shutters. The eyes withdrew into the darkness within; Damatria sat on the stairs to the women's quarters, listening but not intervening. She thought about Andreia's fair good looks when they first met, and her expertise with herbs. When, she asked herself, had she conceived such a hatred for the girl? Never, came the reply: she had no right to interfere in the beating, because it was the prerogative of decent citizens to discipline the families of tremblers. The fault was Antalcidas', for putting his wife in that position. There were other considerations too—her newfound honor in the community as the mother of a hero, for one. Nor could she deny that Antalcidas' disgrace had discouraged her charitable feelings toward him and his family. If not for Epitadas's sacrifice, everything she had worked for would have been for nothing. The thought frightened her.

She stood up and ascended the stairs. The girl would survive, of course; someone would put a stop to it. Everyone knew that Sparta needed spears.

Sure enough, the pummeling stopped when a male voice rang out: "What is this shame? You children, leave her alone!"

An ancient Spartiate, happening by on his way to Limnae, stood there shaking his staff in admonishment. Leonis, who was as submissive before her male elders as she was domineering to low-class females, backed away from the prone Andreia.

"Put the brat down, Gorgo," she said. "We don't want to be late to the gymnasium!"

4.

When it was over, Damatria changed her mind. She sent out two of her helot field hands to collect Andreia from the road and carry her home. Then she realized that she probably needed care for her injuries, and that she was alone. In good conscience, Damatria could not tend her daughter-in-law herself after doing nothing to prevent the incident; someone else would have to do it. Then she remembered that Molobrus' mother, Lampito, was living not far away in Mesoa, equally alone in her widowhood.

The old woman knocked on the farmhouse door and Melitta opened it. The child looked at her great-grandmother's sparse, weedy pate, her milk-stained left eye, and her crumpled posture, and could say nothing except, "My mother is hurt."

"I know that, my dear. Will you take me to her?"

She found Andreia lying on her bed, her chiton parted to reveal the bruises on her abdomen. The other removed the wet cloth from her face, showing a single blood-flecked eyeball as she squinted at Lampito. Her nose was so grotesquely shifted that it almost touched her enlarged, pendent eyelid.

"Who are you?" Andreia asked.

She was seized by a sudden, wavelike tightening in her womb, which had the effect of convulsing the flesh under her bruises, causing her even more pain. When the contractions ended she glared at Lampito again.

"What are you doing here, elder?"

Lampito stood silent until the next spasm, which came hardly a moment later.

"You are in labor. I will help you."

Andreia shook her head in her pain, saying, "It can't be . . . it's too early. . . ." but was in no position to refuse. The old woman took command of the campaign with an assurance that mother and daughter immediately trusted. The girl was kept busy running for cushions and cups of clean water. When she returned Lampito had reached inside her mother up to the third knuckle of her right hand.

"I can feel him," she reported.

As her labor went on Lampito excoriated Andreia for waiting so long without calling for help. "Do you think you'd do this yourself? Don't look at me, *push now.* The selfishness of girls today is a scandal; it's a wonder you bother to make babies at all—PUSH!"

The rhythm of exertion and rest went on for hours, until night came and Lampito had Melitta fetch oil for the lamps. Sometime after midnight, with Andreia so spent that she was falling asleep between contractions, the old woman reached inside her again. As she pushed the birth canal down, blood and amniotic fluid shining on her leathery hands soaked into the earthen floor. Lampito peeped within with her good eye, then winked at Andreia.

"He has red hair."

Melitta watched agape as her brother was delivered, flipped over, and liberated from his cord by a carving knife. After washing him, Lampito put the infant on his mother's stomach. All watched in wonder as he crept toward the breast.

"Our little soldier finds his own mess," the old woman said, pleased.

Andreia slept for thirty-six hours after the birth. Lampito stayed by her side, keeping her clean, guiding the newborn's rooting mouth to her nipples. When she awoke, Andreia was confused by the presence of the stranger, but remembered her arrival when she felt the infant bundled at her side.

"Who are you?" she asked Lampito again.

"Sparta has become too big, when relatives don't know each other."

She explained that she was Antalcidas' grandmother on his father's side, and that Damatria had summoned her after the attack.

"Then the lady Damatria has done us a kindness," said Andreia.

Lampito tossed her head. "Perhaps."

The newborn began to cough; Andreia gathered him closer and rocked him. Then she noticed his color.

"Why is he so blue?"

"His lungs are weak. It is not unusual with children born so early. He may not survive."

Andreia reflexively covered the baby's ears. This

prognosis, however justified, struck her as needlessly cruel to say aloud.

But in time it became clear that something was wrong with the child. In the following days his breathing became more labored, with his color never improving beyond a sickly plum purple. His breaths became so shallow at night that his mother had to put her ear to his chest to see if his heart still beat. The struggle to catch his breath would wake him up after no more than a few minutes of sleep at a time—a schedule that also gave Andreia no time to rest. Lampito watched them suffer, fully knowing the only end that could await the boy. But she kept her thoughts to herself.

Andreia would not raise a hand in surrender. With Antalcidas away, she took it upon herself to give his son a name she thought would please him: Molobrus, after the boy's grandfather. And despite what had befallen her the last time she walked the streets of Sparta, she insisted on going out herself, with Melitta in tow, to register the name at the city magistrate's. As a precaution, she hid the boy's unhealthy color by wrapping him in blankets. This earned her an unexpected bonus: swaddled babies were such a rarity in Sparta that passersby gawked at the baby and hardly noticed the trembler's wife.

Yet the day Andreia dreaded came on with pitiless speed. Over the weeks she and Lampito had exhausted the known remedies, both practical and divine. She hired a professional root-cutter to gather medicinal herbs under the light of the full moon. With Damatria's word as credit, she spared no expense on ointments, including one made with truffles, silver rust, crushed black ants, and the gallbladder of a freshly killed brown bear. She sent expensive dedications to the Sanctuary of Asclepius at Epidauros, and inquired about bringing an adept of the healer-god to tend little Molobrus in Kynosoura. But when they turned to this last recourse it was too late for the priest to arrive in time.

They came for the prescreening at dawn the day before the judgment. The official of the ephorate was as dreary looking as his errand, regarding the child with eyes fishy and lifeless. Andreia prayed inwardly to Apollo as he made the examination—the first time she had done such a thing in her life. She chose to consider her appeal answered when she learned that Molobrus had been slated as number two in the judgment order—that is, only the second most likely to be rejected.

"So it seems our little boy is not the least promising of the bunch!" she crowed.

"So it seems," replied Lampito.

Andreia kept up her optimism on the morning of the judgment. Lampito accompanied her as far as the borders of the sanctuary of the Brazen House, helping her to rewrap Molobrus' swaddling clothes before Andreia went on alone.

"You might as well boil the barley for the baby's lunch," Andreia declared, a smile fixed on her lips. "We won't be long away."

After she was gone, Lampito spied a squad of under-thirties gathered under a tree, with two infant-sized baskets at their feet. When she approached them they fell silent, watching her anxiously; Spartan youths learned early to beware attracting the attention of stern old women.

"I assume *those*"—she indicated the baskets— "mean you are the guard for Langadha gorge."

The leader stood up straight. "We are, elder."

She searched the recesses of her cheeks with her tongue, then bowed her head and disgorged a silver lump into the palm of her hand. The soldiers leaned in to see what she had there: a silver tetradrachm of Argos, thick as a child's finger, the wolf's head emblem on its obverse glistening with her spit. She let them stare at the thing, feeling the thrill of its illegality make a palpable circuit through them. Then she closed her hand.

"I think you can find somewhere to spend this, next campaign," she said, handing the coin to the leader. The others hung on him, jabbing their fingers to get a feel of it.

"This is for the boy, the son of the trembler. Break his neck first. Don't make a mess of it."

5.

The under-thirties, accompanied by a magistrate and half a dozen helot bearers, made the procession up to the gorge before sunset. The soldiers marched with arms ready; in the long history of the city no one had ever interfered with their errand, but the Spartans did not believe in tempting a first occurrence.

For the walk up from the valley floor the helots carried the two baskets. Since not even the Lacedaemonians, who longed to hear the wails of dying adversaries, wished to rouse the cries of what they carried, the helots, on pain of flogging, stepped with care lest they jostle the fated contents.

When they approached the rim, the soldiers took the baskets away. Helots, after all, could never be allowed to kill Spartans, even defective ones. As the end neared, the guard captain felt the hard curve of the Argive coin, tucked in his tunic, warm with the heat of his hand—and fretted. For some time now he realized that he had forgotten which of the two boys was the son of Antalcidas. He was twenty-eight and as mindful of matters of virtue as anyone on the verge of full citizenship. Not to follow through on his promise to Lampito, though illegally made, gave him a vague sense of dishonor. Yet he could not make a spectacle of his confusion in front of the magistrate.

The latter was walking ahead, gazing idly at the hard gray pinnacles that stretched like boney fingers over the place of forgetting. While boys undergoing the Rearing ranged all over the Taygetos, all of them acquired a deep aversion to this spot, seldom looking into the depths where they knew the sons and daughters of Sparta were swallowed up. Their imaginings peopled it with ghosts and ghouls, with faces laid open like melons after sword practice, or mangled pieces of animated cadaver twitching and crawling over the streambed. When the boys grew up, most surrendered their fantasies, but not their dread of the gorge. The magistrate was an exception: with duty taking him up there almost every week, he strolled almost leisurely, peeping down as he whistled the melody of some half-forgotten camp song. He interrupted his performance to spit into the sacred chasm, and then turned back to the guard captain.

"Are your feet stuck in mud? Let's get on with this business before we have to fetch firewood in the dark!"

When the other had resumed his strolling, the captain stepped off the trail and removed the cover from the basket. He didn't look at the face within, and didn't hesitate. Taking the head in one hand and the shoulder in the other, he wrenched them obliquely apart until he heard the crack of the vertebrae. Then, unwisely, he looked down at what he'd done.

The boy's skull was mottled with skin ulcers that were responsible for his rejection. His face, however, was perfectly formed, down to the delicate flutes of his nostrils, the whisper of eyebrows, and the tiny pink lips that now parted for his last breaths. In the brief moment he could bear to look, he saw the death rattle and the ball-less whites of his eyes rolled under half-closed lids, and covered the basket. No one could say he had not tried to fulfill his promise.

6.

If not for the absence of his mother, travel in the warm, rocking basket would have been pleasant to Molobrus. It lulled him, over the miles of his life's journey to the place his fathers had chosen for him, his brows furrowed with the effort of dreaming. He saw the nimbus of gray that he had learned was his mother, her head bent, pouring tears as her fingertips glistened blood from the scoring of her cheeks. He saw another shape in the gloom, still less distinct, who also wept, though he sensed not for any knowledge of a son borne up from her dark, benthic core. He went upward, ever upward, through the soft gates that waited to strangle him, up into the light, the trail, the judgment, and the mountain. Had he known the gorge awaited, he might have wondered to what fresh heights this new caregiver would send him.

When the moment came, instinct triggered a reflex that made him grab for some secure object. Thick arms spread and gathered in empty air; his bladder voided as he fell. After this the sensation seemed familiar—a long-lost weightlessness. In peace, he remained curled into a ball, his feet crossed at the ankles, his right thumb in his mouth, his eyes turned away from the light, for all the time left to him in the world.

7.

The Athenians were hard-pressed to find places for their guests. As criminal penalties at the time more often included death, fines, or exile, prison space was minimal in the city. The likelihood of another Lacedaemonian invasion discouraged the keeping of captives in camps outside the city walls. High-ranking Spartiates like Antalcidas and Frog were therefore kept in a small jailhouse near the marketplace, while less valuable prisoners, such as the under-thirties and the handful of surviving helots, were boarded out to the storage pits and basements of wealthy citizens. The latter, though scattered, did not want for company: it became a popular amusement for hosts to cap the entertainment at their drinking parties by showing their guests the shackled Spartans in their cellars. Cleon kept no fewer than six in his fine home in Scambonidae; Demosthenes a token two. Nicias took none, though his basement was the biggest in town.

Demosthenes earned the military victory on the island, but Cleon reaped the success. The latter's jingoist populism became the dominant political force in the city. The prisoners, he argued, could be used as a check on Lacedaemonian aggression: if the enemy dared invade Attica again, they would watch their countrymen's throats slit and their bodies strung up on the walls. Sure enough, the Spartans sent no invasion the following summer. Instead, they sent a procession of envoys, each newcomer prepared to concede a little more than the last. Cleon—who most now believed could do no wrong—enjoined the Assembly to dismiss the negotiators. With the Athenians holding what they believed were almost three hundred trump cards, they were content to wait for even greater rewards.

Though the Spartans sought the return of their prisoners, their more immediate concern was the Athenian navy. The Athenian ships, based now in Pylos, struck more freely than ever, sacking and burning from the borders of Argos in the east to Helus in the south to Messenia in the west. The Athenians introduced more Messenian exiles into Pylos, encouraging them to ravage the land and free as many of the natives they could find. The Spartan response betrayed their desperation: they organized companies of roving cavalry and archers. Naturally, with no proper citizens willing to do such dishonorable duty, only low-caste Nigh-dwellers and indigent Spartiates joined the new forces.

Meanwhile, Nicias burnished his reputation by leading a successful invasion of Cythera. The loss of this island, where Ramphias had once been governor, cost the Lacedaemonians any semblance of control of their seacoasts; they could hardly spare the troops to protect their territory, much less another adventure to Attica. Yet the Athenians would not negotiate. The mood in Laconia fell to its lowest ebb since Xerxes the Persian threatened Greece with a million men, fifty years before.

The gods have a taste for intervening in such times. On this occasion, during the tenth summer of the war, they puffed Cleon up with such confidence that he coveted another, more ambitious military command. Bringing his powers of persuasion to bear on the Assembly, he was rewarded with a force of thirty ships and several thousand Athenian and allied troops. The green conqueror sailed Thraceward and, after some early successes at Torone and Galepsus, erected trophies to his glory; proceeding around the treacherous waters beneath Mount Athos, he next took it upon himself to liberate the Athenian foundation of Amphipolis, a strategically set town then occupied by allies of the enemy.

This was a harder nut to crack. Opposing him for this siege was Brasidas, son of Tellis, who was a new sort of Spartiate commander—bold, resourceful, comfortable with operating far from home with foreign allies. Against such an adversary, Cleon grew timid, refusing to attack until he could gather all the reinforcements he could. Sensing weakness, Brasidas seized the initiative, storming out with inferior forces to rout the Athenians. In the battle the Spartiate and the demagogue were both killed: Brasidas in delayed fashion after suffering a mortal wound; Cleon cut down from behind as he ran away from the battlefield. Thus ended the remarkable career of a tanner's son.

The antagonists were alike in being little mourned in their home cities: in Laconia, Brasidas' freelancing was viewed with suspicion by his elders, while most Athenians found the manner of Cleon's death—a career politician pretending to be a soldier, meeting his end with a javelin in the ass—as compellingly ridiculous as his oratory. The most important consequence of the battle, however, was that the jingoes were out of the way of a peace settlement. Nicias and the Agiad king Pleistoanax took the lead among their respective cities, negotiating a treaty and joint alliance that was supposed to last for fifty years. One of the key provisions of the agreement was that all prisoners, including the Spartans captured at Sphacteria, were to be let go at last.

8.

After three years in the state jailhouse, Antalcidas had spent more time in bright, cosmopolitan Athens than any of his elders. More time, in fact, than his Atticophile wife, who had so long lectured him on Athenian civic excellence. Of course, his experience there was only of his prison cell and a short patch of exercise ground. The former was windowless, and the latter had a view, partially obstructed by smoke and ramshackle roofs, of the Squeezing Place to the southwest and a cornice of the Propylaea to the east. This was the extent of his sightseeing in the largest, richest city of Greece.

When they were released, no one came from Laconia to escort the prisoners back home. This worried the under-thirties, who hoped that the ephors would understand that they surrendered on orders of their superiors. The Spartiates knew better—Frog, who wore his shame lightly, absorbed himself in organizing the march, refusing to speculate on what reception they should expect. Antalcidas, for his part, envied Epitadas for his honorable exit. He could count on one hand his reasons for not following his brother: namely, his wife, his son, settling accounts with Frog. The latter concerned him most the day they set out on the road home.

There was unease in the ranks when Antalcidas did not join his countrymen for the march. As they proceeded along the Eleusis road, suspicion rose that they were being tracked by something as invisible as the wind and unavoidable as night. "The Athenians are betraying the treaty," Frog declared, but no one believed him. For what was on their trail was nothing as clumsy as an Athenian. Instead, the Lacedaemonians had the strange sense of being like helots under observation by an operative of the Hidden Service.

The air of doom seemed to gather and congeal around Frog; the under-thirties, without knowing why, moved away from him. Despite their night training, the tension over what followed them made the Lacedaemonians afraid of the dark. Frog took to sleeping in trees with a heavy rock. If what trailed him had a name, he would have guessed it was "Antalcidas," but in a broader sense the specific adversary didn't matter. Too many of his comrades wanted him dead for the decision he had so loudly owned for himself, in front of witnesses. When someone suggested he rush ahead to procure a sword at Megara, Frog scoffed, saying, "No Megarian sword should keep a man from his Fate, if he chooses to face it."

They found him the next day at the foot of his tree. His throat had been slit with a very short blade, perhaps even a sharpened stone; his tongue was cut out and, by evidence of the wet spot nearby, was left in the dirt. The crows had claimed their gift before the body was found. Frog could only have been dead for a few hours, but his corpse was swollen, the face chalky, as if he had been rotting for much longer.

Antalcidas proceeded south. The upheavals of the war had disrupted wagon traffic, leaving most of the roads unrutted but trampled by the prints of thousands of bare marching feet. Though he had traversed the mountains into the Peloponnese many times, it had always been in the company of an army. Now, as a lone traveler, he saw the road stretch thin and insubstantial through those spaces, and the sound his breathing something small and absurd in the enormity of silence around him. It was as if the gods had exhausted their palettes in rendering the fuller, more frivolous landscapes of other lands, and for Greece been forced to make the most with pure black, the green of ripening olives, and earth. He saw the blankness in his own shadow—a shadow that was uncompromising, sharing not a shred of gray with him.

Outside Nemea he stopped at a farmhouse for water. The master, who regarded him narrowly from under thick, tufted brows, seemed to recognize him as a Lacedaemonian. When Antalcidas asked for a drink, the Nemean accompanied him to the wellhead, going on about the "peace of Nicias." His real purpose, though, was to ask a question: how could it be that the Spartans had given up at Sphacteria?

"That must be old news by now, friend," Antalcidas replied. "That was years ago."

"It was, but you're the first Lacedaemonian we've seen this far north since word came. I'm hoping you can explain it."

Antalcidas drank; out of the corner of his eye, on the ground, he could see the shadow of the farmer's wife as she listened from around the corner. He drained the cup, handed it back to the Nemean, and took up his staff to resume his trip.

"Some answers are not worth the effort of asking," he said.

Two days later he topped the pass through Sciritis and gazed down into the haze-dressed valley of Laconia. Despite what his intellect told him to expect, he found his breath quickening at the prospect of arrival. In Athens, he had spent much of his time alone, yet had always felt the energy of the place—a low rumble, like the pulse of the earth—rising up from the pavement stones. Near Corinth, he looked up and saw the tentacles of commerce, eternal and lucrative, reach up the acropolis to wrestle with the thousand sacred courtesans who served Aphrodite there. As he passed to the west, he could turn back at night and trace the path by the procession of customers' torches snaking up the illuminated citadel.

But in Laconia all was quiet. Crossing the Eurotas bridge, he came to the first of her five villages, Limnae, and found it little more impressive than a hundred country hamlets he had seen on the road. It was midmorning, and the household helots were out doing the marketing for their masters. None of these met his eyes as they passed; nor was he acknowledged by the knots of schoolgirls on their way to lessons.

Sparta was small enough, though, that one would always recognize someone within a few moments of going out on the street. No sooner had this thought entered his mind than he saw a familiar face. It was, in fact, someone from his deep past, whom he had not encountered in all the years since his childhood. Antalcidas, walking by the man, raised a chin to a man with a conspicuous mole on his right cheek.

"Rejoice!" he hailed the former packmate he once knew as Birthmark.

Antalcidas was arrested by a series of expressions that came over the other's face. First there was surprise—an involuntary widening of the eyes and mouth, a hint of amusement at the pranks of Fortune. Second came the imposition of a memory: Birthmark seemed suddenly afflicted, his legs unable to slow the pace that carried him onward. Finally, there was disapproval: a sanctimonious darkening around the eyes, and a deliberate speeding of his step as he completed the act of ignoring the comrade who had greeted him.

Antalcidas found himself walking stiffly onward, bewildered. Certainly Birthmark had recognized him—nobody forgot the faces of those with whom he had shared the Rearing. Such things always transcended circumstances that might take a man up or down in the esteem of everyone else. If Birthmark had been declared a trembler, Antalcidas would still have greeted him, perhaps even shared a drink with him. And he thought: how cold the Lacedaemonians had become, how petty in their resentments!

This thought put him in mind of his dear Andreia, who once told him that, of all the Greeks, the Spartans had the broadest territory and the narrowest hearts. Remembering her, a smile came over him as he redoubled his pace toward the little house in Kynosoura. *The son of Antalcidas grows.* It occurred to him that the boy must be walking by then, and learning the songs of his ancestors. If he hurried, he might yet be first to put a sword in the hands of his son.

9.

He didn't have to wait long to see Andreia. As he came up the path she was bent to her garden work, picking herbs for the kitchen. Hearing him, she stopped, straightened; when she turned to look over her shoulder at him there was no reaction on her face. The smile died on Antalcidas' lips. He was reminded suddenly of a feeling he'd had on a patrol high in the mountains of Arcadia, when the snows finally broke in late spring. Standing below, he was sure the avalanche would bury them, until the streaming white

comet was diverted into some hidden ravine, and he
and his men stood alone, abandoned by death. Andreia, too, turned aside. Yet the wall of her frigidity
still bore down on him.

In his prison days he had spent much of his time
daydreaming of her. He imagined the time of their
separation—and her latest pregnancy—would have
changed her, and occupied himself with imagining
her appearance on the day of their reunion. As she
conducted him inside wordlessly, he saw that his fantasies had failed him: Andreia's figure had not become plumper with home comforts, nor her hair
grayer, nor her cheeks more deeply lined with age. Instead of matured, she was simply diminished, as if
worn down by the years. He remembered her standing nearly his equal in height, and was surprised to
find that her head barely rose to his shoulders. Instead
of gaining weight, she was thinner. Through the ungirt side of her chiton he could the blade of her hip
protruding, the white of the bone almost visible beneath the taut translucence of her skin. Her hair had
neither the luminance of her youth, nor the gray tendrils of age, but had become only darker, flatter,
duller.

She still said nothing as he washed and dressed the
road blisters on his feet. Playing the proud Spartan
patriarch, he would not deign to engage in domestic
chatter, but would wait for the occasion to measure
out his words. He got his chance when Melitta ran
into the house, and upon discovering her father sitting there, froze in her tracks. Antalcidas, grinning
without reservation, raised a hand to summon the girl
to him. Panic flashed on his daughter's face as she
backed away and fled.

It was not an unusual response of a Spartan girl to

her father. "She looks well," Antalcidas said at the top of Andreia's bowed head. "But where, may I ask, is our son?"

With a sharp upward glance, Andreia met his eyes. All at once, his seigneurial pretentions crumbled; he parted his lips to say something, but his voice died under the blaze of her look. She rose, and after dropping the cleaning rag into the basin, retreated without explanation up the stairs to the women's quarters.

Thus began the long process by which Antalcidas learned the fate of little Molobrus. She never said outright that his son lay with the jackals on the mountain; she let the story out in pieces, by means of frowns and significant silences, until even a proud Spartan patriarch could guess the truth. When he took to going around the house with a stricken look on his face, she said her first words to him since his return:

"And so the father is last to know the fruit of his sins."

Antalcidas thought about this statement for a full day, his brow furrowed, until he attempted a defense the next morning.

"Why do you blame me, instead of the judges who condemned him, or the ephors who stripped us of our dignity?"

Andreia gave nothing but a bitter grimace as she took a clean rag to Melitta's face. The girl, for her part, blamed her mother's unhappiness on the arrival of this presumptuous stranger. The weight of a trembler's disgrace, the gossip, and the loss of privileges, were calculated to fall on his child too, so that he was obliged to explain to her why her father was the lowest sort of man. He came to accept he would never know his daughter, and that in fact she was just waiting for him to disappear. Her cheek screamed the question when he touched it, and her hair, and her eyes: *why are you still here?*

He tried with Andreia again that evening, when she stood at the hearth, stirring the stew pot.

"So this is the homecoming you think worthy of me?"

This was more than Andreia could take. She threw the spoon at him, scalding his cheek with the boiling sauce on its bowl. He touched the burn with this fingers, a look of childlike hurt in his eyes.

"Tell me what I have done to you, woman—except my duty to you?"

"I only wish I had the courage to throw a knife!" she cried, and with eyes welling over, fled upstairs again. Though a wife's quarters were beneath a Spartan warrior's dignity to enter, Antalcidas followed. When he topped the steps, he found Andreia collapsed on her day couch, face buried in her hands. As he approached to sit by her, she spoke from behind her fingers.

"Even now you can't grieve for him."

He thought about this. He was saddened by the news at first, but it passed; he had, after all, never met the boy. Nor was it rare for infants to die in Laconia.

"A fine figure of a man I would be, to shed tears like you."

"Weep for your name, then, which is as dead as you should be now."

He pulled her hands from her face, and said in a voice he usually reserved for correcting subordinates in the field, "You know I had nothing to do with it."

"This was your city," she replied, "yet you let this happen."

"Did you hear what I said?"

"None of that is important. It is what people think."

He sat trying to reason with Andreia for hours, and again the next day, and the day after that, though nothing, not even the surrender on the island, made him feel less a man than the number of words he wasted to convince her. With every day, he could see the crust of her indifference thickening. At last he took the husband's prerogative with her, fighting his way through her stiff limbs. With his eyes, he made the only promise he could, to replace what was taken. Yet with every act of entering her, searching for her center, her could feel her receding ahead, into the darkness.

"I can't. Not in this place—or with you," she told him.

She never flung the ultimate accusation, trembler, but the word seemed poised to follow, like the inevitable conclusion to a syllogism.

He got up, but before he left he paused.

"Then the true coward is you," he said.

10.

Three years later, the Spartan army stood on a plain near the Peloponnesian city of Mantinea, facing an allied army of Argives, Arcadians, Mantineans, and Athenians. A battle was going to be fought because the treaty ending the war with Athens had been a sham: in the ensuing years, neither side had fulfilled its obligations. The Athenians were firmly entrenched at Pylos, and the Lacedaemonians still occupied the Athenian ally of Amphipolis. All the Greek powers sent out secret emissaries to negotiate defensive alliances against their adversaries, frightening each

other with vague fears of Spartan-Athenian hegemony, an Argive-Corinthian plot to take control of the
Peloponnese, or a Spartan-Theban dagger pointed at
the heart of Athens. Each party insisted on terms that
would make it finally, completely secure—until the
hard bargaining pushed the negotiations to collapse
and the diplomats went off to try their luck with the
other side. This, in turn, magnified the fears of everyone else, who redoubled their own underhanded
dealings.

In Sparta, the capitulators of Sphacteria remained
in disgrace. The 120 Spartiates were still forbidden to
attend their dining clubs, hold public office, or engage
in any financial business; the 171 under-thirties faced
permanent status as landless Inferiors. Yet, even as the
people shunned them, there was a general fear that
the survivors might abandon the Spartan cause. The
army was by now undermanned and overstretched,
having fewer than a third of the eight thousand troops
it had in the time of Leonidas. To forestall their loss,
all the ex-Equals were given new panoplies, free from
the state, by magistrates who would barely look at
them. Rumors were allowed to circulate that the capitulators might be pardoned after all—if they
showed themselves worthy on the battlefield.

Antalcidas stood in the ranks of the Inferiors with
his state-granted shield and spear. It was the first time
since his return from Athens that he had left Laconia.
His old Spartiate comrades would barely have recognized him: he had lost his lean, hungry look, his face
having filled out in a sudden lapse into middle age;
his beard, which fell now to his navel, was prema-
turely white. In his shame, forbidden to wear the
crimson of Lacedaemonians in good standing, he
wore gray to the occasion of his death.

The Spartans had been late to realize their enemies were on their way. As the battle would occur on Mantinean soil, the natives took pride of place on their right wing, with the Arcadians, Argives, and Athenians stretching out to their left. Guided by their training, the Lacedaemonians formed their lines rapidly, with the Sciritan Nigh-dwellers facing the Mantineans, the ranks of Inferiors—including Antalcidas—against the Arcadians, and almost all the surviving Spartiates filling out the line opposite Argives and Athenians. The Eurypontid king Agis, who occupied the center with his three hundred knights, would fight with very heavy burden that day: to win the field, or find the Lacedaemonian army broken in his hands. Sparta herself, unwalled and unguarded, lay only two days' march away.

Antalcidas picked up his shield. He had made sure to get command of a twenty-four man platoon, with himself in the front rank. This would make him visible to all his men when his time came. Turning to examine them, he faced a gallery of greenhorns, Nigh-Dwellers, reprobates, and reformed cowards like himself.

"Your orders are simple, scum: keep the pace—and watch how men should die!"

He cracked the head of his spear against his shield, and waited for the others to do the same. He heard their answer, the percussion of iron against bronze, the ancient music of the ranks, stretching back to echo the battle order of the Homeric heroes before the walls of Priam. Satisfied, he raised his cheek guards, spat, and pulled his helmet down low around his ears.

The enemy line came down the hill, approaching on the double-quick. The boy-pipers behind the Spartans began to play. Without thinking, the Lacedaemonians moved their feet to that deliberate cadence, marching at a slower pace but good order. Antalcidas' heart was pounding now, surging with exhilaration, for there was no feeling like being swept before a clanking human beast of ten thousand legs, propelled unstoppably toward that wall of hostile spears. His urine coursed down his legs, but not in fear—in time, with the inevitability of it, he would ejaculate too, for there would be much fucking to do that day. He would rip pussies for them all, the men he would penetrate with his spear. As his men watched in wonder, he charged into the arms of the enemy, letting out as he ran a wail of joy like a man coming into his beautiful bride.

Those who witnessed it spoke for years of Stone at Mantinea.

11.

The lady Damatria laid out Antalcidas on the same table where her youngest was honored a few short years before. Equals from all over Laconia came to marvel at her good fortune: to have a husband acquit himself well in battle was worthy enough, and to see him followed by a heroic son like Epitadas a true bounty. But to live to savor the glory of a second son was a rare thing indeed. With the victory at Mantinea, she became the most envied woman in Sparta. Instead of being known as "Damatria the Grasping" or "Damatria, Queen of Bitches," she earned a new epithet among her peers in Kynosoura: "Damatria the Thrice-Blessed."

She sat by the garlanded head of the corpse with a handkerchief to daub away the tears that could not come. No one could blame her, for what was there to cry about? She received her admirers all in turn—the two kings of Sparta, Agis and Pleistoanax, and Ramphias, the former governor of Cythera, and old Endius, the boy-herd, and the packmates Redhead, Cheese, and Rehash, and all the members of the Hill Wolves. She knew that all of them had shunned Antalcidas when he was alive, but had rushed to see him when they learned the manner of his death. She wondered, would he have forgiven them? Of course he would! The boy was such a fool—he lacked the wits even to keep a secret grudge. She kissed her fingers and laid them along her son's cold temple. No one ever claimed he was sprung from good stock.

But he had served his mother well in another sense. She had been sitting there all morning, accepting the gifts of cake and good wishes from people she relished despising, when she realized she had not imagined the face of *that helot* all day. At some point she had not been aware, the rape had ceased to dominate her thoughts. It was a memory now—painful to be sure, which she loathed to dwell upon—but a memory nonetheless. Somehow repaired now, she loosed a tear for Antalcidas' sake. She would invite Andreia and her little girl to live with her in her big house.

"Rejoice, for you have given your last child to Sparta!" old Isidas, the ex-ephor, told her. Wetting his ancient lips through their thicket of beard hairs, he asked, "So, do you still think him 'the shame of Sparta?'"

Damatria smiled. "Not at all. Both of my sons were good boys. They have exceeded their fathers."

Acknowledgments

The primary source for the events at Sphacteria is Thucydides' *History*, Book Four. This ancient account is concise, substantial, but by no means copious in detail. I am indebted to the scholarship of Anton Powell, Adrienne Mayor, J. K. Anderson, A. H. M. Jones, Robert Flacelière, James Davidson, Victor Davis Hanson, and Barry Strauss in filling out this version at least semiplausibly. Richmond Lattimore translated the Tyrtaeus poem included in Chapter 1; Prof. James L. McGlew of the University of Missouri—Columbia advised me on the ancient Greek in Chapter IX. Thanks to Prof. Paul Cartledge of the University of Cambridge and Prof. David Hollander of Iowa State University for reviewing the manuscript, and to Prof. Joan Ramage of Lehigh University, who was invaluable in helping me to understand the natural history of Sphacteria. Special thanks as well to my editor, Brent Howard, my infinitely-patient agent, Jeff Gerecke, and of course, to my wife Maryanne.

List of Characters

Aeimnestus (Spartan): Renowned slayer of the Persian commander at the Battle of Plataea

Agis II (Spartan): Eurypontid king of Sparta

Alcander (Spartan): A city elder

Andreia (Spartan): Daughter of Ramphias; wife of Antalcidas; mother of Melitta

Antalcidas (Spartan): Illegitimate son of Damatria and an unknown helot; husband of Andreia; half-brother of Epitadas

Arcesilaus (Spartan): A city elder

"Beast" (Spartan): Nickname of Antalcidas' second pack leader during the Rearing

"Birthmark" (Spartan): Nickname of Antalcidas' first pack leader during the Rearing

"Cheese" (Spartan): Nickname of packmate of Antalcidas during the Rearing

Cimon (Athenian): Noble and general; after the Great Earthquake of 464 BC, led Athenian expeditionary force to Laconia to expel the Messenian rebels from Mount Ithome

Cleinias (Athenian): Oarsman of the lowest rank on the *Terror*

Cleomenes I (Spartan): Renowned Agiad king of Sparta in the time before the Persian Wars; famously died by self-mutilation

Cleon (Athenian): Popular politician and would-be military commander; leader of war party after the death of Pericles

"Cricket" (Spartan): Nickname of packmate of Antalcidas during the Rearing

Damatria (Spartan): Mother of Antalcidas and Epitadas; widow of Molobrus and wealthy wife of Dorcis

Damonon (Spartan): Member of the Spit Companions dining club

Demosthenes (Athenian): Noble and general; after suffering defeat in Aetolian mountains, led the successful incursion into Messenia at Pylos (not to be confused with the fourth century orator)

Dicaearchus (Athenian): Oarsman of the highest rank on the *Terror*

Dorcis (Spartan): Wealthy landowner and second husband of Damatria

Dorieus (Spartan): A member of the Spit Companions dining club

Doulos (Helot): Servant and shieldbearer, given by Damatria to Antalcidas upon his maturity

Endius (Spartan): Public official in charge of Rearing of Spartan youth ("boy-herd")

Epitadas (Spartan): Son of Damatria and Molobrus; half brother of Antalcidas; leader of Lacedaemonian garrison on Sphacteria

Erinna (Helot): Servant and mistress of Dorcis

Eudamidas (Spartan): A member of the Spit Companions dining club

Eurymedon (Athenian): Fleet commander and superior to Demosthenes at the outbreak of the Pylos campaign

"Frog" (Spartan): Nickname of packmate of Antalcidas during the Rearing; restive member of Lacedaemonian garrison during siege of Sphacteria

Gorgo (Spartan): Sister of Leonis

Herippidas (Spartan): A member of the Spit Companions dining club

"Ho-hum" (Spartan): Nickname of packmate of Antalcidas during the Rearing

Ianthe (Athenian): Wife of Demosthenes; succumbed to plague

Iphitus (Spartan): Admiral and member of the Spit Companions dining club

Isidas (Spartan): Ex-ephor, member of the Gerousia, and member of the Spit Companions dining club; peace emissary to Athens during the Pylos affair

Lampito (Spartan): Mother-in-law of Damatria, mother of Molobrus

Leochares (Athenian): Officer and subordinate to Demosthenes at Pylos

Leonis (Spartan): Female tough who has a fateful encounter with Andreia

Melitta (Spartan): Daughter of Antalcidas and Andreia

Molobrus (Spartan): Father of Antalcidas, first husband of Damatria; namesake of Antacidas' son by Andreia

Nicias (Athenian): Noble and general; after the death of Pericles, leading figure in the peace party

Oreus (Athenian): Oarsman of the middle rank on the *Terror*

Patronices (Athenian): Oarsman of the highest rank on the *Terror*

Philemon (Athenian): Wealthy sponsor (*trierarch*) of the vessel *Terror*

Pleistoanax (Spartan): Agiad king of Sparta

Praxitas (Spartan): Platoon leader over Antalcidas, who acquitted himself poorly in a fight with Arcadian raiders

Protesilaus (Messenian): At Pylos, leader of the Messenian exiles from Naupactus and ally of the Athenians

Ramphias (Spartan): Father of Andreia and governor of the island of Cythera

"Redhead" (Spartan): Nickname of packmate of Antalcidas during the Rearing

"Rehash" (Spartan): Nickname of packmate of Antalcidas during the Rearing

Sphaerus (Athenian): Ancient steersman of the *Terror*

Stilbiades (Athenian): Bosun on the *Terror*

"Stone" (Spartan): Antalcidas' pack moniker during the Rearing, and a derogatory nickname thereafter

Thibron (Spartan): Mentor to Antalcidas' pack during the Rearing, later disgraced and exiled

Timon (Athenian): Oarsman of the lowest rank on the *Terror*

Xeuthes (Athenian): Captain of the *Terror*

Zeuxippos (Spartan): Ex-ephor, member of the Spit Companions dining club, and personal mentor of Antalcidas

A Novel of Alexander the Great

EMPIRE OF ASHES
by
Nicholas Nicastro

323 B.C. The great Alexander is dead.
Machon—the late emperor's renowned friend and
ally—is being scapegoated for his downfall.
An outsider on trial for his life, Machon will tell
his Greek accusers the stunning, tragic truth
behind the meteoric rise and fall is a peerless
military leader who claimed himself a god—and
lost his humanity.

**"Nicastro takes you by the scruff of the neck
and yanks you into the action of history."**
—*Ithaca Times* (NY)

0-451-21366-1

**Available wherever books are sold or at
penguin.com**